CHRISTMAS AT THE
CAT CAFÉ

JESSICA REDLAND

Boldwood

First published in Great Britain in 2023 by Boldwood Books Ltd.

Copyright © Jessica Redland, 2023

Cover Design by Debbie Clement Design

Cover Photography: Shutterstock

Every effort has been made to obtain the necessary permissions with reference to copyright material, both illustrative and quoted. We apologise for any omissions in this respect and will be pleased to make the appropriate acknowledgements in any future edition.

A CIP catalogue record for this book is available from the British Library.

Paperback ISBN 978-1-80162-484-8

Large Print ISBN 978-1-80162-485-5

Hardback ISBN 978-1-80162-483-1

Ebook ISBN 978-1-80162-486-2

Kindle ISBN 978-1-80162-487-9

Audio CD ISBN 978-1-80162-478-7

MP3 CD ISBN 978-1-80162-480-0

Digital audio download ISBN 978-1-80162-482-4

Boldwood Books Ltd
23 Bowerdean Street
London SW6 3TN
www.boldwoodbooks.com

For my good friends Angela, Carol and Nicola, with thanks for your help and big hugs xx

This book is also dedicated to anyone with a chronic pain condition to whom I send my love and understanding xx

For my good friends Angela, Carol and Nicola, with thanks for your help and big hugs xx

This book is also dedicated to anyone with a chronic pain condition to whom I send my love and understanding xx

CAST OF CAT CHARACTERS

The team at Boldwood Books adore cats so, for the names in *Christmas at the Cat Café*, I turned mainly to the Boldwood fur family, taking some liberties with colour and age. Age shown on the table below is at the start of the book and the age of the kittens will therefore change as the book progresses.

Cats	Breed	Colour	Age	Owner/Carer
Babushka	Norwegian Forest Cat	Silver tabby with black mackerel stripes	6	Rachel
Boo	British Short-hair*	Black	21	Issy
Freyja	Bengal	Brown tabby with black classic stripes	1	Claire
Heathcliff	Norwegian Forest Cat	Silver tabby with black mackerel stripes	6	Rachel
Jupiter	American Burmese#	Silver	1	Isobel & Tristan
Marmalade	British Shorthair	Ginger classic tabby	12	Fictional
Sybil	Bengal/ Maine Coon	Brown tabby with black mackerel stripes	2	Claire
Viking	Moggy (shorthair)	White with black tail	3	Isobel & Tristan
Winnie	Munchkin	Cream/ Chocolate spotted taby	5	Emily

Kittens	Breed	Colour	Months	Owner/Carer
Blinky	Exotic Short-hair*	Grey	3	Nia's friend
Cloud	Persian (longhair)	Blue smoke	5.5	Fictional
Effie	Ragdoll	Grey and white	7	Charlotte
Marmite	Moggy (long-hair)	Black	4.5	Sue
Pebbles	Highlander (shorthair)	Brown spotted tabby with white socks	3.5	Fictional
Rubix	Moggy (shorthair)	Mixed colour tabby	5	Fictional
Ruby	Moggy (Shorthair)	Black	4.5	Sue
Smudge	Aztec	Brown classic tabby	4.5	Fictional

* Breed has been fictionalised
# The real Jupiter is a mix of breeds and I've narrowed it down to one

1

'Tabby?' Matt called, knocking on the open door to the empty flat.

'In the front room,' I called back, scrumpling up the protective plastic covering I'd ripped off the last of the cat beds I'd been unpacking.

'That's a lot of beds,' he said, joining me and doing a double-take at the rows of igloo cat beds and the pile of open ones in front of the bay window.

'I've got a lot of cats!' I said, smiling at him. 'How's it going downstairs?'

'All done and ready for your approval.'

'Ooh, that was quick!'

Matt and his team had done an amazing job refurbishing the empty shop on Whitsborough Bay's Castle Street, turning it into my brand-new business venture – Castle Street Cat Café.

'The lads are loading the tools and rubbish into the van,' he said as I followed him downstairs to the first floor.

I gasped as I stepped through the door.

'Looks a bit different with the chairs and tables,' Matt said.

My heart raced with excitement as I ran my fingers across the nearest table. 'It's amazing. Honestly, Matt, I can't thank you enough for the fantastic job you've all done.'

'A cat café is a first for us and we've loved the chance to get creative.'

I followed him down to the ground floor, another pulse of excitement running through me on seeing everything in place down there. With the building works now complete, I had two and a half weeks to clean and get everything ready for opening day on 15 November.

'It's perfect,' I confirmed to Matt. 'Thank you.'

'I'll head off then. Good luck with opening day and give us a shout if you need anything else doing before then or if you decide what to do with the flat.'

'I'll talk to Leon about the flat when he's back, but it'll probably be the New Year before we make any decisions.'

The building was four storeys, made up of two floors of retail space and a three-bedroom flat. The original intention had been for my boyfriend, Leon, and I to move into the flat ourselves with the cats, but it was one of the many things that had changed over the past six months. Now I wasn't sure what we'd do with it.

'No worries,' Matt said, getting into the van. 'You know where we are. See you soon.'

Waving them off, I locked the door and paused for a moment in the large entrance porch. It was decorated with the most adorable wallpaper covered in colourful cartoon cats. Directly opposite the external door and therefore easily seen from outside was a large welcome sign and a metal plaque stating *Life is better with coffee, cake and cats*. On the other wall, opposite the internal door, there was another metal plaque – *Please keep the door closed and don't let the cats out – no matter what they tell you!*

I wanted a visit to the Castle Street Cat Café to be a special and memorable experience and I could achieve that through three things – adorable cats, delicious food and amazing surroundings. I was confident about the first two and, to accomplish the latter, I'd divided the café into three themed areas, one downstairs and two on the first floor, and had enlisted my extremely talented older brother Rylan – an art tutor at Whitsborough Bay Sixth-Form College – to paint murals on the walls.

The ground floor, in honour of the street name, was Cat Castle. Across the largest wall was a mural of Whitsborough Bay Castle with knights on horseback charging towards it carrying flags with cats on.

The builders had constructed a castle-themed activity centre for the cats, including a drawbridge, a winding staircase and turrets. Walkways across the wall connected cat sleeping platforms.

Also downstairs was an accessible toilet, the kitchen – a closed-off area which the cats couldn't access for hygiene reasons – and a retail sales area. I was starting small and simple with some cat-themed greetings cards, stationery, soft toys and mugs but, if sales went well, there was room to expand the range. I was excited about unpacking the merchandise and stocking the shelves.

I stood for a while, a smile on my face, imagining how Cat Castle would look with customers and cats and how it would sound with the clinking of crockery and the chatter of customers over chilled instrumental music – great for keeping the cats calm.

Removing my phone from the pocket of my favourite cat hoodie, I clicked onto the camera to take photos for Leon, but shook my head and put it away. I'd sent him several photos in the early stages of construction but, once the painting of the murals started, I'd decided not to give him any sneak peeks, preferring him to see it for the first time in person, and I was going to stick to that. Two more sleeps and he'd finally be back. I couldn't wait.

I returned to the first floor for a closer inspection. The front section carried a seaside theme and, although I'd anticipated Cat Castle being my favourite, Kitty Cove had stolen that crown. Matt's team had built a plinth in front of the bay window with a large wooden lighthouse to the left and a sailing boat to the right, both with platforms for the cats to lie on. The space in between looked like a beach with small striped deckchairs and hammocks for the cats, plastic buckets to hold cat toys and teasers, and a few small old-fashioned suitcases with the tops held open so the cats could curl up inside. The mural on one wall depicted a busy beach, people playing in the sea and Whitsborough Bay's RNLI lifeboat bouncing across the waves to a rescue. The opposite wall had a fairground theme with a Ferris wheel, helter-skelter and dodgem cars. Sleeping platforms protruded from the different rides.

Halfway along that wall was a cliff lift with more platforms but, instead of going up to a cliff top, the lift headed into the final themed area – Feline Forest. In a nod to nearby Kittrig Forest – somewhere I'd always loved to visit – the section at the back was full of trees. There were lots drawn on the mural, some had been built with wood, and a few had been sculpted to add variety and depth. There were sleeping platforms in the trees, a treehouse, colourful hammocks and rope bridges for the cats to prowl along. Owls and woodland animals painted on the murals completed the forest look.

At the very back of the room, there were two more toilets, a couple of cat flaps to the litter trays and a quiet room which the public couldn't access but where the cats could go if they needed a little time out.

I pulled out one of the chairs in Feline Forest and sat down, looking around me, marvelling at how my vision had come together. Leon had thought I was too ambitious and there was no need to spend so much money on it, his attitude being that the customers would be coming to see the cats and their experience would be the same whether the cats were curled up in a lighthouse or on a regular wooden ledge. I disagreed. I'd always believed that, if you're going to do something, you might as well do it really well. Besides, it was my money and he'd left me to project manage it all on my own, so they were my decisions to make.

I could happily have stayed there for ages, lost in my daydreams, but I needed to head home to feed the cats. I took one last look around, a huge grin on my face.

'I did it, Nanna,' I whispered. 'You always said I'd achieve my dream of working with cats one day. Thank you.'

Returning to the flat for my bag and coat, I locked up and set off on foot towards home and back to the cats – all sixteen of them.

You know those memes you see on social media about crazy cat ladies? That's me! Okay, so being thirty-four, I'm not the age profile they typically depict, and I'm not single either, but I freely admit to being completely obsessed with cats, and I don't get why anyone would label that 'crazy'. Cats are the most adorable, loving animals capable of bringing such great comfort to their owners, and I've certainly been in need of plenty of that over the past eighteen months.

I've been an ailurophile – isn't that a beautiful word for cat lover? – since I was seven. On the way to our local playground, I'd skipped ahead of Mum but suddenly stopped dead in the lane, my head cocked to one side. When she joined me, she asked what I was doing and I told her I was listening to the cats singing to me. She couldn't hear anything and was about to pull me away when a tiny black and grey tabby kitten tumbled down the bank and onto the track. We found a cardboard box in the undergrowth with another two kittens inside and two more spilling out. Mum scooped them all back into the box and we took them straight home to our house in a village called Little Sandby, north of Whitsborough Bay.

Who does that? What sort of person shoves five kittens in a box and abandons them in a lane? And not even where someone can easily spot them. I'll never be able to comprehend behaviour like that. If a person is going to abandon kittens, can't they at least have the decency to take them to a veterinary practice or rescue shelter instead of just leaving them to their deaths?

Anyway, I begged to keep them all. That was a no, but my parents said I could keep one of the kittens as long as our rough collie, Cassie, accepted it. Cassie was an absolute superstar and readily accepted all five of them, licking them clean and snuggling against them, as though her purpose in life had always been to be their surrogate mother. Sadly, one of the boy kittens didn't make it through the night, but the others were fighters. Mum and Dad relented and let me keep two – a boy called Smoke and a girl called Fluff. Nanna (Dad's mum), who lived round the corner, gave a home to the other two girls – who she named Primrose and Daisy – so I effectively got my wish to keep them all.

Before finding 'the singing cats', my name, Tabitha, often got shortened to Tabs, but I became Tabby from that point.

Smoke and Fluff were my world. I rushed home from school each day to play with them, rolling a ball, dangling feather teasers, brushing and stroking them, and I spent a lot of time at Nanna's too with Primrose and Daisy.

I wanted a job working with cats when I grew up and becoming a vet seemed logical but, on starting senior school, I had to ditch that idea when science turned out to be my worst subject.

Nanna told me never to give up on my dream of a cat-based career.

She reckoned something would present itself one day, even if I had to pursue a different career path first, and that's exactly what had happened.

Nanna excelled at baking. Her Victoria sponge cake was the stuff of legends, winning the first prize rosette at the Little Sandby village fete every year, and any cakes she contributed to the church bake sale were always the first to sell. As a teenager, I became increasingly interested in her expertise. The pair of us began experimenting with new recipes and flavours. Before long, I was as passionate about baking as she was. I studied a diploma in catering before securing an apprenticeship at The Ramparts Hotel, Whitsborough Bay's only five-star hotel. I stayed on as a pastry chef, but I never let go of my dream to work with cats, and now I was eighteen days away from opening my own cat café, combining my two passions of baking and cats.

Without Nanna, this would have been out of reach financially and it was therefore a bittersweet moment that I could only afford to fulfil my dream because Nanna was no longer with us. Last year she'd been plagued by a series of illnesses and health problems, leading to the pneumonia which claimed her in late November. Before she died, she told me there'd be a sizeable inheritance and reminded me of our conversation never to give up on my dream of working with cats. Opening a cat café was something I'd spoken about for years so I knew this was exactly what she'd have wanted me to do with the money, but I so wished she was here to see it.

2

After a short walk from the cat café, I arrived at 37 Drake Street – the three-bedroom terraced house where I lived with Leon. I moved in four years ago after we'd been together for six months. In the early days, we'd talked about selling his house and buying somewhere together out of town with a garden where it would be safer for the cats to roam freely, but the convenience of being able to walk to work and having pubs and restaurants so easily accessible meant it never quite happened.

'I'm home!' I called, pushing the front door open and stepping into the hall.

My two six-year-old Norwegian Forest Cats – a large but gentle breed – appeared at the top of the stairs and ran down to greet me, both stopping a few stairs from the bottom.

'Hi, Babushka, hi, Heathcliff,' I said, bending forward and giving them each a scratch behind the ears. 'Have you missed me? I've missed you.'

The siblings were silver with black markings in a mackerel-striped tabby pattern. Heathcliff was a little bigger than his sister and distinguishable by a white muzzle, whereas she had a white chest, and they were both absolutely gorgeous.

'Where's everyone else?' I called up the stairs. 'Are any of you ready for food?'

That soon brought several cats running. In the kitchen, I dished up wet food into their named bowls. They shared dry food and water but had all been trained to eat their main meal from their own bowl – the only way for me to make sure everyone was eating when there were so many of them.

I watched for a moment, smiling at the different stances they all adopted for eating and listening to the contented lip smacking, but there was one cat missing as usual and I knew exactly where I'd find him.

Marmalade was a red (ginger) British Shorthair tabby cat with the classic pattern of swirling lines. At twelve years old, he was the oldest of the fur family and had been Leon's cat when we met and, boy, did Marmalade let me know that. I knew how affectionate he could be from seeing him with Leon but he tolerated me rather than adored me and had become increasingly aloof in the time Leon had been away.

'Hi, Marmalade,' I said, perching on the edge of his favourite armchair. 'Are you not dining with the others tonight?'

He looked straight at me with his large, round golden eyes, before blinking and looking away. Cattitude! I stroked his back, keen to show him some love even if he didn't show me much in return.

'I know you miss Leon,' I said, softly. 'And I know he's been gone way longer than promised, but he'll be back on Monday.'

Marmalade jumped down from the sofa and padded towards the kitchen. It made me sad, but I knew his disdain for me wasn't personal. When Leon started as a chef at The Ramparts six years ago, he and I became instant friends. He was in a long-term relationship but wasn't happy. Mimi was extremely possessive and couldn't bear the thought of anyone else having a piece of her boyfriend – friends, colleagues and even his cat. Six months after he started at The Ramparts, Leon went home early to find Mimi yelling at Marmalade and the poor cat cowering. After walking away on several occasions but always returning, falling for Mimi's promises to get a grip on her erratic behaviour and jealousy, this was the final straw and Leon walked out for good. Buying the house on Drake Street had been a clear sign to Mimi that it was finally over and he'd never be back. When Leon and I got together in the November, eight months later, and I met Marmalade for the first time, he was wary around me – understandable after how Mimi had treated him. I was sure he'd come round, especially when I loved cats so much, but he never had.

When I moved into Drake Street the following May in time for my thirtieth birthday, I already had Heathcliff, Babushka and Winnie, who was a year old at the time. A cream and chocolate spotted tabby, Winnie was a Munchkin – a breed with extremely short legs but a surprisingly strong ability to run and leap which seemed to defy their leg length.

Together, Leon and I added to the fur family with Viking, Jupiter, Sybil and Freyja and I'd been looking forward to us choosing the kittens for the café together but Leon's absence over the past five months meant that he'd played no part in it and hadn't even met any of them yet.

One of the kittens, five-month-old Rubix, jumped up onto the sofa, licking his lips. His name was inspired by the Rubik's cube because he was a mix of colours, reminding me of a meme of a similar-looking cat and the caption *When you're the last cat made that day and there are no matching parts.* A rescue moggy – a cat with no defined breed – Rubix had one blue and one golden eye. His front right and back left paws were ginger tabby, his other two paws were grey and black tabby, and his body and tail were a mixture of the two colours. His face was grey and black tabby with a spot of ginger around his golden eye and a white muzzle. He was so playful and made me smile every time I saw him.

'Not long until you meet Leon,' I said to Rubix. 'He's going to love you so much and, once he's home and settled, we'll take you to the cat café. I can't wait to see what you all think of it.'

I didn't plan on taking Marmalade to the café as it would be unfair to introduce him to so many people and busy surroundings at his age. I was going to take the other adults and would play it by ear as to which ones adapted well. Their wellbeing was at the forefront of everything so if they weren't happy, they wouldn't be made to spend time at the café. I hoped that, even if Babushka, Heathcliff and Winnie didn't settle, the four younger adults would. The eight kittens should be more adaptable to their surroundings and settle in easily.

Rubix clambered onto my knee and was soon joined by Cloud, a Persian long-haired kitten with a blue smoke coat and brilliant copper eyes. I stroked them both and closed my eyes for a moment, reflecting on the past five months. It had been hard work and I'd far rather Leon had been by my side, but I'd got through it and achieved something amazing. I just hoped it was finally out of his system. Project managing the refurbishment was one thing, but I absolutely couldn't run the cat café without him so if he came back and got itchy feet again... I opened my eyes and shook my head, unable to bear the thought of it.

'He wouldn't do that to us,' I said to the kittens. 'He promised.'

3

FIVE MONTHS AGO

Whenever Leon bit his nails, I knew he had something on his mind. It usually took some encouragement from me for him to open up, but he'd been nibbling on them all week and I still hadn't got to the root of the problem. The purchase of 9 Castle Street had gone through two days ago on 17 May and we'd been out for a meal to celebrate, so I'd asked him what was up then. He claimed it had been nerves about the deal falling apart last minute, which was fair enough – I'd felt anxious about that myself, especially as I'd already left my job at The Ramparts last week – so why was he still biting his nails two days on?

'What's going on, Leon?' I gently prompted after he'd been home for an hour on Friday night, looking increasingly agitated.

'There's something I need to talk to you about,' he said after a pause. 'But not here. Can we go for a walk?'

'Sure.' It felt like a delaying tactic but if it meant he was finally going to open up, so be it. I pulled on my trainers and a hoodie and we set off down to the seafront in silence.

'Do you want to walk or sit?' I asked when we reached South Bay. It was a warm, calm evening, reasonably busy but not a patch on how it would be over the approaching half-term break or the summer months.

Leon looked around, frowning. 'Maybe keep walking. We'll head towards The Bay Pavilion. It'll be quieter there.'

'You're making me nervous,' I said, as we crossed the road onto the same side as the beach.

'Sorry.'

'Come on, Leon,' I said once we'd walked a little further in silence. 'The suspense is killing me.'

'Okay,' he said with a sigh. 'Do you remember me getting offered that job as a cruise ship chef after I split up with psycho Mimi?'

His ex had been relentless in trying to get him to move back in with her and he'd told me that applying to the cruise line had been a knee-jerk reaction to try to get rid of her.

'You turned it down because you'd just bought your house,' I said.

'Yeah, and then we got together and the timing was never right.'

My stomach started churning. There was obviously a 'but' in there and I had a feeling I wasn't going to like where it took us.

'I never regretted that,' he continued, 'but over the years, I've often wondered what it would have been like.'

He fell silent once more.

'Why are you telling me this?' I asked, trying hard not to sound impatient.

'Because they got in touch and asked if I was still interested.'

We'd reached the approach road to The Bay Pavilion and there weren't many people around. I paused on the path with my backside resting against the sea wall, folded my arms and stared at him, eyebrows raised.

'And are you?'

'Yes.'

'Meaning what? You're still wondering what it would be like, or you want to do something about it?'

He lowered his eyes and teased a pebble on the path with his foot. 'They've offered me a three-month contract starting at the end of this month. It's a great opportunity.'

I'd known there was something wrong, but I'd never have suspected this. He couldn't be seriously considering it, could he?

'But we've just taken on the café,' I said, perturbed by the enthusiasm in his tone.

'I know, but you were always going to be the one project managing the refurb. I'm not needed at this stage.'

Leon wasn't interested in the creative side of setting up the business, so we'd already agreed that it made sense for him to continue working full time at The Ramparts, bringing in a regular income. Just because I was project managing it, it didn't mean I wouldn't have appreciated his input. It might be my business on paper, but I very much saw it as our business and the fulfilment of a dream we'd talked about for several years.

'I know it's not what we planned, but I really want to do this,' Leon said, finally lifting his gaze, his eyes pleading with mine.

'What happens at the end of the three months?' I asked.

'I come home and we open the café in September as planned.'

He placed his hands on my hips and pulled me closer to him, planting a soft kiss on my forehead. 'I just feel like I need to get this out of my system and doing it before the café opens is surely better than me wanting to do it after we open.'

'You *really* want to do this?'

'If I don't, I'll always be wondering.'

We both turned to look out at the sea, resting our forearms on the wall.

'Three months is such a long time,' I said.

'But it's not forever. And you'll have so much going on, you'll barely notice I'm gone.'

I glanced at him, eyebrows raised once more. 'You know that's not true.'

'It's just something I need to do.'

I slowly exhaled as I stared out at the sea, imagining how great an expanse of water would be separating us if he went. *When* he went. It wasn't like I could stop him. He'd supported me with the café and it was only fair I support him with this.

'I'll miss you,' I said, softly.

'Does that mean you're okay with it?'

'I'm not okay with it, but I'll support you. Just three months, though. I can't open the café on my own.'

'Just three months. I promise.'

* * *

Present day

That promise was what kept me going. I hung a calendar on the kitchen wall and drew a big red heart on his expected return date. Each evening before bed, I took a black marker pen and placed a cross through the day, telling the cats we were one day closer to Leon returning. An asterisk at six weeks signalled halfway. Except it wasn't.

At that point, Leon called to say that he'd been offered a two-month extension working under Jean-Pierre Duval – a celebrated chef and one of Leon's idols. It was an amazing opportunity and what would be the highlight of his career so far, so he was understandably excited about it. I was thrilled for him, but it hurt that he'd already accepted it. Of course I'd have said yes – what kind of girlfriend would I have been if I hadn't? – but it would have been nice if he'd thought to discuss it with me first, especially when it had an impact on the café's opening date.

I had no choice but to delay opening by two months and continue to manage everything on my own. It was lonely and hard but it was a small sacrifice that I was willing to make for the man I loved. On a positive note, that extra time took the pressure off, which was so much better for my health challenges.

I drew another red heart on the calendar around 30 October and prayed that he'd keep his promise to return when the extension was over, no matter what further exciting opportunities presented themselves.

4

The following day was Sunday lunch with my family – something we tried to do on the last Sunday of every month at my parents' home in Little Sandby.

I hugged my beautiful one-year-old Bengal cat, Freyja, and kissed the top of her head. A classic tabby, Freyja was brown with black stripes.

'Can I trust you to play nicely with the others while I'm out?' I asked her.

She purred contentedly in my arms, looking up to me with innocent green eyes, as though she would never dream of teasing the rest of our fur family – and especially not her half-sister, two-year-old Sybil.

'I'll see you in a few hours,' I said, gently placing Freyja onto her favourite cat bed on the large activity centre in the dining room, where she gave a lazy yawn before curling up for a nap. Sybil – a Bengal Maine Coon cross, same mother as Freyja – was also a brown tabby but with black mackerel-style stripes and a white nose stripe. She was sprawled out on one of the platforms, her front paws dangling over the side. I gave them both a final stroke and left the house, that familiar feeling of loss tugging at me each time I said goodbye to my fur babies.

When I arrived at Bramble Crescent, Rylan's car was on the drive beside Mum's, and Tom's car was on the road. Tom wasn't related by blood, but we all considered him to be part of the family. He'd had a rough start in life, taken into foster care at the age of seven when his mother and her boyfriend were arrested for drug dealing. When he was nine, he was placed with Nanna for a long-term placement. The same age as Rylan, they quickly became the best of mates, inseparable inside and outside of school. The pair of them often let me hang around and I had so many wonderful memories of summers spent riding our bikes, building dens or playing in the stream in the bluebell wood half a mile north of the village, and winters building snowmen and having snowball fights. We were the siblings Tom had never had and he was like a brother to us both.

My parents welcomed him like another son and we were all grateful that Nanna – a fiercely independent woman who hadn't let being widowed at a young age stop her from expanding her family through fostering – had brought Tom into our lives.

I parked behind Tom's car and, as I got out, the front door opened and my parents' rough collie, Sindy, trotted across the lawn to greet me.

'Hello, beautiful,' I said, stroking her soft muzzle. 'I've missed you.'

Mum was waiting in the doorway and gave me a warm hug. 'I'm so glad you could make it. We thought you might need to spend today in the café.'

'Matt and the gang finished up yesterday so I'm nearly there.'

'I'm so excited to see it finished. As soon as Leon's seen it, we'll be there in force.'

I was desperate to show the café off to my family, but it only felt fair for Leon to have the first full viewing.

I hung my coat and scarf over the end of the banister and breathed in the delicious aroma of a traditional Sunday lunch – roast chicken and stuffing blended with roast potatoes and the sweeter smell of cauliflower cheese. I was so ready for a proper home-cooked meal. I could cook but it didn't excite me like baking did and I'd been very lax in the kitchen while Leon was away, finding cooking for one exceptionally tedious.

'Who's on chef duty today?' I asked.

'Your dad and Tom – my favourite combination.'

As well as being a star baker, Nanna had been an amazing cook.

She'd passed on her skills in the kitchen to Dad when he was a child and she'd loved having another apprentice in the form of Tom.

'Tabby!' My sister-in-law, Macey, was seated in an armchair in the through lounge/dining room and held her arms out for a hug. 'No chance of me getting up, so you'll have to come down to me.'

I laughed as I bent over to embrace her.

'How are you feeling?' I asked as I sat beside Mum on the sofa.

'Shattered.' She ran her hands over her growing baby bump. 'Can't believe I've still got seven weeks left. And that's assuming he arrives on time. It's going to kill me.'

Shattered? That was the story of my life!

'At least it's half term now and your maternity leave has started.' Macey was a psychology tutor at the sixth-form, which was where Rylan had met her.

'Thank goodness,' she said. 'Why don't they warn you that pregnancy sucks?'

Mum laughed. 'I think they do, but every woman hopes they'll be the lucky one and glow throughout.'

'Urgh! My only glowing is the slick of sweat after throwing up, or from the night sweats.'

Macey looked at me with sad puppy dog eyes and ran her forefingers down her cheeks to indicate tears, but we all knew how excited she was about the baby despite not loving the pregnancy part. Rylan and Macey were going to be such amazing parents and nobody deserved it more after nearly three years of trying and nothing happening. At the start of this year, they'd decided it was time to explore other options, but that's when Macey found out she was pregnant. I couldn't be happier for them, but their baby news had got me thinking about children. I'd never imagined I'd be in my mid-thirties and childless. Leon and I both wanted children, but there never seemed to be a right time and, with our new venture, I wasn't sure there ever would be. My health challenges added a further complication too. It had been easy to push thoughts of raising a family aside when we had no friends or family with babies or young children, but it had been on my mind a lot during Macey's pregnancy and those feelings were only going to get stronger once Baby Walsh arrived.

'Hi, Tabby,' Rylan called, poking his head through the serving hatch between the kitchen and dining room. 'What do you want to drink?'

'A lemonade, please.'

'Coming right up.'

Rylan appeared moments later with a lemonade for me and a fruit tea for Macey. 'Dad says lunch will be fifteen minutes.'

'I'd better go and say hello to him and Tom.'

In the kitchen, Dad wiped his hands on a tea towel and gave me a welcome hug, but Tom was attending to a sizzling tray of roast potatoes, so I stayed at a safe distance.

'We weren't sure if you'd make it today,' Dad said.

'Mum said the exact same thing but you know how much I love a Sunday roast, especially when I'm not cooking it.'

'How are you doing?' he asked, giving me a concerned fatherly look.

'I'm good at the moment, thanks.'

'You'd tell us if you weren't?'

'Of course! But I really am fine. Having an extra two months to prepare has had its advantages. It hasn't been nearly as full-on as it would have been.'

Although I'd much rather Leon had returned when he'd said – or not gone away at all – it had been good for the café. The company from whom I'd originally ordered the tables and chairs had messed me around so I'd needed to cancel and find another supplier who couldn't have got them to me for the original opening date.

Tom had returned the roasties to the oven. As the heat had steamed up his glasses, he wiped them before giving me a hug.

'Hey, Tabby-cat,' he said. 'It's good to see you.'

'Hey, Tom-cat,' I said, squeezing him back.

I'm not sure when we'd started calling each other that, but it was our special term of endearment which nobody else used.

'How's things?' I asked him.

'Nearly year end so it's all the same old – chasing clients to get their receipts in.'

'Same clients every year too,' Dad said, rolling his eyes.

'And every year they promise they'll be better prepared the next year,' Tom said.

'And every time the next year arrives, they're later than ever?' I suggested, and they both nodded. I did feel for them and resolved to be one of the early ones with the café's accounts, especially when they point blank refused to charge me for being my accountants.

A self-professed 'numbers geek', Tom joined my parents' accountancy practice after college, taking day release to become a qualified accountant. He'd remained a valuable part of their practice ever since and they'd surprised him on his thirty-fifth birthday last year with a partnership in the firm.

Dad and Tom shooed me out of the kitchen, insisting I relax before lunch. I was more than happy to sit down. I wasn't really 'good' this morning – pushed myself too hard yesterday – but it was easier to say that than admit the truth. I just wanted to enjoy the time with my family and try to ignore the pain.

Back in the lounge, Macey was reeling off the contents of her hospital bag which she'd packed yesterday. The excitement in her voice was matched by the expression on my brother's face. They knew they were having a boy but were remaining tight-lipped about names. My parents couldn't wait for the arrival of their first grandchild and I was thrilled about being an auntie.

'I'm really sorry,' I said, waving my phone at everyone when we settled at the dining table for lunch a little later. 'I'm waiting for Leon – last minute as always – to confirm his flight details. Can I bend the rule just this once?'

We had a strict no-phones-at-the-table rule in our family but nobody was unreasonable about it if anyone was waiting on big news.

'I think we can make an exception on this occasion,' Mum said, smiling at me. 'I bet you can't wait to have him back.'

'It's been a long five months.'

My parents liked Leon and had welcomed him into the family right from the start, but they weren't impressed with some of the decisions he'd made this year. They were too diplomatic to come straight out with it but carefully chosen words like 'surprised' accompanied by concerned looks told me that he'd massively gone down in their estimation. I wondered whether I should have been a bit more loyal to him and made out that I was 100 per cent behind everything he'd done, but my parents weren't daft. They'd have seen through it, so I took the same approach as I took with my health – telling them the truth but not the whole truth.

'I'm in awe with how calm you've been about it all,' Macey said.

I gave her a gentle smile. 'I haven't always felt it. But we're through it now and he's back tomorrow, so it's all good.'

'I think a toast's needed,' Dad said, putting his knife and fork down and raising his glass. 'To our amazing daughter and her brand-new venture, the Castle Street Cat Café. To Tabby!'

'To Tabby!' everyone chorused, smiling at me.

As I sipped my drink, I sent a silent toast up to Nanna.

Our meal was exactly what I loved about family get-togethers – lots of laughter and banter. Rylan and Tom shared anecdotes about each other's mishaps during their weekly five-a-side football game, making us all laugh. I loved their bond. They took the mickey constantly but it was all good-natured and I knew they'd do anything for each other. Tom had been the best man at Rylan and Macey's wedding and their baby would refer to him as Uncle Tom.

We were taking a break in the lounge before having our dessert when my phone rang and Leon's name flashed up on the screen, making my heart leap. I slipped out of the room, dying to hear his voice again.

'Hi, Leon,' I said, connecting the call as I walked down the hall. 'Are you all set for your final night?'

There was a slight pause. 'I'm not coming back tomorrow.' His tone was hesitant and my stomach churned.

'Couldn't you get a flight?' I hoped I didn't sound too annoyed, but what had he expected, leaving it until the eleventh hour like this?

There was no response from Leon. I stepped outside and closed the external kitchen door behind me, frowning. 'Leon? Are you still there?'

'Yeah, I'm...' He sighed. 'I'm sorry, Tabby, but I'm not coming back. I'm staying on the ship.'

I sat down heavily on the stone bench beneath the kitchen window. 'For how long?'

'Until Christmas.'

'Christmas?' I cried, feeling sick. How could he do this to me again? I'd supported him leaving, I'd even put the café opening date back to support the extension, but he was taking huge liberties now.

'But you said you'd only extended your contract to work with Jean-Pierre Duval.'

'Yes.'

'So is he staying on board longer?'

'No.'

The one-word answers were so frustrating.

'Then I don't understand,' I said. 'The café's opening a fortnight on Wednesday. You promised you'd be back.'

'I know, and I thought I would be, but things have changed. This is what I want to do now.'

I couldn't think straight. What did that mean? It was what he wanted to do until Christmas or what he wanted to do forever?

'What about the café?' I asked, my voice a little shrill. 'I can't keep putting the opening date back.'

'I'm not asking you to,' he said, gently. 'You should open as planned.' A pause. 'Without me.'

I gasped, feeling panicky at the idea of it. 'Without you? But I don't want to. That's why I shifted the last date. It's not right doing it without you. It's our dream.'

'No, Tabby, it's *your* dream.'

I flinched at the sharpness of his tone. That was spectacularly unfair. We'd spent years discussing it and Leon had been as much into the idea as me.

'Working on a cruise ship is my dream now,' he said. 'I love it and it's what I want to do long term. I'll be home for a couple of weeks over Christmas and New Year, but I'm starting another contract in January, so I won't be working in the cat café.'

My hand tightened round the phone. So it *was* forever and I was on my own with the café. There was an obvious question to ask about what that meant for us, but I couldn't seem to form the words.

'Are you still there?' Leon asked.

'Yes.' It came out as a whisper. Tears pricked my eyes and my throat was burning.

'You don't need to rush to move out,' he said, his voice gentle again. 'I'll let you know the date I'll be back, so as long as you're gone by then.'

I closed my eyes as a chill rippled through me and forced out the question, only managing two words. 'It's over?'

'It has to be. Distance relationships don't work. Not long term, anyway. We've both got very different dreams and they're not going to work in alignment. I'm sorry. I hope we can still be friends. You could email me photos of the cats and let me know how the café's doing. And, as I say, there's no rush to move out. You can stay till I'm back.'

I swallowed down the lump in my throat and somehow found some strength to inject into my voice. 'I won't be doing that, Leon. I'm not housesitting for you or paying half your mortgage. I'll have my stuff moved out by the end of next weekend and I'll post my keys back through the letterbox.'

'Tabby! Don't be like that!'

I was seriously riled now. Jumping up from the bench, I stomped across the lawn towards the decking at the bottom of the garden.

'Like what? How do you want me to be, Leon? I've spent the past five months slogging my guts out getting our business ready and you were meant to be coming home tomorrow to help me prepare for opening day. Now you phone me and tell me that not only do I have to continue going it alone but we're over too. Completely out of nowhere.'

'It wasn't out of nowhere,' he snapped.

'It was for me! How long have you been thinking about this?'

'Does it matter?'

'It matters to me.'

'Ever since you got the inheritance.'

'Leon! That was early December! It's the end of October now. Why the hell didn't you say anything before?'

'Because you kept going on about the cat café being what your nanna wanted.'

'It was, but I'd never have gone for it if I'd thought for one minute it wasn't your dream too. When we viewed it, I asked you if you were 100 per cent in and you promised me you were. You lied to me!'

'I thought I was in. I didn't know this opportunity was going to come my way. I never wanted to mess you about or hurt you.'

'Yeah, well, you managed to do both. Goodbye, Leon.'

'Tabby, I—'

But I didn't want to hear any more apologies or platitudes. He'd already let me down by extending three months to five, and now he wasn't returning at all, leaving me to run the café on my own when he knew that wasn't possible. I didn't want anything from him ever again.

Energy zapped, I sank onto one of the chairs on the decking and rested my elbows on the table. He *had* lied and the worst thing was that I'd known it at the time, but I'd pushed aside the voice of doubt because I didn't believe the man I loved could ever let me down so badly. I'd done the same when he phoned about the extension. What was I going to do now?

5

'Tabby-cat? Are you still out here?'

I heard Tom's voice nearby and swiped at my wet cheeks, but I was too late.

'What's happened?' he asked, rushing to my side, sloshing tea over the side of the mug he hastily placed on the table.

'Leon's not coming back,' I said, bursting into tears again. 'It's over.'

He scraped the nearest chair across the deck so it was closer to me and plonked himself down on it, his legs touching mine.

'He's dumped you?' he asked, sounding shocked.

I nodded. 'Just now on the phone. Apparently the cat café is my dream, not his, so he's staying on the cruise ship and I'm moving out.'

'Oh, Tabby, I'm so sorry.'

He pulled me into his arms and hugged me close as the tears spilled down my cheeks.

'I can't believe he's done that,' he said softly, releasing me when the tears finally subsided. 'What a tool.'

I sank back into my chair, sniffing, wishing I had a tissue on me.

'And to kick you out too?' he added. 'That's low.'

'He said I could stay until he gets back at Christmas but he can piss right off. I'm not paying his bills and keeping his house clean. Probably cutting off my nose to spite my face, but I said I'll move out by the end of next weekend. So now I have to finish getting the café ready *and* move into the flat above it.'

'But isn't the flat unfurnished? And didn't you say it needs work?'

'Yes, but I don't have much choice. Well, I do, but I'm not staying in that house a moment longer than I have to.'

'You could stay with me and sort the flat out later.'

His kind offer brought another lump to my throat. 'That's lovely of you, but you're not allowed animals in your apartment and I don't think there's any chance we can sneak in sixteen cats without someone noticing and objecting. I'll work something out.'

He placed his hand on my arm and fixed his eyes on mine. 'I know you like to be independent, but this isn't the time for principles. I want to help and so will your parents. Please let us.'

I gave him a weak smile. 'I could use some help moving my stuff across later this week.'

'What about finishing off in the café?'

'It's nearly done. It's just the move I need help with.'

'Promise you'll shout up if there's anything else. You don't have to do this alone.'

'I'll be fine,' I said, lifting up my mug and taking a few sips so I didn't have to look him in the eye. There was no way I was going to ask for more help. If I did that, they'd discover the truth and I couldn't let that happen.

'Are you coming back inside or do you need some more time?' Tom asked.

'I need a moment. I'll finish my tea first. Can you say I was still on the phone? I'll tell them myself when I come in.'

'You're sure you'll be okay?'

I shrugged. 'I'll have to be.'

Tom patted me on the shoulder and left me to my thoughts. I stared into my tea, fighting back the urge to slump onto the table, head in hands, and bawl my eyes out once more. In the space of a five-minute phone call, everything about my life had changed. I'd lost my boyfriend, my home and I could be about to lose my business before it even opened. There was no way I could run it without Leon.

I finished my tea and took my empty mug back to the house. As I loaded it into the dishwasher, I heard laughter from the lounge and hated that I was about to put a dampener on things, but they needed to know what was going on.

'There you are!' Mum declared. 'What time's he due back?'

Tom caught my eye and winced.

'He's not coming back,' I said, sinking onto the sofa beside Mum. 'He doesn't want to run the café and he doesn't want to be with me anymore.'

There were cries of disgust from everyone and questions were fired at me, but I didn't have many answers.

'Why don't you stay at the house a bit longer?' Dad suggested when I'd explained the part about me moving out. 'I get what you're saying about not wanting to do him any favours, but wouldn't it be easier on you if you focus on opening the business and then move?'

'Probably, but I don't want to be there anymore so I'd rather be at the flat. It'll make some things easier too like getting the cats used to the café.'

'Just let us know what you need,' Mum said.

'Is there any chance of me borrowing the bed from the spare room?'

'Of course you can. You can borrow the bedside drawers and lamps too if that would help.'

'You could have the sofa bed out of our spare room,' Rylan added, glancing at Macey who nodded her approval. 'It's not much but it'll be more comfortable to sit on than the garden chairs.' They'd already loaned me their garden furniture so I could work in the flat during the refurbishment.

'I can offer you a coffee table and an uplighter,' Tom said, scrunching up his nose apologetically. 'It's not much, but everything's fitted at mine.'

'I'll take it all,' I said. 'Thank you.'

Between them, they reckoned they could cobble together enough crockery, cutlery and pans to keep me going, which I really appreciated.

An hour later, the fatigue was too much for me. 'Sorry to bail out early,' I said, 'but I've got a lot to organise now, so I'd better head home and make a start.'

There were hugs all round and even Macey insisted on getting up this time so she could hug me more tightly. They were all so supportive and encouraging – not that I'd have expected anything else from my amazing family – and I was so grateful for the help with moving.

As I drove home, I blinked back the tears to concentrate on the road. My head was pounding and my body ached. Like my heart.

* * *

When I returned to Leon's house later and stepped into the hall, it somehow felt quieter and emptier than usual now that I knew he wasn't coming back.

Babushka and Viking – an angelic and extremely affectionate three-year-old white rescue moggy with a black tail – greeted me this time. I sat on the stairs and told them I'd missed them – my usual greeting to whoever met me at the door – and sighed as I added, 'But it looks like Leon hasn't missed any of us, especially me.'

A motorbike revved outside, making me jump, and sending both cats running back upstairs. I stayed where I was, feeling weary, but then I heard the slam of the front door next door followed by what sounded like a herd of elephants stampeding up the stairs adjacent to ours. The squeals of the children were drowned out by their mother yelling at them, as usual. I heaved myself up, shrugged off my coat and went into the lounge.

A thumping bass line from music on the other side hit me and I ran my hands through my hair, shaking my head. Leon had claimed the noise from both sides never bothered him but, when I spent all day in a loud environment, I wanted to come home to peace and quiet. I wouldn't miss this house at all, but I would miss Leon and was struggling to believe it was over. I'd felt so lonely without him these past five months and the only comfort had been knowing it was temporary.

I wasn't particularly thirsty but making a mug of tea would give me something to focus on instead of replaying that final phone call over and over in my mind. As I waited for the kettle to boil, my eyes were drawn to the calendar hanging on the wall and the big red heart on the square for tomorrow. Each cross on that calendar had meant a step closer to us being back together. Except it had all been a lie. What each cross really symbolised was how long Leon had been stringing me along, making promises to return which he had no intention of keeping.

On the phone, he'd mentioned having doubts since I received Nanna's inheritance, but I couldn't help wondering if it was way before that. Could it be the reason we'd never bought a place of our own, why he'd never proposed, why we hadn't spoken about having children since our early days together?

Feeling anger stabbing at me, I grabbed the black marker pen I'd been using for the crosses and frantically scribbled over the heart before grabbing the calendar off the wall and ripping the pages, resigning those hopeful crosses to the recycling bin.

There was so much I needed to do, but my priority had to be finding someone to replace Leon in the café. I sat at the dining table with my laptop open, trying to create a job description, but the words wouldn't come. I didn't even know what to call the role he was going to play. After an hour of concentration, I had nothing. Releasing a loud, frustrated sigh, I closed the laptop.

The cats needed feeding so I put food and fresh water out and watched them eagerly tucking in. Marmalade must have been hungry today as he trotted in from the lounge without glancing in my direction and joined the rest of them.

Maybe I'd start packing up the kitchen while they ate. I opened the cupboard door nearest to me, which contained all the crockery, and retrieved two cat-themed mugs. Everything else belonged to Leon, bought before we got together. As I opened more cupboards, I was repeatedly reminded that this was Leon's house. All I owned were the mugs, a chopping board and a couple of tea towels with cats on them. When we'd cleared Nanna's house, I'd kept everything she used for baking – bowls, measuring spoons, a food processor and so on – but they were still in cardboard boxes in the smallest bedroom. Leon had promised me he'd have a clear-out and shift around in the kitchen to give them space, but it had never happened.

I placed my belongings together on the worktop with a heavy heart. How was it over? Tears burned my eyes – tears that Leon didn't deserve. The packing could wait.

I needed a distraction, so I put the television on, but couldn't hear it above next door's music and switched it off again. Sybil draped herself across the sofa arm and Winnie curled up by my feet for a sleep. A couple of the girl kittens – Effie and Blinky – jumped onto my knee. Seven-month-old Effie was a grey and white Ragdoll with beautiful blue eyes, and three-month-old Blinky was a grey Exotic Shorthair with green eyes. With her flat face, she was like the pug equivalent of the cat world. I felt so much calmer as I stroked them and tuned into their gentle breathing, but it wasn't enough to focus my thoughts away from Leon.

He said we'd been drifting apart for a long time, but I hadn't felt that way at all. How had I missed it? Had I been so wrapped up in the cat café that I hadn't seen the signs or had he just said that to ease his conscience over blindsiding me?

I hadn't admitted it to my family earlier, but I was scared. I'd never have gone ahead with the purchase if I'd known I'd be on my own. Leon knew that, so why hadn't he spoken up earlier? I'd given him plenty of opportunity to pull out but he hadn't taken it and now I was screwed. It wasn't going to be difficult without him – it was going to be impossible. And he knew that. He'd always known that.

6

EIGHTEEN MONTHS AGO

I twisted a lock of my long blonde hair round my index finger as I sat in the waiting room at the doctor's surgery. I knew what the verdict would be, but I so wished it could be different.

'Tabitha Walsh to room six.'

With a sigh, I pulled my bag onto my shoulder and shuffled slowly along the corridor.

'Morning, Tabitha,' Dr Amberley said when I sat down in her consulting room. 'Any change in your symptoms since we last met?'

'No. Still exhausted.'

She nodded and tapped something into her computer. 'Last time, we examined your joints and ruled out rheumatoid arthritis. This time, we've had the rest of your test results back and everything's clear so we can rule out diabetes, thyroid problems, lupus and so on. As we discussed before, there's no specific test for it but, with your symptoms, other conditions ruled out, and you having an auntie and a cousin with it, my diagnosis is fibromyalgia.'

My stomach sank. I'd been fairly sure that would be the case, but there'd been a sliver of hope that it would turn out to be something different – something treatable. Fibromyalgia is a disorder which causes chronic pain, but little is known about why it develops. It's believed that people with fibro have abnormal levels of certain chemicals in the brain which change the way pain messages are processed and carried round the body by the central nervous system. It's more common in women, typically develops between the ages of twenty-five and fifty-five and can be hereditary. Big tick in all three of those boxes for me.

'As you know, there's no cure for fibromyalgia,' Dr Amberley continued, 'and it won't just disappear, but there are ways to manage it and it's not degenerative.'

The condition not getting worse didn't feel like much of a positive alongside knowing I'd have it for life. My Auntie Sonia – Mum's older sister – massively struggled with her fibromyalgia, frequently ranting on social media. Her daughter – my cousin Fiona – wasn't quite so vocal, but she shared lots of memes about the condition and it all sounded terrifying. I'd never talked about it in person with either of them. They lived in Leeds, ninety minutes away, so we didn't see them very often.

'Is there anything you want to ask me?' Dr Amberley said, bringing my focus back to her.

'You said it can be managed.'

'You can take paracetamol for pain relief and I'd strongly encourage that, and there are anti-inflammatories which can be taken. Some fibromyalgia patients present with depression but, even if that's not the case, antidepressants can help with sleep problems and pain. Cognitive Behavioural Therapy – CBT – can help a patient with the way they think about the condition, particularly if they're finding they're focusing on the negatives. But the main thing I recommend for now is self-care. Drink lots of water, eat a healthy diet and introduce regular exercise into your routine. Low-impact aerobic activities are best – walking, cycling, swimming – and those which engage the mind too such as yoga and tai chi.'

She glanced at her screen. 'Remind me about your job. You're a full-time chef?'

'A pastry chef at The Ramparts Hotel. I work shifts and I average a forty-eight-hour week.'

She tapped that into her computer then turned to face me. 'I'm sure you don't need me to point out that that's a long working week for someone with fibromyalgia. I'm guessing you're on your feet all day too.'

I nodded. 'Will I need to reduce my hours?'

Dr Amberley held her hands up. 'It's not for me to tell anyone what to do or not to do because I know it's not that simple. Reduced hours mean reduced income and that's not an option for some people. However, if you haven't already done so, I would strongly encourage a conversation with your employer. There may be some adjustments that can be made.'

Adjustments. What if I didn't want to make any adjustments? What if I liked my life exactly how it was?

'What did they say?' Leon asked when I settled into the car after my appointment.

'Just as I thought,' I said, my voice flat. 'Fibromyalgia.'

'No!' He took my hand in his. 'Are you okay?'

'I'm not sure. I don't think it's sunk in yet. I really hoped it wouldn't be that.'

'Me too. I'm so sorry. What happens next?'

I shrugged. 'Lots of thinking to do and adjustments to make.'

'Can you still work?'

'Yes, but the doctor said I might want to think about reducing my hours.'

'How do you feel about that?'

'Pretty pants right now. I love my job. I don't want to cut back.' My voice cracked as I said it. I'd just turned thirty-three and didn't want a life-long potentially life-changing condition. I wanted things back to how they'd been before.

'Let's get you home and we can talk about it some more,' he said. 'It'll be all right. We'll deal with it together. I love you.'

'Thank you. I love you too.'

Leon pulled away and I stared out of the window. It was a warm, bright mid-May day, but I shivered and pulled the sleeves of my hoodie down over my hands. I felt drained and just wanted to crawl under the duvet and wake up tomorrow discovering it had all been a horrible dream.

In some ways, it was a relief to have a diagnosis as I now knew what I was dealing with and I had a doctor who was knowledgeable and understanding. I was one of the fortunate ones there. I'd seen stories online of people waiting for years, being passed from one doctor to another, with some medical professionals even telling patients there's no such thing as fibromyalgia and it's psychosomatic. That had to be such a slap in the face.

It's believed that fibromyalgia symptoms can be triggered by illness, infection, surgery or a traumatic event. If that was true, illness had been my trigger. In November last year, I was off work for a fortnight. What started as flu developed into a stomach bug and I've never been so ill in my whole life. When I returned to work, I still felt drained and put it down to a lack of energy after being bed-bound for the best part of two weeks, and being so busy with the approach to Christmas. I took a week off in early January to give me some more time to recover and it seemed to do the trick but, back at work once more, I kept experiencing bouts of fatigue and pain throughout my body. I tried to push through it, but my body wouldn't let me and I had to have more time off work. I'd hated it.

Leon had been really supportive, doing all the cooking and cleaning and never moaning when I cancelled plans to go out. He'd been the one who pushed me to see the doctor and had been full of reassurances that, whatever the diagnosis, he'd be there to support me through it.

We arrived back at Drake Street and he sent me up to bed while he filled a hot water bottle and made me a drink.

'I'm scared,' I admitted, cuddling the water bottle against my stomach a little later as I lay under the duvet while Leon sat on the bed beside me.

'What part scares you the most?' he asked.

'All of it! Being in pain, feeling shattered, the confusion. And I'm scared of what it means for us. We've already had to cut back on nights out. You didn't sign up to this.'

'And neither did you, but we're in this together. I'm not going anywhere so don't you worry about that.'

* * *

Present day

I stroked Winnie, memories of my diagnosis day swirling round my mind. He'd said all the right things to reassure me, but had he been saying them to convince himself? Could my diagnosis have been the point when things changed for Leon, or perhaps even earlier when I didn't recover from that first bout of illness?

Before that, our relationship had been amazing. We'd both worked long hours and had unwound with regular nights out or day trips between shifts, but I couldn't keep that pace up anymore. Had Leon been steadily pulling away from me since that moment, knowing that the life he loved so much would need to change for me? Had he loved our life-style more than he loved me?

I had so many questions. I brought up Leon's number on my phone and hovered my finger over the call button, then shut it down. There was no point. He probably wouldn't answer and, if he did, we'd argue. If I wanted answers, I'd need to get them another way.

'Sorry, Winnie,' I said, lifting her up as I rolled off the sofa. 'You can have the sofa to yourself for a bit.' I laid her back down and went back to my laptop on the dining table.

To: Leon Dexter
From: Tabby Walsh
Subject: Questions
Your phone call this afternoon was a heck of a shock. As I'm sure you can imagine, I've spent the afternoon trying to get my head round things and I have questions. I might not like some (any) of the answers, but I need to know so I can get some closure. I think you owe me this, don't you?

1. Did your feelings for me change after my fibromyalgia diagnosis? (be honest!)
2. When did you really get offered the job to work on the cruise ship?

3. Did you ever have any intention of running the cat café with me?
4. If you didn't, why did you encourage me to set it up when you know my fibro means I can't run it on my own?
5. Did you ever love me?
6. Is there someone else?

I read through it and deleted the sixth question. I didn't need to know that. If he had met someone else and it came out in one of the other questions, so be it, but it wasn't the important issue here. What I needed to know was how long he'd lied about how he felt about me and our future together. Some might say I was punishing myself by seeking out answers, but I was already thinking the worst, so why not have it confirmed?

7

As soon as I opened my eyes on Monday morning, I felt it. Pain. Fibro flare-ups were unpredictable – sometimes appearing out of the blue for no reason – but doing too much or being under stress typically (but not always) triggered mine. I therefore wasn't surprised to be hit by a more severe one after Leon's news, especially when I'd already had a mild flare-up yesterday from doing so much on Saturday.

I was experiencing stabbing pains, like somebody somewhere had a voodoo doll of me and was laughing hysterically as they viciously jabbed a long pin into my back, my hips, my calves, my neck... There wasn't a part of me they spared. Today was going to be hard.

'Amber,' I muttered as I shuffled across the landing to the bathroom, wincing with each movement. I applied a traffic light system to the pain level of my flare-ups. Green was a mild one, meaning I was in pain but I could just about push through it and go about my normal business, although I'd be completely exhausted by the evening. Yesterday had been one of those days. Amber massively slowed me down as the pain and other symptoms were so much worse and everything was a struggle. Red flare-ups were thankfully rare but they stopped me in my tracks, barely able to move and even in pain while lying still.

I sat down wearily on the toilet seat and closed my eyes, fighting the urge to weep. I had things to do, to think about, to plan, and I was going to struggle to do much today. I might be out of action for today only, for tomorrow as well, or even for as long as a week.

The walk-in shower looked enticing and the hot water would bring comfort, but one of the many frustrations of fibro was that a shower took a phenomenal amount of energy, which I didn't have. Washing my hair was out of the question, and washing myself was a massive challenge. And don't get me started on the effort needed to rub myself dry with my towel – a simple task most of the time becoming my Everest during a flare-up.

Heathcliff, Sybil and Marmite – a four-and-a-half-month-old long-haired black rescue moggy who I'd hand-reared along with his sister from being a few days old – were waiting for me outside the bathroom.

'Good morning, you three,' I said, my voice full of warmth. 'Don't panic! Food's coming!'

All I wanted to do was go back to bed and crawl under the duvet, but the cats had to come first. I padded downstairs, clinging onto the banister, and along the hall into the kitchen, stabbing pain in my joints with every step I took. Freyja, Babushka and Marmite's sister Ruby – also black all over but short-haired instead – trotted out of the dining room, mewing at me. I hated that, on days like this, I couldn't just bend down, scoop them up and shower them with kisses. When I was settled on the sofa or in bed, they'd cuddle against me, and the comfort they brought me was invaluable.

'Morning, everyone,' I called, my voice ten times brighter than I felt. 'Anyone hungry?'

That brought Sybil, Winnie and Effie running. Smudge and Pebbles were already in the kitchen, pacing up and down by the bowls. Pebbles was a short-haired Highlander – a recently developed American breed and therefore quite scarce – so I'd been thrilled to have her join the fur family. A brown spotted tabby with white socks and adorable rounded ears, she was the most playful of all the kittens and so much fun to be around. Smudge was an Aztec kitten – a mix of three specific breeds and only recently recognised as a separate breed – and, like Pebbles, was a brown tabby but with the classic swirly markings rather than spots. He adored being around people and action so was going to really thrive in the café environment.

I topped up the water bowls – several trips with a small plastic jug as I couldn't carry anything heavier – and added wet food to their bowls.

Changing the litter trays was yet another fibro challenge. Last night, I should have changed them in anticipation of how today was likely to be. All I could do for now was scoop, bag and sprinkle some fresh litter on the top.

My family had offered to help and I'd insisted I only needed help with the move, but that wasn't true. I needed help with so much more, but I couldn't ask them. I couldn't let them know how bad things were. I still hadn't come to terms with it myself.

Returning to the kitchen, I found all sixteen cats tucking into their food with satisfying slurping and lip-smacking noises. I was hungry, but devoid of energy. Breakfast would have to wait. It was one of the things that had hit me hard when Leon went away. If he was heading into work when I had an amber or red flare-up, he'd always made sure I had a cup of tea or coffee and some breakfast. He'd leave my lunch in the fridge and bring something for tea home with him. Without him here these past five months, I'd often gone without, and I could feel the impact in the looseness of my clothes.

As I reached the bottom of the stairs, I heard my phone ringing, but there was no way I could get upstairs in time to answer it. When I finally reached it, there were two missed FaceTime calls – one from Mum and one from Tom.

I couldn't let Mum see me on FaceTime, so I lay down in bed and called her instead, putting her on speakerphone – less effort than holding my phone.

'How are you doing this morning?' she asked when she answered.

'Slight flare-up,' I lied.

'Aw, Tabby, I'm sorry.'

'It would have been a miracle if I'd got away with it after yesterday. C'est la vie!' Well, it was my life, anyway.

'Do you need anything from me? I can take a few hours off or stop by tonight to help you pack.'

'Honestly, Mum, I'm fine. I've got some paperwork to sort and a job description to write, so it'll probably be Wednesday before I start packing. The main thing I need help with is the actual move.'

'Okay, but promise you'll let me know if there's anything else we can do. I can't bear the thought of you struggling.'

'I will. Thanks, Mum.'

We said our goodbyes and I disconnected the call. I couldn't face speaking to Tom too, so I flicked my phone onto silent, closed my eyes and willed the pain to go away.

* * *

I was sure I could hear someone whispering my name.

'Leon?' I murmured.

'Sorry to disappoint,' Tom said.

I opened my eyes and glanced in the direction of his voice. He was in the doorway, clutching a mug of tea. I was so parched, it was like seeing an oasis in the desert.

'I knocked but there was no answer,' he continued. 'Hope you didn't mind me letting myself in.'

Tom, Rylan and my parents all had a spare key – a family thing in case of emergencies.

'What are you doing here?' I asked him.

'I was dropping some accounts off with a client in town so your mum asked me to bring you some flowers. I've put them in the sink in some water. I made you a cuppa.' He came round to my side of the bed and placed it on a coaster on the bedside cabinet. 'But don't drink it if you'd rather go back to sleep.'

'I'll have it. What time is it?' I was aware of my words coming out slowly and a little slurred, as though I'd been drinking.

'Half ten. Have you had any breakfast?'

'I was going to make some porridge but I fell asleep.'

'Would you like me to make you some?'

It was on the tip of my tongue to say I was fine and send him away, but he wasn't going to buy that after finding me asleep at 10.30 a.m. and I was so hungry.

'Yes, please,' I said. 'It's in the cupboard by the...' I tailed off, frowning, as I grappled for the word. Another symptom of fibromyalgia was brain fog and it did my head in. It wasn't like I was searching for a difficult word right now. Leon would frequently fill in the blanks for me instead of giving me the time to find the word myself and, while I appreciated his intentions were good, it wasn't helpful. If I asked him to be patient with me, he got in a right huff.

'...by the...' I said, grimacing at Tom.

'Fibro fog?' he asked.

I frowned. 'How do you know about that?'

'I did some research online after you were diagnosed.'

'You did?'

'I'd never heard of fibromyalgia and I wanted to understand it.'

I stared at him for a moment. What a thoughtful thing to do.

'Breadbin!' I exclaimed, as the word suddenly came to me.

'One bowl of porridge coming right up.'

'Thanks, Tom-cat.'

'You're welcome, Tabby-cat.'

I was so touched that Tom had looked into fibromyalgia and that he understood fibro fog. I found it a nightmare. I know everyone jokes about being forgetful, particularly as they're getting older, but when the fibro fog engulfs me, it's not just a couple of 'dippy moments' – it happens again and again and again. I lost my house keys earlier this year and Leon found them in a bag of cat litter. I've found my phone in the fridge, my shoes in the shower, my umbrella in the laundry basket. It's not just misplacing things, either. It's struggling to form sentences, being unable to remember words for everyday objects and drifting off midway through saying something. It's having a panic about early-onset dementia. It's feeling stupid.

I needed to manoeuvre myself into a sitting position which would take ages and wouldn't be graceful. If I started now, I'd hopefully be done by the time Tom reappeared and I could convince him that I was still in bed because I was feeling sorry for myself after Leon dumped me and not because I was in too much pain and too fatigued to do anything. He'd surely buy that, especially when today was the day Leon should have been coming home. That definitely justified a day 'moping' in bed.

With a lot of grunts and gasps, I managed to push the pillows up against the headboard and sit against them. I took a few moments to catch my breath before reaching for my phone to see whether Leon had replied to my email from last night.

My heart pounded as I scanned down the list of messages in my inbox and saw that he had.

To: Tabby Walsh
From: Leon Dexter
Subject: RE: Questions
When I saw your email, I braced myself, thinking you were going to have a go at me and, to be fair, you'd have been justified. Thanks for not making it harder than it already is. I've answered your questions below. I'm sorry if the answers hurt, but you did ask me to be honest.

1. Did your feelings for me change after my fibromyalgia diagnosis? (be honest!) If you'd asked me this before I joined the cruise, I'd have said a resounding no, but I've had a lot of thinking time and I have to say yes. I hate myself for that. I'm so sorry. I loved you but I also loved our lifestyle and, when that changed, I struggled. I was okay with it when you were first ill but when we knew it was going to be a lifetime change, I found that hard to deal with. I know how selfish that sounds but you wanted me to be honest 😔 I'm not cut out for this. You need someone who loves you and will care for you in sickness and in health.

2. When did you really get offered the job to work on the cruise ship? They got in touch with me last October – a circular email to update their database. I had an online interview and I didn't tell you because your nanna was ill. I heard I'd passed the interview just after she died, but there were no vacancies for my skills so I didn't expect it to lead anywhere.

3. Did you ever have any intention of running the cat café with me? Definitely. I got the offer just before the sale of the café went through and it excited me. I assumed I'd get over it when the café was officially ours because the café was exciting too, but I couldn't stop thinking about the offer and realised I wanted to go for it. That's when I told you.

4. If you didn't, why did you encourage me to set it up when you know my fibro means I can't run it on my own? I honestly thought I'd do the 3 months and that would be it – out of my system – and I'd return home. I had no idea I was going to love it as much as I do.

5. Did you ever love me? Yes. I can't believe you'd ever doubt that. But as I said on the phone, we've been drifting apart for some time now. You might not have realised it but, if you look back, you'll see the signs. It wouldn't be fair to either of us to keep a distance relationship going when my heart isn't in it anymore. I don't think yours is either if you're really honest with yourself.

I hope this gives you the closure you need. I know you probably hate me right now but you'd hate me more if I came home and jumped ship in 3–6 months' time. I wish you well with the opening and I'm sure the cat café will be an even bigger success without me than it would be with me. Take care.

'Your breakfast is served,' Tom called jovially, arriving in the bedroom with a tray, but his tone changed to a concerned one. 'What's happened?'

I looked up at him blankly.

'You're crying.'

I hadn't even realised. They say the truth hurts and that email had certainly been truthful.

'I emailed Leon some questions and asked him to be honest. He was. You can read it.'

Tom laid the tray on the bed beside me and picked up my phone. His eyes widened and he pursed his lips several times as he scrolled down the email.

'Wow! Well, isn't he the gift that keeps on giving?'

'To be fair to him, I wanted the truth and he gave it. And I expected it to be bad, so...' I tailed off, unsure where I was going with that sentence.

Tom placed the phone face down on the bedside cabinet, shaking his head. 'He should have had the decency to talk to you before he went away.'

'I think he was confused,' I said, feeling strangely defensive of Leon. 'He says the cruise gave him time to think.'

'Yeah, about how many more lies he could tell you. He doesn't deserve you standing up for him. Even he acknowledges that he's a selfish git who put his social life ahead of the woman he was meant to love.'

My head dipped and I closed my eyes for a moment. Tom was right. That was exactly what had happened and Leon had admitted as much. I just wished it hadn't taken him so long to tell me the truth.

'Sorry,' Tom said, his voice soft. 'The last thing I want to do is hurt you too.'

I looked up and gave him a weak smile. 'You haven't. You're right about Leon. I don't know why I'm trying to defend him.'

Tom's phone beeped and he took it out of his shirt pocket, read the message and replaced it. 'I've got to shoot. Is there anything else you need before I go?'

'No. You get back to work. Thanks for... that,' I said as the word 'porridge' evaded me. 'And tell Mum thanks for the flowers.'

When he left, I pulled the tray a little closer, releasing a squeak of pain as the effort burned my neck and shoulders. No wonder Auntie Sonia took to social media to vent her frustrations. Last night, Fiona had shared a meme: *Fibromyalgia – pain that makes you want to run away from your own body*. Couldn't have put it better myself.

Giving up halfway through my porridge, I dropped the spoon into the bowl with a splat and rested my head back against the pillows. Ruby jumped up onto the bed beside me and I gasped as a thought struck me. Not once during our phone call yesterday or his email today had Leon asked after the cats. He'd made a comment about staying friends and me sending him photos of the cats and the café but that had felt like a throwaway comment from someone trying to lessen the impact of the *you're dumped* message. It hadn't been concern for the cats. I thought he'd loved them as much as me. He'd certainly acted as though he had. Acted. He'd been doing that for a while.

He said he'd told me the truth in his email and, brutal as it was, I couldn't help thinking he'd held some things back and was still acting a part. It didn't matter now. The only important thing was getting out of here by the end of the weekend and opening the café as planned a fortnight on Wednesday. How I was going to run the café without Leon's help was another matter, but I'd work something out. I had to. This was my dream and I wasn't going to let him ruin it.

8

On Tuesday, the pain severity had dropped from amber back down to green, so I could at least start on the packing. I messaged Mum first thing, thanking her for the flowers and telling her I was doing well and would have another head-down day with paperwork. There was no reason for her not to believe me because none of them had any idea how bad my flare-ups could be. How could they when I didn't tell them? The only person who knew was Leon and I hadn't been completely honest with him either, which made me feel hypocritical for being annoyed with all of his lies.

After breakfast, I nipped out to buy some crates and cardboard boxes, then, careful not to over-exert myself and to take several rest breaks, I began packing. My belongings from the lounge, kitchen and dining room barely filled one crate – another reminder of how this had always been Leon's home and never mine.

My recipe books and paperbacks from the spare bedroom upstairs filled three crates – so telling that I could fill more crates with recipe books than I could with my belongings from the whole of downstairs. I wrote my name on the boxes containing Nanna's baking items and pushed them next to the crates.

I returned downstairs for a mug of tea and a longer break. Jupiter, my one-year-old silver American Burmese – an extremely affectionate and needy cat – joined me as soon as I sat down with my drink and mewed loudly, demanding attention. He loved pouncing on the feathers on a teaser, so I spent some time playing with him. We were soon joined by Pebbles and Smudge, so I picked up another teaser and held one in each hand.

Playing with the three of them soothed my soul, taking my mind off the pain and the fatigue. Sybil and Freyja appeared and curled up together beside me. Feeling their warm bodies against my leg was also a tonic. Leon might not love me anymore, but my fur family loved me unconditionally. Well, fifteen of them did, although even Marmalade had his moments.

By the time I'd finished my tea, Jupiter, Pebbles and Smudge had tired of their play and settled down to sleep, signalling time for me to crack on with some more packing. I was about to get up when a message came through and my heart leapt when I saw who'd sent it.

FROM ALISON

Hey you, I'm back in Whitsborough Bay this week. Loads to tell you and dying to hear all about your fabulous cat café. I'm conscious it's only 2 weeks until opening but would love a catch-up if you have time. Happy to help you clean, organise or bake if that helps! xx

I'd known Alison for about twelve years. She'd been recruited as a receptionist at The Ramparts Hotel four years after I started there and she had one of those bright, bubbly personalities that everyone warmed to. I'd always got on well with her any time our paths crossed at work but we'd never spent much time together outside of work, clashes of shift patterns making socialising a challenge.

Six years ago, Alison surprised everyone by handing in her notice to go travelling round Europe for four months with her new-at-the-time boyfriend – and now her husband – Aidan, a travel writer. Alison caught the travel bug and they'd since travelled the world together, only returning to Whitsborough Bay for short stretches at a time to see Aidan's parents, who ran Sunny Dayz Guest House near Hearnshaw Park, and to catch up with friends.

I'd probably seen more of her on her trips home than I had in the whole time we'd been working at The Ramparts and we'd become steadily closer, regularly messaging each other while she was away. Outside my family and former employer, Alison was the only person who knew about my fibromyalgia diagnosis. Writing it in a message to a friend on the other side of the world hadn't felt as difficult as saying it to my local friends.

It would be so good to see her again. She'd known Leon from work and would be shocked by his latest bombshell.

TO ALISON

I'm so excited you're back as I've got loads to tell you! Would tomorrow be good? Meet you at the cat café at 10.30 so I can give you a tour? xx

FROM ALISON

Purr-fect! (Bet you've already heard that one a million times!) See you then xx

I felt so much brighter at the thought of seeing Alison. She was the most inspiring person I'd ever met and I could really use an injection of her positivity. In the meantime, I needed to apply a little self-motivation as that job description for Leon's role wasn't going to write itself. The problem was that it was a big role to fill, needing several different skills, and I wasn't hopeful of finding anyone suitable, especially not on the salary I could offer. I needed them to be an experienced chef or baker who was willing and able to run the front of house and who could step up and manage the team at short notice if I experienced a flare-up. How on earth could I convey that in a job description? And if I did find someone with the right experience, how was I going to sell it during the interview? *I've got fibromyalgia, which means that you might get a phone call from me first thing saying I'm in too much pain to make it downstairs. On those days, I need you to step up and manage the staff, cats and customers. I have no idea how often this will happen, I can't give you advance warning and I can't give you another member of staff to take my place so you'll be doing all this one person down. When can you start?*

Maybe I'd tackle that task after I'd seen Alison.

9

The following day was the first day of November and, as I made my way down Castle Street towards the café, I noticed a few Christmas gifts had appeared in the shop windows. Christmas stock would have been introduced across the past couple of months but would massively build this month.

A quick ask around had revealed that most of the traders decorated their businesses on or just after Bonfire Night. If the café had opened in September as planned, I'd have done the same, but I wanted to showcase the café without the distraction of Christmas decorations so mine would have to wait.

I reached the café shortly after nine and made a slow start on the cleaning before Alison arrived.

'Tabby!' she squealed, launching herself at me as soon as I opened the external door. 'I've missed you!'

'I've missed you too!' I don't know how I managed to sound so bright when every nerve ending was crying out in pain at her touch. Hugs. I loved them but when you have a condition which makes every nerve ending hypersensitive during a flare-up, they don't exactly bring the comfort they should. But I bit back the pain as I'd done so many times before because I wanted to hug my friend.

'Come in,' I told her when we pulled apart. 'I'll give you the grand tour, then make a drink.'

Alison stepped into Cat Castle and gasped. 'Wow! I knew it would be good, but this is off the charts.'

Outside Richards & Sons – my builders – Alison was the first person to see the finished café and her reaction was fantastic.

'There's so much to take in,' she said, excitement in her voice as she worked her way round the ground floor, running her hand across the various platforms and the drawbridge, and gazing at the murals. We moved upstairs and toured round Kitty Cove and Feline Forest, both of which evoked the same awestruck reaction.

'You and Leon designed this?'

'Not Leon. Creativity isn't his thing. I could visualise it in my head, but I don't have the skills to put that down on paper. Thankfully, I have a brother who does.'

Alison slowly turned in a circle, her eyes shining. 'Customers are going to love it.'

'I hope so.'

'Oh, they will! So much thought has gone into it. I've been to a few cat cafés around the world, as you know, and this is by far the most impressive.'

She'd been to Taiwan and visited the world's first cat café, which had opened there in 1998. Six years later, the concept found its way to Japan and she'd visited cat cafés there too so, as soon as my offer was accepted for the premises, I'd pumped her for information on everything she could remember about her visits and what she thought were the plus and minus points to bear in mind.

Alison's positive reaction helped ease the emotional pain from the past few days.

'I'll make us some hot chocolates,' I said. 'Come down when you've explored.'

I'd just placed two mugs on one of the tables downstairs when she appeared, a big smile on her face.

'You, my friend, are incredible,' she said. 'I can't wait to see this place with cats in.'

'Me too. I'm moving them into the flat on Saturday so that'll be their first chance to explore.'

'Oh! So you're moving into the flat after all?'

'I am. Leon isn't.' My throat tightened. It still felt very raw. 'We've split up.'

'Oh, my God!' She clapped her hand to her chest, her eyes wide. 'Why? When?'

'Sunday. He was meant to be returning on Monday and I was expecting him to phone me with his flight time. Instead, he phoned me and said he wasn't coming back...'

She shook her head intermittently as I filled her in on what had happened with Leon.

'I'm so sorry, Tabby,' she said when I'd finished. 'I always thought you two were solid. I'm so disappointed in him. I thought he was better than that.'

'So did I. I'm gutted that we're over and that he's shafted me with this place. We were meant to be doing this together.'

'From what I've seen, you're doing pretty spectacularly without him.'

I gave her an appreciative smile. 'Trying my best.'

'Okay. Let me check my understanding here. Leon decided against selling his house so has contributed nothing financially, design isn't his thing so he contributed nothing creatively either, and the scone and cake recipes are all yours. So what was his superpower? Because it sounds to me like you were doing everything. What was Leon actually going to bring to the party?'

She was smiling as she said it and I knew her intention was to help me see that I was better off without Leon, but it made me feel terrible. For the first time, I put myself in Leon's shoes. He loved cats but he hadn't had a long-held dream to work with them like I had and, even though he'd enthusiastically gone along with the idea of opening a cat café, what would he really have got from it? He'd been a brilliant chef de partie in a five-star hotel with responsibility for managing the menu, a section of the kitchen and the staff who worked there. Why on earth would he want to give that up to be a glorified waiter in a café he didn't even own a share in (albeit by his choice)? He'd be serving scones and cakes that he hadn't even made himself and the only times he'd be in charge – because it was my business, not his – were when I was in too much pain to work. No wonder he'd fled the country!

Alison was still looking at me questioningly. This would be the perfect moment to be honest with her about my condition, but I couldn't do it. Instead, I went into default mode and glossed over it.

'I'm being over-dramatic about it all. It was a shock. I was looking forward to us working together, not having to make all the decisions or deal with all the problems on my own, but I'd rather he wasn't here than he was here and hating it. Anyway, enough about him. How long are you back for this time?'

She smiled at me. 'For good. The past six years have been a blast but Madison's nearly two and we'd like to get her settled into a nursery.' Her smile widened and her eyes sparkled. 'And she also has a brother or sister on the way.'

'You're pregnant? Aw, Ali, I'm so pleased for you both. When's it due?'

'Ninth of April. I'm seventeen weeks. We've been talking about settling back here for a while, but being pregnant again has been the trigger for making it happen. Aidan's still got a few commitments abroad, but he'll be done with those before the baby arrives.'

'I'm so excited you're coming back. Where will you live?'

'With Aidan's parents, Lorraine and Nigel, for the moment, but we're looking to buy somewhere. We've got a few viewings lined up later this week.'

Alison had to head off an hour later.

'I really am sorry about you and Leon,' she said as she wrapped her scarf round her neck. 'Break-ups are hard and it must be extra tough when it feels out of the blue. Are you sure you're okay?'

'I think so. I've had so much to do with the café that I haven't had a chance to think too deeply about it.'

'That might be a good thing, but it might mean it hits you later. I'm here for you if you want to talk about it, whether that's in two days, two weeks or two months.'

'Thanks. I appreciate that.'

She pulled on her coat. 'When you do have some time to think, will you do me a favour? Ask yourself this question: What's the secret to happiness?'

'That sounds a bit profound.'

'I suppose it does.' She smiled. 'Before Aidan and I got together, we had a conversation about it. He knew exactly what it was for him – living each day as though it was his last. He asked me what my secret to happiness was and, when I couldn't answer him, he made it my homework.'

'Did you complete your homework?' I asked, my curiosity piqued.

'I did, although it took me a while. I asked around first and discovered it meant different things to different people and could change depending on what was going on in their life at the time. For me, it turned out that it was learning to love myself. I'd spent years comfort eating and I needed to come to terms with why I did that. It stemmed from losing my family and the guilt I felt for not being with them that day. Letting go of that guilt has been a game changer and the past six years have been incredible. You're making a fresh start, Tabby – new home, new business, new life – and that's such an exciting position to be in. If you work out what the secret is to finding your happiness, you can shape your future around it.' She scrunched up her nose. 'Am I making any sort of sense or am I waffling?'

'No, you're making a lot of sense. I'll ponder on it.'

With another hug, Alison left, promising to visit again soon and to bring Madison with her.

I did another half an hour of cleaning then paused to have a sandwich. As I ate, I reflected on my chat with Alison, particularly about what Leon's role in the business would have been. Even if he'd sold his house and gone into a partnership with me, his role wouldn't have been different. I'd still have been the visionary and the cook. He'd still have been leaving a job he was passionate about just so he could step into my shoes when I was too ill to work. He was going to be me when I couldn't be. What a crap career prospect!

I wished he'd talked to me about his concerns. Or maybe he hadn't cared enough to try. Maybe he'd already checked out by that point. I wasn't going to feel guilty about it. I hadn't forced him to say yes to the café and I'd given him several outs which he hadn't taken, including on the day we viewed the premises.

10

SEVEN MONTHS AGO

Leon squeezed my hand as we turned onto the cobbles of Castle Street. It had always been my favourite street in Whitsborough Bay. The cobbles and Victorian lamp posts gave a feeling of warmth and nostalgia, but the independent shops and cafés were vibrant. I knew from asking around that there was a strong sense of community among the Castle Street traders and I absolutely wanted to be part of that.

'Do you think we should be concerned about there being two cafés on the street already?' Leon asked as we passed the first one.

Aunt Polly's Tea Room was a traditional English café with vintage-style floral china crockery, pretty pale pink tablecloths beneath glass table-toppers, and a massive emphasis on afternoon tea. It was particularly popular with an older customer base. Towards the other end of the street was The Chocolate Pot – a gorgeous café with a friendly, relaxed atmosphere which appealed to all ages.

'I don't see either of them as direct competition,' I said. 'We're more of an experience than a traditional café. Are *you* worried?'

He put his arm round me and kissed the top of my head. 'Not if you're not.'

We approached the empty double-width premises about a third of the way down the street on the left-hand side, sandwiched between Seaside Blooms, the florists, and a hairdressing salon called Hairlequin's. The wooden shutters inside the large ground-floor bay window were closed and a blind was pulled down on the door so we couldn't see inside. I'd peeked through the letterbox as soon as the estate agent gave me the heads-up that it was coming onto the market.

There'd been a few premises available last month, but none of them were right. I'd seen this empty unit – a former clothing boutique – on Castle Street and was convinced it would be perfect. I'd asked round all the Whitsborough Bay estate agents and even those in the surrounding area, but it wasn't for sale and nobody seemed to know what the plans were, so I'd pestered them and it had paid off because I'd had a call to say it was about to go up for lease or purchase and did I want first refusal?

A woman of a similar age to me wearing a grey trouser suit and carrying an A4 zipped portfolio approached us with a smile. 'Tabby Walsh?'

'Hi, yes, and this is my boyfriend, Leon.'

'Good to meet you both,' she said shaking my hand then Leon's. 'I'm Emma. Shall we go inside?'

She produced a key from her pocket and I held my breath as she pushed the door open. 'As you can see, there's a large retail space here. There's a stud wall at the back and, behind that, you'll find a couple of storage rooms, a kitchenette, a toilet and the stairs.'

I gazed around the room, imagining how it would look as a café. The ceilings were high, as I'd hoped – something that I hadn't been able to get a sense of from the sales particulars. Leon and I had paced out the dimensions in my parents' back garden and used Dad's gardening twine to map out the shop floor. I'd been worried it might not be big enough and that the space would feel smaller when we saw it with walls, but it actually seemed bigger.

'Feel free to go through to the back and have a wander round yourself,' Emma said. 'Give me a shout when you're ready to look upstairs.'

'Is it me or, if you took down all the stud walls, is it bigger back here than out the front?' Leon asked as we explored the back of the shop.

I glanced down at the particulars and did a swift calculation of the dimensions. 'You're right. It's about a third as big again.'

We called for Emma and followed her up to the first floor where stud walls had been erected to create two rooms. With the walls taken down, this would be a great space for most of the chairs and tables as the ground floor wasn't enough on its own.

'The flat is on two floors, laid out like a traditional house,' Emma said, leading us up the next flight of stairs. 'I should warn you that, if you're interested in buying rather than letting, the flat can't be sold off separately. There's something in the deeds about the building needing to stay together.'

'That's fine,' I told her. 'We're planning to live in the flat ourselves.'

'Brilliant. Well, it hasn't been lived in for several years so it could do with updating, but the building's sound and it had a new roof four years ago.'

There weren't any photos of the flat on the particulars so I'd been prepared for the worst, but it wasn't actually too bad. The 1980s-style wooden kitchen was dated but serviceable and the exposed floorboards throughout the flat just needed a sand and varnish. The worst part was the bathroom, which was a step back into the 1970s with a turquoise suite, floral wallpaper, contrasting fluffy cerise pink bath, pedestal and toilet mats, and even a toilet seat cover.

'Bathroom's hideous,' Leon muttered, curling his lip up. No doubt he'd be thinking of the amazing walk-in shower at his place.

'But it's a good size, and there's room to install a walk-in shower *and* keep the bath.' I missed having access to a bath, which helped soothe my fibro aches and pains.

'Are you having doubts?' I asked, my stomach lurching at the thought of falling at the final hurdle.

There was a scary moment of hesitation, before Leon smiled and shook his head. 'Don't panic. It's just the thought of all the work that's needed, but it's nothing we can't handle. You'll get your dream.'

'*Our* dream,' I corrected him.

'That's what I mean. *Our* dream.'

'I'll give you some time to look around up here on your own,' Emma said, heading for the stairs. 'Meet you downstairs when you're ready.'

Leon wandered over to the front bay, made up of three arched windows and, when I heard the door close downstairs, I joined him. He had his arms folded and there was clear tension throughout his body.

'Are you sure this is what you want?' I asked tentatively.

'Of course.' His pitch was a little higher than usual, which did nothing to ease my nerves.

'If you're having doubts, you have to tell me. You know I can't do this without you so, if you're not 100 per cent in, we need to walk away.'

There was another agonising pause while I awaited his verdict. His shoulders relaxed and he drew his attention away from the window and back to me, with a smile.

'Don't look so worried. I'm all in.' He slipped his arms round my waist and looked down at me. 'It's just a bit overwhelming realising that something we've talked about for so long is in our grasp. I didn't think we'd ever be able to do it.'

'Neither did I.' My voice caught in my throat and Leon drew me against his chest, stroking my hair.

'So what do you think?' Leon asked. 'Is it purr-fect?'

I laughed at his pun. 'It's pawsitively purr-fect.'

'Not a *cat*astrophe, then? Well, except for that bathroom.'

'No. It's claw-some and I'd like to go for it, purr-lease.'

Leon rolled his eyes at me, laughing. 'Claw-some? I can't beat that. I've nothing left. Let's find Emma and *whisk-her* back to the office to sort out the contract.'

'Oh, my gosh, Leon! That is genius.' I grinned at his very-pleased-with-himself expression. 'How long have you been thinking about that?'

'A couple of hours.'

'Idiot,' I said, ruffling his hair affectionately.

'I'm liking those smiles,' Emma said when we joined her downstairs. 'What did you think?'

'I love it,' I said. 'We need to discuss it overnight, but I'm fairly sure it'll be a yes. You don't have any other viewings lined up?'

'Not yet, but I can only keep it exclusive for you overnight. I'll need to start advertising tomorrow.'

'I understand. I'll let you know first thing either way.'

Emma handed me her business card. 'I look forward to hearing from you tomorrow. If you have any more questions this afternoon, just give me a call.'

She locked up and said goodbye, striding off towards the main precinct. Leon and I stood back and looked up at the building. Excitement bubbled inside me. This was it. This was my dream. Right in front of me was the Castle Street Cat Café. I knew the sensible thing was to reflect on it overnight but it was so difficult not to run after Emma and ask her to draw up the contract.

Leon had to go into work for an evening shift, so I returned to Drake Street on my own on cloud nine, my childhood dream of a job where I could work with cats within my grasp.

When we'd first talked about opening a cat café, Leon bought me a large planner with a picture of a cat-shaped mug on the front and the caption *All I need is coffee and cats*. Over the years, I'd tentatively added information and ideas to it but hadn't wanted to go overboard when it was only a pipe dream. Not anymore! I fed the cats, made myself something to eat, called my parents to give them an excitable update, then spent the rest of the evening at the dining table, scribbling down ideas and drawing rough sketches. I kept glancing at the clock, eager for Leon to get home so I could show him what I'd been doing.

I heard his key in the lock and Marmalade jumped down from the armchair in the through-lounge and ran to the door to greet him, as he always did.

I called out, 'Hello,' but hung back in the dining room so Marmalade could have Leon's attention.

'I thought you'd have already gone to bed,' Leon said, appearing in the lounge with Marmalade in his arms.

'I was too excited. I wanted to show you...' I tailed off, frowning at his dark expression. 'Is something wrong?'

'We need to talk.'

My stomach plummeted to the floor.

'Please don't say you've changed your mind,' I blurted out before I could stop myself.

He placed Marmalade down on the sofa and sat beside me at the dining table, his eyes fixed on mine.

'Say something,' I pleaded, my heart pounding.

'It's not the café,' he said. 'It's the flat. I've been thinking about it all shift. I thought I could do it, but I can't give up this...' he swept his arm round the room, '...to live there.'

'Is this about the bathroom? It's easily changed.'

'It's not the grim seventies bathroom or the eighties kitchen. It's moving from a house I love to a flat above a café. I can't do it. It's a step too far for me. I'm sorry.'

'But we can't afford to do this without the house sale proceeds. My inheritance isn't enough on its own.'

'What about renting instead of buying?'

'That wasn't the plan.'

He flashed his eyes at me. 'Sometimes plans change.'

'But our dream was—'

'No, Tabby!' He looked shocked at the volume of his voice and lowered it as he continued. 'I was dreading coming home tonight because I knew you'd do this.'

'Do what?'

'Try to guilt-trip me into selling this place. I know you've never loved this house, but I do and I want to stay here. Why's that so hard to understand?'

Without waiting for a response from me, he scraped his chair back on the laminate and muttered that he was off to bed. Propping my elbows on the table, I held my head in my hands and took several deep breaths, determined not to cry. I hadn't appreciated quite how emotionally attached Leon was to the house until now, and I should have. It had been the place he'd bought after finally getting away from his toxic relationship with Mimi. It wasn't just a house to him – it symbolised escape, freedom and a fresh start.

Closing my planner, I checked the cat water was topped up, put the lights out and went upstairs. The bedroom was in darkness but there was no way Leon could be asleep already.

'I'm sorry,' I said, crouching down beside his side of the bed. 'I'll speak to Emma in the morning and ask about leasing instead.' I had to find a way to make this work.

'I'm sorry too,' he said. 'I didn't mean to get tetchy about it.'

'That's all right. It's been a busy day.'

When I slipped into bed beside him a little later, I pressed myself against his back and draped my arm across his waist.

'I love you,' I said, 'and I'd never want to push you into doing anything you don't want to.'

'I know.'

'I hear you about the flat, but if you've changed your mind about opening a cat café with me, now's the time to say it.'

'Why would I have changed my mind?' He patted my hand. 'I'm tired. Time for sleep.'

I kissed his shoulder then turned onto my back. So things weren't going to happen quite as planned, but they were still happening.

* * *

'Are you angry with me?' Leon asked over breakfast the following morning.

'I wish you'd said something sooner, but I'm not angry with you. It changes things but it doesn't stop the plan.' I rolled my eyes at him. 'Bit like my fibro.'

As soon as the estate agency opened, I rang and put my offer to Emma. She said she'd get straight onto the landlord but, when she called back shortly afterwards, she had an unexpected blow. If I wanted to run a regular café, the lease could be mine, but the landlord wouldn't consider a cat café, convinced the cats would cause too much damage to his property. I only had three options – open a regular café (which didn't interest me at all), buy the building as originally planned (assuming I could get a mortgage for it because I didn't have enough funds without Leon's contribution), or give up on my dreams.

'I'm sorry,' Leon said, hugging me when the call ended. 'I know we could resolve this if I sold the house, but...'

'It's okay. I'll see if I can get a loan or a mortgage and, if I can't, it obviously wasn't meant to be.'

'I need to go food shopping,' he said. 'Will you be all right?'

'Yeah, I'm fine. See you later.'

As soon as he left the house, I broke down in tears. This was so unfair. I didn't want to have an argument with him about this and I did understand how easy it can be to think you're okay with something when it's hypothetical and not be okay with it when it becomes reality, but I was so pissed off with Leon right now. He had to have had some sort of inkling he didn't want to sell the house and if he'd spoken to me about it, I'd never have got my hopes up for the Castle Street property. I'd have searched for somewhere smaller and toned down my ideas. He'd let me believe this was possible. So close, and yet so far.

Heartbroken, I FaceTimed Mum and told her to forget everything I'd said the night before because it wasn't going to happen.

'I'm so sorry, sweetheart,' she said. 'You sounded so excited last night.'

'I was. It was perfect, but it wasn't meant to be. I'll contact some banks but I'm not hopeful.'

'Don't give up. Something will turn up.'

'I'd best get myself a lottery ticket and hope.'

I was surprised to see Mum FaceTiming me again within the hour, with Dad on the screen too.

'Your dad and I have had a chat and we have a solution for you. Our business has done well, as you know, so we don't need our share of the inheritance from your nanna. We're going to split it between you and Rylan.'

It took me a moment to register what she'd said and I shook my head vigorously. 'That's way too generous.'

'It's what we want to do,' Dad said, bobbing up behind Mum. 'It's what my mum would have wanted us to do too. She was determined you'd get your dream one day so we're not going to stand by and let it slip away.'

I went from devastated to elated. My hands shook as I called Emma again and put my offer in to buy 9 Castle Street after all. Five minutes later, she called me back with the news that it was mine. That had been a very close call.

11

PRESENT DAY

Lunch finished, I took a mug of tea up to the flat and stood by the bay window in the empty lounge, looking out onto the cobbled street below. Leon had stood right here nearly seven months ago and his body language had told me the truth – that this wasn't for him. I remembered how nervous I'd felt, my palms sweating, my stomach churning. Deep down, I'd known that he wasn't fully committed but I hadn't wanted to believe it. I'd let him convince me that his only doubts were about finding the time and energy to refurbish the flat when they'd been so much bigger than that.

Leon's reaction to that amazing lifeline from my parents was another thing that I could now see differently. When he'd returned from food shopping and I'd told him the news, he'd thrown in several objections about it being too generous and feeling indebted to my parents. Had he ever wanted the café or had it just been one of those lovely dreams people talk about like what they'd do if they won the lottery, never believing it will actually happen?

Leon talked about there being signs that we'd drifted apart. Was this what he'd meant? That he hadn't wanted the same things as me and he'd been dropping hints along the way?

I had so many more questions for him, but I wasn't going to email him again. I needed to let that one go and focus on me, my fur family and the business.

Something else Alison said had really resonated with me. When she'd talked about finding happiness, she'd talked about guilt. Oh, my goodness, did I feel that every single day. I could now see that it had been holding me back. I'd tried so hard not to take time off work, somehow battling through my shifts and being completely wiped out by the time I got home. Sometimes I lost that battle and, every time I phoned in sick, I was consumed with guilt for letting my boss and my colleagues down.

I felt guilty if I cancelled plans with family or friends and even guiltier that I sometimes lied, saying I needed to work. I thought that Kelsey, a former colleague from The Ramparts, and Faith, a friend from my school days, would have stuck around but it hadn't taken long before each of them stopped inviting me out and now they'd both drifted away, years of friendship clearly accounting for nothing.

I felt guilty that Leon had needed to do so much for me – looking after the cats and making sure I had food and drink when I was floored by a flare-up. He took control of the shopping, cooking and all the cleaning duties at home so that I could rest between shifts. Knowing I wasn't doing my fair share had weighed heavily on me. I felt guilty that our sex life had suffered. And now I felt guilty that I'd placed him in an impossible position with the business. I'd been dreaming of this for years and, once I received my inheritance, I never stopped to think about whether it was what Leon really wanted.

I sighed heavily. What had I got myself into? I'd planned my 'fantasy cat café' for years, but I'd never adjusted those plans to incorporate the reality of a chronic condition. My head hadn't been completely buried in the sand, but I had been relying on Leon's support.

* * *

Back at Drake Street late that afternoon, I sat down at the dining table with my laptop and cat planner. I was still struggling with the wording for replacing Leon so I hadn't yet advertised the role and I felt even less confident about doing so after speaking to Alison. What was the job? *Sickness cover for café owner with chronic pain condition* didn't exactly sell it, but that's essentially what it was. *Be available to come in two to three hours early to make scones if the owner has woken up with a fibro flare-up.* Honestly! Who'd want a job like that?

If I couldn't find a way to advertise it, I couldn't fill it, so I needed to get my head around what it would mean for the café if it was only me and the waiting staff. I opened my planner to a fresh page and scribbled down the questions that immediately sprung to mind.

1. *Working Wed–Sun – who covers fibro flares? Who bakes when I can't?*
2. *Will still have work to do cooking/cleaning on a Mon & Tues – how will I manage that?*
3. *What about the summer holidays? Wanted to open 7 days a week. Impossible on my own*
4. *More cats = more litter. Can't expect staff to clean it. Heavy to lift*

I dropped the pen and pushed my planner aside. There were other points I could add, but why bother when the first four already felt unsurmountable? Should I halt my plans to open a fortnight today and put the café on the market instead? My stomach did a somersault at that thought. What were the implications of selling? I'd have no job and nowhere to live as the deeds stipulated that the flat couldn't be sold off separately. I'd likely lose most of the money I'd invested as, even if the stars aligned and I found someone who wanted to keep the place running as a cat café, there was no track record of success so the risk would likely mean a knock-down offer. A buyer wanting to run a regular café faced stiff competition on the street, which would likely deter them, and a buyer wanting a shop would need to rip everything out. Whichever way I looked at it, I'd lose out financially. And, even if I did take that hit, I doubted the run-up to Christmas was a good time to try to sell a business.

What if I didn't sell? What if I got a manager in to run the cat café instead? I shook my head. What was the point in having a dream if somebody else lived it for me?

Babushka was curled up on the sofa and Winnie was draped over the back. Winnie looked up at me and mewed for attention. I stroked her head and back, and scratched the sweet spot behind her ears. Alison had asked me what my secret to happiness was. It was my cats. I'd been an ailurophile since I was seven. It completely defined the person I had been, was now, and always wanted to be. I needed to find a way for my ailurophilia and fibromyalgia to work together instead of against each other and the only way I was going to be able to address that was to do something I'd avoided since my diagnosis – seek help. I didn't have any way of making contact other than via Facebook so I returned to the table, opened my laptop and typed in a message.

TO SONIA AND FIONA

Hi both, I hope you don't mind me reaching out to you both, especially since it's been so long since I last saw you, but I could really use your help. I was diagnosed with fibromyalgia 18 months ago and I'm struggling to come to terms with it. If you have any advice, I'd be extremely grateful. Thank you x

I added my phone number and email address and sent the message before I could change my mind. Moments later, my phone rang with an unknown number. My heart raced as I answered it.

'Hello?'

'Tabby, it's Fiona. I've just seen your message. I'm free now if you'd like to talk.'

'I'd love to,' I said, tears rushing to my eyes that she'd responded so quickly. 'Thank you.'

Fiona asked me what had happened to lead me to seeking a diagnosis and how my fibro presented itself. I took the phone over to the sofa and placed it on my lap on speakerphone as I explained.

'You said in your message that you're struggling to come to terms with it,' she said when I'd finished. 'What do you mean by that?'

I sighed. 'Several things. For a start, I haven't been honest with my family about the severity of my flare-ups.'

'Is there a reason for that?'

'I don't want to be a burden to anyone. If they knew how bad it gets, they'd want to help and that's not fair. They have their own jobs and lives.'

'What about Leon?' she asked. 'Does he know the truth?'

'We're not together anymore – long story – but, no, I wasn't honest with him either, although it was harder to hide it.'

'What are the other things you're struggling with?' Fiona asked.

'I can't get my head around there being no cure, that this isn't a bout of illness that I'll get over. This is for life, and I don't want it to be. At the start, I fought as hard as I could not to change anything, but that wasn't realistic. The days I phoned in sick at work were the days I was on empty. On less than empty. I didn't want to be that person. I didn't – still don't – want this thing to control my life but the truth is it does. It dictates what I can and can't do. It doesn't care that I want to work full time *and* have a social life and that makes me so angry.'

'It sounds to me like you're stuck between denial and anger,' Fiona said. 'I've been there. The key to living with fibro is to accept it and, for me, the only way to do that has been to change my mindset about it. Mum has never made it to the acceptance stage, as you can probably tell from the stuff she puts on social media. I don't think she'll respond to your message but, if she does, it's unlikely she'll be able to help you.'

'How has your mindset changed?' I asked.

'It'll probably help if I go back to the start and tell you how I used to be. As I say, Mum is extremely negative about it and I completely understand that. Who'd choose to have chronic pain? She wasn't just angry with the fibro. She was angry with herself, my dad, me, your mum, her best friend, her employer, our neighbours, her hairdresser, the woman who ran the corner shop. I'm not exaggerating here. She blamed everyone for what was happening to her and she still does. She reckons nobody understands what she's going through and nobody cares, which is completely untrue. When I got diagnosed, I thought it would bring us closer together. I'd be an ally. I'd be the one person who fully understood her because I was experiencing it too, but it didn't work out like that.'

'What happened?' I asked when she paused, no idea that there'd been any bad blood between them.

'She'd hate me if she knew I was telling you this. Promise me you won't say anything to your mum?'

'I promise. You don't have to say anything if it puts you in a difficult position.'

'It's okay. I want to help you. So Mum made it into some sort of twisted competition. Who has it the worst? If I was in pain, she was in agony. If I was tired, she was exhausted. If I was feeling down, she was severely depressed. You get the picture. Every conversation included a reminder of how long she'd had this, how alone she was, how horrendous her life was. She wanted sympathy and I gave her it, but she wasn't willing to show any towards me and I realised that if I didn't get to grips with my fibro, this could be me – angry, bitter, hating the world and everyone in it. That scared me more than a lifetime of pain, so I went online and researched the hell out of it. I read hundreds, probably thousands, of articles and blog posts on fibromyalgia and other chronic pain conditions. I watched YouTube videos and joined online support groups. Some of what I found scared the hell out of me, some reassured me I wasn't alone and some of it gave me the way forward.'

I stared at my phone, my heart pounding with anticipation as to what my cousin was about to say. I so desperately needed to find a way forward myself, especially now that I needed to face this without Leon.

'You described your fibro as a nightmare, as something that controls you, dictates your life, stops you doing things. That's a natural reaction and I've been there. What I did was change my mindset from hating and fighting the fibro to accepting that life *does* have to change, but I don't need to feel guilty or angry about making those changes. It's less about the fibro being in charge and more about me taking charge by listening to my body and trying to work with the fibro.'

'How do you even begin to do that?'

'Have you come across the spoon theory?'

'No.'

'It came from a writer in the States called Christine Miserandino back in 2003. She has fibro and lupus, among other things, and she was out for a meal with a friend who wanted to understand what it's like living with a chronic illness. Because a big part of it is fatigue and there-fore lack of energy, Christine looked around for something to physically represent units of energy and ended up with twelve spoons. She then got her friend to talk through her daily activities – even ones she thought were really simple – and Christine took a spoon off her to represent the energy needed to complete each one. Some activities required more than one spoon – two, three, six – which soon left the friend empty-handed. This theory was a game changer for me. It helped me get my head around how I structure my day and it became a way to communicate to my friends and my partner. Graham comes home from work and asks how many spoons I'm on and, if it's six, we might do something but, if I've got an empty drawer or, even worse, borrowed from tomorrow's supply, he knows I'm spent and probably need some help.'

'I'm horrendous at asking for help,' I said. 'We have no idea why, but I've always been fiercely independent. It was a standing joke in our family way before fibro reared its head. How do you get over the guilt in putting someone else out?'

'By not thinking of it as putting someone else out or, to use your term from earlier, being a burden. If it was your brother who had fibro instead of you and he asked you to run the vacuum cleaner round for him once a week, would you do it?'

'Of course!'

'Why?'

'Because he's my brother and I'd want to help.'

'And you've just made my point for me. The people who love us genuinely want to help and those who don't aren't worth hanging onto. I don't know what happened with you and Leon but if it ended because of your diagnosis, then he was worth letting go. Our energy supplies are limited so why waste them on someone who doesn't really care? That's why my marriage fell apart. Neal couldn't deal with my diagnosis. He was a non-believer at first – all the classics like I was making it up, I was just being lazy, I didn't look ill – and when he finally accepted that fibro was a thing, he couldn't cope with it. We say "in sickness and in health" in our wedding vows but, when two people go into the marriage with no health challenges, I'm sure they both hope they won't be tested with the sickness part. If they are, not everyone can keep that vow. I'm not angry with Neal about that. It was a lot to deal with and, of course, I wasn't dealing with it very well myself at the time. Graham couldn't be more different and I count my blessings every day that he came into my life. Fibro *is* a burden, but the person who has it *isn't*. Think of it as a hod of bricks that you've been asked to carry for the rest of your life. It would be difficult to carry them anyway, but you're now expected to do that while in pain, with fatigue, and less energy. There's no way you can keep carrying those bricks on your own, but if your friends and family each took a few from you, you'd be able to manage the load and use it to rebuild your new life as a fibro warrior.'

Fibro warrior? I hadn't heard that term before, which wasn't surprising considering I hadn't done any research into living with the condition, but I liked it. It conjured up strength rather than defeat.

'I'm conscious I've talked a lot,' Fiona said. 'I could keep going for ages, but I don't want to overwhelm you. Is there anything you'd like to ask me?'

'I get the mindset thing and I accept that I need to be honest with my family and let them help, but what I'm still struggling with is how I live with this thing.'

'It's back to the spoons. You can't live your life how you did before and it's natural to grieve for that now and in the future. After all, the things you took for granted before like feeling refreshed after a good night's sleep, being able to work *and* play, planning things and sticking to those plans, remembering things, and even standing and walking, are gone or have changed. But that doesn't mean you can't live a full life. If someone you loved was in pain, you'd tell them to slow down, to relax, to treat their body with respect and compassion, so give yourself that advice and heed it.'

We talked some more about how Fiona had come to terms with her fibromyalgia and how there were still days where, despite a massive mindset shift, she broke down in tears from the pain and frustration.

'I'll send you a link to the website where you'll find the origin story for the spoon theory,' Fiona said as the conversation drew to a close. 'And I'll send you a few memes that I have as a screensaver. They help me on a tough day.'

'I can't thank you enough for calling me, Fiona. That's been really helpful.'

'Any time. Take care of yourself and make sure others take care of you too.'

Five minutes after the call ended, the link she'd promised came through. I clicked on it, but it looked quite long – best read with a mug of tea. Another message came through with four colourful memes. I scanned down them.

Listen to what your body whispers before it starts screaming

Fibromyalgia can feel isolating, but please know you are never alone

It's OK to be angry at your body – you didn't sign up to these new terms and conditions – and it's OK to feel sad when you see someone doing all the things you used to do but now can't

You haven't lost who you are. You're a bit different now, but you're just as fabulous as before

I could see why Fiona found them inspiring and saved them into a new folder on my desktop. I might create a screensaver from them too. She'd also sent a chart with a guide as to how many spoons various daily activities might require. Even without reading the origins story, it made sense to me. Finally, she sent a graphic of the Kübler-Ross change curve in response to a chronic illness diagnosis and a link to an article going through each stage in more detail. A quick glance at the first stages shown on the graphic definitely echoed my experiences so far.

A message pinged up on the original thread I'd sent to Fiona and Auntie Sonia.

FROM SONIA

Sorry to hear you've got it. Not sure what advice you're expecting. Every single day's an uphill struggle as far as I'm concerned and that's never going to change. Ask our Fiona. It doesn't bother her 😔

FROM FIONA

Of course it bothers me, Mum! But I've found a way to make peace with it and still live my life. I've spoken to Tabby already and sent her some info. Tabby – hope you find it helpful x

FROM TABBY

Auntie Sonia – I'm sorry to hear that and send hugs x

Fiona – received and really appreciated, as was the call. You're a star x

FROM SONIA

She's a bloody martyr

That last unnecessary comment from Auntie Sonia didn't warrant a response or even a reaction. I suspected she wasn't alone out there with how she felt about the cards she'd been dealt, but I wanted to be more like Fiona. I'd been an independent, positive person before. Now I couldn't be quite as independent as I used to be, but there was no reason why I couldn't still be positive.

I put the kettle on to boil ready for reading the spoons story and exploring the change curve and then I'd get that job advertised. This was the start of a fresh chapter for me – new home, new business and brand-new attitude.

12

The following day, Mum took time off work to help me clean the flat. It turned out not to be as much work as anticipated. Even though the kitchen and bathroom were dated, the previous tenant had taken good care of them and all that was needed was a good dust and cobweb clearance. Mum, for some unfathomable reason, loved vacuuming so she took control of the café's vacuum cleaner, leaving me to clear the dust from the surfaces – a far less physically demanding job, so hopefully I wouldn't suffer tomorrow.

The front and back bedrooms were similar sizes but, as the front one had a lovely bay window overlooking the street, I decided to make that my bedroom. The one at the back, which I'd christened the 'cat lounge', would be for the cats. There was more space in the flat than in Drake Street and I wanted to do everything possible to make them feel comfortable in their new home. I didn't need a second bedroom so they might as well have a devoted area. The smaller third bedroom would be my office and storage.

In the evening, Rylan and Tom gave five-a-side football a miss to join Dad in moving over the furniture they'd loaned me in a van borrowed from a friend of Dad's. I met them at the flat and, while Dad and Rylan assembled the bed for me, Tom and I put together an enormous activity centre I'd ordered for the cats. I say put together but the pair of us could not have been more incompetent, although, in our defence, the instructions were dire. Rylan and Dad kept coming into the room to see what we were laughing about and, when they'd finished the bed, they joined us in equal incompetence. We managed eventually and it did me the world of good to have an evening of laughter and banter.

* * *

On Friday morning, I went shopping for some essentials – a kettle, toaster, microwave, towels and bedding – and ordered a washing machine for the flat.

My clothes and belongings were all packed and ready for Rylan and Dad to move to the flat in the evening, along with the activity centre and scratching posts from the dining room, and this morning's purchases. Dad would help me transfer the cat beds, bowls, litter trays and the cats themselves in the morning.

With a busy weekend ahead of me, I spent the afternoon relaxing and playing with my fur family.

'This is our last night here,' I said to Sybil and Freyja as I sat on the floor in the lounge with my back against the sofa, rolling a ball to them. 'How are you feeling about the big move?'

Right from finding the 'singing cats', I'd talked to all my cats as though they understood everything I said and I often answered for them, using the tone of voice and accent I imagined them to have.

'I think it will be simply marvellous,' I replied for Sybil in the posh and proper clipped English accent I imagined her to have.

'I'm weally excited,' I added for Freyja, in an excitable young girl's voice. 'We just want to be with you.'

'Aw, I'm pleased to hear it. I just want to be with all of you too. I love you.'

I'd tried to get Leon to join in, but he refused, rolling his eyes when I went into a full-blown conversation with the cats. I hadn't thought anything of it at the time, but perhaps that had been another sign that he wasn't as into the fur family as I was.

Marmalade watched us from his usual place on the armchair.

'How are you holding up?' I asked him. 'I'm so sorry about Leon. I know how hard it must hurt that he's not coming home.'

I'd once seen an episode of *Bagpuss* – a children's TV show from the 1970s. Bagpuss, a pink and cream striped stuffed cloth cat, had a deep, gentle voice befitting an elderly cat and, as soon as I heard it, I knew it was Marmalade's voice.

Marmalade stared at me. 'I'm not talking to you,' I mimicked for him in Bagpuss's voice. 'It's your fault that he's not coming home. He was only with you because you were the opposite of Mimi, but it was a rebound thing. He never loved you. Friends with benefits.' He blinked at me then jumped down from the armchair and padded into the dining room to run his claws down one of the scratching posts.

Sybil mewed at me and I realised I'd stopped rolling the ball, so I returned my attention back to her, frowning. Where had that stuff about Mimi just come from? It had slipped out as the sort of insult Marmalade might hurl at me, but it rang true. When Leon and I first got together, he'd told me he really liked me because I was the opposite of Mimi – calm, relaxed, easy to be around, not a game-player – but perhaps over time that had made me a little too dull. Perhaps he'd enjoyed the fire and passion he'd had with Mimi. Some people thrived on relationships like that.

I shook my head and rolled the ball again. It was pointless speculating. Our relationship was over and I needed to move forward and forget about him – something which five months on my own was going to make a little easier.

13

Moving day arrived and, after showering, I stuffed my nightshirt and toiletries into an overnight bag, watched by three of the kittens – Blinky, Cloud and Smudge. Cloud tried to bat my hairbrush out of my hand as I added it and Smudge jumped into the bag.

'Don't worry,' I said, as I lifted him out, planting a kiss on the top of his head, 'you're all coming with me.'

I zipped the bag up and took a final look round the bedroom. Twenty-three weeks ago today, Leon had flown out to the Caribbean. That was 161 nights without him. I'm not sure how I'd have coped without the company and love of my fur family. They'd made sure I wasn't sad and lonely and I was here to do the same for them. From now on, it was me and the cats versus the world.

Out of the bedroom window, I spotted Dad reversing his car into a space a little way down the street.

'Come on, you three,' I said to the kittens. 'That's your lift. It's time to take you to your new home.'

Jupiter and Viking were also on the bed and Sybil and Freyja were asleep in the spare room, so I called to them all to follow the kittens and me downstairs. I had six cat carriers already laid out and was borrowing Mum and Dad's two. For the short distance to the café, siblings Sybil and

Freyja could comfortably travel together, as could Viking and Jupiter, who were the best of friends. Two of the carriers were extra-large and could take four kittens each, with Marmalade, Babushka, Heathcliff and Winnie in carriers of their own.

Dad arrived with his carriers and, between us, we rounded up the cats. They were all fairly compliant but Marmalade ended up being a double-handed job after he kept splaying his legs out so I couldn't fit him through the 'door'. Dad had to lift the lid off and do some careful manoeuvring of it back into place while I gently pinned Marmalade to the bottom of the carrier.

While Dad loaded all the cat beds into his car along with a couple of bags for life containing the bowls and some food, I did one final look around. Surprisingly, I felt nothing. Even though I'd never loved the house, I'd enjoyed living here with Leon before my diagnosis, but I couldn't conjure up those happy memories now as this was the place where he'd left me alone for over five months. This was the place where he'd fallen out of love with me – if he had ever been in love in the first place. I'd be glad to see the back of it.

We secured six of the carriers into my car and two on the back seat of Dad's and he watched the cars while I did one final scoot round to check all the windows were closed, the doors were locked, and I hadn't left anything behind.

'Straight to the flat?' Dad asked when I'd closed and locked the front door for the final time, then posted my keys through the letterbox in an envelope. My family had already surrendered their emergency keys and I'd placed them in a kitchen drawer.

'Yes,' I said. 'Straight to our new home.'

* * *

Mum, Tom, Rylan and Macey had beaten us to the café. Macey had already unpacked the kettle and was on tea-making duty.

'How was your last night in Drake Street?' she asked as I placed Marmalade's cat carrier down on the floor.

'Uneventful. Played with the cats as usual. I was ready to leave.'

'Fresh start,' Mum said.

Dad, Tom and Rylan returned with two cat carriers each and I was about to go down for the last one but they insisted on carrying everything else up for me, which was a relief as I suspected today was going to use a lot of energy. I counted my blessings that my body had allowed me four days in a row without a flare-up, although I had worked at about a third of the pace I would have done before my illness and subsequent diagnosis, and my amazing family had done all the hard physical work.

My priority for today was to get the cats settled and familiar with the location of their litter trays, water bowls and food. The litter trays were in the utility room next to the kitchen, which had a couple of cupboards, a sink and plumbing for a washing machine. The kitchen was a good size but nowhere near big enough to feed sixteen cats, so I set up a water and feeding station in the cat lounge against the wall opposite the new activity centre. The bathroom was on the other side of that wall so, when I got round to having it refitted, Matt should be able to extend the pipes to add a sink to the cat lounge as well as fitting some cupboards for cat food storage.

While Dad and Tom helped me settle the cats, Mum unpacked my clothes and hung everything up on a couple of rails she'd borrowed from the church in Little Sandby which got used for jumble sales, and Macey supervised Rylan unpacking everything for the kitchen.

The afternoon sped by and, although sparse, the flat did start to feel more like home and a little less echoey. I treated everyone to a takeaway to say thank you for their help and, at half six, they all said their goodbyes.

'I did it,' I said to Winnie as she weaved round my legs in the lounge. 'I told Leon we'd be out by the end of the weekend and we are. It's our first night in our new home. Excited?'

'I'm just happy to be wherever you are,' I answered for her in the soft Cornish accent I imagined she had.

'And I'm happy to be wherever you are too,' I told her. 'Let's go and find the others and make sure they're settling in okay.'

Smaller activity centres, scratching posts and beds had been placed around the flat. Tom had observed that the cats had way more furniture than me, but it was the way it needed to be for now. My absolute priority was making them feel safe and settled. All I needed was a bed and somewhere to sit. Everything else could be sorted later.

Pebbles and Smudge were both stretched out asleep on their old activity centre in the lounge, Heathcliff was using one of the scratching posts and Marmite and Effie were curled up on the sofa bed together, with Ruby draped over the back of it, looking out of the window. Winnie jumped up onto the other end of the sofa bed.

I found Viking cleaning himself in the dining room while Jupiter watched from a radiator bed in there, so that was four cats and five kittens accounted for downstairs.

Upstairs, Sybil was in the cat lounge curled up in a bed on the new activity centre and Freyja was lying in a long padded tube. Rubix was in one of the igloo beds but came out to weave round my legs on his way to lapping up some water. Blinky and Cloud were on my bed, but there was no sign of Babushka or Marmalade anywhere. Trying not to panic, I went back downstairs and worked my way more carefully through every room, trying to remember the last time I'd seen either of them. With my family coming and going at various times today, what if they'd nipped out of the flat onto the stairs, and then out onto the street? There were so many doors for them to get through that it shouldn't happen, but that didn't mean it couldn't.

When I returned to the cat lounge, Freyja crawled out from the tube and trotted over to me with a soft meow. I picked her up and hugged her.

'If you've seen Babushka or Marmalade, now would be a good time to speak up,' I said, scratching her ears.

At that moment, Babushka padded into the room, paused for a stretch, then wandered over to the toy box. She lifted out a small pink mouse with her mouth, dropped it on the floor and batted it about with her paw.

'Where've you been hiding?' I asked her. Presumably she'd been exploring the flat, moving into rooms after I'd checked them.

Freyja evidently wanted to play with Babushka's mouse too, jumping down from my arms and joining her, so I left them to it and continued my search for Marmalade.

Half an hour later, I was on the verge of tears, unable to find him anywhere. I was going to have to go outside and pray that, if he'd somehow escaped, he was waiting by the front door. Cats had homing instincts, but Marmalade was an indoor cat so the likelihood of him finding his way home and doing so safely was extremely remote. The thought that he might have attempted the journey back to Drake Street in search of Leon terrified me, but I was going to have to check.

I needed to nip to the toilet before going out. I closed the door behind me and jumped when a pair of green eyes met mine.

'Marmalade! There you are!'

I hadn't thought to look behind the bathroom door.

'Are you okay?' I asked, crouching down beside him and stroking his back. He gave no objection, but he didn't purr. 'Do you want a cuddle?'

Marmalade dipped his head and walked past me, out of the bathroom and down the hall with a couple of flicks of his tail. He was *not* a happy cat right now, but it wasn't just down to today's move. He hadn't been happy since the day Leon left us. I no longer thought of it as *when Leon went to work on the ship* or *when Leon took his overseas opportunity* or however I'd labelled it before. The reality was he'd left us that day and he'd known it but had been too gutless to admit it.

I still couldn't believe that he hadn't asked after the cats on the phone or in his email, or at least Marmalade. How did you tell a cat that their beloved owner had abandoned them? I hoped the move to the flat wouldn't turn him completely against me or cause problems between him and any of the others. They had their occasional moments but generally lived harmoniously together.

Chasing Marmalade round the flat wasn't going to help matters, so I'd leave him to it. The main thing for now was that I'd tracked him down and he was safe inside.

I went into my bedroom and admired the amazing job that Mum had done with the unpacking. Dresses, tops and T-shirts were all hanging on the clothes rails, organised by colour. Underwear, socks and nightwear were in the bedside drawers, and everything else like hoodies and loungewear was organised and beautifully folded in my suitcases. She'd taken my new towels, toiletries and make-up into the bathroom and had even unpacked the everyday items. There was nothing left for me to do, so I took my laptop down to the lounge.

As soon as the purchase of the premises went through, I'd set up a website, email account and social media presence for the café. In addition to project managing the refurbishment, getting the website design right and thinking about the types of posts I wanted to create had been a much-needed distraction during the first couple of difficult weeks without Leon. At the point he told me about his extension, I thankfully hadn't announced a mid-September opening date as that wouldn't have looked good to potential customers but, in early October, I'd gone live with the announcement that the Castle Street Cat Café would be opening on Wednesday, 15 November.

There'd been a couple of comments about cat cafés being unethical – something I'd hoped wouldn't happen but had been prepared for after discovering that the UK's largest cat charity was opposed to cat cafés – but the response had been overwhelmingly positive and the following had steadily built.

I'd advertised for waiting staff and had a small team ready to start next week, getting acquainted with the cats, the menu and the role ahead of opening day. I'd taken on five students aged seventeen and eighteen to work across the weekends and school holidays – Arwen, George, Lena, Sienna and Max – all of whom had previous work experience in retail or hospitality and who loved cats. I had a team of three for weekdays. Twenty-three-year-old Mark and fifty-five-year-old Wendy both had hospitality experience at a more senior level, but each had specific reasons for wanting part-time hours and no management responsibilities. My third weekday team member was Arwen's older sister, Fay, who was taking a year out before going to university and had previously worked in a fish and chip takeaway on the seafront. I felt confident with my recruitment decisions for all of them, although only time would tell.

I checked the cat café's email account. There were no applicants so far for Leon's role, which I'd advertised as 'Café Supervisor'. Feeling my anxiety levels rising, I shut down the emails and closed my laptop.

'It's early days,' I said to Marmite and Effie, who were still on the sofa bed beside me. 'And still some way from the closing date. We'll be fine, won't we?'

I'd already accepted that I wouldn't find a supervisor in time for opening day and was trying to think of it as a good thing because I'd have a more realistic view as to what I could and couldn't do once the café was up and running and therefore what the supervisor's role needed to be.

I put my laptop down on the coffee table and stretched my arms. I'd tried to limit what I'd carried yesterday and today but even two flights of stairs with Marmalade in his cat carrier had taken its toll on my muscles and my body was aching. It was time to take advantage of having access to a bath once more.

Twenty minutes later, I felt the tension leaving my body as I dipped down under the relaxing sage and sea minerals muscle soak bubble bath. I'd dotted some tealights along the edge of the bath and the sink, and streamed some mindfulness music on my phone. Heathcliff pushed open the door, padded several times on my new bathmat (I'd ditched the cerise pink bathroom set) and evidently decided it was comfortable as he tucked his paws in and settled down to sleep. I closed my eyes and could easily have drifted off too. It had been a busy day and I hoped my body wouldn't take that out on me tomorrow. Even though I'd steered clear of anything too physical, mainly focusing on the cats while everything went on around me, my body did what it liked.

'It's going to be fine,' I said. 'Think positively. You've got this!'

14

When I woke up on Sunday morning, the first feeling was momentary confusion as to where I was. The second feeling was relief that my fibromyalgia had spared me again today.

Sybil and Freyja were curled up together on the other side of the bed by the pillow. Freyja opened one eye and looked at me, but closed it again. Viking, Jupiter and Cloud were sleeping at the end of the bed. Cloud stretched in her sleep, then curled up once more. They all looked so comfortable, which made me feel happy and relaxed.

'It's going to be great,' I whispered to them.

Several more of the fur family were sleeping in the cat lounge, looking very much settled and at home in their new quarters. I put food and fresh water out and it didn't take long for the others to join them, but there was no sign of Marmalade. I checked the activity centre and the beds in the cat lounge, but they were empty, as were the rest of the beds around the flat. I thought I might find him behind the bathroom door, but he wasn't there either. Eventually I found him behind some boxes in the smallest bedroom.

'Your food's out,' I told him.

No reaction.

'Come on, Marmalade. You know you love your food.'

When he still didn't move, I bent down to pick him up, watching for signs that he objected. He didn't wriggle, so I stroked his head and back as I held him in my arms.

'I know I'm not your first choice,' I said, gently, 'but I love you and I promise to take good care of you.'

I carried him through to the cat lounge and placed him down next to his food bowl, but he walked away, taking a quick lap of water before leaving the room. It was new and unsettling for him, so I'd give him lots of extra attention over the next few days and hopefully he'd be all right.

I made myself some tea and toast for breakfast, showered and dressed, then took a few photos of the cats, which I added to the café's Facebook page, telling our followers that the cats were really excited to start meeting their fans a week on Wednesday. Ten days. Was that really all we had left until opening day? Macey had asked me yesterday if I was excited, and I'd smiled and said, 'Of course! I can't wait!' but the truth was I was far more nervous than I was excited, and that made me angry. I *should* be excited. How many people were fortunate enough to do the thing they'd dreamed of doing for decades? And I was scared. What if I woke up on opening day with a flare-up? Even a green one would be difficult when I had a business to run and a team to manage without my safety net of Leon. For someone who liked to be fiercely independent, I hadn't appreciated quite how much I'd grown to rely on him, and that made me angry too.

There was one person capable of calming me down, so I sent her a message.

TO ALISON

Just a quickie to let you know I'm settled in the flat now. If you don't have any plans this afternoon, you're welcome to come round for a cuppa xx

FROM ALISON

Would love to but it's Nigel's birthday so we're off out for the day shortly. Could do Tues, Wed or Thurs this week if you're free either of those days xx

TO ALISON

11am on Thursday? Happy birthday to Nigel.
Hope you have a lovely cake-filled day xx

It had been a long shot hoping that Alison would be free today and maybe it was just as well. I'd have a quiet day in the flat with the cats, do an online supermarket shop and prepare myself for the week ahead. I was training the weekday team on Wednesday and the weekend team next Sunday and there was a huge list of other things I needed to do like unpacking, washing and organising everything for the kitchen now that the dust had all settled and the café had been thoroughly cleaned. The retail stock needed displaying, the stock cupboard organising, the human toilets stocking and the litter trays placing in the cat toilet. There was more than enough time to do all of that before we opened, but I had to be realistic and allow for my fibromyalgia to stop me in my tracks somewhere along the way.

I was playing with Effie and Pebbles and a feather teaser after lunch when a message came through from my cousin.

FROM FIONA

How did the move go? Hope it hasn't been too draining x

TO FIONA

The move went well. Trying to have a relaxing day with the cats. Scared of a flare-up stopping me in my tracks next week 😔

FROM FIONA

I have some thoughts on this and probably easier to talk than type. Are you free for a quick chat?

Taking that as confirmation that Fiona was free now, I rang her.

'I can completely relate to the flare-up fear,' Fiona said after we'd exchanged pleasantries and established that we were both having a good day. 'The problem with the fear is that you can get stressed about it and potentially bring on a flare-up.'

'A self-fulfilling prophecy?' I suggested, adjusting my position on the sofa bed when Effie and Pebbles clambered onto my knee.

'Exactly! Fibromyalgia is so unpredictable that it's not worth investing any energy into worrying about a flare-up. Fibro flares can be triggered by so many things such as stress, over-exertion, illness, changes in the weather and temperature, but sometimes those things don't trigger a flare, and other times you can have a flare and none of those things are present.'

'Tell me about it! It's so frustrating when they seem to come out of nowhere.'

'But isn't it a blessing when you know you've done too much and you're not hit by one? I used to be a big planner with weekends packed full of activities. Now I embrace spontaneity. If I wake up on a Saturday or Sunday morning feeling great, Graham and I jump in the car and go somewhere. We say yes to invitations with friends but always with the caveat that we'll only be able to confirm for definite on the day and they understand why that's the case because they've all seen me at my worst, mid-flare-up.'

'Really? Was that intentional?'

'Absolutely. We have a condition which is invisible to others and, when we're at our worst, we hide ourselves away because we physically have to, so our friends and colleagues never see how bad it gets. I didn't really want the people I care about to see me in bed in pain or to attempt a conversation with them while brain fog stole my words, but I decided that my fibro was something I wasn't going to be ashamed of or embarrassed about, so I chose to show my friends a bad day. They didn't need to see me to believe me, but it felt like the right thing to do for me.'

'That's brave! How did your friends react?'

'They were really shocked, but they appreciated the eye opener and it's actually brought us all closer together. Now, when I have to pull out of something last minute, they completely get it and I don't feel guilty, so I'm glad I did it, although I appreciate it's not for everyone.'

'You're so positive about it all,' I said, full of admiration for her.

'I try to be, but I'm not infallible. I have days when I wish I could run away from my body, when I don't know which symptom to cry about first, when I want to scream and swear at the injustice of it all. I allow myself to have those moments, but I don't allow my life to be all about them. I'm grateful for every day I don't have a flare-up. I'm even grateful for the days where I have one but it's mild because I can still function, even if it's in slow motion.'

'I probably do need to be more grateful for the good days,' I admitted, 'and stop panicking about a bad one being just around the corner.'

'It'll take time to get there – it's all about baby steps – but it does help. Really sorry, Tabby, but I need to shoot. We're taking advantage of a good day and going for a walk with some friends. Are you okay?'

'Yeah, thanks. I appreciate the chat – really helpful again.'

After the call ended, I stayed where I was for a while, stroking the two kittens. It was interesting what Fiona had said about letting her friends see her at her worst. I'd been so disappointed with Faith and Kelsey for drifting away, but I should have been disappointed with myself instead. I hadn't even told them about the fibro, let alone thought to let them see it. In their shoes, how would I view myself? Like an old friend who wasn't interested in maintaining the relationship anymore, and who couldn't even be bothered to explain why. No wonder they'd stopped getting in touch. I'd thought they'd rejected me but I was the one who'd rejected them first.

'I should probably get in touch with them and apologise,' I said to the kittens. 'And I should probably do it now, but if they suggest meeting up, the timing is wrong and we'll be back to square one. I'll get the café up and running first and then I'll reach out. Another few weeks isn't going to make any difference.'

Babushka padded into the lounge and jumped up onto the sofa bed beside me, purring as she pressed her body against my legs.

'Fiona's onto something with embracing spontaneity,' I said, stroking Babushka's ears back. 'I'm not sure how easy that's going to be with the café to run, but I'll do my best.'

I thought about one of the four memes she'd sent me earlier in the week – *You haven't lost who you are. You're a bit different now, but you're just as fabulous as before.* The new me was going to work hard at accepting the unpredictability of my condition and being grateful for the pain-free moments. I could liken the unpredictability to the British weather and how frequently plans had to change when a summer's day brought rain rather than sunshine. I recalled many trips to the beach, picnics, bike rides, camping trips and village fetes from my youth being called off thanks to the weather. Fibro was just like that – disrupting the best-laid plans – but it didn't mean that I couldn't plan those things. I just needed to think differently about everything around those plans and hope that being good to my body beforehand would lead to my body being good to me on the day. Sometimes that strategy would win and sometimes it wouldn't and that was how life would be from now on, but better to make and cancel plans than not make any at all.

15

I slept well during my second night in the flat and woke up feeling unusually refreshed. Following my conversation with Fiona yesterday, I took a moment to acknowledge that and to feel grateful that I'd been blessed with a pain-free day.

The cats seemed to have responded positively to their new home in the flat – with the exception of Marmalade – so the plan for today was to let them into the café and get them familiar with the surroundings there and where to find their water and litter trays. Matt had installed a clever eco-friendly water fountain system where the water at various drinking stations around the café was constantly refreshed.

After breakfast, I shook a tub of treats and encouraged the cats to follow me down to the first floor, propping the door to the flat open with a cat-shaped crocheted doorstop.

It was so lovely watching my fur family exploring Feline Forest and Kitty Cove. Freyja sprawled out on one of the flower-shaped beds while her sister Sybil settled on a platform in one of the trees. Smudge looked adorable curled up in a red and white spotted toadstool igloo bed until Rubix pounced on her and they tumbled out of it, play-fighting. Winnie headed for the lighthouse, Heathcliff and Babushka for the boat, and Effie launched herself onto one of the deckchairs on the beach while the others prowled around sniffing and prodding. When I went downstairs a little later, I found Viking and Jupiter on the castle and Blinky sprawled out on the drawbridge.

I spent all morning moving between the two floors, checking they were all okay and that there were no toileting incidents, but all seemed to be well.

At lunchtime, I kept the door to the flat propped open while I made myself a sandwich. A couple of the cats came back upstairs at that point. Even though I'd created a quiet area on the first floor, they might like to fully escape into the flat while the café was open. I couldn't leave the door propped open, so a cat flap needed to be a priority. When I'd finished eating, I sent Matt a text.

> **TO MATT**
>
> I've had a slight change of plan and have moved into the flat. Could you quote me for installing a cat flap in the door and a sink and cupboards in the back bedroom? Thanks

> **FROM MATT**
>
> I'm having lunch with Charlee over the road so can be with you in 10 mins

> **TO MATT**
>
> Perfect. See you shortly

As well as being part of a superb construction team, Matt had turned out to be a really useful contact. His wife, Charlee, owned Charlee's Chocolates – the chocolate shop directly opposite the café – so he'd introduced me to her and her business partner Jodie. They'd then introduced me to several other business owners on Castle Street who'd all been really welcoming and happy to share their tips and experiences.

I put my empty plate and mug next to the sink and went downstairs to meet Matt.

'I feel bad dragging you away from your lunch,' I said, when I let him in a few minutes later.

'It wasn't a planned lunch. I had a plumbing job in town which wasn't nearly as complicated as expected, so your text was timed perfectly.'

We headed up to the flat.

'You changed your mind about living here?' Matt asked, as he measured the thickness of the door.

'I had it changed for me. Leon decided that his future is working on cruise ships and not with me.'

He looked up, grimacing. 'Sorry about that.'

'Thank you.' I shrugged. 'One of those things sent to test us. Do you think you'll be able to fit a cat flap without changing the door?'

Matt tapped some measurements into his phone. 'Should be able to.'

I took him upstairs to the cat lounge and explained my vision for up there.

'Shouldn't be a problem either,' he said. 'I'll come back to you with a quote tonight. I'll be able to fit the cat flap one evening this week, but this is a bigger job. We'll squeeze it in, but it might not be until the end of the month. I'll look at the schedule and confirm that with the quote.'

'Thanks, Matt. I really appreciate it. I need the bathroom replacing and a few other things, but I'll see how I get on living here first.'

'No probs. I'll be in touch later.'

When I let Matt out, I paused in the doorway and looked up and down the street, a light breeze ruffling my hair. I hadn't been outside since moving in on Saturday morning and a quick stroll wouldn't go amiss. As it had been Bonfire Night last night, I was curious to see which businesses had been decorated for Christmas.

In the window to Hairlequin's next door, boxed hairdryers, straighteners and other styling tools and products were displayed with sparkly pink and silver bows on them. Pink fairy lights were draped over the gifts and strung round the window and I could see a small pink tree on the welcome desk and a larger one in the back corner.

A couple of doors on, Bay Books had a small Christmas tree in the middle of their window with children's Christmas books fanned round the base of it. A display on one side showed further children's titles and the other side had adult books, including the seasonal classic *A Christmas Carol*. Red fairy lights twinkled around the window and on the tree. The tree was decorated with bookmarks, pens and colourful bottles of ink which all looked so effective.

Castle Jewellery had a large shop window with several display tiers, each of which had fake snow, sprigs of holly, swathes of ivy and sparkly Christmas baubles. Next door to them, the Wedding Emporium had a stunning red bridal dress in the window with a cream fur-lined cape, and bridesmaid dresses in red, green and gold. Fake snow and warm white lights finished the look perfectly.

There weren't many shops that hadn't put their decorations up – or at least started to – and I felt all cosy and festive when I returned to the cat café. I still wanted to showcase the café without the distractions of Christmas decorations, but perhaps I'd add some fairy lights round the window for opening day or I'd look out of place.

Christmas was going to be very different this year but one of the massive benefits of having my own business would be not working on Christmas Day. The Ramparts Hotel was very popular for Christmas Day and New Year's Day lunch, and Leon and I had worked both the whole time we were together, tending to celebrate Christmas on Boxing Day and write off New Year's Day. It would be lovely to have a normal Christmas Day this year – well, as normal as it could be without Leon.

Early that evening, I was thinking of making myself some tea when my phone rang.

'Are you home?' Rylan asked.

'Yes, why?'

'Because I'm outside with Macey and Tom. I've got my key with me. Are we okay to come in?'

'Of course. Come up. The flat door's open.'

'This is an unexpected surprise,' I said, leaning against the door-frame when I heard their footsteps and voices. 'Didn't I just see you all two days ago?'

'We've got something for you,' Rylan said from the bottom of the stairs. 'It's a surprise, so go into the lounge with Macey while Tom and I bring it up.'

I led Macey into the lounge and she sank down onto the sofa bed with a sigh.

'Close your eyes,' Rylan called.

I did as asked, intrigued by the shuffling sounds. Whatever the surprise was, it sounded like it was heavy.

'Open them!'

I opened my eyes and gasped at the enormous box – a brand-new smart television.

'We wanted to get you a housewarming gift,' Rylan said. 'This is from the three of us and Mum and Dad.'

'A TV? Oh, my God! I was thinking some pasta bowls or a cutlery set. This is way too generous.'

'I told you we should have bought her some dishcloths instead,' Tom said, his voice exaggeratedly dramatic. 'Best take this back to the shop, then. Are you going to carry it down, Macey?'

'Yeah, no problem.'

They all raised their eyebrows at me.

'Honestly, you lot, I don't know what to say. Thank you so much. That's amazing.'

'We know you don't want to rush into any big furniture purchases until you've decided on styles and colours,' Macey said, 'but we figured a TV has a fairly standard look.'

'And you know you're clueless about this stuff,' Rylan added. 'You'd only have roped one of us in to help you choose anyway.'

'That's true,' I admitted.

'I know you've only just moved in,' Macey said, 'but I bet you've already missed having a telly.'

'I have, actually. I've had a lot to do, but there have been moments when I could happily have plonked myself down in front of something – especially last night – and I haven't been able to. I'm so grateful. You've made my evening.'

'Wait till you see what else we've got,' Tom said.

He and Rylan left the room and I glanced at Macey, but she did a zipping motion across her mouth. They returned moments later and Tom handed me a bag for life.

'A tuna pasta bake, garlic ciabatta and salad,' he said. 'Homemade.'

'You absolute star, Tom-cat. Thank you.'

'You're welcome. If you want to pop the oven on, we'll fix the wall mount and get the TV set up.'

As Rylan and Tom were technical and I wasn't, I was more than happy to leave them to it. I took the food through to the kitchen, put the oven on and poured drinks for everyone. The laughter coming from the lounge made me smile. I'd been feeling a bit lost and lonely yesterday, but Fiona had lifted me then. A look in the shop windows earlier and now this had given me a further lift. Leon wasn't in my life anymore, but there were plenty of people who were who did care and I was going to do more to let them in.

* * *

'That was so delicious, Tom-cat,' I said, placing my knife and fork down on my empty plate a little later. 'With your cooking skills, how are you still single?'

'Because he's a geeky accountant,' Rylan quipped.

'Says the scruffy artist married to the nerdy shrink,' Tom responded, 'with geeky accountants for parents.'

Winding each other up about our professions was something we'd always done, but always with affection.

'I don't get why you're single either,' Macey said, cocking her head to one side and studying Tom's profile. 'You're a catch.'

'The next time I go on a date, how about you come with me and tell them that?' Tom said. 'I don't seem to have much luck convincing them myself.'

Rylan affectionately patted him on the back. 'That's because you can't talk to women.'

'Rubbish!' I protested. 'He can talk to me and Macey. He can talk to his clients.'

'That's because he's not on the pull,' Rylan said.

I glanced at Tom, feeling defensive towards him, but he nodded. 'He's right. Put me in front of a client and I'm fine. Put me in front of a date or potential date and I lose the ability to form sentences.'

Macey unsuccessfully stifled a yawn. 'Sorry. Nearly bedtime for me.'

'I'll finish setting up the telly,' Rylan said, 'and then we'd better head home.'

Tom helped me clear the table and grabbed a tea towel as I filled the washing up bowl. The dinner table conversation was playing on my mind.

'Does it bother you being single?' I asked as I placed the first clean plate on the draining board.

'Nah. I'm used to it.' Tom picked up the plate and started drying it. 'I've been single for so long that I'm probably too set in my ways now to make room for anyone else.'

He finished drying the plate and dipped his fingers in the bowl and flicked some water at me. 'Could you be any slower at washing up?'

I flicked some water back at him. 'What are you? The washing up police?'

He scooped up a handful of bubbles and blobbed them on my nose, so I scooped some up and splatted them on his forehead. He scooped up more so I did the same and we stood facing each other, bubbles at the ready.

'Are you sure you want to do this?' he said, his eyes sparkling mischievously.

'Are *you* sure you want to do this?' I challenged back.

He splatted them on my head as I caught his mouth, laughing as he blew them away.

'How are you finding it without Leon?' Tom asked after we resumed washing up.

'Weird. I'd already got used to him not being around, so his absence hasn't affected me as much as it might have done and, at the moment, my big focus is on the café. It's not just about getting ready for opening day – it's about how I run it without him. Once we're open and in a routine, I reckon it'll hit me more.'

'Are you sure there's nothing I can do to help you with the café?'

'I appreciate the offer, but the only thing the café needs now is a replacement Leon. If you spot one of those roaming the streets, send them my way.'

The three of them left shortly afterwards, so I rang my parents to thank them for my new television. I was eager to try it out but it was getting late and I wasn't sure if I could concentrate on something new, so

I found a film I'd watched several times before. The sofa bed was comfy, so I put my pyjamas on and settled down to watch.

Babushka curled up by my feet and Viking tucked in beside me. I managed maybe half an hour of the film before worries about running the cat café without Leon pushed their way in. I hadn't said anything to my new team during the interview process about my fibromyalgia, but I would have to mention it during their training because it would affect them at some point and I didn't want them thinking I'd lied to them.

'I have to be honest with my family before I tell the team,' I said, stroking Viking's belly. 'I'll do some baking and invite them round for a trial run on Saturday and tell them then. Do you think that's a good plan?'

'It is a very good plan indeed,' I replied in the sing-song Scandinavian accent I imagined Viking to have. 'It is about time they know the full details.'

'You're right, Viking. I'll message them tomorrow.'

17

The first training session on Wednesday with my weekday team went really well. Taking Fiona's advice about listening to my body and not trying to do everything on my own, I asked them to unpack, wash and put away all the crockery, cutlery and kitchen supplies. It got them working together and I ran bite-sized training sessions while each dishwasher load was on.

Mark, Wendy and Fay all adored cats – currently owning or having owned cats in the past – and were brilliant with them. All the cats, except for Marmalade, came into the café at some point and I loved how quickly the team had picked up their names. I'd prepared a coloured cat guide containing a photo and short bio for each cat including their name, date of birth, breed, names of any siblings or close friends and a few personality quirks.

When the team left, I looked round the kitchen, delighted that everything was unpacked and in its place. It all looked so shiny and new and lovely. I picked up my planner and scanned down the to-do list, ticking off what we'd finished today.

Everything was going smoothly so far. Time was on our side – no last-minute panic anticipated – and I hadn't had a fibro flare-up in nine days. Whenever I went for this long without one, the idea that it might have gone nudged at me. It had been a mistake, a misdiagnosis, I'd just been really tired for a long time and the pain was... well, I wasn't sure what it was, but it was gone. And then it would return, my body not caring that it had given me false hope. Therefore, at the back of my mind, there was a worry that I might get struck down very soon. I had two further worries – what was going to happen when I had a flare-up once we were open (whether or not I'd found a replacement for Leon because it would still be an issue even if I had) and Marmalade.

I locked the inner door downstairs, switched the lights off and went up to the flat. I opened the fridge, scanned the contents and closed it again. I wasn't hungry yet and wasn't sure I could be bothered to make something even if I had been. The cats would be, so I went up to the cat lounge to dish up their tea. As had become the norm, Marmalade didn't come running like the others. I found him tucked behind the bathroom door.

'Hey, Marmalade,' I said softly, crouching down and stroking his back. 'Have you missed us today?'

Across the week, I'd come upstairs several times to give Marmalade some attention, but he hadn't been massively responsive. He'd typically let me stroke him for a minute or so, then he'd wander off. He did that now.

'Do you not want some food?' I asked, but he left the bathroom. It broke my heart that Marmalade was clearly so unhappy without Leon. I removed my phone from my jeans pocket and quickly tapped in a text.

TO LEON

I'm worried about Marmalade. He hasn't been right since you left

As soon as I sent it, I regretted it. What did I expect Leon to do from a cruise ship in the Caribbean Sea? He evidently felt the same as a reply came back minutes later.

FROM LEON

What do you expect me to do about it from 4.5k miles away? If you're that worried, take him to the vet

It was a fair comment, although I wasn't impressed by the lack of concern for his beloved pet. How could he disown him so easily? Another text arrived which had me grinding my teeth.

FROM LEON

Is he really out of sorts, or was that just an excuse to get in touch? I thought I was clear about it being over

'Get over yourself,' I snapped, angrily typing in a response.

TO LEON

Your message was received loud and clear and I can assure you that the last thing I want to do is be in contact. You made it very clear that you don't care about me anymore but I thought you might actually care about your cat. Apparently not. I won't disturb you again

I stared at the phone, challenging him to respond. The dots kept appearing, as though he was composing a message, but nothing came. With a frustrated sigh, I shoved the phone back in my pocket and returned to the cat lounge. Marmalade wasn't there. Leon might not care, but I did. I'd ring the vet in the morning and make an appointment to get Marmalade checked over in case it wasn't just Leon's absence making him withdraw and there was something more serious going on.

Leaning against the doorframe, watching the cats, I had a sudden feeling of loss. How many times had I watched them eat back at Drake Street only for Leon to slip his arm round my waist and make a joke about me being like a waiter on standby? Since that phone call, I'd thought a lot about what he'd said about us drifting apart. Although it was clear now that we'd wanted different things, I still couldn't see that distance on a personal level. I genuinely thought we'd been happy together and I was struggling to go from a loving relationship, counting down the days until Leon returned, to being single again. He might have fallen out of love with me months (years?) ago, but I couldn't just flick a switch and magically switch off those feelings, much as I wished I could.

I wasn't sure what to do with myself this evening. I didn't need to attend to any café admin, so it would make sense to use the free time to find some design inspiration online for the flat and maybe start a Pinterest board. I took my laptop through to the lounge and opened up a new board, but I wasn't in the right frame of mind and found myself scrolling aimlessly. Leon's attitude towards Marmalade had really narked me, but so had his attitude towards me. I thought I knew him so well, but so much of what he'd done this year bewildered me. Perhaps I shouldn't be mourning my loss. Perhaps I should be celebrating a lucky escape.

18

I was in luck with the timing of my phone call to the vet's the following morning. They'd just had a cancellation, so I managed to secure that slot and took Marmalade down for a blood test first thing.

'He seems healthy enough,' the vet said, after she'd given him a thorough check. 'As you say, it could be the loss of a loved one and the change of scenery that's put him off balance, but you're right to check there's nothing more serious. We should have the test results back tomorrow afternoon, so we'll give you a call then.'

As soon as I returned to the flat and opened the cat carrier, Marmalade ran out and upstairs, presumably to hide behind the bathroom door again or some other place where he felt safe.

I went into the kitchen to make a hot drink. Pebbles was on the worktop, batting an empty plastic drinks bottle back and forth. I watched her, smiling, as the bottle got closer to the edge and eventually tumbled on the floor. She looked forlorn as she looked around for something else to play with – or should that be push onto the floor?

'Down you get while I boil the kettle,' I said, picking her up and giving her a cuddle.

Pebbles clambered onto my shoulder and draped herself across it while I filled the kettle.

'You've found your balance now, haven't you?' I asked, snuggling my cheek against her head. 'Good girl.'

Matt texted to say he could come round this evening to fit the cat flap. He confirmed that the kitchen cupboards I'd approved for the cat lounge were on order and could be fitted the week after the café opened, so that was one big task sorted.

Shortly after, Alison rang to say she was outside. With Pebbles still perched on my shoulder, I went down to let her in.

'Aw, how adorable are you?' she said.

'Thank you. And what about Pebbles?'

She laughed as she stepped into the porch. 'You look fabulous too, Tabby.'

We'd only made it across the café and up a couple of stairs when there was a knock on the door. I extricated Pebbles from my shoulder and handed her to Alison while I answered it.

'Delivery for Castle Street Cat Café,' a courier said, indicating three large boxes.

I glanced at the side of one of the boxes and smiled at the image of a Christmas tree on the side. This must be the last of my Christmas decorations for the café. I signed for them and shuffled them inside.

'Do you want a hand upstairs with them?' Alison asked.

'You're pregnant, I have fibromyalgia, and they're heavy. They can stay here for now.'

'Anything exciting?' she asked as she handed me Pebbles, who immediately scrambled back onto my shoulder.

'Christmas trees. I've ordered a few alternative ones which the cats should enjoy rather than destroy.'

'Are you going to have Christmas decorations up when you open next week?' Alison asked as we headed upstairs.

'No. I really want to show it off like it is, even if that's only for a week. It's another thing Leon's messed up. If I'd opened when I was meant to two months ago, I'd have had them up by now. Do you want to see what I've bought?'

'Ooh, yes, please.'

I took her into the dining room and showed her the igloo beds I'd sourced in the shape of a Santa hat, reindeer, snowman, Christmas tree and Christmas pudding, some cat-themed Christmas bunting I'd had especially made, and various other festive decorations. There'd been so many amazing Christmas items that I could easily have spent a small fortune but I'd set myself a budget and stuck to it.

'It's a shame your Christmas will be cut short,' Alison said as we packed everything away. 'There's always next year, though.'

'Yeah. I'll probably add extra bits each year, but I won't be replacing the beds unless they're past it.'

I took Alison on a tour of the rest of the flat and she had a good giggle at the bathroom suite, especially when I showed her photos with the cerise mat set in situ.

'That's nasty. Who thought those two colours together would ever be a good idea? Are you going to get it refitted?'

'Probably in the New Year if I can face the noise and the mess, and if I have the money. If the café tanks, it'll be staying turquoise.'

'The café won't tank. Are you worried it will?'

'I'm trying not to think about it. I've only released booking slots up to Christmas and they're looking pretty good, but who knows what'll happen in January when everyone's skint, they're all staying in and the novelty has worn off? Hopefully we'll be okay, but I am prepared that trade might dip quite a lot until Easter.'

We went back downstairs and I made a couple of drinks, which we took into the lounge.

'Are you looking forward to Christmas back in Whitsborough Bay?' I asked when we'd settled on the sofa bed. 'It was Thailand last year, wasn't it?'

'It was, but it was Whitsborough Bay the year before, although Madison was only five weeks old, so I'm looking forward to her experiencing her first proper British Christmas. Lorraine and Nigel are really excited about it. What will you do?'

'I'm not sure. We haven't discussed it yet. It only just struck me this week that it'll be my first not working in years.'

'That'll be lovely. You won't be on your own?'

'No. My family won't let that happen.'

We chatted some more about my Christmas plans for the café and
the Christmases Alison had spent abroad. All too soon, she had to head
off, but it had been a great visit. I hadn't given Christmas that much
thought until this week but after my tour of the shops and the conversation with Alison, I was feeling quite excited. Christmas at the Castle
Street Cat Café was going to be magical and I was going to enjoy every
moment of it. Without Leon.

19

Marmalade's blood tests came back the following day and didn't reveal anything untoward. That was a relief, but he wasn't right. Withdrawn and unsociable, I wondered whether it wasn't just Leon's absence that had affected him. Could it be that the expanding fur family had become too much for him in his advancing years? He'd never shown aggression or impatience with the kittens, but he hadn't shown any interest in them either. Much as it would break my heart to do it, could rehoming him be the fairest thing for him? He'd always adored my parents, so maybe they'd take him. They already had an elderly cat – a black British Short-hair called Boo who was a whopping twenty-one years old but in great health. They'd been talking about getting another cat, ideally an older rescue one as a young cat would be too much for Boo. If Boo and Sindy responded well to Marmalade and vice versa, that might be the solution. At least that way I could still see him. I'd put the idea to them during the test run tomorrow.

I spent the day in the café baking a couple of cakes and tray bakes, in my absolute element, using Nanna's food mixer and her beautiful pastel-coloured spoons and spatulas once more. It was great seeing how the kitchen worked for me and I shifted a few things around to what felt like more logical positions now that I was using the space. In the morning, I'd bake some scones.

When I'd finished washing and putting everything away, I took a tub of treats out to lure the fur family back upstairs. Sybil, Babushka, Marmite, Effie and Rubix were all in Cat Castle so I called their names as I shook the tub. Jupiter joined us on the first-floor landing so I led them up to the flat, fed them each a couple of treats and closed the flat door behind me.

Three of the remaining kittens were in Kitty Cove – Ruby and Blinky curled up together in the boat and Cloud in one of the suitcases. I could see Freyja on one of the Ferris wheel platforms and another rattle of the treats brought Viking out of a toadstool igloo, pausing to stretch before he ran over to me. Smudge was on one of the flower beds. The six of them followed me up to the flat and were rewarded with their treats, and I did a quick check to make sure the other three adult cats – Marmalade, Winnie and Heathcliff – were already in the flat with Pebbles, giving them each a couple of treats when I found them. Marmalade was behind the bathroom door again. I'd placed a cat bed there to make him more comfortable.

'You're not happy, are you?' I asked, sitting beside him and stroking his back.

He seemed relaxed enough with his paws tucked in and made no effort to move away from me, but it wasn't right seeing him removing himself from the other cats like this. Guilt crept in once more that my expansion of the fur family had pushed him out, but I shoved it aside. Marmalade's behaviour had changed when Leon had been away for a fortnight. If I went out, he'd rush up to the door when I returned, then slink away when he saw that Leon wasn't with me. Then he stopped. Leon hadn't just broken my heart, he'd broken Marmalade's, and I was so annoyed with him for that. Had he even considered Marmalade's welfare when he'd accepted that cruise contract or had he been that desperate to get away from me that it had never entered his head? I'd be fine without him and I'd make damn sure Marmalade was too.

20

One of the many frustrations about fibromyalgia was its unpredictability. Sometimes I knew I'd pushed myself and done far too much and expected my body to punish me for that. It usually did, but not all the time, which was confusing. Other times I could do everything right and it would still floor me, reminding me that there was no such thing as 'right' and 'wrong' and that my body was in charge and would do what the hell it liked.

A fibro symptom I only experienced intermittently was restless legs. It's a really uncomfortable itchy creepy-crawly feeling in the legs which gives overwhelming urges to keep moving the legs in an attempt to stop the sensation. Of course, it doesn't stop it at all and all the kicking about makes sleep pretty much impossible. I'd felt the start of it late on Friday night with pins and needles in my feet, and it had spread up my legs for a full attack in the early hours of Saturday morning. I'd never had an occasion of restless legs without a fibro flare-up and today was no exception.

'At least the restless legs have stopped,' I said to Marmalade as I sat on the toilet with him watching me from his usual spot. 'Small mercies.'

The pain level was amber, although it was very close to red. When I made it back to my bedroom, I'd have to message my family to tell them the test run was off. Typical. I'd been looking forward to it, but also to being honest with them about my condition.

As I fed the cats a little later, I thought about the spoon chart Fiona had sent me. How many spoons were needed to feed sixteen cats during an amber flare-up? Probably more than I had at my disposal today.

Back in the bedroom, I picked up my phone and started to compose a WhatsApp message.

> **FROM TABBY**
>
> Really sorry about the short notice, but I need to cancel today's plans. Nothing to worry about but I've had a fibro flare-up. It's only mild but

I stopped typing and looked at my message. Lie, lie, lie! The whole point of today had been to open up to them and admit that I needed help. How were more lies going to help that? Shaking my head, I deleted the message and put my phone down, thinking about what Fiona had said about letting her friends see her mid-flare-up. The one thing more powerful than me telling my family about my condition would be letting them see it for themselves.

I lay back in bed, tears spilling down my cheeks and soaking into my pillow. Letting the people I loved see me so vulnerable was a terrifying thought, and I knew it would be upsetting for them, which, in turn, would be upsetting for me. But it was a step I needed to take to prevent me from glossing over how bad things could get. Full transparency.

Ten minutes before they were due, I sent a fresh message.

> **FROM TABBY**
>
> Slight change of plan. Can you meet outside the café and, when you're all here, let yourselves into the flat? Grab a chair each from the garden table in the dining room and come up to my bedroom (Macey can sit on the bed). There's something I need to show you xx

I'd seen Tom attach his spare key to the same keyring as his apartment keys, so I knew they'd be able to get in. My heart pounded as I watched the clock. From four storeys up, I wouldn't be able to hear them when they arrived outside – especially over the general hubbub on the street on a busy Saturday – but I'd hear them on the stairs once they were inside the flat. And, when that point came, it would be too late to change my mind.

Viking, Cloud and Marmite were all on the bed with me. 'Do you think this is a stupid idea?' I asked them.

Viking took that as an invitation to clamber onto my knee. I winced as he padded on me, every movement shooting pain through my legs, but I could just about bear it once he'd settled. The comfort of his soft fur and his purrs was worth the discomfort.

Footsteps and voices alerted me to their arrival.

'Tabby?' Mum called.

Viking shot off the bed and out the room, but Cloud and Marmite stayed where they were.

'Upstairs,' I called back. 'Don't forget your chairs.'

Mum arrived in the bedroom first and stopped dead.

'Don't panic!' I said before anyone could speak. 'As you can see, I'm not very well today. I need to tell you all something which is why I asked you to get the...' I drifted off, the word 'chairs' evading me, so I waved my hand in the direction of the one Mum was holding. 'Sit down. It's story time.'

Exchanging concerned looks, they opened out the chairs and sat round the foot of the bed as Macey perched on the end. For a moment, I wanted to laugh at the ridiculousness of it all. It felt like a scene from a film where a dying monarch has gathered their family round their bedside to inform them of their succession wishes.

'I was going to cancel, but the reason I invited you today wasn't just for a trial run of my baking,' I said. 'It was so I could tell you something. When I said I'd been diagnosed with fibromyalgia, I told you it was mild. That isn't true...'

* * *

I wished I'd told them sooner. It felt as though they hadn't just taken some bricks off that hod I was carrying – they'd taken the entire hod from me, loaded the bricks into a wheelbarrow and wheeled them far away. Obviously the pain hadn't gone, but the weight of the guilt, the lies, and the deceit had and it felt good.

They'd all been shocked to hear how bad it really was and there were lots of expressions of guilt that they should have noticed, which I swiftly quashed.

'You couldn't have noticed because I didn't let you. I avoided you all on the really bad days and lied on the others. Leon didn't even know how bad it was and he lived with me. So no guilt, please. I couldn't bear it.'

I talked about my symptoms, my traffic light scale, the unpredictability of it all, and started trying to explain about being stuck on the change curve between denial and anger, but I was soon losing a battle with fatigue and brain fog. I kept losing track of my point, forgetting words and was struggling to keep my eyes open.

'I think we should give you a break,' Dad said. 'We'll leave you in peace for a bit and make some tea.'

'You won't leave?'

'We're not going anywhere,' Mum reassured.

'Is there anything we can do for you right now?' Rylan asked.

'Cat litter needs changing. Sorry.'

'Consider it done.'

Mum stayed behind, and sat down on the bed beside me, lightly stroking my hair back from my face.

'I wish I could hug you, but I don't want to hurt you.'

'I wish you could too.'

'You get some rest.' She blew me a kiss and left the room, pulling the door to with just enough room for the cats to get in and out.

* * *

When I opened my eyes, I was shocked to see it was quarter past one. The unbroken sleep had been welcome, but didn't make any sort of dent in the fatigue. I missed the days when feeling tired could be sorted out with a few early nights. Fatigue was something else.

I needed the toilet. They must have heard me moving around because, when I returned to the bedroom, Mum was in there with a tray containing a bowl of tomato soup, a soft white roll and a glass of fresh orange juice.

'Have you been shopping?' I asked, knowing I hadn't had any of those things in the flat.

'Tom nipped out. He's made us all lunch.'

'That was kind of him. It looks good.'

'I brought you a tea towel in case of slops,' she said, draping it across me once I'd settled back into bed.

'How's your morning been?' I asked as she sat on one of the garden chairs.

'Good. Rylan and your dad have cleaned the litter trays, I've given the bathroom a once-over, Tom's cleaned the kitchen, and Macey and I have been playing with the cats. That Rubix is such a character. Well, they all are, but him especially.'

'Did you see Marmalade at all?'

'He sat on my knee for a bit. He's such a softie.'

'I have a huge favour to ask. I don't suppose you'd consider taking him, would you? He's been so miserable since Leon left and I think he blames me for it. I'm really worried this isn't the right environment for him anymore. If Sindy and Boo accept him, I think he might be better off at yours.'

'I'll speak to your dad, but I'm sure it won't be a problem.'

'I feel like I've failed him.'

'You haven't. Failing would be ignoring it. Instead, you've noticed an issue and you're working on a solution that's best for him. If anyone has failed him, it's Leon. That lad has a lot to answer for. I know you said he didn't know the full extent of your condition, but he knew enough. He had no right to...' She paused, evidently conscious of her raised voice. 'What's done is done. He's not worth wasting our energy on.'

When I finished my soup, Mum took the tray away with instructions from me to ask everyone to return to the bedroom so I could finish my explanation.

Once they were settled, I explained the change curve again and how

I could see the way forward to acceptance following my conversations with Fiona. Finally, I talked them through the spoon theory, showing them the visual Fiona had sent me.

'You all know how much I struggle to ask for help and that's not going to miraculously change. I'm still finding this really hard to admit but I do need help. There are things I can't do or which are a huge struggle when I have a flare-up. Leon picked up most of them and, even though I know he's nobody's favourite person, I will say in his defence that he never complained about it. He's not here anymore and life's difficult living on my own when I have a flare-up. I know it's a huge ask—'

'Whatever you need, consider it done,' Dad said, which was echoed around the room. 'Write a list and we'll sort it between us.'

We agreed I'd put a list on WhatsApp when my flare-up had passed and I could think properly.

'We had a chat over lunch,' Mum said. 'We think you might need some extra help over the next month or so while you get the café up and running and settled into a routine, so we have a proposal for you. Your dad and I will help where we can, but Tom's going to take this coming week off work to—'

'That's too much,' I protested.

'I want to do it,' Tom said. 'It's basically just an excuse to play with the cats.'

I gave him an appreciative smile.

'I wish I could help,' Rylan said, 'but if there's anything you need doing after college hours, just shout. Or I can help on a weekend until the baby arrives.'

'I'll be worse than useless,' Macey said, shrugging apologetically, 'but I'll be here in spirit.'

I was so touched by their generosity that I couldn't speak. There'd already been several tears today as I told them my story and I didn't want to shed more. I touched my hand to my heart and blew them all a kiss with the other to show how grateful I was.

'And on that note,' Mum said, standing up and folding up her chair, 'you need some more rest, so we'll leave you for now.'

Mum, Dad, Rylan and Macey left the bedroom, taking their chairs with them.

'You look a bit overwhelmed,' Tom said.

'It's so much. I don't want to be a—'

'Don't you dare say "burden". You could never be that to the people who love you.'

'But you're changing your lives for me.'

'If it was Rylan or your mum who was ill, what would you do?'

'Help.'

'Exactly! So that's what we want to do for you. Look at it another way. If you were visually impaired, would you refuse a guide dog?'

'No.'

'If you had a hearing impairment, would you refuse hearing aids? If you had paralysis in your legs, would you refuse a wheelchair?'

I could see where he was going with this and shook my head.

'So why would you refuse help? The guide dog, the hearing aid, the wheelchair all assist those people in living their lives. Accepting help from us will assist you in living yours.' He smiled and winked. 'Of course, the downside of that is having to spend more time with you but, as I say, we get to play with the cats. Every cloud.'

I wished I could hug him. Ever since childhood, if I was poorly or had hurt myself, I could rely on Tom to throw in that one quip to make me laugh.

'Thank you,' I said.

'You might not be thanking me in a minute. My help comes with terms, conditions and a privacy notice.'

That made me smile again.

'There's a perfectly comfortable sofa bed going begging, so I'm moving in for the week to keep you out of mischief. No protests. It's happening. So I'm nipping home to get some clothes and bedding. I'll go food shopping while I'm out too. Is there anything you need me to bring from home or get from the supermarket?'

I stared at him for a moment, blown away by the kindness.

'I can't think of anything at the moment,' I said, my voice husky with emotion.

'No worries. Text me if you do. I'll lock up behind us and let myself back in, so you get some rest. See you later.'

He folded up his chair and gave me a little wave as he left the bedroom. I pushed down the lump in my throat and snuggled down under the duvet, stroking Freyja, who'd curled up beside me. I felt bad that they were going out of their way to help me, but I needed to get over it because they clearly wanted to do it. Tom was right that I'd have done it for them. Taking a week off work was an imposition but at least I knew it wasn't getting him into trouble with his employer when he worked for my parents. Moving in with me was huge too, but also a relief. I talked to the cats all the time and got so much love back from them in return, but I'd been lonely since Leon left. I'd never lived on my own before and I missed having someone to talk to, even if it was just a bit of chitchat about how the day had been. It would be so good to have that back, even if only for one week.

21

On Sunday morning, my flare-up had eased somewhat. The restless legs thankfully hadn't made a reappearance during the night, so I'd managed a little more sleep.

There was a knock on my bedroom door and Tom poked his head round it. 'How are you feeling this morning?'

'Down to green level today.'

'That's good news. Can I get you some breakfast?'

'Maybe later. I need a shower and, if I don't do that now, I won't have enough time to recover before the weekend team arrive.'

'Do you need to wash your hair?' he asked.

'I'd skip the shower if I didn't, but it's overdue.'

'Do you have a swimming costume?'

'Yes, why?'

'Your shower's over your bath, so what if you have a bath and I kneel by it and wash your hair for you? If a shower usually uses two spoons, maybe me helping will just use one.'

I smiled at him. 'You've been studying the chart.'

'You know me. Anything with numbers.'

'A bath and you washing my hair would be great.'

'I'll set it away running.' He headed towards the door, but paused, screwing up his face. 'Will putting a swimming costume on use an unnecessary spoon? I don't mean you shouldn't wear one, but should I help you put it on? Oh, but that's...' His cheeks were bright red and he looked ever so flustered. 'I'll just stop talking.'

'I've got a looser costume,' I said. 'If you could get it out for me, that would help.'

I pointed out a holdall and told him which colour costume to look for. He started the bath running as I slowly pulled it into place and slipped on a soft knee-length dressing gown over the top.

Tom's embarrassment had made me smile but, when the bath was ready, the roles were reversed. He eased off my dressing gown and I suddenly felt very self-conscious wearing a swimming costume in front of him, especially as the neckline was lower than I'd remembered from when I'd worn it on holiday with Leon. Rylan, Tom and I had regularly gone to the beach and swimming pool together during our childhood, but I was now aware that he hadn't seen me in so few clothes as an adult. I shouldn't be embarrassed. It was only Tom. But my cheeks were ablaze as I took his hand to steady me as I stepped into the bath and sank down beneath the bubbles, trying not to look like I was deliberately arranging them across my cleavage.

'Do you want to soak for a while or should I wash your hair straight-away?' he asked.

'Hair first, please.'

He reached the shower hose down from the wall mount and draped it over the taps, then whipped off his T-shirt.

'Didn't want to get it wet,' he said, when his eyes met mine.

I didn't mean to look, but he was right there, torso naked, and what could I do? For someone who never went to the gym and whose only form of exercise was a five-a-side kickaround with my brother and a few of their former school mates (which sounded more like an excuse to go to the pub than anything else), he was surprisingly toned.

I averted my eyes and dipped my head ready for the water, grateful to be able to hide my flaming cheeks from him.

'I've never washed someone else's hair before,' Tom said as he rubbed shampoo through my hair and massaged my scalp. 'Tell me if it hurts.'

'It's soothing,' I said, closing my eyes and relaxing. 'You've got the job!'

Leon had been good with me, but he'd never once offered to wash my hair. What a difference it made to my post-shower recovery having Tom doing it for me, brushing it and drying it too.

He made me some porridge while I got dressed and we ate our breakfast together at the garden table.

'I can't believe you've packed the bed away,' I said as we relaxed in the lounge for half an hour before the weekend team were due.

'I wanted you to have somewhere comfortable to sit. It's no bother.'

'I really appreciate all of this, and I have another favour to ask. Do you mind helping me with the training? I'm still foggy and I might need an interpreter. I don't want them thinking I'm stupid.'

'Are you going to tell them what's going on?'

'I don't know.'

'Obviously it's your call, but it's going to come out at some point so why not just put it out there right at the start? Own it!'

I raised an eyebrow at him. 'Did you really just say "own it!"?'

He laughed. 'Yeah, and I can't get away with that, can I?'

'No, but I like that you tried. And you're right. It *is* going to come out at some point so I might as well get it over with.'

* * *

I sat on a stool in the kitchen while Tom made drinks.

'I'm going to tell them now,' I said, watching the team through the kitchen window.

Several of the fur family had followed us downstairs and two of the kittens – Effie and Blinky – were pouncing on a feather teaser George was dangling while Sienna stroked Jupiter who was stretched out on one of the castle turrets. Arwen and Lena were rolling a ball with a bell in it between them which Rubix was watching intently and trying, but failing, to pounce on, and Max was dangling a catnip mouse in front of Viking. The engagement with the cats was a great start.

Tom took their drinks out and I asked them to gather round one of the tables while I sat with Tom at the next one over.

'Good to see you all here for your first training session,' I said, smiling at them. 'Before I go through the plan for today, I want to introduce you to a good friend of mine, Tom Headley. He'll be helping me out today and the rest of the week.'

I paused briefly while they acknowledged each other, trying to still the butterflies. I hated that I felt so nervous about this, but it was perhaps to be expected considering it was information that wasn't generally out there.

'Tom, my parents, or my brother might be here for your first weekend shift, supporting me,' I continued. 'There are two reasons for that. The first is that I was going to be running the café with someone else but they decided last minute that it wasn't for them. You've probably seen my advert for that role. I've not had any success in filling it yet, so my family are helping out. The second reason is...'

I glanced at Tom, who gave me an encouraging smile.

'...I have something called fibromyalgia. Have any of you heard of it?'

Lena told me one of her best friends had recently been diagnosed with it, so she had some knowledge of it. The others were unfamiliar, so I briefly outlined what it was and how it affected me.

'I had a bad flare-up yesterday and it's still with me today, although not as strongly. I can't stand for long, which is why I have stools in the kitchen, I can't carry anything heavy and, as you'll have noticed when I was explaining about my fibro, words can evade me. Is there anything you'd like to ask me?'

'What can we do to make things easier for you?' George asked.

Tears pricked my eyes at his thoughtfulness and maturity. 'On difficult days, you won't see me leaving the kitchen very often. I need to limit the time on my feet and going up and down the stairs so it's about you all keeping on top of clearing tables and checking the toilets, particularly upstairs, so that I don't need to.'

'We can do that,' Lena said, and the others all agreed.

'Thank you, all. I really appreciate it. Today, I want to go through the menu with you, show you where to find everything and talk about how your role will work. I have a couple of tasks for you too – stocking the shop part and sorting out the store cupboard. Before we do any of that, I'll formally introduce you all to the cats.'

The only one who'd never owned a cat was George. I pointed out the cats in Cat Castle, then took them upstairs to introduce them to the cats there, after which I gave them fifteen minutes to play with the cats, giving me a chance to re-energise before going through the menu.

We took a break for lunch at half twelve, and it warmed my heart to hear that they were all going to McDonald's together, friendships already forming. I stayed downstairs while Tom nipped up to the flat to make us both a sandwich.

'I think you've found a good team,' he said when he returned.

'Me too. I might not have had any success in finding a Leon replacement, but the rest of the recruits are good.'

But when they returned from lunch, I took one look at George and my heart sank.

'Are you all right?' I asked him, wincing at his red eyes.

'My eyes are really itchy.'

'He keeps sneezing too,' Arwen said. 'I think he might be allergic to cats.'

George shook his head. 'It's probably just a cold.'

'Can the rest of you go upstairs with Tom to start organising the store cupboard while I talk to George?'

They headed upstairs and I sent George into the accessible toilet to wash his hands and splash his eyes with cold water. It was possible he'd rubbed salt in his eyes at lunchtime, but it was more likely that Arwen was right. This wasn't the first allergic reaction to cats I'd seen.

'Are you asthmatic?'

'No. Why?'

'Research suggests people with asthma are more likely to be allergic to animals and it can trigger a bad reaction in someone who's asthmatic.'

'Am I going to lose my job?' he asked.

'I'm not going to dismiss you for having allergies, but I don't think it's very practical you working here if you do. Your eyes look so painful and sneezing is obviously an issue when you're handling food all day.'

'What if it isn't a cat allergy? Or what if it is and I take antihistamines?'

'Let's address whether it's a cat allergy first. My suggestion is that you go home, take a shower, put on fresh clothes and see whether the symptoms go when you've removed all traces of cat. If they do, then I'd suggest it *is* a cat allergy and not a cold. Antihistamines should help but do give serious consideration as to whether that's what you want to do.'

'I really want to work here.'

'And I want you to stay, George, but I don't want you to suffer. Have a think about it. And don't worry about pay. I'll pay you for the full shift today.'

A sombre George went upstairs to say goodbye to the others. I'd completely winged that. I had no idea where I stood with this. Could I dismiss him for being allergic? Was it my duty to pay for antihistamines for members of staff who were? Having employees was so complicated!

'I'm really sorry for letting you down today,' George said as he returned to the ground floor. 'Especially after what you told us this morning.'

'Aw, George, don't think like that. It's one of those things. Message me later to let me know how you're doing and we'll take it from there.'

I let him out and had only just closed the door when he sneezed several times. I couldn't imagine him returning. I knew several people with hay fever and had seen how much discomfort it could cause. It was difficult to avoid pollen and other hay fever triggers, but cats *could* be avoided. It might be different if someone owned a cat and discovered an allergy, but this was work.

If George left, I needed a replacement, I needed one fast, and they'd need to learn on the job. There wasn't anyone else I'd interviewed who I'd want to take on, but I'd received a few more CVs since filling the positions. I opened my laptop and looked through them, but nobody stood out.

The rest of the afternoon went well. Max and Sienna stayed with

Tom to finish sorting the store cupboard while Lena and Arwen came down to stock the shop.

After they left, Tom appeared as I was loading the dishwasher.

'I'll do that,' he said, shooing me over to a stool. I didn't have the energy to object.

'Do you think George will be back?' he asked.

'Nope. So that's another position to fill. He looked gutted about it.'

'So do you. I have an important question for you. How many spoons do you have left?'

'Thanks to you, maybe three or four.'

'What would you say to a spot of fresh air? We can go for a short walk, then I'll make tea and we can watch TV.'

'That sounds great.'

'I'll get your coat to save you doing the stairs. Is it okay to round the cats up when we get back?'

'That's fine. We won't be out long.'

I stroked Freyja's belly while I waited for Tom to get my coat, pausing when my phone beeped with a text.

FROM GEORGE

Looks like I am allergic to cats. Symptoms cleared but Mum took me to see a friend of hers who has two cats and they started again. I wanted to give it a go but Mum says it's not fair on you and she's right. Really sorry to let you down. Hope opening day goes really well

First Leon and now George. Two team members lost and we hadn't even opened the doors to the public! I'd already experienced more problems with staffing than I had with the ambitious refurbishment. Fingers crossed it would be smoother going from now on. Thank goodness my family had offered to help at the weekend because I was going to need them.

22

'Are we just baking for the next two days,' Tom asked as we settled on the sofa bed after a delicious tea following a short walk round the block, 'or is there any more prep to do for opening day?'

'I've got some balloons and bunting to put up outside on opening day but I didn't get anything for inside other than a balloon sculpture for the porch, which will arrive readymade. So, yes, all baking but, now that you're here, there's something else I can do which I'd had to ditch...'

When Matt introduced me to his wife, Charlee, she suggested going for drinks and a chat after she closed that day. Her best friend and business partner, Jodie, joined us and they told me how they'd both ended up relocating from Hull to Whitsborough Bay. They enthused about being on Castle Street and said that the other traders were really supportive and welcoming and a good tip to get them even more onside was freebies. Charlee had distributed sample bags of chocolates before she opened, which went down a storm.

It had therefore been my intention a couple of weeks ago to make a huge batch of cat-shaped shortbread biscuits and distribute them with a discount voucher exclusive to Castle Street business owners and employees. When Leon told me he wasn't coming back, my priorities had changed and the welcome biscuits had gone to the bottom of the to-do list. With Tom on board, we could do it together, better late than never.

'Sounds like a great idea,' he said. 'Do you have the discount vouchers ready?'

'All printed off. They just need cutting up. I've got boxes for the biscuits, some paper gift bags to put them in, and stickers and curling ribbon to make them look pretty.'

'Tell me where to find everything and I'll do the cutting and sticking now to save time tomorrow.'

'You're so good to me. There's a bag for life in the dining room. Everything's in there with a list of the businesses and my guesstimate of how many staff they have so I know how many biscuits to hand out. There's a paper cutter in the small bedroom.'

Tom brought everything he needed into the lounge and set up the garden table and a chair so he could work. Guilt poked me once more because I wasn't helping, but the walk – although very nice – had taken a couple of my spoons and I didn't want to borrow against tomorrow's supply.

'Stop it!' Tom said jovially, looking over after he'd cut up the first batch of vouchers.

'Stop what?'

'Feeling guilty. I can feel it emanating from you. I *offered* to do this, I *want* to do this, and I don't want you to feel bad about it. Please.'

'But it's hard not to. I hate not being able to do things for myself.'

'No kidding! Remember once on holiday, we visited a stately home with a maze? Rylan and I found the way out but you couldn't and we were all standing on this platform trying to direct you, but you refused to look at us. You said it was your problem and you didn't need any help. It took you an hour to get out and you were all mardy with us because we'd had ice creams during that time.'

'Oh, God, I remember that! I was so scared, but I was determined to do it myself.'

'And there was that time we went on a bike ride and you got a puncture. Rylan knew how to fix it but you snatched the repair kit off him and said you'd do it. Your repair didn't stick so you tried again, still refusing help.'

I grimaced, recalling that situation too. 'The second repair didn't stick either and there was nothing left in the kit, so I had to ride my bike home with a flat tyre. My backside was killing me for days!'

Tom laughed. 'You didn't tell us that.'

'Because I'd have never heard the end of it.' I shook my head. 'Am I really that stubborn?'

'Independent. Determined. Persevering.'

'Also known as stubborn!' I cried, laughing. 'I wish I knew why I was like this.'

'Your nanna said you were a typical Taurean.'

'Nanna and her horoscopes. I'm not sure I believe in any of that, but I don't have a better explanation.'

'Being all those things I mentioned is a good thing,' he said. 'Look at what you've done here. Leon took himself out of the picture and you kept going. A lot of people would have crumbled under the pressure, but you knew what you wanted and you refused to let a setback – a huge one at that – stand in your way. Look at how you've handled your fibromyalgia. You haven't let that stop you either, but you have learned to ask for help.'

'Only took me thirty-four years to do that.'

'Not true. You asked Rylan to fix your puncture properly the following day, you asked me for help when you were struggling with your maths at school and you've asked for help with your fibro now. I think you need to know you've tried your hardest on your own first, and there's nothing wrong with that. It means that when you do ask for help, we know you *really* need it.'

Cloud appeared and jumped up onto my knee so I stroked her, thinking about what Tom had said and wondering what I could do to repay his kindness. I thought back to the recent comment Macey had made about him being a catch. I'd never thought about it until then – he was just Tom, my brother's best mate and part of the family – but I could see now that he would make an amazing boyfriend for someone. He was kind, thoughtful, generous, good-looking.

My cheeks flushed as I had a sudden vision of him in the bathroom this morning when he'd whipped his T-shirt off. I surreptitiously glanced across at him. I'd never formed an opinion about his looks before, so why was I thinking it now? He reminded me of the actor Ben Whishaw, although Tom was a bigger, taller build. His thick, unkempt dark hair was very similar to Whishaw's and, when he wore a suit and glasses, Tom had that same geeky appearance Whishaw had as Q in the James Bond films. Thick dark lashes framed hazel eyes and, although I preferred the freshly shaved look which Tom usually sported when working, there was an appeal about his unshaven jaw today.

And then it struck me what I could do to thank him for his kindness to me. He'd said he couldn't talk to women and that's why he was so unlucky in love. What if I gave him some pointers? Although he had said he wasn't bothered about meeting someone. I might need to quiz him a bit more about that.

I flicked the TV on and found a sitcom I'd seen before on one of the streaming services so watched a random episode while Tom worked, but I wasn't concentrating on it. All I could think about was a spot of match-making for Tom. I didn't have that many friends, so that narrowed down the pool of matches. Alison was happily married, Kelsey had been in an on-off relationship for over a decade so it was messy and complicated and Faith was single but not right for him. And it wasn't like I was in contact with Kelsey and Faith anymore.

None of my staff were suitable – mainly far too young – but, even if they were, I wouldn't want to go down that road as it would make things awkward at work if anything went wrong. I had no idea how he'd met previous dates, but I could help him set up a profile on an app if he didn't already have one, or give him some pointers if he did, and I could give him a few tips on what to talk about if he went on a date. We could even try some roleplays, although I suspected we'd both end up in fits of giggles if we did that.

'All done,' Tom said, joining me on the sofa bed with a mug of tea each. 'You didn't look like you were watching any of that.'

I glanced at the TV and realised the closing credits were rolling. 'I wasn't. Miles away.'

'Were you thinking about George leaving?'

'Among other things.'

'I had an idea about that. When we take the biscuits round the other businesses tomorrow, I was wondering if it was worth asking the owners of the other two cafés if they'd taken on any weekend students recently who they could trade for George.' He rolled his eyes. 'That sounds like he's a Top Trumps card. I promise it sounded better in my head.'

'Top Trumps? There's a blast from the past!' I said. 'It's a long shot, but it's worth trying. I spoke to both the managers – Tara from The Chocolate Pot and Eileen from Aunt Polly's Tea Room – when the refurb started as I didn't want them to think I was going to be competition. They're both friendly.'

'What do you want to do now?' Tom asked. 'If you're done in, don't feel any obligation to stay up with me.'

'I'm fine for a bit longer,' I said. 'It's nice to have the company. Friday just gone was exactly twenty-four weeks since Leon left.'

'Do you miss him?'

'I did. Despite having an enormous fur family living with me, the house felt empty without him. I cried myself to sleep every night for that first fortnight and several more times after that. But I kept myself busy during the day – when my fibro let me – and I kept telling myself that it was just a bit of short-term pain because he'd soon be back and we'd be running this place together.'

'And now?'

'Now I just miss the company – having someone to talk to on an evening, to laugh with, to slob in front of the telly with. To be fair to the cats, we do all of those things, but the conversation isn't always stimulating.'

'I thought he was a tool for what he did to you, but I can't help thinking now that it was for the best that you found out what he was really like and you could make the café completely your own.'

'I'm just grateful that he got me to put it all in my name. It could have been so messy. Of course, looking back, I now know why he did that.'

'Why couldn't he have been honest with you back then? Why tell a half-truth?'

I shrugged. 'You could ask me the same about my fibro. Why tell you and Rylan and my parents that I have it and not tell you how bad it is? I didn't want to face up to it and I think Leon was the same. His feelings changed for me and he was struggling to accept what that meant for us. Being on the cruise gave him the time and space to work it out.'

'Maybe. But he could still have let you know sooner than the day before he was due to fly home. That's really shitty.'

'Yeah, it is. But the fact that he could do that to me has made it easier to move on. Someone so last minute and unreliable is not someone I want in my life.'

'Do you want to meet someone new?'

Did I? I took a sip of my tea while I contemplated my response. 'One day, yes, but not right now. It's too soon after Leon and I've got way too much on my hands with the café, but I'd like to think there's someone out there for me.'

'I'm sure there is.'

'Are you? Because I'm not. I thought it was Leon, but he had other ideas and I can't say I blame him. I didn't sign up to fibro, but neither did he, and that's when his feelings changed, as I showed you in that email.'

Tom curled his lip up. 'It's so shallow of him.'

'I know, but that reaction doesn't bode well for meeting someone in the future. If someone who supposedly loves me can walk away because it's too much to deal with, what about someone who's only just getting to know me? And not only do they have the fibro to deal with, they have to love cats. Who in their right mind would take on a girlfriend with health problems, a business to run and a million cats?'

'There's so much more to you than that,' he said softly.

I grinned at him to lighten the mood. 'Oh, yes! I forgot to mention the stubbornness.'

'Independence, perseverance and determination,' he corrected. 'Although the inability to play Top Trumps could be a deal breaker. You were rubbish at it when we were kids.'

'I probably still am.'

'Probably didn't help that Rylan and I cheated, arranging the pack to our benefit before getting you to join us.'

'You horrible boys!' I cried. 'I can't believe I never realised you cheated.'

We sat in companionable silence for a little while, sipping on our drinks. I was pondering on whether it would be a good moment to give him my proposition when he spoke.

'Seeing as we're being honest, last weekend you asked me if being single bothered me. I said no and that I was used to it. I lied.'

His eyes met mine and the sadness in them broke my heart.

'It does bother you?'

'Not all the time. I *have* got used to it – I've had to – but I look at what Rylan and Macey have and sometimes I wonder why I don't have that, why I've never had that. Not even close. I think my record is four dates. How pathetic is that? I'm thirty-six and I've never had a relationship last longer than a fortnight and do you know what the worst thing about that is? It scares women off! My last date asked me about my relationship history. I'd always glossed over it before, but I decided to tell her the truth. She thought I was winding her up and didn't do a very good job of covering her shock when I said I wasn't. She said she needed to nip to the loo and she legged it. I saw her running past the restaurant window.'

'No! That's awful.'

'She'd picked the restaurant, and it was really pricey. Our food arrived just after she scarpered and I was too embarrassed to sit on my own and eat it, so I paid the bill and left. That was last year and I haven't been on a date since – or back to that restaurant.'

He sounded jovial but it was obvious how much the experience had hurt him.

'Just before she went to the loo, do you know what the last thing she said to me was? *What's wrong with you?* It wasn't just the question, but the way she said it, as though I was some sort of freak.'

'She's the one in the wrong for behaving like that,' I said, lightly touching his arm. 'There's absolutely nothing wrong with you. Well, except your cheating at Top Trumps.'

That made him smile. 'Believe it or not, it wasn't the worst date I've been on.'

'Really? What was?'

'It was years ago. I was out with your brother celebrating passing my accountancy exams and we spotted a group of the popular lasses from school. I used to really like one of them but would never have dared to speak to her. I bumped into her at the bar, I'd had a few drinks and I stupidly told her I'd fancied her at school. She asked me if I was still interested because I could take her out the following night if I was. I was sure she wouldn't turn up, but she did. She asked me what I did and instead of just telling her I was an accountant, I prattled on about what I'd been studying and I must have been boring her senseless but she kept smiling and laughing and moving closer. I hadn't noticed how much she was drinking until she ordered a second bottle of wine and I realised I hadn't even finished my first glass. A bit later, she got up to go to the loo and was really unsteady on her feet, so I went to help her and she puked all over me.'

'Ooh! That's nasty.'

'Turned out her boyfriend had ditched her and started seeing someone else. They were going to the same restaurant and she'd only gone out with me to try to make him jealous.'

'I can't beat either of those, but I do have a couple of grim experiences of my own...'

We spent the next hour or so laughing about various dating disasters and the laughter did me the world of good, but it also exhausted me.

'I'm going to have to call it a night,' I admitted shortly after nine.

'It's been fun,' he said. 'Is there anything you need me to do for you tonight?'

'If you could top up the water bowls in the cat lounge and scoop any nasties out of the litter trays, I'd be really grateful.'

'Consider it done. Night, Tabby-cat.'

'Night, Tom-cat, and thanks for everything.'

As I put my phone onto charge, I spotted a text message from Mum.

FROM MUM

Thought I'd sent you a text this morning but it's not here so no idea where it went! Hope you've felt a bit better today and that having Tom there is helping. Spoke to your dad about Marmalade and we'd love to have him. How about we pick him up tomorrow evening and see how he gets on with Sindy and Boo this week? Big hugs to you xx

TO MUM

Improved today but off to bed now. Tom has been amazing. That's a relief about Marmalade. Fingers crossed he settles. Let me know tomorrow what time to expect you. Thank you xx

It was brilliant news about Marmalade. Sindy had visited Drake Street before and had responded well to the cats, so hopefully she wouldn't be an issue, and Boo was such a gentle soul that I couldn't imagine him being bothered by Marmalade or vice versa.

I went to the bathroom and found Marmalade on his cushion behind the door. My eyes filled with tears as he looked up at me. It was going to hurt to get down, and hurt even more to get up again, but I needed to be near him. I lowered myself onto the bathmat and ran my fingers through his fur.

'I don't want to let you go,' I whispered, tears spilling down my cheeks. 'I love you, Marmalade, but it breaks my heart to see you like this. Mum and Dad are going to take you and hopefully you'll settle in at theirs. I'm sorry I failed you. Will you forgive me?'

He blinked a few times, then stood up and left the room. I'd take that as a no.

I stayed on the floor for several minutes, letting the tears roll. Feeling cold and in danger of seizing up, I twisted onto my side and hauled myself up against the side of the bath, gritting my teeth against the pain.

I brushed my teeth and returned to the bedroom with a weary sigh. I just about had enough energy left to slip out of my clothes, leaving them where they fell, and into a nightshirt. Winnie, Babushka and Ruby were already on the bed and, as I settled under the duvet, I felt the mattress dip. The kittens were too light to have an impact, so it was one of the adult cats. I had a quick glance to see who it was before I switched the light off, and the tears started again as Marmalade padded over to me and curled up against me, purring.

'Last night together, eh?' I whispered, stroking his ears. 'Thank you.'

23

I slept reasonably well that night. The situation with Marmalade had been weighing heavily on me and it had been such a gift to have him cuddle up to me, as though he'd understood what I said about finding him a new home. Having Tom around to take on some of the work had helped massively, as had having some company. I didn't want to think about what would happen at the end of the week when he returned home. After only two nights, I already knew I was going to miss him.

There was a gentle knock on my door, which I'd left ajar for the cats to come and go freely.

'I'm awake,' I said. 'Come in.'

'How did you sleep?' Tom asked, pushing the door fully open and leaning against the frame.

'Pretty good. You?'

'That sofa bed's surprisingly comfortable, although one of the kittens face-planted me in the early hours, which was a heart-stopping moment.'

'They do that a lot. You'll get used to it.'

'I didn't mind. You know I love cats.'

'I do. It's such a shame you can't have one.'

'Yeah, I messed up there, so it's nice staying here and being surrounded by them.'

'Any time you want your cat fix, you're welcome to come on a playdate.'

He laughed. 'Don't make offers like that. You'll never get rid of me! Porridge for breakfast?'

'Yes, please.'

'I'll bring it up shortly.'

As he headed downstairs, I reflected on his comment about never getting rid of him. That wasn't an unappealing prospect.

* * *

'Oh, my God! These are delicious!' Tom could barely speak over the huge chunk of cat-shaped shortbread he'd shoved into his mouth.

I gave him a nudge in the ribs. 'They're meant to be gifts.'

'Yeah, but somebody has to quality check them.' He winked at me as he whipped another biscuit from the cooling rack in the café kitchen.

'Just as well I've made plenty of extras. And that isn't a reason to swipe another one.' I placed myself between him and the biscuits with my arms folded and a stern expression on my face.

'You look like a bouncer.'

'That's the intention. Got to keep the riffraff out.'

A buzzer sounded and I removed the final biscuits from the oven and placed them on a tray while Tom finished scoffing his stolen goods.

'Right, that's all the biscuits done. I could do with some lunch now, although I suspect somebody might be full already.'

'Two stomachs,' he said, patting his middle. 'Savoury one and pudding one.'

'I believe you. Thousands wouldn't.'

We headed upstairs and Tom ate his lunch without any struggle, after which we returned to the ground floor to pack the biscuits ready for distribution. While I'd been baking, Tom had put the flat-pack boxes together and spread them across several tables with a gift bag ready beside each one, sticker and curled ribbon on one side, business name on the other. He'd lined each box with serviettes and placed the discount vouchers in the bags, so we only needed to add the biscuits.

'How do you want to do this?' Tom asked a little later when everything was packed.

'It would be quicker if we took a side of the street each, but I'm thinking it would be more fun if we did it together.'

We decided to start with Seaside Blooms next door and work up and down the street in an anti-clockwise direction, nipping back for fresh supplies.

As well as speaking to the two café owners, I'd made a point of visiting my neighbours on either side before the building work started, to apologise for the noise. Both Sarah, the owner of the florist's, and Harley who owned Hairlequin's, the hair salon, had said a bit of noise was worth it if it meant having a neighbour again as empty units didn't look good.

Harley had only moved into her salon in the spring so was still settling in, but Seaside Blooms had been around for my whole life. Sarah had taken over from her auntie a decade ago and her auntie had run it for twenty-five years before that. I'd known Sarah to say 'hello' to from working at The Ramparts as she had the contract to supply flowers there, but it had been good getting to know her a little better, although I hadn't seen her for several weeks.

Sarah and one of her colleagues, Cathy, were behind the counter, pricing up some vases. They looked up and smiled as we pushed the door open, the overdoor bell gently tinkling.

'Tabby!' Sarah said. 'Your ears must have been burning. Cathy and I were just talking about you, wondering how the final preparations were going.'

'I feel surprisingly on top of things. I'm baking today and tomorrow and I've brought you some samples.'

'Aw, that's so lovely. Thank you.' Sarah took the bag Tom handed her and she and Cathy peeked into the box.

'That's our afternoon cuppa sorted,' Cathy said.

'They're delicious,' Tom said. 'I might have tested a couple.'

'Four!' I corrected. 'This is my friend, Tom. He's helping me this week.'

Sarah and Cathy introduced themselves to him.

'It looks gorgeous in here,' I said, looking round the shop at the beautiful Christmas decorations. A mix of red and white fairy lights were strung round the ceiling, window and across the display cabinets. Crimson, white and cream festive-looking flowers and shiny green foliage nestled in brushed steel buckets. Some of the buckets contained glittery twigs and other sparkly flourishes. Christmas wreaths hung on the wall and there were poinsettias and Christmas cacti.

'We love it when Christmas arrives,' Cathy said. 'Can't beat a bit of sparkle with your Christmas bouquet.'

'Charlee said you've moved into the flat,' Sarah said.

'Yeah, Leon ended things, so big change of plans. I've moved into the flat and I'm running the café without him.'

'Aw, no! I'm so sorry. Are you okay?'

'Getting there. How was your fortieth, by the way? Where did you go?'

Sarah had turned forty in late September, which had to be the last time I'd seen her. She'd told me that her husband, Nick, was taking her away for a week but was keeping the destination a secret.

'We went to the Algarve and it was amazing. He'd booked this huge villa and my family and closest friends had flown out on the previous flight so they were all there to surprise me. I had absolutely no idea.'

'That's so romantic,' I said. 'Something like that would never have entered Leon's head. I moved in with him around my thirtieth but, on my actual birthday, he forgot to book the shift off work. If it hadn't been for my family, I'd have spent the evening on my own.'

'Just as well you're shot of him, then,' Cathy said. 'If a man can't be bothered to make any effort on a special occasion, he's not worth bothering with.'

A customer appeared so we said goodbye and continued up the street. The owners of the next four shops were really appreciative of the biscuits, and it was lovely seeing all the Christmas decorations in place in the shops, but we received our first negative reaction from Eileen, the owner of Aunt Polly's Tea Room.

'Why would you bring me cakes when I make my own?' she asked, snubbing the bag Tom held out towards her.

'They're cat-shaped shortbread biscuits,' I said, surprised by her reaction after she'd previously been so friendly.

She shrugged. 'Cakes, biscuits, semantics. I don't want them, thank you, especially if they've got cat hair in them.'

So that was what this was all about? She'd thought about it and decided she didn't approve of cat cafés. I didn't want to start an argument but there were customers within earshot, so I couldn't let that accusation go. I'd worked very closely with the local food safety officer to ensure everything was in place to get a top rating during our first inspection.

'The cats can't get into the food preparation areas and we have the highest hygiene standards.'

Eileen stared at me, her arms folded, her facial expression a mixture of boredom and disbelief.

'Thanks for your time, anyway,' I said, smiling brightly. 'I hope you have a great week.'

I turned to the elderly couple nearby, who'd stopped eating their afternoon tea and weren't even trying to disguise that they were listening. 'That looks delicious, so I'm sure you'll be full when you leave, but can I tempt you with some free cat-shaped shortbread?'

'Ooh, yes, please,' the woman said.

'Margaret!' Eileen snapped.

'Don't Margaret me. If she's offering free biscuits, I'm happy to accept them.'

'Don't you dare!'

Tom looked at me uncertainly, but the man resolved it, taking the bag from Tom with an eyeroll and one word. 'Sisters.'

I beat a hasty retreat, with Tom hot on my heels.

'Wow, that Eileen's a feisty one!' he said as we crossed over to the cat café to get the next batch of bags.

'I don't get it,' I said. 'She was friendly when I first met her.'

'You maybe took her by surprise then, or there were too many customers around who weren't family. Don't let her get to you. There's always going to be someone who wants to spoil things. You've had five positive reactions and one negative one, so focus on the good ones.'

I nodded, trying to push aside that confrontation. Our next visits were to Sweet Sensations – an old-fashioned sweet shop – and specialist teddy bear shop, Bear With Me. The owners of both businesses were as lovely as they'd been on the other occasions I'd seen them, eager to hear how preparations were going and appreciative of my praise for their lovely Christmas decorations.

The rest of our drop-offs on that side of the street went well. Some business owners wanted to chat about the cat café or plans they had for their own business, whereas others gave a quick thank you and good luck wishes. The main thing was that they were all positive.

'See!' Tom said as we took a breather on one of the benches in Castle Park at the end of the street. 'Everyone's excited for you and rooting for you. Eileen's all alone on the angry step.'

'I'm glad you're with me. If I'd been on my own, I might not have continued after Eileen's reaction. I hope she doesn't bad-mouth me to her other customers.'

'If she does, it says a lot more about her than it does about you. You've got this, Tabby-cat. I'm really proud of you.'

'You are?'

'Of course I am!' He put his arm round me and rested his head against mine. 'We all are.'

It was an unusually mild day for November, with calm seas and a pale blue sky, so I didn't feel at all chilly – just cosy and comfortable snuggled up close to Tom. My eyes were drooping and I could easily have drifted off to sleep, but Tom released me and stood up.

'We need the next batch of biscuits, so I'll save you a spoon and grab them and we'll finish off your side of the street.'

I twisted on the bench and watched him cross the main road and set off along Castle Street. An attractive woman walked towards him and turned her head to look back at him after she passed, but he kept going, clearly oblivious to the attention he'd drawn. It was amazing to think about all those disastrous dates he'd been on. As we'd moved round the businesses this afternoon, he'd been so at ease chatting with any women we met – friendly and engaging without being flirty – so he definitely could talk to women. I suspected it was the date itself which was the sticking point, nerves and past experiences getting the better of him. I'd love to be able to help him with that. He deserved to find someone special.

Tom returned and we continued our deliveries, but I hesitated outside The Chocolate Pot.

'What's up?' Tom asked. 'I thought you said the owner was friendly.'

'Tara? Yeah, she is. She was a lot friendlier than Eileen from the outset but what if Eileen had a point about the biscuits? Is it insulting to give food samples from my café to the owner of another café?'

'If you were in direct competition with them, it might be a bit strange, but you're offering something completely different. People are coming to see the cats and they'll grab a drink and quick bite while they're there. It's not like you're offering full meals or afternoon tea.'

'Okay. Let's do this!' I pushed back my shoulders and stepped through the door.

There was a slimline Christmas tree between the window and the serving counter and Tara was passing it with a mug of hot chocolate.

'Tabby! How's it going?'

'Good, I think. Have you got a minute?'

'I do indeed. I was just about to take a break. Would you like a drink?'

'We're fine, thanks.'

I introduced Tom as we followed Tara to an empty table near the back of the café. Twinkly warm white fairy lights were wrapped round the pillars and there was another larger Christmas tree in the back corner, beautiful needle-felted and other hand-crafted decorations hanging from the branches. Charlee had told me that Tara made them all herself and customers could buy them.

'You look worried,' Tara said when we sat down. 'Is everything okay?'

'I made some biscuits to take round the shops and I've got some for you but...' I tailed off, wondering if she might be insulted if I said I wasn't sure what her reaction would be.

Tom stepped in. 'One of the business owners wasn't impressed with the gift and she's knocked Tabby's confidence.'

'Let me guess. Eileen?'

'How did you know?' I asked.

Tara rolled her eyes. 'She's the only one I can think of who'd be like that. There are a couple of traders who are quiet and keep themselves to themselves, but the rest are really supportive, as I hope you've discovered. Eileen's very hit and miss. Some days she's lovely and other days it's like she got out the wrong side of the bed and everyone knows it! Best approached with caution. So, what sort of biscuits are they?'

Tom handed her a bag containing two boxes. 'Cat shortbreads.'

She removed the top box and smiled at the contents. 'Cute. And they smell amazing.'

'I hope there's enough in there for everyone,' I said. 'But if you don't feel comfortable giving them out...'

'I'm guessing Eileen claimed to be insulted and refused them,' Tara said. When I nodded, she grabbed one and took a large bite, making noises of approval as she chewed.

'More fool her for missing out,' she said when she'd swallowed. 'It's melt-in-your-mouth delicious. Thank you. Opening day's Wednesday, yes?'

'Yes. The café's ready. I've just got the baking to do.'

'Are you nervous?'

'Not so much about opening day or even the first week because I know we have bookings, but there's that slight niggle that it might be a novelty that wears off.'

'I felt the same when I first opened The Chocolate Pot, but here we are, still thriving. It'll be twenty years next summer. I still remember those first-day nerves. I was all fingers and thumbs and managed to drop a four-pint carton of milk on the floor, which exploded everywhere. Luckily that was before any of the staff arrived so nobody saw the mess.'

'I bet that took some cleaning up.'

'Ages! Hopefully you won't be as clumsy as me but, if there's anything I can do to help, just let me know.'

'Why don't you ask her about George?' Tom said.

Tara ate her shortbread as I told her about George's allergy and mooted the idea of a staff swap.

'It sounds even more of a long shot now that I'm saying it out loud,' I said as I finished.

'Maybe not. I had an eighteen-year-old student called Hattie start a couple of weeks ago and I know she loves cats. She might be interested. Leave it with me.'

'I haven't said anything to George about it.'

'That's fine. I'll tell Hattie it's just an idea at the moment and it'll only happen if all parties are in agreement. If they are, I'm happy to do a swap. And don't worry, she's a good worker. I wouldn't recommend a problem employee.'

'Thanks. I really appreciate that.'

'Completely different to Angry Eileen,' Tom said as we left the café after Tara and I exchanged mobile numbers. 'Sounds like she's had a run-in with a few people.'

'That does make me feel better. And everyone else has been so kind. It's going to be all right.'

'It's going to be more than that,' he said, smiling at me. 'It's going to be brilliant.'

And, at that moment, I believed it really was. My latest flare-up had cleared, I'd opened up to my family and had their help, Fiona was at the end of the phone with more helpful advice if needed, preparations for opening were ahead of schedule, I had the support of (most of) the street and my parents were collecting Marmalade tonight. Life on Castle Street was good.

24

On Monday evening, Mum and Dad came to collect Marmalade. I was fine about it at first, telling myself it was the right thing for him, but then he wandered into the lounge when they were preparing the cat carrier, jumped up on my knee, and purred. After spending the night before snuggled up to me, that was me completely gone, tears everywhere. I'd never felt so torn. Had Marmalade finally accepted that Leon wasn't returning and pledged allegiance to me instead, or had he somehow known he was moving out and was thanking me for it? If it was the former, would sending him away cause further damage?

'We could always leave him here for a few more days and see how it goes,' Dad suggested.

'I'm not sure. I just want what's best for him.'

Marmalade jumped down from my knee and trotted over to Mum, weaving round her ankles and purring more loudly than I'd heard in months.

'I think he knows,' I said, wiping my cheeks with my sleeve. 'You'd better take him. It's not like I'm never going to see him again.'

I felt drained after they'd gone. Tom ran a bath with lavender bubbles to relax me and I went to bed afterwards but I couldn't drift off, my mind switching between Marmalade leaving and the earlier unpleasant encounter with Eileen in Aunt Polly's Tea Room. I was normally calm and rational but I kept catastrophising about the damage Eileen could do to my business if she decided to pass on her thoughts to her customers about what she perceived to be a lack of hygiene. It made me so mad. I'd done everything I was meant to do and more. The kitchen was pristine and a cat-free zone, and food covers would be given to all diners so that they could keep their food and drink covered when the cats jumped onto the tables – which they absolutely would do and which was part of the charm. There were antibacterial wipes available for customer use or my team were on hand to wipe the table. I'd like to think that anybody who was completely averse to cats being in the presence of food was not our demographic.

At 1.11 a.m. on Tuesday morning, I was still awake. I looked at my phone and felt a sense of satisfaction at the matching numbers, but hoped I wouldn't still be up when 2.22 a.m. arrived. At some point in the early hours, I finally drifted off.

An almighty crashing sound yanked me from my sleep, heart pounding in the darkness. I ran to the top of the stairs and flicked the light on just as Tom appeared at the bottom.

'Did you hear that?' I asked.

'It came from downstairs.'

I followed him to the flat door.

'It sounded like glass,' he said, pulling on his trainers and reaching for the handle. 'Keep the cats in.'

I closed the door behind him and slipped my feet into a pair of boots before following him downstairs. The cold draught hit me when I reached the first floor and I knew what I was going to see when I made it down to the ground level. I'd known when I heard the crashing, but nothing quite prepared me for the sight that greeted me. I opened my mouth, but no words came out.

'I'm so sorry,' Tom said, pale-faced as he turned to me. 'I'll call the police.'

I pressed a shaky hand across my mouth, unsure whether I was going to throw up or scream. Not only had the window been smashed but somebody had doused the place with bright red paint. The beautiful castle mural was covered, paint dripped like blood from the turrets of the activity centre, and from the tables and chairs. Pieces of toughened glass caught the light, sparkling like diamonds. If it had only been a smashed window, I might have thought it was an act of mindless vandalism, but the paint had to mean it was deliberate and targeted.

As though in a dream, I shuffled closer to the window, taking care not to step on any paint or glass, vaguely aware of Tom's shocked voice as he conveyed to the police operator the details of what had happened. My beautiful café! Who'd do something like this?

I glanced through the window towards Aunt Polly's Tea Room at the top of the street and bit my lip. No, she wouldn't. It was my catastrophising last night that was taking me to her. All she'd done was refuse some free biscuits and make a snide comment about cat hairs in front of her sister. It was a giant leap to go from that to an attack on my café. It was more likely to be the work of someone who'd already taken a swipe on social media.

'The police will be here soon,' Tom said, placing his phone on one of the paint-free tables and taking a couple of steps closer to me.

'What if there'd been cats sleeping down here?' I murmured.

'You can't think like that,' he said, enveloping me in his arms. I gratefully rested my head against his chest. What were we going to do? There was no way we could be ready to open tomorrow. It would take days to clear up this mess and repair the damage, and I still had baking to do.

'You're shivering,' Tom said, pulling away. 'I'll get your coat.'

He raced upstairs while I stood limply staring at the mess.

'What happened here?'

I looked up at the sound of the man's voice. He and a woman, both wearing dressing gowns, were peering through the window. Presumably they lived in a flat above one of the shops and had heard the commotion.

'Someone's trashed the place,' I said. 'I don't suppose you saw anything?'

'No, sorry,' the woman said. 'The sound woke us up.'

'Police are here,' the man said.

I saw flashing blue lights reflected in the windows across the street before I saw the police car.

'Are you the owners?' one of the police officers asked the pair on exiting the car.

'I'm the owner,' I called.

He peered through the empty window.

'There's paint and glass everywhere,' I said. 'I'll get the keys and let you in the door.'

As I started up the stairs, Tom appeared at the top with my coat. 'I picked up your keys and phone too.'

'The police have just arrived.'

Unlocking the external door, I spotted the words spray painted across it – FREE THE CATS – in bright red capitals. If there'd been any doubt, that confirmed it was a targeted attack. Just what I needed!

25

The window had been smashed at about half three in the morning. By the time the police had taken statements and an emergency glazer had boarded up the window, two hours had passed. Wearily, Tom and I traipsed back up to the flat. My head was thumping so, while Tom made us both a hot drink, I went up to the bedroom and swallowed a couple of paracetamol.

It felt really cold in the flat and I shivered as I clambered under the duvet.

'You've still got your coat on,' Tom said, placing my drink on the bedside drawers.

'I'm so cold. I can't face taking it off.'

'I'll put the heating on.' He put his tea down beside mine and left the room, returning a couple of minutes later, rubbing his hands together. 'How are you feeling?'

'Scared, devastated, gutted we won't be able to open tomorrow as planned and, to top it all, I've got a fibro flare-up.'

'No! When did that start?'

'Not sure. I think the adrenaline kept me going downstairs and now that I've stopped, my head's pounding and my bones are aching.'

'Can I do anything?'

'Not with the fibro, but I'm really freaked out about what happened.'
I patted the bed. 'Will you stay with me?'

He climbed in beside me.

'I wish I'd installed CCTV,' I said.

'You heard what the police said. They'll check with the other owners,
but whoever did this probably had a hood up and avoided all cameras.'

'Do you think they timed it deliberately to ruin opening day?'

'Probably.'

'Mission accomplished.'

'We might have to open later than planned, but we'll still open,' Tom
said, his voice reassuring. 'Whoever did this hasn't defeated you. We'll
rally the cats and show them we're here to stay.'

I gave a pathetic 'Yay!' and a half-hearted fist punch in the air. Right
now, I felt as though they had defeated me. I hadn't even opened for
business, and already somebody was making it clear I wasn't welcome. I
couldn't bear that much hate.

* * *

After I finished my drink, I dozed off but was awake again at seven and in
full flare-up mode. I still had my coat on and it felt like it was wrapped
tightly round my skin. My attempts to wriggle free from it without crying
out in pain woke Tom up.

'Are you okay?' he said.

'Trapped in my coat. It hurts.'

'Hang on. I'll help.' He scrambled to his knees and carefully eased
the coat from me. 'I've got it. You're free now.'

I burst into tears.

'Where does it hurt?' Tom asked.

'Everywhere.' It was one of those *I don't know which part of my body to
cry about first* days, except today I had *and somebody trashed my café and
wrecked my dreams* to throw into the mix.

'There's so much to do,' I cried. 'And I don't think I can do it.'

'You don't have to. I'm here. It's five past seven so your parents will be
up. I'll give them a call and we'll get a clean-up team sorted.'

'People have booked for tomorrow. I'm letting them down.'

'They'll understand. I'll go on your website later and put a notice up, and email everyone who's booked to let them know what's happened.'

'We'll need to give...' I grappled for the word, but it wouldn't come. 'Argh! Giving money back. What is it?'

'Refunds?' Tom suggested.

'That's it!'

'Again, I can sort all that out for you later. I might need some guidance on how the system works, but there's nothing you need to do.'

'This isn't how it was meant to be.'

'I know. It's a pile of shit and if I find out who did this...' He bit his lip and shook his head. 'Not helpful. What are your thoughts? Open on Saturday instead – gives us four days to clear up and get sorted – or play it by ear?'

'Forget the whole thing,' I muttered.

'I know you don't mean that,' he said gently.

'Don't I? I can't do this, Tom. I've been kidding myself all along that I can, but I can't and I've been too stubborn to accept it. This was my dream, but fibromyalgia has stomped all over it in its bloody giant clown shoes and now the anti-cat-café brigade are out in force and I'm too ill to even clear up the sodding mess.'

'You can't let whoever did this win.'

'What's left to win? Fibro has already beaten me.'

'You're only saying that because you're tired and upset.'

'No, Tom. I'm saying it because it's true.'

I stared at him, silently challenging him to try to put a positive spin on it all when, right now, there was nothing positive about the situation.

'I'll ring your parents,' he said, lowering his eyes as he left the bedroom.

I sank back onto my pillows with a sigh. That was awful. I'd raised my voice – something I hardly ever did – and I'd sworn too, which was also extremely rare for me, and all in front of a man who I cared about deeply who'd put his life on hold to help me this week. He hadn't deserved that outburst. Clearly it hadn't been directed at him, but he'd have felt the sting of my frustration and that wasn't fair.

'I'm sorry,' I said as soon as Tom returned to the bedroom a little later.

'That's okay.'

'No, it isn't. You're trying to help and I shouldn't have shouted.'

'I knew you weren't shouting at me.'

'Even so.'

He perched on the edge of the bed. 'Look, Tabby, you really don't need to apologise to me. I know you think you were out of order to get angry but I think you were incredibly restrained in the circumstances. You must feel like yelling and screaming at the top of your voice. I would.'

'I want to, but it takes too many spoons.'

My voice sounded so weak and mournful that I couldn't help laughing at it. And suddenly the word 'spoons' seemed hilarious.

'Spoons,' I repeated, laughing harder.

'Why's that funny?' he asked, looking bewildered.

'I don't know. It's...' But it wasn't at all. None of it was. And I dissolved into tears once more.

* * *

'I know you're in pain, but do you think there's any way you can pull some clothes on and make it downstairs?' Tom asked, poking his head round my bedroom door shortly after half ten.

'Do the police need me?'

'No, but there's something I think you'll want to see.'

I didn't have the energy to ask him what it was. It must be good because he wouldn't have disturbed me otherwise. Perhaps somebody had some CCTV footage clearly showing the vandal's face, although he'd bring them up to the flat if that was that case. My head hurt speculating.

'I need soft clothes,' I said, wearily, pointing towards my suitcases lined up against the wall, lids open. 'Middle case, soft pink bottoms, pale grey top.'

I'd never been a fan of clothes shopping, but I'd intermittently drag myself round the shops and scour online for anything with cats on. I had enough pairs of cat socks to keep me going for a month, and a wide range of T-shirts, dresses and hoodies. Since fibro, my new obsession was PJs and loungewear, the softer the better. If they had cats on them, it was a bigger bonus.

After a bit of rummaging, Tom retrieved the items and helped me into them.

As we left the flat, laughter and chatter drifted up to me from downstairs. Clinging onto the banister, I followed the sound and paused on the bottom stair, tears welling in my eyes.

'Did you organise this?' I asked, looking up at Tom.

'I didn't need to. They all came for you.'

The ground floor of the café was a hive of activity. The window boards had been removed to let light in. Matt and his brother Tim were sweeping the broken glass onto shovels and loading it into a wheelbarrow. Matt's wife Charlee was at the front door with Mum and the pair of them were scrubbing the graffiti off the door. Several other business owners – Sarah from Seaside Blooms, Jemma from Bear With Me, Carly from Carly's Cupcakes, Ginny from The Wedding Emporium and Lily from Bay Books – were carefully scraping paint off the tables, chairs and floor.

Tara appeared on the cobbles with a tray of takeaway cups. 'Drinks are ready,' she called.

'Your dad and Matt's dad have gone to get a replacement activity centre and a few other materials.'

I hadn't been spotted yet but, as the helpers came back into the café with their drinks, they saw me and gathered round, expressing their sorrow for what had happened.

'I can't believe you're all here,' I said, easing myself into a nearby chair – one of the few that had escaped the paint. 'What about your own shops?'

'We've got staff to cover,' Sarah said.

'We had to help,' Jemma added. 'This is awful.'

'Do the police know who did it?' Lily asked.

I looked up at Tom, as I had no idea what the update was.

'They've gathered some CCTV,' he said, 'but I don't know whether it's any good yet.'

'How are you feeling?' Mum asked.

'Horrendous.' I looked round the room at everyone's sympathetic expressions. 'I can't thank you all enough for this. It's so kind of you to give up your time. I'm so sorry I'm not helping. I would if I could, but...' I glanced up at Tom once more.

He crouched down beside me with his back to the others. 'I said you weren't well today,' he murmured. 'I haven't mentioned the fibro.'

I looked round the group again. It was confession time. They'd have accepted that I was poorly and one look at me right now would absolutely confirm that, but it was important to me that they understood that I meant it when I said I'd help if I could.

'The reason I'm not shovelling glass or scrubbing paint alongside you is that I physically can't. I've got a chronic condition called fibromyalgia which causes pain, fatigue and brain fog. I'm not in pain all the time – just when I have a flare-up – but when and why that happens is unpredictable. Stress and doing too much can be factors and I think it's safe to assume that this...' I wanted to say 'mess' but I couldn't find the word so I feebly swept my arm round the room to illustrate what I meant, '...this has been the trigger. Worst flare-up I've had in a long time. I need to go back to bed. I'm sorry.'

There were lots of comments about not needing to apologise and how they were happy to help, but I wasn't sure who said what. I rose from the chair and Tom took my arm to steady me when I unbalanced. His touch made my nerves scream in pain, but better that than fall and be unable to get up. I adjusted position so that I was holding his arm instead and shuffled towards the staircase, but a voice stopped me in my tracks.

'Bacon and egg butties are served. Get them while they're warm.'

I twisted round, eyes wide. 'Eileen?'

She placed a tray of food down on the table beside her and took a couple of steps closer as the helpers moved in on the butties.

'Oh, honey, I'm so sorry about what's happened. What a shock! I wanted to help, but one of my team phoned in sick and I don't have enough staff today. I figured some butties was the least I could do.'

She looked and sounded so sincere and I felt guilty that I'd thought, even for a few seconds, that she could be capable of this.

'Thank you. That's really kind.'

She shook her head. 'It isn't. I was rude to you yesterday and I'm sorry. I've got a few things going on in my life at the moment and you got the brunt of them, which was wrong of me. My sister gave me a right earbashing after you left and I deserved it. Believe it or not, I love cats. I've got two of my own.'

I certainly hadn't expected that. I loved hearing about other people's cats, but I had no energy to even ask their names today.

'You'll have to tell me all about them sometime. I need to...' I couldn't even finish the sentence. I had three flights of stairs to climb and I wasn't sure how I was going to manage it, although I wouldn't have missed seeing this for the world. I'd heard great things about the community on Castle Street and none of them had been exaggerated. Even someone as grumpy as Eileen could pull out the stops when help was needed. Most of the time I preferred cats to people, but I loved that people still had the ability to surprise and delight me. Seeing this right now had been worth my final couple of spoons.

26

At one o'clock, Mum came up to the flat and asked if I wanted my lunch in the bedroom or downstairs.

'In here. There's soup in the cupboard if you don't mind heating me some up.'

'No need. Your dad's picking up your lunch now. Are you okay if we join you to eat ours?'

'That's fine.'

'I'll be back shortly.'

Dad appeared soon after with a couple of chairs, followed by Mum with a tray of food.

'Jacket potato with cheese and beans,' she declared. 'Courtesy of Eileen from the tea room over the road.'

'Eileen provided lunch?' I asked, stunned by her further generosity.

'I tried to pay,' Dad said, 'but she wouldn't hear of it. She said that, when you're on your feet again, she wouldn't say no to some cat biscuits. I'm presuming she doesn't mean biscuits for cats.'

I smiled. 'Long story.'

Mum draped a tea towel over my top and I hungrily tucked into my lunch, scooping the potato out of the skin as it was too much effort to cut it and I couldn't bring myself to ask Mum to cut up my food as though I was a toddler.

'Where's Tom?' I asked.

Mum shrugged. 'Not sure. He said he had an errand to run.'

'How's Marmalade?'

'Settling in really well,' Mum said. 'I'll show you some photos when you've eaten. Sindy adores him and Boo doesn't seem fazed. He's eating and he isn't hiding anywhere, so I think he's going to be absolutely fine.'

At least something was going well.

Dad finished his potato first so he updated me on the progress downstairs while I continued eating. The glass had been taken away and the café thoroughly vacuumed to catch any final fragments, the graffiti had been removed from the door and most of the paint had come off the floor and furniture. A little more elbow grease was needed this afternoon to remove the final traces and my parents were going to do that. My insurance company, who I'd asked to liaise with Tom, had arranged for a glazer to come this afternoon and the team from Richards & Sons were going to stick around to help if needed, repair some damage to the window frame and replace the activity centre. Mum had messaged Rylan to let him know what had happened and he was going to stop by after college to assess the damage to the mural and make a start on repairing it.

'Any news from the police?' I asked.

'Not yet,' Dad said. 'A couple of officers called round about an hour ago to check whether there'd been any more trouble, but they didn't have any news.'

'A reporter from the *Bay News* stopped by too,' Mum said. 'She took some photos of everyone helping with the clear-up. She was keen to get a quote from you and ideally a photo but I said you weren't very well. I've put her business card in the kitchen. If you were willing and able to speak to her tomorrow morning, she thinks she can secure front-page coverage in Thursday's edition. It could be great publicity for the café.'

When I didn't respond, Mum added, 'Tom told us you were having doubts about opening up.'

'You probably think that's mad after all the money I've spent on this place.'

'It's not about the money,' Mum said. 'You're the most important part of this and it has to be right for you.'

'Did you have doubts when you set up your business?'

'Loads of them,' Mum said.

'We'd talked about it for years,' Dad said. 'There were so many reasons not to do it – guilt for leaving, bad timing with having a family, worries about reduced income, fear of failing – but we couldn't push the dream aside. We really wanted to run our own business our way, so we had to silence the doubts and just go for it.'

'Any regrets?' I asked.

Mum shook her head. 'None, but we had a lot of problems at the start. When your dad resigned, our employer got shirty about our future plans and made my life hell, so I ended up leaving early and, because we had a non-compete clause, we had no income coming in for months, which was worrying.'

I'd finished eating so Mum took my plate and added it to the tray with hers and Dad's. 'The problems didn't end there. Remember that first office, Ray?'

Dad laughed. 'Mice infestation. They set up home in the filing cabinet and we had to return receipts to a few brand-new clients with pieces munched out of them. That was embarrassing. Luckily, they saw the funny side of it and they're all still clients today. What was worse, Joanna? The mice or the naked people?'

'Naked people?' I asked as they laughed together.

'Definitely the naked people,' Mum said when she'd composed herself. 'The first office – the mice-ridden one – was above a shop and we moved out to a purpose-built suite of offices with shared toilet and kitchen facilities. There was a lovely photographer in a small studio next door who did family photos and portraits. He retired and another photographer moved in and we assumed he was going to do the same. Until I walked into the kitchen and was confronted by a couple of naked men making coffee.'

'This new photographer took more of a... shall we say *artistic* approach to photography,' Dad explained. 'There were some interesting outfits too.'

'You don't want to know,' Mum said, shaking her head. 'How they got in and out of some of those masks and straps, I'll never know. Anyway, the point is that most people who set up businesses have low points at the start, partway through, or both, when they consider walking away. I was talking to Charlee downstairs and she had water pouring through her ceiling just before she opened and Tara said she was duped about the condition of the flat. Stuff happens. It's horrible and stressful when it does, but we all kept going to achieve what we really wanted and I know you can too. I suppose the big question is whether you do still really want this. Ignore the fibro, Leon leaving and what happened downstairs. Do you still want to run a cat café?'

Right now, I really didn't know, but I was saved from answering by Tom calling up the stairs that he was back.

'There's a jacket potato in the kitchen for you,' Mum said when he appeared in the doorway.

'Thanks. I'll have that shortly.'

'Where've you been?' I asked.

'To get you this.'

He reached behind him and lifted up a boxed television. 'You said that watching films soothes you when you have a flare-up, but it's hard work getting downstairs, so I got you a smaller telly for your bedroom. And I don't want to hear anything about it being too much and you can't accept it because it's going on the wall and you're going to enjoy it so that's that.'

'No spoons left to argue,' I said. 'Thank you.'

While Tom ate his lunch, Dad went downstairs to borrow some tools to wall mount the TV but returned with Matt's brother Tim, the electrician from Richards & Sons.

'I've put up hundreds of TVs,' Tim said. 'I'll have it done in a jiffy.'

While he worked, Mum showed me photos of Marmalade settling in and they were reassuring. I especially loved one of him curled up against Sindy in Sindy's bed.

Ten minutes later, the TV was up and working – way quicker than

Tom and Dad would have managed between them. Mum and Dad went
back downstairs with Tim to finish scraping the paint and Tom sat on
the bed with my laptop.

'Do you know what you want to say to your customers?' he asked,
logging onto my website.

'Not really.'

'Do you want me to cobble something together and you tweak it?'

'Yes, please.'

He opened up a Word document and tapped out a message with a bit
of frowning and deleting.

'How does this sound?' he asked eventually. 'Tell me if it's too cheesy.
We were so excited to welcome you to our paw-some new home this
week but there's been a cat-astrophe. Somebody smashed the window
and trashed our beautiful café. We weren't hurt but our home was so,
sadly, it's not paw-ssible to open as planned. Please give us a meowment
to issue refunds for bookings on Wednesday to Friday inclusive. We
hope to open on Saturday but watch this space for confirmation as we
need to make sure everything's purr-fect first.' He looked at me, his brow
creased uncertainly. 'Is it pants? I can start again if you hate it.'

'It's amazing,' I said. 'Sounds like numbers aren't your only
superpower.'

'Are you still thinking of Saturday for opening? Everything will be
ready downstairs and there's time to bake. Even if you're not feeling up
to baking, your dad and I can do it.'

'I don't know. Can I make a decision tomorrow?'

'Yeah, no problem. I'll leave it as an intention for now and I can
always change it later.'

'Sounds good.'

I switched the TV on, found a family film I loved and put the sound
on low while Tom worked. He created a graphic using the café's
branding and posted it onto my website and social media channels, and
he put a stop on accepting bookings for the rest of the week, but kept it
open from Saturday onwards. He also sent an email to everyone who'd
booked this week, with the graphic attached, giving them a bit more
detail about what had happened and when to expect a refund.

It wouldn't be right for the team to find out by word of mouth or coverage in Thursday's *Bay News*. To save me a little energy, Tom composed a text on my phone for the weekend team telling them what had happened, explaining that the current plan was still for them to work their weekend shift, and I'd let them know if anything changed.

As Fay, Mark and Wendy would be directly affected by the café not opening this week, it didn't feel appropriate to send them a text. They didn't know about my fibro yet either. Tom offered to call them for me. Even though I didn't feel up to three conversations, it felt like a cop-out on my part so I rang them and couldn't help feeling relieved when none of them answered. I left a short message saying there'd been an incident at the café which meant we couldn't open this week as planned, and I'd fully explain the impact of that in an email. Tom then composed a variation of the cancelled bookings email, added in an explanation about my fibromyalgia, and sent them all that.

'Have we missed anyone?' I asked him.

'I don't think so. Police, insurance, customers, staff... I think that covers it. Oh, and I let the cats know. They offered to help with the clearup, but I told them to look after you instead. I hope they've been doing a good job.'

I smiled at him, grateful for everything he'd done for me and the ability to lighten my day. 'Great job, but you know who's doing the best job? You are. I don't know what I'd have done without you this week.'

'I'm glad I'm here. If you'd been...' He stopped and bit his lip before closing the laptop. 'That's that done, so I'll leave you to get some rest. Anything you need before I go back downstairs?'

'I'm fine, thanks.'

'See you later then.'

I looked at Viking, curled up by my feet. 'We know what he was about to say, don't we? If I'd been on my own last night. Thing is, he can't stay here forever. I *am* going to be on my own from next week. That's not good, is it?'

Thank goodness for that television and the distraction it gave me for the rest of the afternoon. I had so much spinning round my mind and I couldn't make any sense of it. Mum's question about whether I really wanted this was a good one, but it had taken me by surprise. I'd assumed my doubts were because of the three things she'd listed – my fibromyalgia, Leon's departure and this morning's shocking attack – but I now had a niggling sense there was more to it than that, which scared me. What also scared me was the thought of Tom leaving and me being on my own. Even though I hadn't liked living there, I'd never felt unsafe or vulnerable on my own in Drake Street and I hadn't felt that way when I'd first moved in here. Hopefully it was just the shock of what happened and the jitters would settle, but what if it had a lasting impact? For someone who struggled to sleep anyway, I could do without adding in fear of further attacks in the early hours.

27

On Wednesday morning, I shuffled to the bathroom, took one look at my matted hair and bloodshot eyes in the mirrored bathroom cabinet, and wished I hadn't. Ignorance was sometimes bliss. I was still in two minds about speaking to the reporter. With *Bay News* coming out on a Thursday, I understood why there was a deadline of this morning, but I could use at least another day.

Returning to the bedroom, I checked my emails. Mark and Wendy had both been in touch to express their shock and anger about the attack, their empathy for my fibro, and said to let them know if there was anything they could do this week to clear up. Wendy said I mustn't pay her if she didn't work the hours, but that wasn't an option for me. I'd offered her a job and a start date and it wasn't her fault it had changed.

But among those two positive emails was a bad news one.

To: Castle Street Cat Café
From: Sienna Hilton
Subject: Weekend job
I'm really sorry but my mum says I can't work at the cat café anymore. She's worried about me being safe after what happened yesterday. I didn't tell you last night because I hoped she'd change her mind this morning but she still

says no. I'm gutted. Really sorry for letting you and the cats down. Hope you can find a replacement quickly.

Sorry again, Sienna

Sienna was the youngest team member, having only just turned seventeen at the point she applied for the role. I hoped the other parents wouldn't feel like hers. Even my students who were eighteen and officially adults still lived at home so might not have complete free rein over their decisions. Frustrated, I tossed my phone onto the duvet beside me with a loud sigh.

'Bad news?' Tom asked, coming in with a mug of tea.

'Sienna just quit. Her mum thinks it's too dangerous working here.'

'You're kidding? That's crap.'

'Especially after already losing George. If I do open on Saturday, I'm now down to three students. It's not enough, especially when I need to factor in breaks.'

'There'll be enough of us. I'll be here and your parents have said they can work too so, between us, we'll pull it off. And I have some George-related news from Tara. She says Hattie would be up for a swap. She knows George from college so she's going to speak to him today. If George wants a job at The Chocolate Pot, the swap's on and you'll be back up to four students.'

'Fingers crossed.'

'How are you feeling this morning?'

'Better than yesterday, still not great, but I'm going to have to get up. I've got so much to do.'

'What do you need to do that I or someone else can't do for you?'

'I need to sort out the refunds, find out what I owe Matt for the work yesterday, thank everyone else for helping, see how the police got on, get in touch with that reporter...' There were more things I'd thought of during the night, but I couldn't bring them to mind.

'You don't owe Matt anything – he made that very clear. You thanked the others yesterday so they won't be expecting more thanks today, so you can knock that off your list for today. The police said they'd be in touch if there was news, so you don't need to contact them.

The refunds, I can sort. Which just leaves the reporter. She does specifically want to speak to you so I can't help there, but you could always phone her.'

'She wants a photo.'

'So invite her up to the flat. I'm sure she'd want cats in the photo and this is where they are. And I'm going to stop telling you what to do and make you some porridge, if you want some, that is.'

'Yes, please. And I like you taking control. Takes the pressure off when I can't think straight.'

He paused in the doorway. 'You will tell me if I overstep and get too bossy?'

'I will, but you're fine. Honestly, I appreciate it.' I was still struggling to ask for help.

'I just keep thinking about that meme your cousin sent you – the one about listening to what your body's whispering before it starts screaming. I know what you're like for wanting to get on with things and I'd hate for you to push yourself too far just because you're feeling a little bit better, only for the screaming to start again.'

'That meme resonated a lot with me too and, you're right, I do push myself and it nearly always backfires. I need you to keep me in check.'

Looking placated, he left the bedroom with a smile.

'That man's a saint,' I said to Rubix, who'd scrambled onto my lap. 'I owe him so many favours after this.'

I glanced towards the window but, being four storeys up, I couldn't see anything except the buildings opposite, so I had no idea whether there was anyone around – probably not as it was only just 9 a.m. and a lot of the shops didn't open until ten on weekdays out of season. Between the buildings, I could see patches of dull grey sky.

'It should have been opening day today,' I said, returning my attention to Rubix and stroking his back. 'We're not doing very well with opening days, are we?'

Babushka jumped onto the bed and settled beside me, so I stroked her too.

Tom returned a little later with my porridge. 'The cats are all fed, by the way, so don't let them tell you otherwise.' He picked up Rubix and wandered over to the window with him while I slowly raised my first spoonful to my mouth.

'Anything happening?' I asked.

'A couple of people cutting through. Jemma's just unlocking Bear With Me. The lights are on in Charlee's Chocolates but I can't see anyone.'

'They're probably in the workshop making chocolates.'

He turned to face me. 'How are you feeling about it being opening day but not opening day?'

'Bit weird. Sort of relieved because I couldn't have got through it like this, but I probably wouldn't have been like this if it hadn't been for the attack.'

'Are you still up for a Saturday opening? I realised downstairs that I was full of reassurances that we'd have enough staff, but I didn't even ask if you definitely want to open then.'

'Can I come back to you on that? I'm not feeling at all excited about it at the moment and I hate that.'

'It's understandable,' he said, perching on the end of the bed and giving me a sympathetic look. 'You've been through so much. But if you do go ahead and open on Saturday, I'm sure you'll feel a lot different when there's a queue of excited customers outside and you're about to open the door to the public for the very first time.'

'I hope you're right. This is my big dream but, right now, it feels more like a nightmare. I promise I'll make a decision by lunchtime so we can let people know.'

* * *

Tom went down into the café after breakfast, saying he wanted to give the place a clean now that the dust had settled. He'd only been downstairs for about half an hour when he phoned me. 'Would you be up for a visitor?'

'The reporter?'

'No. Alison Thorpe. She says she's a friend of yours.'

I smiled at the uncertainty in his voice, as though he was worried it might be somebody trying to be underhand and he needed to be my bouncer.

'Ali's fine. Can you send her up to my bedroom, but warn her I look scary?'

'You don't. I'll send her up.'

A couple of minutes later, Alison arrived with a beautiful vase of flowers.

'I heard what happened. I'm so sorry. I got you these.'

'They're gorgeous.'

'I didn't know if you had any vases but Sarah has a lovely range, so I asked her to put them straight in one. She says the flowers are all cat friendly.'

'Thank you.' I looked either side of me but there was no room on the bedside drawers. 'You might have to put them on the floor for now until I clear some stuff. Furniture shopping hasn't been a priority.'

She placed the vase on the floor beneath the television and joined me on the bed.

'I was going to ask you what happened but tell me about you first. What's going on?'

'You know when I messaged you to say I have fibromyalgia but it's mild? It's not mild.'

I stumbled through my explanation of my symptoms, feeling like I was stuck in Groundhog Day after saying the same thing to so many people recently.

'When you told me, I'd never heard of it, so I looked it up online. It sounded scary and I was so relieved you only had it mild. I'm sorry that isn't the case.'

'It's making me question what the hell I'm doing trying to set up the café. For something I've been thinking about and planning for years, it feels like no real thought has gone into it. It's so impractical. I've got Tom living with me, doing all the stuff Leon used to do and a heck of a lot more, but I can't keep him here forever. He has his own job, home and life to lead and I'm trying hard not to, but I feel so guilty about getting him to help. And it's not just him. He's taken a week off work, but my parents took yesterday off, my brother has been here after college repairing the mural despite having a pregnant wife at home, I've had the Castle Street traders helping clear up the mess, my builders doing some work for free, and here I am lying in bed, unable to contribute anything. I spoke to my cousin who has fibro and I'd started to find my peace with it, but the broken window has messed all that up. I'm angry, sad, guilty, confused and so damn tired.'

'I'm not surprised,' Alison said. 'You've already been through so much and having your café wrecked is bound to stir up loads of emotions. Guilt's a bugger. I felt it heavily after the car crash. I had a shocking case of survivor syndrome and questioned every aspect of my existence. It took me a hell of a long time to accept that, even though I'd always miss my family, it was okay for me to be alive and I was permitted to be happy again. I know bereavement isn't the same thing as chronic pain but, from what I've read about fibromyalgia, the reaction process to a chronic condition is the same.'

'My cousin talked about that and it made a lot of sense. I was so determined to make my way towards acceptance. I told my family, I asked for help and that little bit of progress spectacularly fell apart. I don't even know if I want to open the café – not just on Saturday but ever. I've got a reporter wanting to speak to me this morning who might be able to get the story on the front page of the *Bay News*. I'm telling myself it could be amazing publicity for this place, but do I want that publicity if I'm going to walk away?'

I shook my head, concerned that all I'd done since Alison arrived was whine. 'Bet you're really glad you stopped by with some flowers now. Sorry.'

'I *am* glad. At the risk of adding another dollop of guilt onto your plate, I want to help too because you're my friend and I care about you. I'll come back to the walking- away issue in a minute. Last week I asked what you thought was your secret to happiness. It was a rhetorical question – sort of – but you might have given it some thought and, if you have, that might be a good starting point for what to do next.'

'I did think about it. A lot. And it's these guys.' I stroked Effie who'd joined Rubix on my lap and nodded towards Sybil who'd clambered onto Alison's. 'They're everything to me.'

'What about baking?'

'It's the second love of my life. The cats come first.'

'This might seem like a daft question, but just go with it. Why do you love the cats so much?'

'Oh, gosh! So many reasons. They're affectionate and loving. They can be independent and do their own thing, but can't we all? Every single human I know relishes a little alone time, so why do people judge a cat when they want the same? Besides, when you have as many fur babies as I do, there are always several wanting company even when others want quiet time. They're soft, cute and cuddly. Their eyes are so beautiful and expressive. I feel much calmer when I'm stroking them – I swear my fibro would be even worse if I didn't have them – and when they press their forehead against mine and purr, it's the best thing ever. What else? They don't judge. They don't lie to you and break your heart. They all have individual personalities so it's a joy getting to know them. Jupiter's loud and needy, Winnie looks like she's in a permanent grump but is the most affectionate cat ever, and Babushka and Heathcliff are really staid and dignified most of the time but will then suddenly have crazy time, racing around like little kittens, pouncing on each other and doing parkour on the furniture. Sorry, Ali, I could talk about them for hours.'

'And I'd happily let you, but I don't want to wear you out. So my next question is what do you like doing with them? I'm picking up that stroking them and the cute forehead-touching thing is a big comfort, but what else?'

'I brush them, which is really therapeutic too. I talk to them, sing to them – but don't tell anyone else I said that because singing is not one of my skills – and I play games with them. I love watching films and reading, but I'd rather play with the cats. If they didn't sleep twelve to eighteen hours a day, I'd play with them a lot more.'

'Okay. Playing devil's advocate here, but how does opening a cat café fit alongside all that? Correct me if I'm wrong, but won't your customers get to do the stroking and playing while you're in the kitchen making drinks and cakes?'

My stomach lurched. 'Erm... I... Well...' *Oh, hell!*

Alison's voice softened. 'Sorry. I shouldn't have asked that, especially when you're not well.'

'It's a good question. Everyone's asking me good questions at the moment, and I don't have many answers.'

'Do you want my take on it?'

'Yes, please.'

'Walking away is huge and you're fully aware of that. This is your home, your job and a big financial layout that you probably won't recoup. You've got staff to think about too so no wonder your head's a mess. I reckon that all the doubts you're having right now stem back to Leon leaving. You had plans in place for how the café would run when you were ill and now that can't happen, which has you questioning whether it's what you really want anyway. What happened yesterday is only exacerbating those worries. I personally think you *should* open on Saturday, grab all the help your family can offer, and do your best. If you hit Easter or next summer or this time next year and it's not what you thought, your heart isn't in it, or it's too much for you, you'll know you gave it your best shot. If you decide not to open at all, will you regret that you didn't have a go? Of course you will! You'll be forever wondering how it might have been and, knowing you, you'll beat yourself up about that, so I say give it a chance. What do you think?'

'I think your travels have made you very wise.'

'Or full of bullshit,' she said, laughing.

'Definitely wise, although...' I sniffed the air and winked at her.

She lightly placed her hand on mine. 'I'm going to leave you to get some rest now but have a talk to Tom and your parents. If they're on board – and I'm sure they are – then I think it's worth a try.'

She rolled off the bed.

'Thanks for the advice and the flowers,' I said.

'Thanks for being honest with me about what's going on. I'm not one for spouting quotes – I usually can't remember them – but there's a Nelson Mandela quote that always sticks in my head. He said, "It always seems impossible until it's done." Look at everything you've done so far! You've designed and built a stunning café, trained your cats, come up with a delicious menu, established a strong presence on social media and so much more. You've already completed the part which many would think is impossible. Opening on Saturday is the final flourish.'

Alison said goodbye to me and the cats and left with a wave. She'd talked a lot of sense and most of it had inspired me, but that part about being stuck in the kitchen with limited cat contact scared me. It was so obvious when she spelled it out, yet I really hadn't paused to think about it. Yes, I wanted to share the cat love and have others experience the joy of being around felines, particularly if they didn't or couldn't have cats of their own, but was just being with the cats on an evening enough for me? Was it any different to what I'd had before? When I worked full time at The Ramparts, I only saw the cats between shifts. Could I find I had even less time with them now because I'd still have paperwork to do after the café closed? I had a horrible feeling it wasn't going to turn out as I'd thought, but she was right about me always wondering if I didn't give it a try.

I heaved myself out of bed and slowly made my way down to the kitchen to retrieve the business card for the *Bay News* reporter. I *would* do that interview and pull out all the stops to give the Castle Street Cat Café the biggest plug ever because we were opening on Saturday. I wasn't going to let that vandal take this from me. And I wasn't going to let Leon. Alison was right about that too. If he hadn't left me, none of these doubts would have materialised.

28

Tom came back upstairs shortly after Alison left.

'You're looking brighter,' he said.

'I feel it. We had a good chat and you've both helped me get my head straighter. I *am* going to open on Saturday.'

'That's great news.' He frowned at me. 'Isn't it?'

'Yes, it is, but something Alison said has made me wonder about the whole idea. I'll tell you about it later. For now, I need your help again. The reporter from *Bay News* is coming and I could really use a shower, but I don't have the time or energy. Do you think you could brush my hair for me and spray in some dry shampoo?'

'I have no idea what that is, but I'm happy to be directed.'

I freshened up in the bathroom first and put some clean clothes on, then sat on one of the garden chairs in my bedroom while Tom worked his magic with a detangler before spraying the dry shampoo.

'I've warned her that I'm not very well and that it's nothing contagious,' I told Tom. 'I'm going to tell her about my fibromyalgia.'

He stopped brushing for a moment but, as he was behind me and there was no mirror, I couldn't see his expression. 'Are you sure about that?' he asked, his tone hesitant. 'You weren't even going to tell your team until recently.'

'I want the police to find who did this. What if they weren't caught and they put a brick through the window when we're open and the cats got hurt? I need to know it isn't going to happen again. Ideally I don't want the newspaper-reading population of Whitsborough Bay to know my health challenges, but I think it'll make it a bigger story if there's that added human interest element – café of disabled person can't open due to vandalism.'

'Disabled? You've never called yourself that before.'

'Another part of the denial process. I don't think of myself as disabled, but fibro is long term and it substantially affects my ability to do my normal daily activities, which means it falls within the UK definition of disability.' I chewed on my lip, doubts setting in. 'Maybe I shouldn't mention it. I don't want anyone to think I'm milking it.'

Tom resumed brushing. 'It's probably worth sharing your concerns with the reporter. It's a local newspaper, not a scandal-seeking tabloid, so I'm sure she'll be able to present it in a sensitive way.'

'Hopefully. I can't help thinking that somebody knows who did this and being honest about my fibro might generate a little bit more sympathy and hopefully get them to shop the vandal before they try something else.'

* * *

The *Bay News* reporter – a woman in her mid-to-late-forties called Laura – arrived with a photographer and she couldn't have been nicer. As soon as I mentioned my fibromyalgia, she knew what I was talking about and shared that her younger sister had recently been diagnosed with it after a five-year struggle and umpteen different doctors, which made me appreciate all the more how fortunate I'd been to have a doctor who hadn't dismissed my symptoms as imaginary or the result of being overworked and not getting enough sleep. Laura assured me she would strike the right balance with how she presented my situation, ensuring it didn't come across as exploitative.

The photographer, as suspected, was keen to get some cats in the photo. Several of them were in the cat lounge, so we went in there. They were also keen to take photos of cats in the café so, tightly gripping the banister, I ventured downstairs. A shake of some treats brought Sybil, Freyja, Heathcliff, Marmite, Blinky and Ruby running and they were most obliging in posing for photos on various platforms on the first floor.

'Can we do the same on the ground floor?' Laura asked. 'These different sections are so creative. I'd love to include a photo from each in the article.'

'Of course!' I forced a smile, but I was flagging. I might make it down another flight of stairs, but I wasn't sure if I'd make it back up three.

Tom evidently picked up on my hesitation. 'Tell you what, why don't I do the ground floor bit?'

Laura clearly realised why he'd offered. 'I'm so sorry, Tabby. I should have thought. You get some rest and I'll finish up with Tom. It's been a pleasure to meet you and I promise some good coverage.'

They went downstairs but Blinky stayed with me and settled on my knee.

'I've used a lot of spoons this morning,' I said to her as I stroked her back. 'It's going to have to be a relaxing afternoon in front of the telly. Tell me off if I try to do anything else.'

* * *

'Everything's ready downstairs,' Tom said, returning to the flat later that morning. 'All we need now is food. Before I make lunch, I'll update the website and socials to say we're definitely opening on Saturday. Is there anything else you can think of?'

'My head's mush. Thank you for everything.'

'I've really enjoyed it. Not the vandalism part, obviously, but I've enjoyed being here with you and the cats, and getting the café ready. Baking was fun. Sampling was even better!'

'Bit different to spending your days in front of a spreadsheet?'

'Just a tad. Couple of bits of news for you. Tara popped in and the swap's on. She's spoken to George and he's going to start at The Chocolate Pot on Saturday. He's very grateful to you for recommending him.

Tara's emailed you Hattie's CV and says can you contact Hattie with the hours you want her to work?'

'Will do. That's one less thing to worry about.'

'She says Hattie has a Friday afternoon off college too so, if you want her to come in for training then, she'd be happy to do that.'

'Even better.'

'The second bit of news is that there might be a suitable candidate for Leon's job. A woman called Amelia Sharpe dropped this off.'

He handed me a CV and I scanned down it, noting her experience as a chef and a recent stint managing a small restaurant in Fellingthorpe a few miles down the coast. The combination of catering, front of house and management experience was what I'd been struggling to find.

'This looks promising,' I said, 'although working here is a step back from what she's been doing. It doesn't look like she's working at the moment. Did she say anything about that?'

'There's been a family bereavement so she's taken some time out. She says this job would be ideal because she wants to get back into working but doesn't want the sort of hours and responsibilities she had at the restaurant.'

'Fantastic! I'll give her a ring shortly and see if she can come in for an interview. Things are finally looking up.'

Tom left to update the website and socials and I scanned down Amelia's CV once more. She did look like a very viable prospect. I reached for my phone. Beside me, Blinky stretched out and gave a small mew.

'Yes, I know I said you were to stop me from doing anything, but it's only a quick phone call. After that, I promise I'll relax.'

Amelia sounded lovely on the phone and was available to come in for an interview on Friday morning. I found Hattie's CV on Tara's email and rang her too. I caught her between lessons so confirmed her hours for the weekend and a two-hour session on Friday afternoon to meet the cats and find out more about the role.

I clicked back into my emails and was relieved to see one from Fay confirming that she was fine to start the following week, so at least my weekday team was still intact. I closed the laptop, feeling drained once more. How could two short phone calls and reading one email take it out of me like that?

Tom brought up a couple of bowls of pasta salad for lunch shortly afterwards.

'As we're on top of things here,' he said after we'd eaten, 'I'm going to nip home to get some more clothes. Do you need anything while I'm out?'

'Not that I can think of.'

'You wanted to talk to me about something Alison had said.'

'I did but I'm low on spoons. I'll tell you later.'

He took the bowls away and I flicked the television on, but soon my eyes grew heavy and I drifted off to sleep, feeling so much more relaxed now that I might have found a supervisor.

29

The following morning, I felt a lot better and went into the bathroom for a much-needed and longed-for shower.

'Oh, that's so good!' I muttered, closing my eyes as the water cascaded over me.

Tom had offered his assistance but I couldn't face the whole swimming costume palaver so I declined, although I did ask if he could brush and dry my hair again.

While I was in the shower, he went to Nibbles & News – the newsagent's on the corner – to pick up some copies of *Bay News* and I couldn't help a little knot of apprehension as to whether I'd done the right thing in opening up about my fibromyalgia. Nothing I could do about it now, though.

'It's a brilliant write-up,' Tom called, knocking on the bathroom door a little later. 'You can breathe again.'

I read the article while he brushed and dried my hair and it was more than I could ever have hoped for. The vandalism was the main story on the front page, with a double-page spread focusing more on the café inside. Laura had done me proud, getting the tone exactly right, evoking empathy rather than pushing a sob story. She'd included quotes from me about how grateful I was to the team at Richards & Sons and the Castle Street traders for helping my friends and family with the clear-up while I was incapacitated. I really appreciated the way she conveyed my long-term passion for cats, starting with the story of finding the abandoned kittens through to caring for my large fur family today.

'She's even got a quote from the food safety officer,' I exclaimed, thrilled that she'd also covered the strict food preparation standards and how I'd been working closely with the local authority. 'I wasn't expecting that.'

'It's great publicity,' Tom said. 'I bet there'll be a flurry of bookings on the back of it. But, more importantly, let's hope someone shops whoever did this.'

He'd finished drying my hair and was about to tie it back into a pony-tail when my phone rang. Wendy's name flashed up on the screen and my stomach clenched. *Please don't be bad news.*

'Hi, Tabby,' she said. 'Sorry to call so early but I wanted to give you as much notice as possible...'

My stomach sank even further. After all that stuff about me not needing to pay her and her offering to come in and help get everything ready, she surely wasn't going to give me backword.

'I've just seen your email so I nipped out to get the paper,' she said. 'Brilliant coverage. I bet you're really chuffed.'

'I am. The reporter was really good.' *Please get to the point!*

'It struck me that you might be even busier than expected this weekend because I'm sure loads of people will be booking a table after reading this. I was going away but the friend I'm going with is ill and has had to cancel so I wanted to let you know that I can work this weekend if you need me.'

Relief flowed through me. 'Oh, Wendy, that would be amazing if you don't mind.'

'I don't mind at all. I can do full shifts both days or I can do a few hours – whatever suits you.'

'A definite yes from me, but can I come back to you in the morning with the hours? I need to see how much the article affects bookings overnight.'

'As long as I know by late afternoon, that's fine.'

I thanked her and ended the call.

'Wendy can work over the weekend,' I told Tom. 'She thinks the same as you – that there'll be loads of bookings on the back of the article.'

'I'm convinced of it.'

There were. By early evening, we were fully booked for Saturday and Sunday and across the late morning to early afternoon slots on Wednesday to Friday.

'I reckon the following weekend will be booked up by the end of tomorrow,' Tom said as we scrolled through the bookings diary.

'I hope we don't run out of anything.' Tom and I had spent the day baking cakes and tray bakes and would make more tomorrow. The scones, which didn't keep fresh for as long, would be baked on Saturday morning. Not opening until 10 a.m. each day gave that bit more prepara-tion time and meant I had to be up early but not at stupid o'clock each morning.

'I think there'll be plenty and if one cake sells out, so be it. There's other choices.'

'Yeah, and you've taste tested half of them.'

He grinned at me. 'It's a tough job, but somebody has to do it! Although I don't think I'll be doing much running at five-a-side tonight.'

* * *

I'd asked Amelia to come in at 11 a.m. on Friday morning for her interview, giving Tom and me a few hours in the kitchen to bake first. Yesterday and today, we'd left the flat door open to let the fur family roam freely. From opening day tomorrow, we'd need to coax them down into the café and they'd have to use the cat flap if they wished to return to the flat. From what I could see, they all enjoyed being in the café and trying out the different sections, but that might change when it got busy. My number one priority was their comfort and wellbeing, so when we opened, I'd be watching for changes in behaviour, signs of skittishness and anything else that might suggest the café was no longer a happy place for them. I didn't have any concerns about the kittens adapting quickly, but the adults were an unknown and none of them would be made to come into the café if it wasn't what they wanted. Hopefully that wouldn't be the case as eight kittens weren't many for the size of café we had over two floors. I wasn't working on a ratio of cats to customers, but I'd read about some cat cafés in Taiwan and Japan which only had a few resident felines and nearly all the reviews commented on how disappointing that was. I certainly didn't want that to be the overall impression of Castle Street Cat Café.

There was a knock on the door shortly before eleven, so I hung up my apron and left Tom mixing the batter for a coffee and walnut cake.

'Amelia?' I asked, opening the door.

'Hi, yes. Tabby?' She tucked her long dark wavy hair behind her left ear, revealing several delicate piercings. 'Thanks for seeing me.'

'Thanks for dropping in your CV. Come through.'

'Ooh, it smells delicious in here,' she exclaimed, stepping into Cat Castle. 'You're the chef?'

'Joint effort today with us opening tomorrow. Tom, who you met on Wednesday, is holding the fort at the moment.'

She stepped aside to peer through the kitchen window. 'Hi, Tom!' she said, smiling and waving at him.

He smiled back. 'Coffee?'

'I'm fine for now, thanks. What are you making?'

'Coffee and walnut cake, but we've got brownies and blondies in the oven.'

She slowly breathed in and closed her eyes for a moment. 'Mmm, smells incredible. I could get used to working somewhere which smells like this every day.'

'I'll never get tired of the smell of cakes baking,' I said. 'I thought I'd take you on a tour of the café and talk you through the role, and then we can sit down and go through your CV in more detail.'

'Sounds good. See you later, Tom.' She gave him a dazzling smile. It seemed the smell of cakes wasn't the only thing that appealed to Amelia.

'Aw, who's this little one?' she said.

Cloud had just leapt onto a chair and then the table beside us.

'This is Cloud, one of eight kittens we have. She's a six-month-old Persian and a bundle of fun.'

'Can I pick her up?'

'You can today if you like, but it's a no-no in front of the customers unless it's essential. We have some rules to make sure the cats don't get hurt and one of them is that nobody can pick them up, so we don't want customers seeing us picking them up and copying.'

'Completely understand.'

I gave Amelia a tour of the ground floor and couldn't fail to spot a couple of glances towards the kitchen, although Tom was too busy to notice. He'd definitely made a positive first impression on her. I'd forgotten to mention the woman who'd turned back to look at him when we were halfway through the biscuit deliveries so I'd tell him later about her and Amelia, which would hopefully give him a boost to getting back out there on the dating scene. I wasn't sure if Tom had a type, as I'd never met anyone he'd dated. With her dark hair, dark eyes, perfectly manicured eyebrows, flawless skin and full lips, Amelia was stunning so I couldn't imagine him not finding her attractive.

We went up to the first floor and I felt myself glowing with pride from Amelia's reaction to it.

'I can't believe what you've done in here,' she gushed. 'It's so beautiful and your cats are adorable.'

'Do you have a cat?' I asked.

Her eyes lowered to the floor and she sighed. 'I used to. Well, it was my boyfriend's really so, when we split up, the cat went with him.'

'That must have been hard.'

'It was. I missed them both so much but he'd found someone new so what could I do? I wasn't going to beg him to come back.'

'Break-ups are horrible. I've been through one myself recently. My boyfriend was meant to be running this place with me but he wanted to take his career in a different direction, and that didn't include me. The position you've applied for is what he'd have been doing so I've had to rethink a lot of things and enrol family and friends like Tom to help out.'

'He's not one of the staff?'

'No. He'll be here over the weekend and then it's back to his day job.'

Amelia looked disappointed, which would definitely be a boost for Tom. 'Let's sit down, have a chat about the job and run through your CV.'

* * *

'Bye, Tom!' Amelia called as we walked through Cat Castle after the interview.

'Bye!' he called back, giving her a wave.

'Thank you so much for offering me the job,' she said as I closed the inner door behind us.

It had been an easy decision. Her work experience, her interest in cats, and what she was looking for from the role all aligned with what I was after. I also really liked her and could see us working really well together. And she'd reacted with empathy to my fibromyalgia and understood the impact on her job of its unpredictability.

She'd squealed with delight when I offered it to her and accepted immediately. I had a feeling that it wouldn't be a long-term role for her, but that suited me when I still had a few niggles as to whether the cat café really was going to be viable in the long run.

'Thanks for accepting,' I said, shaking her hand. 'I'll confirm it by email and look forward to seeing you on Wednesday.'

'I take it that squeal meant you offered her the job?' Tom said when I joined him in the kitchen after Amelia left.

'Yes, and she's accepted. Although she was clearly disappointed when I said you don't work here.'

'Why would she be disappointed?' He looked genuinely flummoxed.

'Because I think she has a little crush on you.'

'No! You're making that up.'

'Why would I make it up? Did you not witness the flirting?'

When he looked at me blankly, I closed my eyes and said an exaggerated, 'Mmm, smells incredible.'

'You're hilarious!' he said, rolling his eyes. 'And that wasn't flirting.'

'Aw, come on, Tom! That *was* flirting and if you couldn't see that, it's no wonder you're single. When we were giving out the biscuits and you left me in Castle Park to restock, an attractive woman walked towards you and turned back to look and you didn't see that either.'

Another blank look.

'It's kind of sweet that you don't realise how hot you are.'

'You think I'm hot?'

Heat flowed through me from head to toe.

'No, I... It's Amelia and the woman on the street who think...' I knew my cheeks were burning so there was no use trying to deny it. 'Okay! You're not too bad.'

'Woah! Don't go overboard on the compliments,' he said, laughing.

'You're very attractive and you're a lovely person too. There. Happy now?'

'Very. Thank you. Shame I can't return the compliment.'

There was a bag of icing sugar open beside me and, before I had a chance to weigh up the pros and cons, I grabbed a handful and threw it at him, sending a cloud of powder flying as it landed on his cheek.

'You did *not* just do that!' he cried, licking icing sugar from his lips. 'Right!'

He grabbed a spatula from the bowl of chocolate cake batter he'd been mixing and flicked it in my direction. I squealed as it splatted across my forehead, nose and cheeks.

'If it's war you want, Headley...' I grabbed an egg and threw it at him, giggling as it smashed against his apron.

'You fight dirty, Walsh!' He dipped the spatula in the batter and catapulted a blob towards me, which splatted on my chin and dripped down into my cleavage.

I grabbed another handful of icing sugar as he ran to the end of the kitchen. We had a stand-off at either end of the island, my hand raised, his spatula poised.

'You'll be sorry,' he said, laughing.

'I already am!'

He took a couple of paces closer and I ran round the table. He chased after me but I foxed him by changing direction and flinging the icing sugar. He retaliated with another splat from the spatula and we dissolved onto the floor in fits of giggles.

'Ooh, that hurts!' I said, clutching my stomach.

'Are you okay?' he asked, suddenly serious.

'Yes. Not my fibro. My stomach from laughing. It's a long time since I've laughed like that. That was fun. Messy, but fun.'

He smiled once more. 'It might surprise you to hear this, but you've got a bit of cake mixture on your face.'

That set us both off again.

When we'd calmed down, we looked round the kitchen, shaking our heads at the dusting of icing sugar on the floor and worktops and the chocolatey splats of cake mixture pretty much everywhere.

'We'd better get this cleared up,' I said, scrambling to my feet.

'You might want to...' He pointed to his forehead, then his nose, cheeks, chin, neck.

'Hand me some kitchen towel.'

Tom dampened a couple of pieces and passed them to me. I wiped at my forehead.

'You're smearing it,' he said. 'Let me.'

He took the kitchen towel from me and wiped what I assumed was the worst of it.

'Fresh piece for the last few bits,' he said.

He cupped my chin in his hand and tilted my face upwards as he dabbed my skin. His hand was warm and soft, his touch gentle. I gazed into his eyes, noticing for the first time beautiful amber flecks and a tiny freckle below his lower lashes on his right eye. His eyes were absolutely gorgeous. *He* was absolutely gorgeous. He lightly brushed his thumb over my cheek and an unexpected wave of electricity pulsed through me, making me gasp.

'Did I hurt you?' he asked, jumping back.

'No. It was nothing. I'm fine.'

He resumed his position and I experienced another pulse as his hands touched me. I imagined him running them across my cheeks and into my hair, lowering his lips to mine and... He shifted his gaze from my cheek to my eyes and there was a heart-stopping moment where we seemed to drink each other in. I had no idea what to do. This was my brother's best friend. He was like a brother to me. I'd *never* thought about him as gorgeous before and I'd certainly never had a fantasy about him kissing me. So what was going on right now?

'All done?' I asked, my voice coming out croaky.

Tom released me. 'Yes. Sorry. Done.'

He'd evidently lost the ability to connect words into a sentence. What had been going through his mind? Had he felt something too or was he simply wondering why I was staring at him?

'You might want to do that bit yourself,' he said, his cheeks flushing as he glanced at my cleavage and swiftly averted his eyes.

'Erm, yes. Thank you.'

'I might nip into the toilet and sort myself out,' he said.

'Okay.'

'Just because I might need to give my hair a shake.'

'Okay.'

'Not because I don't want you to touch me.'

'Okay.'

'I'll just...'

He scuttled off and I sank down onto my stool. What just happened?

* * *

The rest of the day raced by. Hattie came in for a couple of hours in the afternoon and was a delight. Confident and funny, she was a natural with the cats. With two positions now filled, I just needed one more student to replace Sienna although, with Wendy now working this weekend, that wasn't an immediate priority. I'd ask the others if they had any friends who were looking for work and, if not, I'd place another advert early next week.

Mum, Dad, Rylan and Macey came round in the evening. Before sharing an Indian takeaway, Rylan did some final touching up on the mural while the rest of us blew up the balloons ready to put round the door in the morning. Everything seemed very calm and on track and, even though I kept having that awful sensation that I'd forgotten something, a glance down my to-do list confirmed that we were ready for opening day. At last!

'Good luck for tomorrow,' Macey said, giving me a hug at the door. 'It's going to be amazing.'

'I hope so.'

Rylan, Mum and Dad also gave me hugs goodbye and checked again that I was sure I didn't need them to help over the weekend.

'We should be okay with Wendy working it now, unless my fibro decides it's going to spoil everything.'

'Fingers crossed it doesn't,' Mum said, 'but we'll be on standby if it does, or if you do find you need more help.'

It was a little after 8 p.m. when Tom and I returned to the flat. Everyone had intentionally visited early so I could get to bed and rest.

While Tom made mugs of tea, I checked the bookings.

'Look at this!' I said, shaking my head in disbelief. 'So many more bookings.'

Tom peered over my shoulder. 'You'll have to send some opening day photos to Laura at *Bay News*.'

'Good idea. I can thank her for her amazing article. There's no doubt this is a direct result. I just hope it achieves my main aim of catching the vandal.'

I took my tea and laptop through to the lounge and Tom and I sat on the sofa bed together, scrolling through and responding to the comments beneath the article on the *Bay News* Facebook page.

'Such lovely comments,' I said, refreshing them. But as I scanned the next one down, my stomach lurched.

The owners of this café should be ashamed of themselves, exploiting cats like this. Anyone who goes to this café should be ashamed of themselves too.

'Ignore it,' Tom said.

A little further down there was something similar.

Cat cafés should be banned. They're unethical. You people disgust me!

I sighed. 'I know there are stacks of positive comments and hardly any negative ones, but I can't help focusing on the bad ones. I wonder if one of them could be the vandal.'

'It's possible.'

Clicking onto our own Facebook page where we'd shared the *Bay News* post, it was a similar story – well over a hundred positive comments but a couple of negatives.

'Ooh, that's nasty,' I said.

Reading this article has just made my day. To the owner – I'm glad you have a chronic illness. Serves you right. To the person who trashed the café – loving your work! Shame you didn't do even more damage cos they're still opening 😒

Tom leaned across me and clicked on 'hide' then softly closed the laptop.

'It's okay,' I said with another sigh. 'That one's easier to stomach than the others. It's horrible and it's personal but it says more about them and what a nasty individual they are than it does about me. The posts about exploitation of cats and being unethical hurt a lot more. The cats are my number one priority.'

'Anyone who comes to the café will be able to see how healthy and loved they all are. There'll always be somebody who doesn't like what you do, no matter what it is you do.'

I glanced at my watch. 'It's half nine and I can hear my bed calling.' I stood up and stretched my back out. 'Night, Tom. And thanks again for everything.'

'Any time. Night.'

I'd have given him a hug but he hadn't stood up and it would be a little awkward leaning over him, so I blew kisses to the cats in the lounge and headed off to bed.

As I closed my eyes, I thought those cruel messages would be playing on my mind, but it was actually Tom's face I saw, so close to mine, and my heart started to race.

30

'Happy opening day!' Sarah said, emerging from Seaside Blooms as I held the bottom of the ladder the following morning so Tom could string the cat bunting across the windows. 'All set?'

'Just about. I'm nervous.'

'I was too when Seaside Blooms re-opened with me as the owner, but that first day was brilliant. You'll be fine. Are you fully booked?'

'Today and tomorrow.'

'That's fantastic. Have an amazing day.'

Several more traders stopped by while we were outside to wish us luck. The frontage looked fabulous with the bunting and balloons round the windows and door, and the giant cat-shaped balloon sculpture in the porch made for a lovely welcome.

As well as being surrounded by cats, there were other differences between the cat café and a regular café – one-hour sittings at fifteen-minute intervals and no guarantee of a table for late arrivals, a limited menu to facilitate speedy turnaround, and an entry fee per person which contributed towards the food, cat litter and veterinary care. Although this was all very clear on our website and I'd love to think everyone who came to a cat café would be a warm and fuzzy cat-loving person, that would be a naïve assumption and there were bound to be customer objections about how we operated.

On days when we weren't fully booked, we welcomed walk-ins. I'd created homemade tables/no tables signs for the window and door and would get more professional ones made once I was satisfied they were working.

As requested, the team were ready to work fifteen minutes before we opened and I gave them a final briefing. A queue was already building outside and I hoped there was nobody in it without a booking as they were going to be disappointed.

'Everyone ready?' I asked Wendy, Arwen, Lena, Max and Hattie, my voice sounding more confident than I felt. My heart was pounding and the nervous butterflies in my stomach were chasing each other and doing somersaults. I was excited, but also terrified.

Max was wide-eyed and clearly nervous, but the others looked calm.

'Ready,' they all chorused.

They looked fabulous in their colourful aprons with the café logo on them – a mischievous-looking grey tabby sitting in a coffee cup, with Whitsborough Bay Castle in the background.

Tom was in the kitchen, ready to help me with the orders, so I gave him a thumbs up and he responded with a nod and a big smile.

'Here's to a successful first day,' I said, pulling the internal door open. 'Enjoy yourselves!'

I closed the door behind me and, heart thumping even faster, opened the external one. So many people! The chatter from the crowd outside hushed as heads turned expectantly in my direction. *Please let this go well. Please let everyone be friendly.*

'Good morning, everyone!' I called. 'Welcome to Castle Street Cat Café and thank you for supporting us on our opening day. We have a double-door system to avoid escapees, so I need to let you in one group at a time. Please listen out for the surname of the person who booked. If you don't have a booking, we're full all weekend but there are some slots next week. Can anyone with a 10 a.m. booking make their way to the front, please? First in is Cavendish, table for four.'

'That's us,' said the woman at the front with a man and two children who were maybe eight and ten. 'That was handy.'

I welcomed them into the entrance porch, closed the door before opening the inner one and smiled at the gasps of delight from the children.

'You're in the Feline Forest upstairs. Hattie will take you to your table.'

Hattie stepped forward with a big smile. 'You're our very first customers! The cats are excited to meet you. As you can see, there are a few of them down here and there are more waiting upstairs if you'd like to come with me. Just a quick reminder of the rules...'

* * *

An hour in, we'd had no customer issues but I'd realised I was short-staffed. Lena and Hattie were covering Feline Forest upstairs and Max and Arwen were responsible for customers in Kitty Cove. Wendy and I were managing downstairs between us, but I was also trying to let customers in and sort out the orders, which was too much for one person.

'Have you turned into an octopus?' I asked Tom when I joined him in the kitchen. 'Because I swear you must have more than one pair of hands in here.' I had no idea how he was managing to keep on top of everything with so little help from me.

'Multi-tasking,' he said. 'Some men are good at it.'

'I think we might need to call in the back-up troops.'

'Already made that call. They'll be here in ten minutes.'

'You absolute star.'

'I figured there's no way we can both keep this pace going and the team need breaks and lunch.'

'Mum and Dad aren't trained, so how should I use them?' It was a rhetorical question but Tom already had the answer worked out.

'I thought your dad could be doorman, your mum can help me, and you can flit between helping Wendy and checking upstairs. It'll give you a better insight into how it's all working and how the cats are coping.'

'Genius! Thanks for being my brain today.'

'I'm also going to be your doctor. You need to make sure you have some rest time today because, if you don't, there's a risk you won't be doing this tomorrow.'

I nodded and sighed. I'd already thought about that myself. While it was amazing to be fully booked, it was full-on. After tomorrow, I'd have a couple of recovery days, but then there'd be five café days on the trot. The old me would have thrived on being so busy and powered through it all with time and energy for a social life. The new me physically couldn't do that and I still needed to work out the practicalities of those restrictions.

On a positive note, it was wonderful to see the place full of people and be part of the excited buzz of something new and different. The cats were loving the attention and I'd had so many compliments about the décor, the cats and the food so, despite the concerns about the logistics and pace, there was so much that was good and I was glad I'd opened today. My face was already aching from smiling.

31

After the excitement and pace of opening day, I feared I'd have a flare-up on Sunday morning but, by some miracle, my body had decided to be kind. However, as Tom and I made scones together first thing, it was obvious to me that the past week had taken its toll on him. Even though he did his best to disguise it, he yawned an alarming number of times. His eyes were red, his movements were slower and the atmosphere was subdued.

When he yawned again, I put down my pastry cutter and faced him. 'Right, that's it! As soon as we're finished with the scones, you need to go back to your apartment and get some rest before returning to the day job tomorrow.'

'I'm fine.'

'Not being rude, but you don't look it.'

'Cheers! I thought you said I was hot.' Despite the obvious tiredness, he still managed a twinkle in his eye as he spoke.

'Don't let it go to your head because, right now, you're looking a bit rough. You need some sleep, Tom. You've been incredible all week but I can't keep you here.' I didn't add the additional words that had crept into my head – *even though I want to.*

He looked as though he was going to protest, so I pre-empted it.

'Mum and Dad are coming back today and I've got Alison on standby. There'll be plenty of us.'

Alison had FaceTimed last night to ask how it had gone and to offer her services for today if I needed any help. She'd been into town yesterday afternoon and had spotted how busy the café was.

'If I do go home, are you sure you'll be okay?' Tom asked.

'I'm sure. Your neighbours will have forgotten what you look like.'

'I doubt it. None of them speak. But I probably could do with some sleep before I attack the spreadsheets tomorrow.' He yawned – not trying to stifle it this time – and stretched. 'I'll only go on one condition.'

'What's that?'

'That I can take a couple of scones with me.'

I smiled. 'After everything you've done to help, I think I can rustle up more than a couple of scones. I'll do you a goody bag.'

We continued working in silence for a while. Tom put a couple of trays of scones in the oven while I was washing my hands. When I turned round, he was leaning against the oven, watching me. I raised my eyebrows at him quizzically.

'You remind me so much of Betsy,' he said. 'Not in looks, but in personality. I think you get your strength and determination from her.'

Nanna had been such an inspiring woman. Widowed at thirty-three when her beloved husband Arnold, a fisherman, lost his life in stormy seas, she refused to bow to family pressure to remarry and was determined to raise my dad on her own. He'd been six when Granddad died. Nanna and Granddad had hoped to have more children and Nanna hadn't seen why his death should stop that, which was how the fostering came about and how Tom ended up in her care. I liked the thought that I'd inherited part of her personality. I'd never considered it before but maybe that was where my independent, determined streak came from.

'She'd have been so proud of you for doing this,' Tom continued.

I swallowed down the lump in my throat. 'I hope so.'

He drew me into his arms. 'I know so.' He kissed the top of my head and I closed my eyes for a moment, feeling his heartbeat as I rested my head against his chest. I swear it was thumping as fast as mine. That fizz was back in the air and I imagined tilting my head towards his and melting into a kiss. I wasn't brave enough to make the move. Was he thinking something similar because this hug was going on way too long otherwise? One of us was going to have to let go sooner or later, and I didn't want it to be me.

Tom cleared his throat and loosened his hold, so I had no choice but to release mine.

'What's next?' he asked, his voice a little higher than usual.

I searched his face to see if I could work out what he was thinking, but he wouldn't catch my eye.

'Raspberry and white chocolate,' I said, reluctantly returning to business.

* * *

'Oh, wow, I've loved today!' Alison said, smiling at Hattie and me as soon as the last of the Sunday customers in Cat Castle had paid and left. 'Thanks for letting me help.'

'Thanks for helping. You are *so* good with customers.' I was actually in awe. I'd known she had a great reputation for fantastic customer service at The Ramparts Hotel and she'd been sorely missed when she left, but I'd never seen her in action.

'I hadn't realised how much I'd missed the buzz of it all.'

'Do you want a job?' I asked.

'If I wasn't pregnant, I'd bite your hand off.'

The final customers from upstairs appeared to settle their bill so I dealt with that while Hattie cleared the tables in Cat Castle and Alison went upstairs to help the others.

As I loaded the dishwasher, I imagined working with Alison every day. She was a bundle of energy, so much fun and clearly a huge hit with the staff, the customers and the cats. What an asset she'd be.

'Have you got time for a quick cuppa before you go?' I asked Alison while the others retrieved their coats and bags once the cleaning was complete.

She glanced at her watch. 'I've got twenty minutes until Aidan stops by with Madison, so yes to that.'

I let the others out and thanked them for their amazing work across the weekend while Alison made a couple of hot chocolates.

'I can't stop smiling,' she said as we sat down with them. 'I'm buzzing.'

Freyja jumped onto her knee. 'Hello, beautiful,' she cooed. 'I love you sooo much, yes I do!'

'She loves you too,' I said, listening to Freyja's contented purrs. 'And I loved having you here. I can only offer a waiting job, but are you sure you wouldn't be interested, even if just until the end of the year?'

'I'm so tempted, Tabby, but I can't. I need to find us somewhere to live as we can't stay with Lorraine and Nigel forever, and I've got Madison. It would cost me more to find a childminder than I'd earn.'

'I can't believe I didn't think about Madison. What a numpty!'

'Don't worry about it. Stuff relating to kids would never have been at the forefront of my mind until I became a mum. If you're stuck, give me a shout. The odd day here and there, I can manage, especially at the moment as the in-laws can't get enough of their granddaughter being home.'

We chatted a little more about the day until there was a knock on the door.

'That's Aidan,' Alison said, waving. 'Do you want to see Madison?'

'Definitely.'

Alison gently placed Freyja on the floor, giving her a kiss on the head first, and let Aidan in. Madison was strapped into a buggy and cried, 'Mummy!' as soon as she spotted Alison, thrusting her arms out to be picked up.

Aidan lightly kissed Alison before she bent down to release Madison and shower her with kisses. It was such a happy family moment which made me go all gooey inside. Would I ever have that with someone?

'Kitty!' Madison cried, pointing at Heathcliff sprawled across one of the castle turrets. Freyja ran along the drawbridge, evoking another cry of 'Kitty!'

Aidan turned to me with a smile. 'If you were hoping for a cuddle, you might have to wait a while. She adores animals.'

My heart melted as Alison carried her over to Heathcliff and showed her how to stroke him gently. She did the same with Freyja and ended up taking her on a cat-hunt with Aidan in tow so he could see what I'd done to the place.

I took our empty mugs into the kitchen, set the dishwasher away and finished wiping down the kitchen surfaces. The kitchen felt empty without Tom in it, so the flat was going to feel really strange.

When Alison, Aidan and Madison left a little later – after I managed a quick cuddle – I returned upstairs with my fur family in tow and was engulfed by the silence. Rubix looked up at me with a plaintive mew. 'I know, sweetie, I miss him too, but we couldn't keep him forever.'

I made some tea and sat in the lounge on the sofa bed to eat it, but it didn't look right in there without Tom's duvet folded up, pillows on top, neatly packed case to one side. I thought about FaceTiming him, but it felt needy. I had to give him some space.

'Come on, you lot,' I said to the cats who'd joined me in the lounge. 'Let's have an early night.'

A couple of them stayed where they were and the others followed me up to the bedroom, finding a spot on the bed. I gazed around the room and my eyes fell on the vase of flowers still on the floor. I really needed to get cracking with ordering some furniture and now would be as good a time as any. I brought up a furniture site on my phone but, after ten minutes of aimless scrolling, I closed it down, feeling listless without Tom.

I drifted off to sleep but woke up in the early hours, thinking I could hear someone downstairs. Lying on my back, heart pounding, I called out, 'Hello?' I'm not sure what I'd have done if somebody had responded. Legs shaking, I went downstairs and opened the flat door. I couldn't hear anything and there wasn't a cold draught like there'd been when the window got smashed.

If someone was down there, I wasn't going to creep up on them. Full lighting was essential. I flicked on the switch, but there was nobody there, no window put through, no graffiti on the door – I even went outside to check. And there was nobody there the second time I checked. Or the third.

32

After a busy opening weekend and a tense disturbed night, I wasn't surprised to wake up on Monday morning with a fibro flare-up, although, as it was green intensity, I could still do what I'd planned – visit the traders who'd helped with the clear-up to give them my personal thanks.

I went to see Eileen in Aunt Polly's Tea Room first as she scared me a little and I didn't want to talk myself out of visiting her in case she'd stepped up in a crisis but was back to snarky mode now that it had passed. She was surprisingly lovely. She gave me a hug, which I accepted despite the pain, and apologised again for her comments. We ended up sharing a pot of tea and chatting about her cats.

It was lovely and Christmassy in Aunt Polly's. The pale pink table-cloths had been swapped out for cream ones with a holly and berry print on them. All the decorations on a large Christmas tree near our table were café-themed – cups, cakes, macarons, gingerbread people, tarts and even glittery triangular sandwiches. The tiered plate stands for after-noon tea had a sprig of holly on the top of them and a menu on the table advertised a special Christmas afternoon tea selection which sounded delicious. I was quite reluctant to leave.

Everyone else I visited insisted it had been no bother helping. It was clear that the vandalism had sent a shockwave through the community as there'd never been an incident like that before. Even though there was no suggestion that I was to blame for bringing trouble to the street, I couldn't help feeling guilty for the drama and had to remind myself of Alison's advice about letting go of guilt.

I hadn't been back long when the police stopped by with disappointing news. They'd examined all the CCTV coverage but the vandal had been careful as expected, keeping their face away from the cameras and wearing no distinctive clothing. They'd followed up a couple of leads with some individuals known for their animal rights activism but those hadn't come to anything. The case would stay open, but it didn't sound like the perpetrator was going to be found, which meant they were free to do further damage. It was disappointing that the newspaper coverage hadn't flushed them out but I'd try not to dwell on that and focus instead on how much extra business it had generated.

I sat at the table in the flat after the police left, looking at the sales printouts for our first two days to see what food and drinks had been most popular. I had a fairly good idea already but wanted to make sure. It would be helpful to have a spreadsheet to keep a track of it but spreadsheets took my thoughts back to Tom, who'd be able to set something up so much quicker than I could. My hand hovered over my phone, but I stopped myself from picking it up. Too needy. I needed to figure this out for myself.

Becoming frustrated with the spreadsheet when I couldn't get my head around a simple formula, I closed it down and opened up a new secret board on Pinterest for 'Flat Refurb' but I didn't know where to start. With moving from my parents' house straight to Leon's, I'd never had decisions to make about painting and furnishing a house. Leafing through a book might be easier than searching online, so I locked up and went to Bay Books a couple of doors along.

'Back again?' Lily said, smiling at me.

'I need some inspiration for refurbishing the flat. Do you have any home design books?'

She directed me towards the appropriate section. They didn't carry an extensive range but even what they had flummoxed me. Did I want a modern interior or something more in keeping with the age of the building? Drake Street had been modern and I hadn't loved it, so I opted for a traditional design book and one about colour.

Returning to the flat, I flicked through the first twenty or so pages in the design book before casting it aside. It wasn't just the fibro preventing me from focusing on anything – it was being here alone that was the problem.

I emailed Laura at *Bay News* to thank her for the amazing coverage last week. I told her it had made a huge impact on sales, and attached some opening day photos. After that it was lunchtime, so I made a sandwich and spent the rest of the afternoon talking to and playing with the cats, asking them how they'd enjoyed their first couple of days with the customers, amusing myself by giving their responses in their own unique voices.

'Do you think I've morphed into a crazy cat lady after all?' I asked Winnie as I sat on the floor, leaning against the sofa bed.

She was too busy batting a catnip-filled fish toy to pay any attention, but I answered for her in her soft Cornish tone. 'I do indeed, my lover, especially now you're single. It's just you and us from now on.'

I couldn't help thinking she was right and while I did want to spend the rest of my life surrounded by cats, it would be lovely if there was a special human to share it with too.

* * *

After tea, I retreated to the bedroom and put a romcom on, but switched it off after ten minutes. I didn't want to watch a film about a couple getting their happy ever after when I didn't anticipate getting mine. I went for the other extreme with a Tarantino film and half-heartedly watched that while adding a couple of opening day photos to the socials, thanking everyone for their support and flagging up that there were still some bookings available for the week ahead.

Shortly after 8 p.m. my phone rang and my heart did an unexpected leap at Tom's name.

'What are you up to?' he asked when I accepted his FaceTime request.

'Doing some stuff on the socials and watching *Kill Bill*.'

He looked surprised at my choice. 'Which one?'

'The first one.'

'Fancy some company?'

It was my turn to look surprised.

'I didn't sleep well last night,' he said, screwing his nose up. 'That sofa bed is comfier than my own bed. I miss the cats. I've got used to having a few of them on the bed with me. And I...'

I held my breath, wondering if he was going to say he missed me. There was a definite pause before he continued, as though he wasn't sure of the right words.

'...I'm worried about you on your own in case... Not that I want to scare you, but—'

'I'm worried about the same thing,' I said, cutting across him. 'I barely slept last night, thinking I could hear someone downstairs.'

'That's not good. Would you have any objection to me coming back to the flat and staying with you for a bit longer – at least until they've caught who did it? I can do my work from there.'

'I don't think they're going to catch anyone. The police came round earlier and they're not hopeful.'

Tom grimaced. 'I was hoping they'd been caught on CCTV somewhere.'

'They were, but they had a hood up.' I shrugged.

'Does that mean a no to me coming back?'

'It means I'd love you to come back, but if you think they might catch someone within a few days... You might be here for quite some time.'

He smiled. 'I'll take my chances. See you in about twenty minutes.'

'Don't you need time to pack?'

He panned the camera round to his duvet, pillows, case, laptop and a crate of paperwork then back to his face. 'I was hoping you'd say yes.'

I smiled back at him. 'See you soon. But we're not watching *Kill Bill: Volume 2*. The dead body count after the first one is enough for me for one evening.'

33

It was so good to have Tom back. On Monday night, he sat on the bed beside me with *Kill Bill: Volume 1* on mute as I filled him in on my disrupted Sunday night, up and down the stairs. He told me how he'd struggled to settle in his empty apartment and had had to stop himself from ringing me in the middle of the night to ask if he could come back. That night, I slept much more peacefully.

On Tuesday, Tom kept coming down to the cat café kitchen for a chat while I baked. Worried about the impact on his day job, I took charge and sent him upstairs to do some work, telling him he could have a reward of a scone or a piece of cake if he promised to do a full two hours without appearing. Two hours later, on the dot, he was back. He claimed it was purely for the cake, but it was obvious to me that he was craving company, just like me.

Today – Wednesday – was the start of the first full week of trading. The lunchtime period was fully booked, but there was capacity for walk-ins at the start and end of the day.

Before we opened, Matt arrived to do the plumbing work in the cat lounge. Depending on how long that took, he said he'd either get the storage units fitted today or tomorrow morning. I hoped the noise didn't disturb Tom too much.

Amelia arrived shortly afterwards for her first day, half an hour earlier than expected.

'I know I'm early, but I was so excited to get started,' she said, shrugging off her coat. 'Is there anything I can do to help?'

'Thanks, but I'm all sorted. You're welcome to spend some time with the cats if you want.'

'That would be lovely. I've been trying to learn their names, but I can only get a few of them to stick.'

'Don't worry if it takes a while. I won't be testing any of you.'

I smiled as she took out her cat guide and started working her way round Cat Castle with it, flicking through the pages.

Before long, the rest of the team arrived and soon we were open for our first customers. Despite still being busy, it didn't feel quite as hectic as it had done over the weekend. We had fewer staff, but some adjustments to how we worked helped things run more smoothly.

Amelia's first day went well. She picked everything up quickly and, although she didn't ooze Alison's warmth – who did? – she was pleasant and efficient, so I felt confident with my recruitment decision.

Towards the end of the day, I answered the door to a tall, slender woman with thick, curly black and grey hair. Wearing minimal make-up, she was naturally attractive and radiated a sense of calm. I guessed her age to be maybe late fifties.

'I haven't pre-booked, but the sign says you have some tables,' she said, her voice soft and warm.

'We do,' I said, welcoming her inside. 'We've got tables in each section available, so you can sit down here where, as you can see, we have a castle theme, or you can go upstairs where there's a forest section and a seaside section.'

'I intend to visit regularly, so I'll sit here today and try upstairs next time.'

'I take it you're a cat lover?'

'What gives it away?' she said, laughing as she hitched her cat tote bag onto her shoulder. Her T-shirt had a cartoon cat on it and there were cat badges pinned to her baggy cardigan.

I led her to one of the free tables, ran through the rules, then left her to peruse the menu. When I returned a few minutes later to take her order, I found Cloud and Ruby both curled up on her knee and several cats round her feet.

'I don't have anything on me,' she said, catching my surprised expression. 'My mother calls me a cat whisperer. Cats have always been drawn to me.'

'You have cats of your own?' I asked.

'Sadly, not anymore. My mother has dementia and I needed to move back in with her as her carer, but she has ailurophobia so my fur babies needed rehoming. It was heart breaking but they all went to wonderful homes.'

'I'm sorry to hear about that and about your mum.'

'Thank you.' She gave me a gentle smile. 'I'll go for passionfruit cake and a large latte, please.'

'Coming right up.'

When I delivered her order a little later, she was still surrounded by cats. I'd never seen anything like it. Her mum was right about her being a cat whisperer.

'My name's Shelley, by the way,' she said. 'You're Tabby, the owner? I saw your picture in the paper. I'm so sorry about what happened to this place. People can be so wicked. Better to surround yourself with cats.'

'It was pretty awful. I'm just hoping it doesn't happen again.'

'It's spectacularly unfair for anyone to make assumptions about this place. One look at what you've done here and at these beautiful cats and kittens and it's obvious you love them and they're happy and healthy.'

'Thank you. I really appreciate that.'

We'd had loads of compliments but this one felt extra special coming from someone who so clearly had an affinity with felines. What a shame about her mum and needing to rehome the cats. It had been hard enough sending Marmalade to live with my parents. I couldn't imagine what it must be like parting with an entire fur family, especially in circumstances like hers.

When Shelley's time was up, she came over to the till without being asked. I'd been surprised at how many customers did that as I'd anticipated needing to give most of them a nudge.

'Thank you for creating this place,' she said as she settled her bill. 'You're so lucky. It would be my dream job to run a cat café.'

'Would it?'

'Oh, yes. I've thought about it so often over the years, but I don't have vision like you. I could never have created something like this. It's spectacular.'

'Did you look upstairs?'

'No. I've made myself resist it. All being well, I'll be back next Wednesday and I'll sit upstairs then, but I'll be thinking about it in the meantime. Lovely to meet you, Tabby.'

'And you. Look forward to seeing you again next week.'

Several of the cats followed her to the door and I laughed as she told them they needed to stay here but she'd see them again next Wednesday. Obediently, they stayed in the café but watched her through the glass. What a fascinating character.

A couple of women were the last to leave and, by the strong resemblance, I guessed they were probably sisters.

'Have you enjoyed your visit?' I asked, smiling at them both.

'We've loved it,' the older one said. 'My sister's glad I persuaded her to come, aren't you, Lou?'

The way she said it and the nudge she gave Lou suggested there was a story behind it.

'Lou didn't think it would be safe,' the woman said, rolling her eyes. 'But now she knows everything's fine. So she has a question to ask you.'

'Okay,' I said, having no idea where this was going.

Lou scowled at her sister then turned to me with an apologetic smile. 'My daughter was meant to be starting a job here, but I was a little concerned after the window got smashed—'

'By a little concerned, she means full-on hysterical meltdown.'

'Thank you, Hannah, helpful as always,' Lou said sarcastically. 'Anyway, I had my moment and Sienna hasn't forgiven me for it. With hindsight, I realise I may have overreacted. You've probably already backfilled her role but if another vacancy does come up, I'd be grateful if you'd consider Sienna for it.'

The looks between them now made complete sense. Hannah had

obviously been on her niece's side and had dragged Lou down to see for herself that there was no danger working here.

'You have a lovely daughter and, as it happens, I've been too busy to organise a replacement. Sienna would be very welcome back, starting this weekend.'

'That's wonderful,' Lou said. 'She might start speaking to me again now. Thank you.'

'Take my number,' I said, handing her a business card, 'and let me know when you've spoken to Sienna as I'll ring her then to confirm the hours.'

They both thanked me profusely and left. That had been unexpected, but very welcome, especially as it had completely slipped my mind at the weekend to ask the others if they had any friends who they'd recommend.

34

Across our first week, we received lots of lovely comments about the café on our social media accounts. So many customers tagged us into the cat photos they'd taken, although I felt a little sad that I spent so much time in the kitchen and didn't get to see all the cuteness and antics myself. The objectors on social media appeared to have lost interest. I doubted it would stay that way, but the break from negativity was welcome.

I'd released January's bookings online and there were already several slots filled, which I hadn't expected this far ahead. Tom thought that some of the customers might be celebrating their birthdays that month and were keen to visit as a birthday treat. I added a post to social media suggesting that coffee, cake and cats was the perfect way to spend a birthday, which generated lots of positive responses from customers naming their birthday month and saying they'd definitely be booking in for then.

I'd taken the opportunity to capitalise on Christmas too, creating a series of graphics suggesting that a visit to the cat café would be a purrfect break from Christmas shopping, for pre-Christmas celebrations with friends or family, or as a gift. I also showcased some of the stock for sale as fabulous Christmas gifts. The posts received a really positive response so I took some of the photos of the cats and spruced them up in a graphics package with Christmassy borders and Christmas hats or reindeer antlers to create a series of countdown to Christmas images.

I still hadn't done anything about furnishing the flat, but Matt and his team had done an amazing job fitting the sink and cupboards in the cat lounge and it had already made such a difference having the storage space and access to water in there. As long as the cats were happy, I was happy.

Saturday arrived and our one-week anniversary. It felt like the cat café had been open so much longer, although that was probably down to the whopping seven months of preparation and years before that thinking about it.

Even though Tom insisted he could help all day, and his assistance in the kitchen was greatly appreciated, I was very aware that he was probably still playing catch-up from taking a week off. When everyone had taken their afternoon break, he finally relented to my nagging and went upstairs to do some work.

I recognised two of the final customers of the day as staff from Castle Jewellery. Both women looked to be in their late twenties, one with dark hair in a fishtail plait and the other with blonde hair in the sort of elaborate styled up-do that I'd seen on TikTok but had no patience to try to recreate myself. They were seated in Cat Castle and kept looking over towards the kitchen. Thinking they might be trying to catch my attention, I went out to see them.

'Hi, did you want something?' I asked, smiling.

The blonde-haired one flushed pink and lowered her eyes, but the brunette smiled back at me. 'We work in Castle Jewellery and were there when you handed out some biscuits. They were awesome, by the way.'

'Thank you.'

'There was a guy with you and we were wondering if he's your boyfriend.'

'Tom? No. He's a friend. A very good friend.' I wasn't sure why I felt the need to add that last part.

'Does he work here?' she asked. 'We've been looking but we can't see him.'

That explained the looks towards the kitchen.

'He's been helping out. Why?' As if I couldn't guess.

'Brodie fancies him,' she said.

'Trish!' the blonde cried.

'Well, you do. You've never shut up about him.' Trish looked at me. 'Is he seeing anyone?'

'He's single.'

Brodie looked up, her eyes sparkling. 'Do you think...?' Her smile slipped and she lowered her eyes once more, presumably losing her confidence.

'Stop doubting yourself,' Trish said, squeezing Brodie's arm. 'You're gorgeous. Unless he's gay?' She looked at me questioningly.

Trish was right – Brodie really was a beautiful woman and her vulnerability was endearing. I'd wanted to repay Tom for his kindness by giving him some lessons in how to talk to women on a date, and sitting in my café right now was the perfect opportunity to put those lessons into practice.

'He's not gay,' I said. 'I'm happy to have a word with him. But please don't get your hopes up. If he's not interested, I promise it won't be any reflection on you. He's had a few bad dating experiences and it's kind of put him off.'

'Haven't we all?' Brodie said, shrugging sadly. 'Should I give you my number, just in case?'

'Yeah, that's probably the best bet. And, again, don't read anything into it if he doesn't get in touch immediately. He's got a lot of work on at the moment.'

'That's okay. I'd already convinced myself it would be a no-go because I thought you two were together.'

I thought you two were together. The words echoed round my mind as she scribbled her number down on a serviette. I picked it up and she thanked me for my help, and crossed her fingers.

Returning to the kitchen, I placed her number safely in my pocket. I should feel excited about having a potential date lined up for Tom and an offer to give him some tips so he didn't mess it up, but I didn't. I felt distinctly uncomfortable. I tried to picture Tom and Brodie together but, like a montage from the movies, I pictured Tom and me instead. Images swirled through my mind of him hugging me in my parents' garden after Leon dumped me, him popping round the following day with flowers from Mum and making me breakfast, flicking water and bubbles at me the day they brought the TV round, washing my hair in the bath, laughing as he tried to get to grips with using dry shampoo the day Laura the reporter came round, our food fight last Friday and so many more warm laughter-filled moments.

I glanced across at Trish and Brodie laughing together and butterflies stirred in my stomach. Why was I being weird about this? Tom was single, she was single, she was attractive and lovely and I just wanted Tom to be happy. Why was I making this anything to do with me?

* * *

Back in the flat after work, Tom chewed on his lip thoughtfully. 'Nope. Can't picture her. I only remember speaking to the owner.'

'I think she might have been serving someone when we stopped by.'

He looked at the number on the serviette. 'I'm not sure it's a good idea. You know my track record. I'll start talking about maths problems or taxation changes and she'll do a runner.'

'Is that the only thing that's stopping you ringing her?'

'Well, that and the fact that I didn't notice her in the jewellers so it's like going on a blind date and I swore I'd never do one of those after last time.'

I narrowed my eyes at him. 'I don't remember you telling me about a blind date when you were running through your dating disasters.'

'Urgh, don't! Someone on my accounting course set me up with a friend of hers and, to this day, I have no idea what possessed her to think we'd be a good match. We had nothing in common and I mean nothing. I know they say opposites attract but this wasn't one of those occasions. We struggled our way through forty minutes of awkward silence, punctuated with the occasional question from me in the hope of finding some common ground, before I suggested we call it a night. I've never seen anyone look so relieved.'

I shook my head. 'I can't believe how many bad dates you've been on.

I can't vouch for whether Brodie's a good match because I don't actually know her, but she seemed sweet and she's very pretty.'

'I dunno. I'm bound to mess it up.'

'What if you had a practice date first? What if we go out for a meal and you pretend you don't know me—'

'But I do know you.'

'Yes, but for the purposes of the practice date, you pretend you don't and you ask some getting-to-know-you questions like you would with a stranger. We can take it from there.' I laughed. 'You even get to walk me home at the end of the night.' I didn't add, *and you get to come in for coffee*, because that would be moving into euphemism territory and I'd never had a conversation like that with Tom before. It would be weird.

He looked down at the serviette. 'Go on, then. If you say she's okay, I'll take your word for it and yes, please, to a practice date with you, but no climbing out of the window or drinking so much that you puke all over me.'

I smiled at him. 'It's a date.' And for some reason, my heart leapt at that idea and I was back in the kitchen after the food fight, that moment of chemistry fizzing between us. It wasn't meant to be an actual date, but my body was reacting as though it was. This was new territory.

'So, are you going to ring Brodie now?' I asked.

'Why? You've only just given me her number.'

I rolled my eyes at him. 'You do realise that women don't appreciate games? She knows you have her number and, if you don't get in touch, she'll assume you're not interested.'

He picked up his phone, grimacing. 'Do I have to call her? I might make a mess of it before we even go on our date. Can I text instead?'

'If you must but let me approve the text before you send it.'

He tapped something in and showed it to me.

TO BRODIE

Hi, it's Tom. Tabby gave me your number. Would you be interested in going out for a drink next week? I'm free on Wednesday or Friday

'Yeah, that's good to go,' I said.

Brodie replied immediately to say that she had a family thing on Wednesday so Friday would be best. They exchanged a couple of brief messages confirming a time and place.

'Your wish is my command,' he said, switching his phone to silent and putting it face down on the coffee table. 'Date organised.'

'It's not my wish if you really don't want to do this,' I said, concerned that he wasn't particularly enthusiastic at securing the date.

'No, it's fine. Would you judge me if I said I'm looking forward to the practice date more than the actual date?'

'You're only saying that because you know it'll go well.'

'I'm only saying it because it's with you.'

His voice was so soft and he held my gaze for a moment. That thing was back again, a tension hanging in the air. My heart raced and I felt my palms sweating. Why did this keep happening? This was Tom-cat. He was attractive, but I wasn't attracted to him. Was I?

The ping of the oven broke the moment and Tom headed into the kitchen to take our meal out of the oven.

'It's just Tom,' I said to Babushka who was sprawled across my lap.

I could hear her respond in her husky Eastern European accent. *Just Tom? But of course. You keep telling yourself that.*

35

The following day was the last Sunday of November, which usually meant Sunday lunch at Mum and Dad's, but my family had unanimously agreed to shift it to an evening so I could still attend after the café closed for the day. I was so excited about seeing Marmalade in his new home. It was hard to believe that it would be a fortnight tomorrow since they'd collected him. So much had happened during that time.

Marmalade ran to the door to greet me, just like he used to with Leon, which made me a little tearful. He sat purring on my knee for about twenty minutes but then he jumped down and curled up on Mum's knee and I heard his Bagpuss voice in my head – *I love you and forgive you, but this is my home now so don't even think about reclaiming me.*

I wondered whether I should drop Leon a quick email to let him know that my parents had Marmalade, but soon dismissed the idea. He'd shown little interest in Marmalade's wellbeing when I'd been worried about him at the start of the month and I didn't want him to think that I was pining for him and using Marmalade to stay in contact. Leon was well in my past now. I'd barely given him a second thought since Tom moved in. It confirmed to me that I hadn't so much been missing him but missing human company. I certainly didn't love him anymore. Had that happened because he'd dumped me or was it a case of absence not making the heart grow fonder?

The roast dinner was courtesy of Dad and Rylan this time and, as always, it was delicious and eaten in great company.

Rylan and Macey headed back home straight after we'd eaten. Baby Walsh was due three weeks tomorrow and Macey was really struggling with back pain.

'I nearly brought my enormous pregnancy pillow with me,' she said as I hugged her goodbye. 'But I didn't want to subject you all to the sight of me splatted out on the rug. I save that joy for Rylan.'

'You look so sweet curled up with it,' Rylan said, looking at her with an expression full of love.

'You weren't saying that at three this morning when you were teetering on the edge of the bed because my pillow and me were taking all the space.'

Tom and I only stayed for another half an hour, allowing me time to relax back at the flat before bedtime, saving some spoons for Tom's practice date tomorrow.

* * *

Rummaging through my suitcases for something to wear the following evening, nervous butterflies stirred in my stomach.

'It's not a real date,' I told Effie, who'd decided to clamber into my suitcase and settle onto one of my potential outfit choices. 'I shouldn't be nervous. It's just Tom. And I'm doing this so he can have a successful date with someone else so I *definitely* shouldn't be nervous.'

But I was.

'You know why I'm nervous?' Effie didn't look like she cared, but I was going to give her my theory anyway. 'It's because I think I might have set myself up as some sort of dating guru when the truth is I haven't a clue what I'm doing. My dating track record pre-Leon is nearly as bad as Tom's.'

Gentle snores came from Effie. 'Am I boring you, Effie? This doesn't bode well!'

'I've made a wardrobe bodge,' I said, striding into the lounge a little later and plonking myself down on the sofa to pull on my favourite high-heeled electric-blue boots over my black leggings. 'Most things need ironing and I haven't got an iron or a board so I've had to go casual.'

I'd pulled on a black cami top under a cream slouch sweater with a wide neck which revealed one shoulder, and I'd added a large pendant necklace. Boots on, I looked up to see Tom smiling at me.

'Doesn't look like a bodge to me,' he said. 'You look amazing! Will I pass?'

'Smart jeans, shirt, clean shoes.' I smiled back, trying to ignore the leap of my heart. 'Big ticks all round. Are you ready?'

'Let's do it!'

I pulled on a smart pink wool coat instead of my everyday padded winter one and noticed that Tom had also gone smart with his coat choice.

'I'm not going to pretend to be Brodie,' I said as we wandered down towards Le Bistro – a cosy restaurant between Castle Street and the seafront. 'I don't know her so I'm going to be me, but I might throw in a few curveballs here and there to keep you on your toes and check you're really listening.'

'Will there be a quiz at the end?' he asked.

'There might be. So what do you think would work well on a date?'

Tom laughed. 'Clearly I haven't a clue or we wouldn't be doing this right now.'

'Fair point. Bear in mind that I'm no expert, but from a female perspective, I'd want my date to have made an effort to look and smell nice, which you have done. If I'm meeting them somewhere, I'd want them to be on time or, more ideally, a bit early, so I'm not on my own waiting. But the biggest, most important thing is the conversation. The whole point of a first date is to get to know each other and find out if you like each other enough to go on a second date. The only way to do that is to ask your date questions.'

'And that's where I fall down. I'm one extreme or the other. I either feel like I'm interrogating them or they ask me one question and I go off on a billion tangents.'

'The questions are just a lead-in to a conversation so it's vital you're listening to your date's answer instead of thinking about what your next – potentially unrelated – question is going to be. Listen to her, ask some additional questions, but also throw in some things about you which relate to what she tells you.'

'Sounds easy enough, until there's an awkward silence and I can't think of any more questions.'

'Then you're not entirely to blame. Your date needs to do some of the legwork too. So, what topics do you think you could talk about?'

'Her job.'

'And...?'

'And I have nothing else.' Tom ran his hands through his hair. 'And therein lies my problem.'

I wasn't convinced it was, but previous bad experiences had clearly made him think that way.

'I think Brodie has a local accent,' I prompted.

'Oh! I could ask her if she's originally from Whitsborough Bay.'

'Brilliant! And what else could lead on from that?'

'Whereabouts she lives, which school she went to, whether she went to college...'

'And the fact that you live in Whitsborough Bay...?'

'I can ask which pubs she likes going to and favourite restaurants. That's a great start.'

We'd reached Le Bistro, so we went inside and settled into our seats in a candlelit corner. It had been a while since I'd dined here and I'd forgotten how romantic it was.

'We've just settled down for our very first date,' I said when our drinks order arrived. 'Over to you...'

If it had been a real date, it would have been pretty much perfect – great company, romantic restaurant and loads of laughter. Granted, some of the laughter was when Tom lost it and looked like a deer in the headlights, but I was generally impressed with some of the thoughtful questions and his ability to listen.

It was great fun coming up with surprising answers like my job as a goat herder, that I was the youngest of seventeen siblings whose names all began with the letters X or Z, and that my ambition was to base jump off the Statue of Liberty.

Tom looked so alluring in the candlelight that I came close to reaching out to take his hand on several occasions, and had to keep reminding myself that this wasn't a real date. He'd be on a real one with Brodie on Friday night, and I wasn't sure how I felt about that.

'I've had a great time tonight,' he said as we set off slowly up the hill. 'Thanks for all the tips.'

'I hope they help on Friday night.'

'If I don't go blank and resort to old habits.'

'If you go blank, you go blank. It's two-way, like I said. It's not up to you to do all the work. And if it doesn't go well, you don't have to stay out late. Most of all, relax and enjoy it.'

'I'll try to.'

We continued in companionable silence for a while.

'Can I ask you a question?' Tom said, pausing as we reached the end of Castle Street and turning to face me. 'Why are you doing this?'

'Because I don't know what I'd have done without you this past fortnight. Saying thank you isn't nearly enough. You've done so much for me and I wanted to do something for you.'

'But why specifically this? Why dating?'

'Because you looked so sad when you talked about wanting what Rylan and Macey have. You *should* have that. You're the best of the best, Tom-cat, and it's criminal that none of those other women have stuck around long enough to find that out.' I could hear the emotion in my voice and feel it in my throat. 'I just want you to be happy.'

'And you think Brodie will make me happy?'

The word 'no' instantly sprung to mind and I wasn't sure why.

'Impossible to say,' I said, trying to sound positive. 'I don't know her so I can't comment on whether she's your ideal woman or not.'

A blast of cold air made me shiver. 'I'm freezing. Can we continue this inside over a cup of tea?'

Tom nodded and we returned to the flat, our pace quicker than before. Several cats greeted us at the door, flooding my heart with warmth, even if my body was feeling the cold. Tom volunteered to make the drinks while I took the cats into the lounge for some attention.

'We've talked about how to act on a date,' Tom said, placing two mugs of tea on the coffee table a little later, 'but we haven't actually talked about my ideal woman.'

Pebbles and Marmite were draped across my lap and Heathcliff was on the sofa bed beside me. Tom picked him up and placed him on his knee instead. Heathcliff stretched out, padded for a bit, then settled.

'That's probably because I've made an assumption about who I think your ideal woman is.'

He raised his eyebrows in a clear expression of curiosity. 'This should be good. Enlighten me.'

'I imagine you settling down with someone who's your best friend. There'll be attraction and chemistry, of course, but that deep connection is what'll really work for you. She'll make you laugh and act like a little kid, but she'll be strong and level-headed during the difficult times. She'll find your passion for numbers and spreadsheets endearing and she'll understand that the reason you love a balance sheet is not just because of your job, but because it makes sense to you when there are so many things in this world that don't. She'll be fiercely loyal to her family and friends, just like you are, and will fully understand and accept that a family is more than blood ties. And she'll love you for being you and not try to change you because you're perfect as you are.'

My voice broke and tears rushed to my eyes. I cleared my throat and blinked them back. 'Ooh! Getting all emosh there. Think I might have had too much wine with the meal.'

Tom didn't say a word – just stared at me. I couldn't read his expression so I flippantly added, 'But I may be way off the mark.'

He shook his head ever so slowly and slightly. 'You nailed it,' he said, his voice low and husky.

The only light in the lounge was from the uplighter I'd borrowed from Tom and, despite being so sparsely furnished, the room suddenly felt warm and cosy. I imagined him shuffling closer to me, his eyes fixed on mine, his hand reaching out to touch my cheek, sink into my hair, draw me into a kiss, and my breath caught in my throat.

Don't go out with Brodie.

The words were poised on my lips, but I couldn't say them because that sentence wasn't complete. It ended with *go out with me instead*, which confused, scared and thrilled me. But the fear was the strongest. *This is Tom. He's your friend. Don't ruin it.*

'Erm, I might take my tea up to bed,' I said. 'Bit tired. Do you mind?'

'No, you get some rest. Thanks again. Tonight was great.'

He held my gaze and I wished I knew what he was thinking. The same as me? It was too scary to come straight out and ask him.

'You're welcome,' I said.

I hoped I didn't look like I was fleeing but I needed some space before I did anything stupid. Where was my head, thinking about kissing him when I'd spent the evening preparing him to date someone else? It was the wine. I'd only had a couple of glasses but I didn't drink very often so it had obviously gone to my head and scrambled my thoughts. Normal service would be resumed by the morning.

36

I barely saw Tom the following day – snowed under with work as the year end inched ever closer. It was probably just as well as I hadn't yet made sense of my mixed feelings about his date with Brodie.

On Wednesday, I was struck by a green-level fibro flare-up, but I didn't tell Tom. I went downstairs to make scones, sitting as much as possible. I still didn't have a people-based solution in place for waking up on a café day with a fibro flare-up strong enough to keep me from working, but I did have a freezer full of scones, cakes and tray bakes. Amelia knew from her interview that she might get a text from me on a morning asking her to step up as supervisor for the day and we'd spoken about that in more detail last week after she'd had a couple of days to settle in. When Tom moved out again, as he'd surely have to at some point, I'd need to get a set of keys cut for her in case I had a flare-up so bad that I couldn't make it downstairs to let her in. For now, it wasn't necessary.

'Ooh, are you okay?' Amelia asked when she arrived for work.

'I've got a mild flare-up today,' I said, locking the door behind her.

'Oh, no! Do you need me to run things?'

'I'll manage the kitchen but I need you to supervise the team today.'

'No problem. We've got this.'

I gave her a grateful smile before returning to the kitchen. We had some bookings but plenty of space for walk-ins. Across the day, there were more of those than I'd expected, but nothing the team couldn't handle. We'd all quickly settled into our stride with how to work most efficiently.

By mid-afternoon, I was having a rest on a stool with a glass of water, thinking about the festive cakes and biscuits I'd add to the menu in December. It had started raining and Smudge was trying to dab the droplets trickling down the front bay window, looking bewildered when he couldn't do anything to stop them. Everything felt so calm and right with the world when I watched cats playing. But a raised voice interrupted the moment.

'What do you mean, my hour's up?' the woman shouted at Fay, drawing glances from the tables around her. I recognised her as one of our walk-ins – maybe in her late fifties with an elderly woman accompanying her, possibly her mother.

My heart sank for Fay, but we'd gone through this scenario during our training and I was confident she'd be calmly reminding the customer that she'd explained how the café worked when she arrived and the customer had confirmed that she understood and accepted that.

'But it's raining.' The woman gestured towards the window. 'You'd kick us out in the rain?'

The older woman with her looked decidedly uncomfortable and rose, pulling on her coat.

Fay had her back to me so I couldn't see her face or hear her words, but it was clear that whatever she was saying wasn't having any impact.

'It's not like you need the tables,' the angry customer cried. 'Bloody jobsworth. We won't be coming back and I'll tell all my friends to avoid this dump.'

My stomach sank. I hated confrontation, I hated unnecessary and untrue criticism, and I hated how some people seemed to think it was acceptable to shout at anyone working in retail as though they were some sort of inferior beings who needed putting in their place. I slid off my stool ready to rescue Fay, but Amelia, who'd been taking an order from another table, ripped it off her pad, slid it through the counter to me and walked over to the customer.

She also had her back to me so I couldn't hear what she said either but, whatever it was, it worked. The customer stood up and pulled her coat on as Fay grabbed the portable card reader to take payment, rolling her eyes at me in the process.

Amelia and Fay joined me in the kitchen when the customer had gone and the friendly chatter in the café had resumed once more.

'Are you two both okay?' I asked.

'Amelia was amazing,' Fay said. 'Thank you.'

'I hope you don't mind, Tabby, but I told her I was the manager,' Amelia said. 'In my experience, customers like that will only listen if they think they're speaking to the top person. I didn't say anything Fay hadn't already – reiterating that she'd already been told how things work, that the cat café is an experience rather than a regular café and therefore has time slots, and that she'd already been permitted to stay for an extra fifteen minutes for free.'

'It was telling her she was more than welcome to stay but they'd both be charged for another hour that did it,' Fay said.

'We were both really polite,' Amelia said.

'I'm sure you were. Thank you. Hopefully shouty customers will be rare.'

Our next walk-in customer was the other extreme – Shelley, the cat whisperer, arriving for the last sitting of the day. She decided to try out Feline Forest this time. Fay took her order up to her, but I was intrigued to speak to her again, so I nipped upstairs to say 'hello' when I saw on our internal CCTV that she'd finished her cake.

'I see you've worked your magic again,' I said, smiling at the cats gathered around her.

'They're all so beautiful,' she said. 'I thought I wasn't going to make it today. Mother had a fall and I had to take her to hospital.'

'Oh, no! Is she all right?'

'Badly bruised but, thankfully, nothing broken. They want to keep her in overnight for monitoring. Her blood pressure is very low. Anyway, how's it going here?'

'Good. The cats seem to be really happy with it. I was curious about your cats. How many did you have?'

'Over my lifetime, dozens, but only four at the time I needed to move in with Mother. Funnily enough, I wasn't particularly into cats when I was younger.'

'What changed?'

Shelley indicated that I should pull out a chair, so I gratefully sat down opposite her.

She looked around, presumably to check whether anyone was in earshot, and leaned a bit closer. 'I discovered that my husband was having an affair with my sister.'

I winced. 'Sorry to hear that.'

'It was a difficult time. Classic cliché of catching them together in our bed so I lost my home, my sister and my business that day because my husband and I owned a restaurant together. I moved in with a friend while I tried to get my life back together and there was this cat – a ginger moggy – which kept visiting her. She wasn't a cat person either but her neighbours told her he'd belonged to the previous owners and they'd left him behind when they moved. Isn't that dreadful? He was living in her shed and she put food out for him every day. I don't know whether it was the idea of him being cast out like I'd been, but I started spending time in the shed playing with him and, oh, my goodness, that little angel stole my heart. I called him Tiger and, when I moved into my own place, I took him with me. The unconditional love that little creature gave me helped rebuild my shattered heart.'

I'd been hanging on every word and felt quite emotional when she finished. 'Cats are such a gift,' I said.

'They certainly are. Better than husbands any day.'

Some customers nearby were getting ready to leave, so I excused myself to go downstairs, ready to take their payment.

I thought about what Shelley had said while I loaded the dishwasher. What a horrible thing for her husband and sister to do to her. I had so many questions. Was she still in touch with the sister? Were the sister and husband still together? Had she sworn off men after that? I didn't have the energy to traipse back upstairs. Maybe I'd have an opportunity to find out more about her next time she visited.

It was still raining when the last customers of the day left. I was on my stool cashing up while the team mopped the floor when there was a knock at the window. I looked up and saw Sarah from Seaside Blooms waving at me.

'I'll let her in,' Amelia said, going to the door.

'Ooh, it's a bit soggy out there,' Sarah said, joining me in the kitchen.

'Do you want a drink?'

'No, I won't keep you. I just wanted to make sure someone has mentioned the Christmas lights switch-on on Saturday.'

I was momentarily confused by her question as the lights switch-on had happened for decades and everyone knew about it. Then I remembered that one of the business owners had said something about there being an alternative version.

'I've a vague recollection of someone mentioning something special. Is it in Castle Park?'

'That's it! I'm so glad I stopped by if you don't know the full details. So, the big public switch-on is outside the shopping centre at half six, which triggers the rest of the lights coming on around town. The Castle Street traders gather for a private do round the tree in Castle Park. Tara supplies hot drinks, Carly makes cupcakes, and Charlee makes chocolates and it's really lovely. Everyone mingles and catches up from about six and there's a pub crawl afterwards.'

'Sounds lovely.'

'You'll come?'

'Yes. I was going to wander up to the main tree, but this sounds much better.'

'It is. It's my favourite event of the year. You can invite the rest of your staff. Partners and kids are welcome, although the space isn't huge as you know, so it usually ends up being mainly the business owners, with their staff going to the big tree.'

'Thanks for letting me know. I'll see if Tom fancies joining me.'

'And you'll join the pub crawl too?'

'If my fibromyalgia lets me. It'll be nearly the end of the working week for me so I might not have enough spoons left.' When I'd visited the various traders to thank them individually for their help in the big clear-up, Sarah had been keen to learn more about fibromyalgia so I'd explained the spoon theory to her.

'Completely understand,' she said. 'Maybe we can go out for a drink in the New Year if you can't make it on the crawl. Right, best get back to finish up. See you on Saturday.'

I loved the idea of a smaller, private lights switch-on. The council workers had been out last week putting up the Christmas lights in preparation. The ones in Castle Street each year were simple but beautiful – white ones strung in a zigzag from one side to the other all the way down the street. Looking round the café, I cursed myself for being so late with my Christmas decorations. My stubbornness to showcase the café without Christmas meant it wasn't going to be decorated in time for the switch-on. I had no spoons available to do it tonight and the next two nights were out because I'd need Tom's help. He had five-a-side football tomorrow night and his date with Brodie on Friday. Mind you, Saturday would only be 2 December, so it wasn't as if I'd missed most of December. I'd definitely introduce Christmas on Monday or Tuesday next week, which would still give three weeks of festive feels in the café before the big day. With festive treats on the menu then, it wouldn't be too late to embrace Christmas at the cat café.

* * *

Tom was in the dining room, talking to a client on the phone when I returned to the flat with the cats. He gave me a smile to acknowledge my return and I waved.

Sybil, Freyja, Rubix and Ruby had all beaten me upstairs and were on the bed. I chatted to them while I stripped off my work clothes and slipped into some soft loungewear.

Fatigue had caught up with me so I sank down onto the bed with the cats and flicked the television on, losing myself in a teatime quiz show. Pebbles jumped onto the bed and clambered onto my shoulder. It might have hurt if I'd been sitting upright but, as I was slouched against the pillow, she was part draped over the pillow and part over me.

'You're so beautiful and affectionate,' I said, stroking her as she tucked in against my neck. 'I love you so much.'

'You two look very cute together.'

I hadn't heard Tom coming upstairs. 'She's the love of my life,' I said, smiling at him. 'Well, they all are.' I turned the TV volume down. 'How's your day been?'

Tom sat on the end of the bed. 'Busy. I've got a few more hours to do tonight. How was yours?'

'Green day, so Amelia stepped up.'

'Why didn't you say? I could have helped.'

'That's why I didn't say. You've just said you have a few more hours of work to do tonight. Imagine how many you'd have to do if you'd helped in the café. It was fine. I stayed in the kitchen on a stool most of the day and Amelia was brilliant. She kept it all running and sorted out a snotty customer.'

I told Tom about the customer and also about Shelley's visit.

'Oh, and Sarah popped in at the end of the day. You know it's the Christmas lights switch-on on Saturday? There's a do for the Castle Street businesses in Castle Park and a pub crawl. I know you've got loads of work on, but I wondered if you'd like to take a break and come with me.'

He sighed. 'I would have, but Brodie texted earlier. She asked if we could swap Friday to Saturday night. I'm going to the switch-on with her.'

My body tensed and I tried to sound casual, but my voice sounded a little high to me. 'Oh! That's fine. Don't worry about it.'

'Sorry.' He grimaced. 'I could tell her I'll meet her later and come to the Castle Park thing with you.'

'No! You can't change your plans for me. I'll go on my own. It's not like I don't know anyone. I've already told Sarah I probably won't have enough spoons for the pub crawl afterwards.'

'I'm sorry,' he repeated. 'If I'd known...'

'Don't be sorry. It's all good.'

But it didn't feel good at all. Last night's feeling hadn't gone away today. I didn't want Tom to go on a date with Brodie. I wanted him to go on one with me. A real one.

37

There was a definite buzz about Christmas in the cat café on Saturday. I tuned in and out of conversations about the lights switch-on tonight, progress with Christmas shopping and plans for the big day. I still didn't have anything confirmed with Mum and Dad and had better speak to them next week to sort something out.

As dusk fell, I stood by the window in Cat Castle and looked up and down the street, absorbing how it looked with just the Victorian lamps lit. It was pretty now, but it would look stunning this evening once the Christmas lights came on.

I'd barely seen Tom this week other than having a quick bite together before he disappeared into the dining room to work. I felt for him without a proper desk and had offered him a table and chair from the café, but he swore that the height was perfect for working from the garden table and the chair was actually comfortable. I didn't want to keep challenging him on that as I feared he might turn around and say I was right and, actually, he'd be better off back at his apartment. I really couldn't bear the thought of him leaving. Even though we couldn't spend our evenings together at the moment, I liked that he was in the flat with me.

'Any last-minute tips?' Tom asked, pulling on his coat, ready to go and meet Brodie.

'Just be you.'

'I thought we'd established that was where I went wrong before.'

'It wasn't you. It was them.'

'Do you think you'll manage the pub crawl?' he asked.

'We'll see. I'm aiming to be there for quarter past six so I don't have much standing around beforehand. If there's not too much standing afterwards, I might manage one drink.'

'Okay. Well, have a good time, although I'll probably be back before you are.'

'You won't be. Enjoy yourself.'

Tom left and I sank down onto the sofa bed with a sigh, feeling drained from sounding so positive when, inside, my feelings were torn. For Tom's sake, I wanted the date to go well to give him a much-needed confidence boost. For my sake, I hoped it wouldn't go *that* well. If only I could trade places with Brodie.

* * *

'I'll see you all in a bit,' I said a little later, blowing kisses to the cats. I'd worn so many layers, I had to breathe in to pull the zip up on my coat, but I didn't want to get cold as that didn't help my fibromyalgia. Better to go out looking like the Michelin Man than risk the cold seeping into my bones.

As soon as I stepped out onto the cobbles, I could hear the music playing outside the shopping centre and the excitement of a large crowd. The local radio station, Bay Radio, hosted the event and ensured a big build-up to the lights being switched on. This year's 'celebrity' guest was someone who'd appeared on one episode of a TV dating show a couple of years ago and was still dining out on their fifteen minutes of fame. The lights would illuminate the enormous Christmas tree outside the shopping centre first, then ripple down the town in sections.

I could see quite a crowd gathered round the smaller Christmas tree in Castle Park. Pulling on my gloves, I strolled down the cobbles to join them, feeling a little nervous at being the newbie, despite the warm welcome I'd already received.

'Tabby!' Jemma from Bear With Me spotted me and waved me over. 'Come and get a hot drink and one of Carly's amazing cakes.'

She led me over to a table where Tara was handing out drinks and there were boxes of Christmas-themed cupcakes. I removed my gloves and took a bite of one of the cakes, widening my eyes appreciatively in Carly's direction as I ate.

'Oh, my God! They're delicious, Carly!' I said, when I'd swallowed my first couple of mouthfuls.

Sarah joined us. 'Glad you could make it, Tabby.'

'Thanks for giving me the details. I asked Tom, but he had plans already.'

'Yeah, hot date with Brodie, eh?'

'How do you know that?'

'Because they're over there.'

I followed her eyeline and my stomach did a somersault as I clocked Tom and Brodie at the other side of the tree. She was holding her phone out in front of them, head close to his as she took a selfie. She put her arm round his waist and twisted him round so that she could do the same but with the tree in the background this time.

'Are you okay, Tabby?' Carly asked.

'Yeah, sorry. Just surprised to see Tom here. I assumed they were going to the main switch-on.'

'They did,' Sarah said, 'but Brodie's ex-boyfriend was there, so they came here instead.'

A loud cheer from the direction of the shopping centre told us that the switch had been flicked. The chatter muted as heads turned towards Castle Street. Section by section, the lights illuminated. At our end of the street was a sign with the words 'Welcome to Castle Street'. Once the street lights were all lit, the sign followed, letters first and then the stars on it.

'Look at the tree now,' Sarah whispered.

The white star at the top of the Christmas tree lit up followed by white, then red, then green lights draped round the branches. The crowd burst into song and I joined them singing 'We Wish You a Merry Christmas'.

It was such a lovely, festive moment which made me feel all warm and fuzzy inside. But then I spotted Tom and Brodie again. He had his arm round her shoulders and they were laughing and it was absolutely right that he was enjoying his date and it was clearly going well, but it gave me a chill inside because, at that moment, I knew without a shadow of a doubt that my feelings had changed towards Tom. I wanted to be the one who he had his arm round, who he was laughing with, who he'd share a kiss with later, and I wanted that for more than just one date.

The song came to an end and everyone clapped and cheered. Tom glanced in my direction and raised his hand in a wave. I smiled and nodded at him. I wanted so badly for him to be happy and, if Brodie was right for him, I wished them well. But I couldn't stick around and watch. It was a little too raw for now.

'Are you coming for a drink?' Sarah asked.

'I'm beat. I'm so sorry. But we'll definitely do something in the New Year.'

'Okay. Take care of you.'

'Thank you. Is there anything I can do to help clear up?'

'You get home. It's all in hand. See you soon.'

I was so relieved she'd said no because that meant I could get away before Tom reached me. I didn't want him to see the tears in my eyes.

* * *

11 p.m. came and went, quarter past, half past, and there was still no sign of Tom. Could he have gone back to Brodie's? During our practice date, we hadn't discussed what might happen at the end of the night, although why would we? That was very personal.

It was nearly midnight when I heard his key turning in the lock. I lay rigid in the bed, listening for his footsteps on the stairs. He paused downstairs, presumably removing his coat and shoes, then continued up to my floor. Was he going to come in? The bathroom light clicked on and the buzz of the fan started, echoing round the flat. Sometime later, the light went off. I slid a little further under the duvet, my heart thumping. I didn't want him thinking I'd been waiting for him to get home.

'Tabby?' he whispered.

I stayed perfectly still.

'Are you awake?'

If he asked again, I'd answer him, but he moved away from my door and I heard his footsteps going back down the stairs.

I chewed on my lip, frowning. What difference would it make if I had waited up? He knew I was skittish in the flat without him so it wouldn't be that unusual for me to admit that I hadn't gone to sleep. As a friend, I should have been eager to hear how his date had gone. But as someone who'd just realised that they'd fallen for their best friend, I couldn't. Not yet anyway.

38

I didn't see Tom at all on Sunday. I was working and so was he and, in the evening, he and my parents took some of their major clients out for a Christmas meal. Shattered, I fell asleep before he returned.

He spent Monday working in Little Sandby with my parents. I stayed in the flat catching up on café admin and social media posts and playing with the cats but, by late afternoon, it was time to get the Christmas decorations up. I'd wanted Tom's help but I hadn't even seen him to ask for it, so I'd just need to crack on by myself.

I took the Christmas beds downstairs and swapped them with some of the regular ones. I hung cat-themed wreaths on the doors, and added decorations to the window ledges along with flame-free candles.

Knowing from previous experience that even the strongest of artificial trees had no chance of surviving with this many cats, I'd tracked down some brilliant variations which had the look of a Christmas tree without actually being a tree. They included a green scratching post with four increasingly narrow round tiers and a wall-mounted light-up tree frame with cat ledges sticking out from the trunk. The various items needed some construction and I was debating whether to start building or put up some Christmas bunting when Tom arrived back.

'What are you doing?' he asked, looking at me curiously as I stood, hands on hips, in the middle of Feline Forest.

'Putting up the Christmas decorations and trying to decide what to tackle next.'

'Do you want a hand?'

'Not if you've got work to do.'

'I've done plenty for today. Give me ten minutes.' He nodded towards the stepladder I'd got out ready. 'And no climbing up that without me.'

'Yes, sir!' I saluted him, making him laugh.

He'd changed into a fresh T-shirt when he appeared a little later. His hair was even more unruly than usual from him pulling his clothes off and on, and I longed to reach out and run my hands through it.

'Decision made?' he asked.

'Bunting.' I'd sourced some gorgeous Christmassy cat material and asked a local crafter to make me several metres of bunting in two different designs. Green material made into square pendants showed cats and kittens in jumpers and scarves posing with Christmas gifts, playing in the snow, peeking out of stockings and wearing reindeer antlers. Red material made into triangular pendants had cats wearing Christmas hats and lots of holly and mistletoe. It had been expensive but it would be used year after year so was ultimately better than buying cheaper paper bunting which I'd need to keep replacing.

'We'll start in Cat Castle,' I said. 'Can you carry the ladder down?'

I got him to hold it for me while I climbed up with the first piece.

'Are you sure you don't want me to do it?' he asked.

'I'm fine. I'm feeling good today.'

After putting up the last piece of bunting, I was a little too quick descending the ladder and lost my footing near the bottom. I wasn't in any danger of a bad fall, but Tom's speedy reactions saved me from a small tumble. He had his arm round me like one of the knights on Rylan's mural catching a princess. I was safe and he could have released me, but he didn't. Something fizzed in the air between us once more as we gazed into each other's eyes. My heart thumped and I so badly wanted him to kiss me, but this was a man who'd just been on a date with Brodie and, for all I knew, already had a second date planned.

'How was your date with Brodie, by the way?' I asked.

'Erm, yeah, it was good,' he said, letting go of me and stepping away.

'She didn't climb out the window?'

'That would have been difficult at the lights switch-on.'

I laughed. 'I mean when you went for drinks afterwards. Or at least I presume you went for drinks as you weren't back when I went to bed at eleven. Not that I was clock watching. You can stay out as long as you like, but it would have been a bit cold staying outside all that time.'

Tom's eyes crinkled with amusement as I wittered on, wishing I could stop the verbals.

'We went for a drink and she didn't do a runner or vomit on me.'

'Best date you've ever had, then,' I said.

'I wouldn't say that.' His voice was soft as he held my gaze once more and I wondered if he could possibly be meaning our practice date had been, but surely not. He'd never given me any indication that he might see me as anything other than a friend. Even those couple of moments could have been purely in my head. Just because I'd felt something, it didn't mean he had.

I led him back upstairs and decided the bunting up there could wait for now – we'd construct the scratching post Christmas tree instead. Sitting on the floor, I opened up a plastic packet containing the screws and an Allen key.

'So are you seeing her again?' I asked.

Tom unfolded the instructions. 'I don't know. Your tips worked really well –stopped me being the worst version of me – but the conversation still felt a bit stilted and there were a few awkward silences.'

He sounded disappointed so, of course, I felt guilty for pushing him into a date when he hadn't been sure.

'I got the impression Brodie was a bit shy, so could it have just been first-date nerves for her? And you've lost your confidence for dating...'

'You can't lose something you never had in the first place.' He picked up the Allen key and twiddled it back and forth in his fingers, shrugging. 'It's probably me. Maybe I'm destined to roam the earth without ever finding love.'

He said the last part in a dramatic tone so I could tell he wasn't too gutted, but he didn't completely fool me.

'There's someone out there for you just like there's someone out there for me. Or at least I hope there is. I want to believe that.' I picked up the instructions but I couldn't take anything in and laid them down again. 'So, Brodie wasn't your ideal woman?'

'She was lovely, but I imagined there'd be more of a friendship vibe, that we'd never be able to stop talking. You were right when you said that's important to me.'

'The friends thing takes time to build. Was the chemistry part there?'

'She's a good-looking lass, but there weren't any butterflies.'

'That's a shame. So how did you leave it with her?'

'She's down in London for a few days – her sister's thirtieth – and then she's got a few Christmas things when she gets back like her work party, so she'll maybe text me when she's back and see if we can fit something in.'

'That's very non-committal for someone who's meant to fancy the pants off you.'

'Which probably means she didn't think it went brilliantly either.'

'Did you kiss her goodnight?' Heat rushed to my cheeks and I couldn't believe I'd just voiced what I'd been thinking since the conversation started. That was none of my business.

That amused look was back once more. 'I walked her to the taxi rank and I think she was expecting a kiss, but she'd just told me she was going on holiday and *might* get in touch when she returned so it didn't seem the right moment for me. She obviously decided to go for it, but I'd turned my head away and she headbutted me on the nose. She couldn't get away fast enough after that. Next second, I'm dripping blood everywhere. I haven't had a nosebleed since I was a kid.'

'Oh, no! Was it bad?'

'I couldn't stop it bleeding. When I got home, I was in the bathroom for ages trying, but nothing seemed to be working. I hoped you might still be awake to give me a hand, but you were in a deep one so I lay on the lounge floor with a bag of frozen peas on my nose and hoped it would stop eventually.'

How awful did I feel now? He'd called to me and I'd ignored him because I hadn't wanted to hear glowing reports about an amazing date, but he'd really been injured and needed my help.

I picked up a random pole with no idea what I was going to do with it. I didn't know how to process the jumble of thoughts in my head – disappointment for Tom that the date hadn't been amazing blended with a sense of relief, sorrow that he'd been physically hurt, guilt that I hadn't helped and delight that the evening hadn't ended with a good-night kiss.

'This isn't getting the tree made,' Tom said, picking up the instructions and studying them for a moment. 'We need to start with that big base piece.'

In an effort to hush the conversation in my head, I took my phone out to put on some music. Seeing as we were four days into December and we were dressing the shop for Christmas, it had to be Michael Bublé's album *Christmas*.

'You did *not* just put Christmas music on,' Tom said, eyebrows shooting up as the first twinkly sounding orchestral notes filled the room.

'No! I wouldn't dream of it,' I said, my tone all innocent.

He rolled his eyes at me as Michael's velvety voice sang the first line to 'It's Beginning to Look a Lot Like Christmas'.

'How did that happen?' I cried, feigning confusion.

The Christmas music absolutely did the trick. The mood lightened and my thoughts settled as we constructed the trees and reminisced about our childhood Christmases.

'You know, I don't have a single childhood Christmas memory that doesn't include you and Nanna,' I said as I unpacked a box of white fairy lights for Feline Forest. I'd been seven when Nanna fostered nine-year-old Tom. Despite only living round the corner, she and Tom had stayed at our house on Christmas Eve so that he could wake up on Christmas morning and experience the excitement and hubbub he'd never had before. The pair of them staying over became a Christmas tradition after that.

'Do you remember Christmases from before?' I asked, as it struck me that we'd never really talked about his life before Little Sandby.

'Tracey didn't do Christmas,' he said, making his way up the ladder with the end of the lights. 'She barely knew what month it was, never mind what day.'

The first time we met Tom, Rylan and I had been curious about his parents. He'd told us then that he didn't know who his father was and had learned not to ask because it made Tracey angry. I'd asked him who Tracey was and he'd replied, 'The woman who gave birth to me, but she didn't want a baby so I'm not allowed to call her Mum.' It was a massive eye opener to a world from which I'd been completely sheltered.

'The worst Christmas ever with Tracey was also the best,' he continued. 'It didn't feel like it at the time – seeing your mother and her boyfriend start Christmas morning beating the crap out of each other and being carted off by the police for that and drug dealing isn't the festive dream – but that's when I went into care and ultimately ended up with Nanna Betsy and you lot.'

He descended the ladder and moved it ready for the final loop of the lights, but didn't climb up it.

'I'm sorry your childhood was so tough,' I said. 'No kid should have to go through what you went through.'

'No, they shouldn't, and I'm forever grateful that I was one of the lucky ones who got out without any lasting damage and found a real family. That chapter in my life is closed now.'

'If you ever do want to talk about it...'

He nodded. 'I'm good, but I appreciate the offer.'

Taking the lights from me, he clambered back up the ladder and attached them to the hooks. I didn't know much about Tom's past but I'd never felt like it was something that hung over him. All I could do was put that offer to talk out there if he ever felt the need.

As we strung up the mixed-colour lights I'd chosen for Kitty Cove, we discussed my plans for Christmas in the cat café, including the specialist festive cakes and drinks I'd be introducing from Wednesday.

When the lights were finished upstairs, Tom also hung the bunting, then took the ladder downstairs to add red fairy lights to Cat Castle.

'Christmas has arrived at the Castle Street Cat Café,' I said, switching them on when he'd finished.

'It looks amazing.' Tom smiled as he looked round the room. 'I still can't believe you had the foresight to ask the builders to put hooks round the ceiling. You're so organised.'

'They did it at The Ramparts and I stored it in here as a genius idea.' I tapped the side of my head.

While I switched the downstairs lights off and double-checked the doors were locked, Tom took the stepladder back up to the first floor to store under the stairs. When I joined him, he'd switched off the main lights, leaving the room only illuminated by the fairy lights and candles.

'Are you pleased with it?' he asked.

'It's exactly what I hoped for. Thanks so much for your help.'

'What else is needed?'

'I've got some Christmassy cat toys to dangle from the trees and some toys and teasers to add to the buckets, then I think we're done.'

Michael Bublé had finished crooning so I picked up my phone to make another selection.

'*Not* Christmas music,' Tom said.

'I can't hear you!'

'Tabby!' He tried to snatch the phone from me but I was too quick for him and the melodical first bars of 'O Holy Night' sounded from Celine Dion's Christmas album, *These Are Special Times*. I wondered how long before Tom recognised it.

'Celine Dion?' he cried as she started singing.

'It's Mum's favourite Christmas album and I happen to like it.'

'Urgh! Is that song from *Titanic* on it?'

I raised my eyebrows at him. 'Is that a Christmas song?'

'No, but—'

'Then it's not on her Christmas album, is it? Although I haven't heard it for ages, so I might just...' I started scrolling and squealed as he made another lunge for the phone before I could change the track. I scooted between the tables as he chased after me.

'Spare me!' he cried.

We chased each other round the tables, but I refused to let go of my phone.

'Sing, Celine, sing!' I cried as she reached a rousing chorus and I tried – and failed – to hit the high notes with her. I wouldn't call myself tone deaf, but I wasn't far from it. My cats could sing way better than I could.

'Ooh! My ears!' Tom cried, laughing as he put his hands over them.

'How very dare you!'

He lunged again and this time he caught me round the waist, but he didn't try to grab my phone. Instead, he pulled me a little closer and placed his hand gently across my mouth.

'How about a compromise?' he said, grinning at me. 'Celine can sing but you don't accompany her.'

'But my singing is beautiful,' I mumbled.

'Your singing is something.'

The song reached an end and I must have hit shuffle because my favourite track from later in the album came on, instantly bringing a lump to my throat and tears to my eyes. The lyrics to 'Another Year Has Gone By' were beautiful.

'Are you all right?' Tom asked, looking at me with concern as he removed his hand from my mouth, his arm still round my waist.

'It's this song,' I said. 'It gets me right here every time.' I placed my hand over my heart.

'Why?'

'It's the lyrics. It's about a couple still deeply in love many years down the line.'

He listened for a while.

'It's a nice song,' he admitted.

'It's gorgeous!' I whispered, as a couple of tears broke free.

'Why does it affect you so much?'

'It's how I imagine true love to be and it scares me that I might never experience it.' I sniffed and swiped at my tears. 'I know it's silly.'

'It's not silly,' he said softly, his eyes sparkling. 'I feel that way too.'

As he gazed down at me, I felt as though he could see right into my soul and that he knew that I had feelings for him which ran much deeper than friendship and gratitude.

He lightly brushed his thumb across my cheek, never breaking eye contact, and next moment we were in each other's arms, our lips pressed together. My heart pounded as he drew me closer, taking my breath away with the passion of his kiss. The kisses I'd imagined us sharing weren't a patch on this, so full of longing. It could have felt strange – this was, after all, the man I'd thought of as a second big brother for most of my life – but it was as though suddenly everything fit together and this had been the plan for us all along.

He drew back for a moment, his eyes searching mine, as though seeking my confirmation that this was okay. It was more than okay. I ran my fingers into that gorgeously dishevelled dark hair of his and drew him back into another deep kiss.

I'd never wanted anyone more and my body yearned for him, but I didn't want to rush into anything one or both of us might regret. I knew I'd had feelings building for him for a while now but I had no idea whether he was simply being swept away in the moment, romanced by the fairy lights and beautiful music. Although surely he knew the stakes were high and he wouldn't be kissing me if he didn't feel something.

The song ended, but a shift change into 'Feliz Navidad' drew us apart and we both burst out laughing.

'Well, that was unexpected,' Tom said, still smiling.

'The song change or the kiss?' I said, smiling back.

'Both, but more the kiss.'

'Good unexpected or bad unexpected?'

'Good unexpected.'

He pulled out a couple of chairs from the table my phone was on and we sat down, legs touching. He flicked the track on my phone back to 'Another Year Has Gone By'.

'There's a reason I didn't give Brodie a goodnight kiss and it wasn't just because of her going away and the vague interest in another date. It was because she wasn't you.'

My heart leapt. 'You wanted to kiss me instead?'

'Our date was so much better. I know it was meant to be a practice one, but it felt real to me.'

'And to me,' I admitted.

He drew me into another kiss, slower this time, more sensual.

'I've wanted to do that for ages,' Tom said when we finally came up for air.

'Same here.' The track ended and 'Feliz Navidad' began again. I paused it and picked up my phone. 'Let's go back up to the flat. I think we've got a lot to talk about.'

We put the lights off and were halfway up the stairs when my phone rang. 'It's Mum,' I said, frowning as I connected the call. It was nearly 10 p.m. and she'd never call me this late unless there was something wrong.

'Macey's waters have broken and they're on their way to the hospital,' Mum said when we'd exchanged greetings.

I paused on the stairs. 'That means he's early.'

'Only by a fortnight, so I don't think we need to be concerned.'

'Okay. Let me know if you hear anything else.'

'Will do.'

'The baby's coming?' Tom asked when I'd disconnected.

'Yes. Early but Mum says not to worry. Macey'll be relieved.'

Tom smiled. 'Yeah, I don't think she's enjoyed the pregnancy part much. Can't believe Rylan's going to be a dad. He's still like a little kid himself most of the time.'

'Says the man who chased me round the tables trying to change my music and who had a food fight in the kitchen.'

'Erm, excuse me! I think you'll find it was you who started that one.'

When I didn't respond, he took my hand and led me up the rest of the stairs.

'It's late,' he said gently, once we were back in the flat. 'Why don't you go to bed and try to relax? You'll have a new nephew to visit tomorrow and I'm sure the last thing you want is a flare-up stopping you.'

'We were going to talk about us.'

'We can do that tomorrow. Get some sleep.' He tilted my chin upwards and gently kissed me. 'See you in the morning, Auntie Tabby-cat. Oh, actually, I might not. I've got a few client meetings tomorrow including a breakfast one. But we will talk. I promise.'

'Okay. Look forward to it.' I gave him a soft kiss then went upstairs, a big smile on my face.

In bed a little later, I played the Celine Dion track once more and brought up the lyrics on my phone, noting that one of the songwriters was Bryan Adams. That man certainly knew how to write a love song.

39

I slept in on Tuesday morning and woke up to find a message on the family WhatsApp group.

FROM RYLAN

Meet Hudson Elliot Walsh, 5lb 6oz, born at 2.07 a.m. by emergency c-section. All a bit dramatic but everyone's fine. They'll be staying in tonight so Macey would appreciate visitors as she's already bored

He added a laughing emoji and a picture of my new nephew, who had a mass of dark hair.

'Have you heard the news?' I called, wandering down the stairs. When I was met with silence, I remembered that Tom was at a breakfast meeting. I found a note in the kitchen.

Good morning and congrats to the new auntie! Checked hospital visiting times & should be able to squeeze in a visit between meetings. May see you there. If not, see you this afternoon x

I was relieved to see the kiss, but wished he was here to deliver it in person. My heart leapt as I thought about the kisses we'd shared last night. Amazing! It was a shame we hadn't had the chance to talk last night as I was a little nervous about what would happen next. Would it be weird starting a relationship when we were already living under the same roof? Would he feel the need to leave? Would I want him to? There was a lot to discuss.

* * *

When I pulled into the hospital car park, I spotted Tom's car and my heart raced at the thought of seeing him again. I'd picked up an 'It's a boy!' helium balloon from Forget-me-not Cards on Castle Street so I grabbed that from the back seat. As I approached the main entrance, I saw Tom pacing up and down, talking on his phone. He smiled warmly when he spotted me and mouthed, 'One minute,' so I loitered with intent a little distance away until he'd ended the call.

'I was hoping I'd see you here,' he said, smiling tenderly as I approached him.

'I was hoping I'd see you too.'

He placed his hands lightly on my hips and gave me a gentle but heart-melting kiss.

'Much as I'd love to stay out here and do that again, we'd better go in and meet the baby,' I said.

We entered the hospital and made our way along the corridor to the maternity wing.

'I was thinking it's probably best not to say anything about last night,' I said. 'Not until we've had a chance to talk properly because you know what they're like – especially Macey. They'd fire questions at us.'

'I'm glad you said that as I was thinking the same. Plus, the focus should be on the baby rather than us.'

'Agreed. Did you see how much hair he has? Already looking like his mum.'

As it was visiting time, the ward was busy. Mum had messaged to say she and Dad would visit this evening as they were at a client lunch. Macey's parents were on holiday, deliberately timed for before the baby arrived, so they'd be disappointed not to be here, and her older sister lived in Durham and would be at work, so Tom and I were the first visitors and probably the only ones for now.

'It's the end bed,' I said, surveying the ward.

We exchanged big hugs with Rylan and tentative ones with Macey, conscious she'd had a caesarean. Rylan tied the balloon to the end of the bed then handed me the adorable bundle in a blue blanket.

'He's so tiny,' I said, stroking my finger across my nephew's soft cheek. 'Hello, Hudson. I'm your Auntie Tabby and I might as well say it before anyone else does. I'm the crazy cat lady.'

'Very crazy,' Tom said, huddling close to me as he stroked Hudson's tiny hand.

Rylan perched on the bed so that Tom and I could have a chair each. Between them, my brother and Macey explained that labour had progressed quickly after Macey's waters broke but there'd been signs that Hudson was in distress and a c-section was going to be safest.

'I take it there's no concerns about him being early?' I asked.

Macey shook her head. 'I was thirty-eight weeks, so he's not classed as premature. He's smaller but not small enough to need special care. He was just desperate to meet us all, which I'm thrilled about because I'd had enough months ago.'

Tom and I exchanged smiles as that was exactly what we'd both said last night.

'There's something different about you two,' Macey said. 'What is it?'

My stomach lurched and I probably looked really shifty as I attempted an innocent shrug.

'Can't think of anything,' Tom said.

'Did you get the Christmas decorations put up last night?' Rylan asked.

'Yes,' I said. 'The café's looking great.'

'She put the Bublé on,' Tom said, giving me a gentle nudge. 'And she followed it up with Celine Dion's Christmas album. Seriously, eh?'

'You loved it!' I protested.

His eyes sparkled as he held my gaze. 'I did.'

'Oh! My! God!' Macey cried. 'There's something going on between you two!'

'No, there isn't,' I insisted as Tom vigorously shook his head.

'There so is!'

'I bloody well hope not,' Rylan said, curling his lip in disgust.

'What's that look for?' Macey demanded, poking him in the ribs.

'These two getting it on. That would be gross.'

'Why?' she asked.

'Because they're like brother and sister.'

'But they're not related.'

'They're as good as. Tom's family. It would be so wrong.'

'Rylan!' she protested. 'That's nasty. What if they are together?'

'Why would they be together?' he said. 'I think you've had too many meds.'

I couldn't bring myself to look at Tom but I hadn't missed that he'd shifted position so that he was leaning away from me rather than towards me.

Rylan seemed to finally remember that we were there. 'Tell me she's imagining it,' he said to me, eyebrows raised, no shadow of a smile on his face.

I gulped and cuddled Hudson a little closer to my chest. 'There's nothing going on,' I said, my voice flat. 'It would be...' I tailed off, shrugging. I couldn't add any of the derogatory terms to the end of that sentence that echoed my brother's thoughts because it wasn't like that at all.

'Definitely nothing,' Tom added. 'But I'm going to have to head off now.' He rose to his feet.

'But you haven't had a cuddle with Hudson yet,' Macey protested.

'I'll come and see you when you're settled back at home. I can hold him then. Congratulations again. See you all later.'

And then he left.

'You're such an arse sometimes,' Macey said, giving Rylan a shove.

'Honestly, it's fine,' I said, not wanting to be the cause of conflict between them on what should be a special day. 'There's nothing between us. We're just good friends.'

'Glad to hear it,' Rylan said. 'My best mate and my sister?' He gave a shudder, making me feel sick. Was that what he really thought?

* * *

I was in the cat café kitchen adding the ingredients for a red velvet cake into a mixing bowl when Tom returned.

'Hi,' he said, joining me in the kitchen but staying by the door. His brow was furrowed and that one word seemed to carry the weight of the world.

'Hi. Meetings finished?'

'Yes. I've got some work still to do, but do you need a hand?' His hesitant tone suggested to me that he would prefer not to spend the next couple of hours in the kitchen with me.

'All under control.'

'Erm, I'm seeing the five-a-side lads tonight.'

'I thought you played five-a-side on a Thursday.'

'I do, but they want to celebrate the baby arriving. Any excuse. Macey's in hospital overnight so Rylan's keen to take advantage.'

'Okay. Sounds good.'

I added a couple of teaspoons of bicarbonate of soda to the flour and cocoa powder, trying to convince myself that this was nothing to do with Tom wanting to avoid me. Drinks before Macey and Hudson came home was a very Rylan thing to do.

'A couple of them suggested grabbing food first,' Tom added, 'so I'll probably be going out before you're done down here and I'll be back late.'

So he *was* avoiding me.

'Okay.' I reached for the packet of brown sugar without looking at him. 'Have fun.'

'I'm sorry,' he said, sighing deeply before leaving the kitchen.

I braced my hands against the worktop and dipped my head, willing myself not to cry. What did I'm sorry mean? *I'm sorry for going out tonight. I'm sorry for what your brother said. I'm sorry because your brother was right and it is gross so it's over.*

'I'm sorry too,' I whispered.

40

Tom was still asleep when I went downstairs to bake scones on Wednesday morning. I hadn't heard him return last night, or rather the early hours of this morning, as I'd still been awake at half past midnight and he hadn't made it back at that point.

The last thing I wanted was for things to be awkward between us so I decided to nip upstairs half an hour before opening time to see if I could clear the air. I could hear the shower going so I waited in my bedroom for ten minutes, hoping to catch him when he came out, but the shower was still going and I needed to get downstairs for the team arriving, so I had to abandon that plan.

I wished I'd said something to him yesterday when he joined me in the kitchen. I'd been rehearsing things I could say for a couple of hours and had settled on a casual, *So, not a great reaction from Rylan but Macey didn't seem fazed so that's one out of two. The cats are excited so that's another fifteen positives...* But then he'd said that stuff about going out with the lads and my feeble attempt at humour hadn't seemed appropriate.

At lunchtime, the kitchen door opened and my heart leapt when Tom came in.

'How's it going?' he asked, his body rigid as he hovered uncertainly by the door.

It wasn't the time or place for a deep and meaningful, especially when I had orders to prepare, but that didn't mean things needed to be uncomfortable between us. Nobody had declared their undying love or made any promises so there was no need for us not to be friends.

I gave him a warm smile. 'Busy. So hands washed, apron on, help me clear these orders and you can tell me about your night out while we work.'

His shoulders relaxed and it was great to see that smile back. We chatted easily about his evening and I told him about a couple of lovely customers that morning, but then an alarm sounded on his phone and he said he had to go as it was a reminder to phone a client.

I sighed as he left. Would we get a chance to talk later and resolve things? I'd been so looking forward to us talking about what had happened, especially after that kiss outside the hospital which told me he hadn't regretted it overnight, but what sort of conversation would we be having now? Something that had evolved so naturally and felt so simple and right suddenly felt complicated and, if my brother was to be believed, wrong.

Why, after all these years, had something changed between us? I'd never felt even the slightest inkling of desire for Tom in the twenty-seven years I'd known him, so why now? But that answer seemed fairly obvious. I'd never spent anywhere near this long in his company without the rest of the family being around, but living and working with him had meant I'd fully let him in. I'd let him see me at my most vulnerable. He'd been there through the pain and the fear and he hadn't run away. He'd given me more of him too, sharing his fears and vulnerabilities. And I really didn't want to lose that.

* * *

Finishing time couldn't come soon enough. After a lovely morning, this afternoon had been horrendous. I wasn't sure whether there was a full moon or something in the water, but we had the most awful customers. It started with a walk-in customer who shouted and swore at me because she refused to pay the entrance fee, despite agreeing to it on arrival. She threw a £10 note at me and stormed out. A tenner didn't even cover the food and drink bill for her and her companion, never mind the entrance. After that, I spotted another customer shoving Viking off his table with such force that Viking yowled and shot upstairs. I had to leave Amelia to have words with him while I raced after Viking to check he wasn't hurt and try to placate him. Poor cat was cowering in the lounge, shaking, and it took me half an hour to settle him. Thankfully, he wasn't injured. When I returned to the café, Fay alerted me to the most foul mess all over one of the upstairs toilets which an unidentified customer had left. She said she'd clean it and just wanted me to know about it, but no way could I expect her to see to that. Even though it was a Wednesday, I didn't even have the pleasure of Shelley the cat whisperer to provide any balance. I hoped she was okay and that her mother hadn't had another fall.

When the team had all left and I'd finished clearing up, I locked the internal door and pressed my head against it, taking deep breaths. Worst day ever!

I rounded up the fur family to follow me into the flat. I could hear Tom on the phone in the dining room so I continued upstairs. I needed cheering up. This morning, when the customers were nicer, one who I'd recognised from a previous visit had mentioned leaving a glowing review on Tripadvisor. I'd seen some great reviews on the café's Facebook page but had stupidly never thought to check Tripadvisor so I logged on to take a look, expecting to be uplifted by what she'd put. Instead, my heart sank. There were thirty-one reviews, which was amazing considering we'd only been open a fortnight, but they had a 3.4 average rating, which wasn't so good.

I hardly dared read any of them but I felt compelled to see what people hated so much in case it was something to do with the service or food which I could rectify. I really wished I hadn't bothered.

DO NOT VISIT!!!!
Took my family to the Castle Street Cat Café at the weekend. My 8-year-old daughter came away in tears after seeing how badly they treat the cats. One of the kittens was limping and others had matted fur and even

faeces hanging from them. The whole place stinks. We had to leave our food, unable to stomach eating it. This place needs condemning. Stay away!

Unhealthy and cruel
I feel sick. Just been. Cat hair all over the sofas and chairs and pooey paw prints on the tables. Ew! My friend said cat cafés are cruel and I should have listened to her

Those poor cats!!!!!!!!!!!
Someone needs to do something about this place. Cats can't have cream or milk but that doesn't bother the owners of the cat café on Whitsborough Bay's Castle Street. Tables were left uncleared for ages and the cats were allowed to lap up the milk out of the jugs. We complained to a waitress but she wasn't interested. Never going back. Hope the place gets shut down.

And so it continued. There were glowing five-star reviews too which contradicted everything the negative ones said, but I couldn't seem to take them in and my eyes kept flicking back to the nasty ones. My head thumped and my stomach churned. Reviews like this could ruin us.

I was vaguely aware of Tom in the doorway but I couldn't tear my eyes away from my laptop.

'What are you looking at?' he asked, plonking himself on the bed beside me.

I tilted the laptop so he could see the screen.

'Full of lies,' he said, shaking his head.

'How could anyone coming to the café think I treat the cats badly? They're not dirty or matted.'

'That's because they're written by people who haven't been to the café.'

'How can you be sure?'

'Because this one says there was hair all over the sofas. We don't have any sofas. And this one talks about cats licking the milk jugs but ours have lids on. I bet you these are the same people who've been vocal on Facebook and I bet the vandal's one of them.'

I loved it when Tom used 'we' or 'our' when referring to the café, showing how much he felt involved and cared about it.

'But who'd do something like that?' I asked. 'It's horrible.'

'People can be really horrible. They sit behind their keyboards and spout their venom without any care for who it affects. I suspect they get their kicks out of knowing their words will hurt. Or, in this case, their lies.'

'I knew there were people out there who don't agree with cat cafés, but I never expected such a backlash.' I closed the laptop as tears pooled in my eyes. 'I don't know if I can do this anymore, Tom. Every time I think it's going well, something bad happens. This isn't what I expected.'

Tom gathered me in his arms and held me as tears ran down my cheeks and I sobbed for the how hard certain aspects were – the angry, rude and disgusting customers, the haters on social media, the negative reviews, staffing problems and vandalism. They say be careful what you wish for. I'd never imagined that would apply to my long-held dream of owning a cat café, but I was starting to have serious doubts as to whether I'd done the right thing.

41

On Friday, Alison stepped in to help while Mark attended a funeral. I was curious to see how Alison and Amelia would work together and whether Amelia would feel pushed out by Alison's larger-than-life personality, but they seemed to gel really well. After the week I'd had, I concluded I was creating problems where there weren't any.

Alison stayed back for a hot chocolate after everyone left.

'You're not yourself today,' she declared when we sat down. 'Spill it.'

'It's been a tough week. I had some horrendous customers on Wednesday afternoon and then I saw some shocking reviews on Tripadvisor – really nasty ones – which upset me.'

She narrowed her eyes and studied me for a moment. 'That's not it. You're upset about them, yes, but there's something else. What's going on?'

I hesitated for a moment, but I could really use some advice and Alison had been great at that so far.

'It's Tom,' I said with a sigh. Out it all tumbled about my feelings building, the moments of chemistry, the fantastic practice date and the incredible kisses.

'I'm guessing there's a big "but" coming,' she said.

'A massive one.' I told her about Rylan's reaction at Macey's accusation that something had happened between us, and how awkward that had made things.

'I just keep thinking that if Rylan's that weirded out, how's everyone else going to react?'

'Who cares? If Tom was your *actual* brother I'd be like, *woah, stop, ew, ew, ew!* But he's not related to you at all. He's your nanna's foster child. Your family love him so I'd have thought they'd be thrilled to see you pairing up.'

'To be honest, I never even thought about their reaction until we saw Rylan.'

'Remember, as well, that you're his little sister. Big brothers are meant to be protective of their little sister – that macho *you hurt my sister and I'll kill you* kind of thing. And he was only reacting to a hypothetical situation. You both denied you were together.'

'I suppose.'

'I bet if you told him you really were together, he'd realise that's a great thing. Who wouldn't want their potential future brother-in-law to be their best mate already? Okay, jumping ahead of myself here and already buying the hat.'

'You might as well put the hat back because nothing's happened since then.'

'And the thing with your brother was on Tuesday?'

'Yep.'

'Oh.'

'Exactly.' I sighed again. 'It was tricky at first but we're back to being friends now and I'm just as confused as before. It's as though Monday night never happened.'

'You *really* haven't talked about it since?'

'He went out with Rylan and the lads on Tuesday night to celebrate Hudson's arrival so I thought we'd talk on Wednesday, but that was the day from hell and I ended up in tears. Last night he was at five-a-side football and drinks afterwards. There hasn't been an opportunity for a heart-to-heart.'

'And there never will be. Tabby, you've got to pin him down and have that talk. Unless you regret that kiss and the thing with your brother is an excuse to forget about it all.'

I shook my head vigorously. 'No regrets.'

'Then tell Tom how you feel. Take the lead. They're *your* family so Tom might be waiting for you to do that.'

'Okay. You've convinced me. I'll talk to him tonight.'

'Good. So tell me more about your afternoon from hell.'

I told her about Wednesday, all the other negative things that had happened before and since opening, and how I was having serious doubts about the whole thing.

'I told you that the cats were my secret to happiness.' I paused and smiled weakly. 'It could be Tom too, but we'll see how that conversation goes tonight. But with the cats, you're right about the café not being what I expected. This isn't about me spending time with the cats – it's about me facilitating other people doing that while I serve up coffee and cake. And it's not even like that's as rewarding as I'd hoped because they're not building meaningful relationships with the fur family. They're here for a drink, a cake and a selfie for the socials.'

I paused again, thinking about Shelley. 'That's not strictly fair. I'm sure that, over time, we'll have regulars who get a lot out of being with the cats and they'll likely become friends, but for most of them it's an Instagram moment and, saying this now, I don't know why I thought it would be anything other than that. I don't know what I thought. I probably sound like I'm hating it and I'm not, but I'm not head over heels loving it either.'

'What could you do instead that would give you what you want?'

'I wish I knew. Win the lottery so I have no financial worries and can spend my day playing with the cats? That's never going to happen.'

Alison shrugged. 'I'm sorry. I wish I could suggest something.'

'I need to do some serious thinking while we're closed between Christmas and New Year. Anyway, enough about me. Thank you for helping out again today. What did you think of Amelia?'

'I didn't spend much time with her, but she seems really nice. Are you pleased with her?'

'Yes, definitely. It's just that...' I smiled at her. 'It's just that she's not you, but I can't have you full time so I need to make the most of you on the occasional day.'

'Aw, bless you. If things were different, I'd love a job here.' She checked the time and tutted. 'Sorry, Tabby, but I'm going to have to love you and leave you.'

'Thanks for listening.'

'Any time. You'll have that conversation tonight, whatever happens?'

'Definitely.'

* * *

Tom wasn't in the dining room when I went upstairs. The piles of paperwork he'd had strewn over the table were neatly packed away in a crate and his laptop was in a case on top of it. Butterflies stirred with the idea that he'd packed to leave, but I dismissed them. It was Friday night so he could have packed away his paperwork as a declaration that he'd finished work for the week and we could use the table for eating once more.

I wandered into the lounge to see if he was in there, but it was empty. As I turned to leave, the butterflies took flight as I clocked his suitcase beside the door with his bedding stacked up beside it.

'Tabby!' I whipped my head round at Tom's voice. He looked sheepish as he stood in the hall holding his washbag.

'You're leaving?'

'I'm... It's... I thought it would be for the best.'

'Did you? Without discussing it with me?'

'We both knew I'd have to go home at some point. There haven't been any more attacks on the café and...'

This was nothing to do with the vandalism and I was so disappointed with him for making the decision to walk away without discussing what had happened. I thought better of him than that. I tightened my jaw and shook my head.

'Make sure you lock the door on your way out,' I muttered, storming past him.

'Tabby! Can't we talk?'

I paused at the foot of the stairs. 'Why? You've already made your mind up.'

'It's for the best. You saw how your brother reacted. I don't want to be the one who causes a rift in your family. I care about you all too deeply for that.'

'Walking away isn't caring.'

'But I want us to be friends. I couldn't bear to lose you. Can't things go back to how they were before?'

'No, Tom, they can't. Because before, you would *never* do anything to hurt me.'

I started up the stairs.

'I didn't mean to hurt you.'

'Well, you did. I know we hadn't talked about the kiss and what it meant for us, but we both know that we'd never have kissed each other on a whim – it had to mean something special. But at the first sniff of anything challenging, you've packed your bags and run away. I don't need someone like that in my life so it's just as well you're going. No wonder you've stayed single all of these years.'

It was a cheap shot, but I wanted to hurt him like he'd hurt me.

'Tabby!' he called, but I ran up the stairs and into the bathroom where I slammed and locked the door, tears raining down my cheeks.

I stood with my forehead against the door, listening intently for the flat door closing. When it did, I ran to my bedroom window and peeked out onto the street. Tom emerged from the shop and ran down the cobbles. A few minutes later, he drove his car up the street, loaded his boot and drove off. I sank down onto the floor, my head between my legs, and proper ugly cried. Even Heathcliff and Babushka weaving round my legs and nudging me for attention and Pebbles clambering onto my shoulder couldn't bring me any comfort.

42

I decided I'd throw myself into work on Saturday. I was used to wearing a mask to hide my physical pain so a mask hiding the emotional pain wouldn't be too difficult to conjure up. Smile, laugh, be friendly and bubbly and nobody will ever know.

As it happened, I didn't have to fake it as it turned out to be the loveliest day I'd had in the café so far. The spirit of Christmas had arrived with an air of excitement all day, lots of laughter from the customers, gorgeous compliments and generous tips. A regular customer called Maggie brought in a fabulous cat-shaped vase which she'd made for me, telling me she'd been having a tough time recently but several visits to my cats had helped her immeasurably and she wanted to thank me for opening up. Another regular called Eliza presented me with five beautifully crafted felt cat decorations she'd made for my Christmas tree, instantly recognisable as Viking, Winnie, Marmite, Rubix and Smudge. She told me she hoped to make all the cats before Christmas and that spending time in the café and crafting were helping her get through a recent bereavement.

It was so touching to hear these personal tales of how time at the café meant so much to these customers and I wondered how many others felt the same but hadn't shared their stories with me.

Towards the end of the day, I opened the door to Brodie.

'Hi, Tabby,' she gushed. 'I'm not here for a table. I just wondered if I could speak to Tom.'

'He's not here.'

'Oh! Is he upstairs?'

'No. He's gone back to his own apartment.'

'No worries, I'll give him a call instead. I told him the wrong venue for tonight.'

I looked at her blankly. 'Wrong venue?'

'For the staff Christmas party. Tom's my plus one. Thanks again for putting in a good word for me.'

With a final beaming smile, she left, scrolling through her phone. Tom was going on another date with Brodie? He certainly hadn't wasted any time.

* * *

I was sick of crying and my poor fur family had to be fed up with the sound of me wailing. Last night when Tom left had been horrendous and tonight wasn't shaping up to be any better now that I knew about his date with Brodie. Lying in bed, surrounded by cats, I tormented myself with questions about the pair of them. When had they arranged for him to attend her work Christmas party? Had they been in contact the whole time she was away? Why was he going on another date with her when he'd told me he wasn't convinced about their compatibility? But the question that haunted me the most was: did my parting shot push them together? I went over that last exchange of words – heated on my part – and hated myself for it. Tom had turned his life upside down to be there for me over the past month and this was how I'd shown my gratitude. Yes, I was hurt and disappointed with him, but the outburst hadn't been fair.

Between the questions, I imagined them together. I had no idea whether the Castle Jewellery Christmas party was a low-key meal out or one of those big party nights at a local hotel where several companies took tables. My thoughts veered towards the latter and I pictured them slow dancing at the end of the evening, eyes closed, cheeks together and, worst of all, I pictured them kissing.

If I could go back, I wouldn't change the kiss but I wished I could change what had happened since. I'd have said something to Rylan at the hospital for a start – defended my right to be with Tom and proudly declared that we were a couple. If I'd done that and shown that I was there for him, no matter what, he'd still be here right now. I wouldn't regret the kiss, but I did regret not standing up to my brother.

43

An amber flare-up hit me on Sunday and I had no choice but to push through it. Alison had plans with her family, my parents and Tom needed to do client work, and it wasn't an option to ask Tom anyway when things were difficult between us.

Tom had been a godsend and a rock while he was here. Although I'd never taken his help for granted – especially as it was still a struggle for me to accept that I needed support – I had become reliant on it, which wasn't good.

When the team arrived for work, I told them that my fibro was playing up – it seemed fairer to get it out in the open because no amount of smiling could hide my slower movements and my short-term memory challenges – but reassured them that I was okay and to bear with me if orders came out a little slower than usual. They were incredibly supportive but it was a harsh reality check. I'd specifically taken on Amelia to step into my role when I had a flare-up so that I could rest, but taking myself out of the business would mean we were short-staffed. I really hadn't thought this through.

As I trudged back upstairs after the hardest working day of my life, the only positive I could find was that we were closed for the next two days. I just hoped that was enough time to recover as I had already used up today's spoons, tomorrow's and probably Tuesday's too.

* * *

Pushing through Sunday raised the severity level to red on Monday and I had no choice but to listen to my body and spend the day doing as little as possible. I'd anticipated that Tuesday wouldn't be much better and could have wept with relief to discover that my body had been kind and reduced the pain level to green. I knew better than to push myself too far but I found baking soothing. I'd make good use of the stool in the café kitchen to reduce time on my feet and I'd take a couple of long breaks between cakes.

'Tell me off if I try to do too much,' I said to Babushka and Pebbles as they followed me down to Cat Castle.

'You've got this!' I replied in Babushka's voice, which made me smile. Thank goodness for my cats and the meaning they brought to my life.

I'd just placed a chocolate and salted caramel sponge in the oven and settled onto my stool for a breather when my phone rang. My heart leapt, wondering if it might be Tom, but it was Macey.

'What are you doing today?' she asked.

'Baking cakes for tomorrow.'

'Could you cope with a visitor? Rylan's not officially back at college till tomorrow but he's gone in for a meeting today. I thought I'd take Hudson for a walk round town and it would be great if we could do a feeding stop-off at yours.'

'Who'll want feeding? You or Hudson?'

She laughed. 'Him, but if a scone happened to roll in my direction, I wouldn't protest. And I am partial to a piece of cake too.'

'I'm sure I can manage something.'

'I'll probably be with you between eleven and half past.'

'Okay. I look forward to seeing you both then.'

It was only when I hung up that I realised that I hadn't bought a card or gift for Hudson yet, which was so remiss of me. While the cake was in the oven, I could nip out now – it wasn't like I had far to go and surely newborn babies weren't difficult to buy for.

I nipped back up to the flat to grab a coat and my bag then headed out onto Castle Street to do some shopping. It was a calm day, but the chill of winter wrapped itself round me the moment I stepped outside and, shivering, I zipped up my coat. It felt like ages since I'd been outside the café, and it struck me that it had been. Aside from trips to the rubbish bins out the back, I hadn't actually left the premises in a week, my last venture out being to see Macey in hospital. That was bad.

A card would be an easy purchase, so I crossed the cobbles and walked down to Forget-me-not Cards, making a speedy selection.

Teddy bears were a good gift for a newborn, weren't they? I headed back up the street towards Bear With Me, intending to cross to Bay Babies afterwards – the baby clothes shop beside Seaside Blooms – to get a cute outfit too.

Jemma was arranging some teddy bears dressed in Santa and elf outfits on a shelving unit completely dedicated to festive teddies. Red fairy lights were strung across the front of each shelf and a large tree in one corner had teddy bears of all sizes peeking out between the branches.

'Morning!' she said cheerfully. 'How are you?'

'Not too bad, but I'm a bad auntie. My nephew arrived a week ago and I've completely forgotten to buy him a present. My sister-in-law is on her way to the café with him so I'm thinking I can't go wrong with a teddy bear.'

Jemma smiled. 'First time you've bought a baby gift?'

'Is it that obvious?'

She pushed the box she was unpacking to one side and joined me.

'This is a really popular range,' she said, pointing to a display of adorable pastel and traditional-coloured teddy bears. 'They're ideal for babies because they wash beautifully in a machine. Other makes are still great as they're baby safe but you'd need to sponge clean rather than shove them in the wash.'

'What are these?' I said, pointing to a dresser where every bear displayed appeared to be different and most of them were wearing clothes.

'They're artist bears. My mum makes them and I make the miniatures in the glass cabinet. They're all one of a kind but they're not suitable for babies or children because they're hand-crafted. That said, some customers like to buy an artist bear or a collectible bear from one of the specialist bear manufacturers like Steiff as a keepsake to sit on the shelf rather than join the child in their bed.'

'They're lovely,' I said, captivated by their expressive faces.

'Thank you. I should point out that they're significantly more expensive than the plush teddies because of the time and the materials needed to make them, but it depends what you're looking for.'

'Now I'm even more confused. It would be nice to get something special and one-off, but I've got a cake in the oven so I don't have time to study each one. How do other customers choose?'

'Sometimes the bear speaks to them – not literally, of course – but there's something that really catches their eye. When they're buying for someone else, it's often something about the way the bear is dressed which has a connection to them or the recipient, making the gift a lot more personal.'

'Hmm. Hudson's only a week old.'

'You could get something that represents his cool auntie. I've got a cat in my miniatures.'

'You're kidding me! I *have* to see that.'

She unlocked the glass cabinet and removed the most incredible cat. Made from grey mohair with black tips, it wore a crocheted burgundy scarf and had the cutest facial expression. I didn't care how much it cost – this was the perfect gift and, thanks to Jemma, it looked like some actual thought had gone into it.

* * *

I hadn't been back long when Macey arrived with Hudson in his buggy, looking flustered.

'He's just started to grizzle so he'll be fully awake at any moment.'

Sure enough, she'd only just applied the brake when he released an almighty cry, sending a couple of the cats running for the stairs.

'Sorry,' Macey said, grimacing. 'Can you grab him and give him a cuddle while I get sorted?'

I was happy to oblige and rested him against my shoulder, stroking his hair and making what I hoped were soothing sounds.

'You're a lifesaver,' Macey said, removing some cloths from the baby bag before settling into a chair and reaching for her son.

The cries ceased seconds later as Hudson contentedly settled for his feed.

'So, what's going on with you and Tom?' she asked, without any preamble.

'There's nothing going on.' Right now, that was the truth.

Macey narrowed her eyes at me. 'Maybe not now, but there was. At the hospital, something was different between you two. You were a lot closer than usual.'

'We'd been living together for weeks,' I said, trying to sound innocent. 'That's it.'

She smacked her lips together, shaking her head. 'That's not it. Come on, Tabby. You can tell me.'

'There's nothing to tell.'

'There is! Come on! Please! This is killing me!'

'Oh, for God's sake. We kissed, okay? We were putting the Christmas decorations up, it was a one-off and meant nothing. End of story.'

She studied my face for a while. 'Nah! Not buying it. It meant something to you and I'm pretty sure it meant something to him too.'

'Obviously not because he went on a date on Saturday night.'

Macey winced. 'Who with?'

'That lass from the jewellery shop, Brodie. The one he went out with the other weekend.'

She shrugged. 'I've obviously missed that one. Why was he on a date when he's into you?'

'Because, like I said, he's not into me.'

'I disagree and I'll be having words with him about this Brodie next time I see him. What's he playing at?'

'Please don't say anything. I'd rather forget the whole thing. And don't say anything to Rylan. I could do without his judgement. He made me feel so dirty.'

Macey gave a knowing smile. 'The penny drops! So that's what it's all about. Why do you care what your brother thinks?'

'Because he's my brother and he's Tom's best mate.'

'And he's full of crap sometimes. Despite what he said, he's *not* grossed out by the idea of you two as a couple. He was shocked, which is understandable – you've known each other forever and there's never been a hint of anything other than friendship. After you left the hospital, I told him off for being so insensitive and pointed out how horrendous he'd have made you both feel if I was right and there was something going on. He was mortified. Now that he's had time to think about it, he reckons it would be pretty cool having a best friend as a brother-in-law.'

'We'd only just kissed!' I cried.

'Yeah, but I know you both really well and you wouldn't have done that if something hadn't massively shifted in your feelings, even if you hadn't admitted that to yourselves yet. Am I right or am I right?'

I lowered my eyes, reimagining that kiss, thinking about the words to the lyrics of 'Another Year Has Gone By' and how that kiss had made me feel like that couple could be us.

'You're right,' I muttered. 'But it's too late now.'

'It's never too late.'

* * *

Back in the flat later that day, I picked up my phone to call Tom, then put it down again a ridiculous number of times.

A message came through from Macey with a photo of Hudson's cat.

FROM MACEY

New family member proudly displayed on the nursery shelves. Thanks again. We love it! Very thoughtful of you. Have you sorted things with Tom? I won't interfere but I will keep pestering you until you have good news for me xxxx

I tried to compose a message to Tom, but couldn't find the right words. Macey's comment that it was never too late rang in my ears, but I had this nagging doubt telling me it was. On time would have been at the hospital, when we got home, any time that week. I'd accused him of jumping ship when things got hard, but what had I done? I'd taken myself out of the game too. The big thing to do would be to reach out and say sorry, but the one thing stopping me was him going on that date with Brodie. I couldn't get my head around that. It felt like such a betrayal and I'd already been betrayed by Leon. I couldn't cope with Tom doing the same.

44

Thursday brought another challenge for the cat café when the food safety officer paid a visit in response to reports of serious hygiene concerns. Of course, he found absolutely nothing to back that up and the five-star rating I'd been awarded a week ago remained proudly displayed in the window, but the whole episode left a sour taste in my mouth. When would it stop?

Amelia caught me in the kitchen having a pity party, trying to wipe away my tears, and she couldn't have been nicer. She gave me a hug then sat me down and made me a hot chocolate.

'There's always somebody intent on causing trouble,' she said. 'It's nasty and smallminded but, if you let them get to you, they've won.'

'I know, but it's hard not to be affected by it.'

'I get that, I really do, but look at what you've created here. Look at how many happy customers we serve every day. Don't let the keyboard warriors and troublemakers take that away from you. Promise me?'

'I promise. Thanks.'

'You take a break, enjoy your drink, and I'll sort out any queries, okay?'

I felt so much better after taking that bit of time out, hiding round the corner, sipping on my drink, listening to the happy chatter. I tried to focus on Christmas instead. The family Christmas plans had finally been discussed. Macey and Rylan were seeing her parents on Christmas Day and having Boxing Day at Mum and Dad's. I was welcome to join my parents in Little Sandby for one or both days. They told me the same offer applied to Tom. I hadn't heard a peep out of him since Friday night and I missed him so much, it hurt. Someone had to make a move and it probably should be me. He'd let me down, but I'd taken it a step further, saying things that were cruel. I owed him an apology and every day that passed where I didn't reach out made it harder and scarier to do so. What if he hated me? What if he wanted nothing more to do with me?

* * *

At the end of the day, the team gathered their coats and bags.

'Do you mind if I nip to the loo before I go?' Amelia asked.

'Of course not. I'll let the others out.'

There was no point going back into the kitchen so I stayed in Cat Castle, straightening up the notepads and cards in the retail area. Sales had steadily increased since we hit December with customers saying they'd make stocking fillers and gifts for the cat lovers in their lives. A range of festive soft toy cats had sold incredibly well and were likely to sell out within the next week.

'I assumed you were in the accessible toilet,' I said when Amelia surprised me by appearing from upstairs.

'Force of habit. My mum always told me never to use the disabled loo in case someone came along who was disabled.'

She moved towards the door and I was about to open it when I heard a stifled mewing. It sounded like it was coming from Amelia's handbag.

'Is there something in your bag?' I asked, moving closer to Amelia, my ears cocked.

She stepped back, tightening her hold on her bag. 'Are you accusing me of stealing?'

I reeled at her snappy response, but kept my voice calm. 'I can hear squeaking. I thought one of the kittens might have clambered into your bag without you realising. Did you leave it outside when you went to the toilet?'

Another plaintive mew, louder this time.

Amelia looked shocked as she placed her bag on a table and opened it. Pebbles popped her head out, making us both jump.

'Oh, my God!' she cried. 'I'm so sorry, Tabby. I *did* leave my bag outside the loo. He must have got in then.'

'She,' I corrected, picking Pebbles up and giving her a stroke.

'Did I say he? Sorry. End-of-day brain.'

'That's okay. You might want to check she hasn't peed in there. I don't think she would, but if she was scared...'

Amelia tentatively put her hand in her bag. 'No, I think we're safe.'

I placed Pebbles on one of the turrets before moving into the entrance porch with Amelia.

'Sorry if I snapped,' she said. 'It was the thought of a bag search. There was a theft problem at my last but one job and they'd do these spot checks. I get that they wanted to catch the thief, but they could have done the searches in a less humiliating way. They found the thief, but motivation was rock bottom by then, which was why I left.'

'Must have been difficult.'

'It was so, as I say, apologies for the reaction. I can't believe there was a kitten in there. They get everywhere!'

I let Amelia out and returned to Cat Castle. Pebbles had climbed onto a higher turret and was already asleep, seemingly unscathed by her time trapped in Amelia's bag. I sat down and watched her for a few minutes. While I had no reason to believe that Pebbles being in Amelia's bag was anything more than a curious kitten getting up to mischief, her reaction disturbed me. I could completely understand that she'd be defensive about a bag search after a bad previous experience, but she could have conveyed that without snapping at me.

Rubix jumped on the table beside me and I picked him up for a cuddle. 'It's me,' I told him. 'Amelia's been helpful and lovely and I'm on edge after the food inspector's visit.'

I checked the locks, called for the fur family, turned the lights off and headed upstairs to my empty flat. I really didn't want a conversation with

Tom after the day I'd had, but I could easily find an excuse every day to put it off, so I settled on the sofa bed and called him. As soon as it connected to his voicemail, I tutted to myself. It was five-a-side night. He'd be on the football pitch or possibly in the pub. I disconnected without leaving a message.

45

Amelia arrived for work on Friday with a box of chocolates from Charlee's shop and a gushing apology, reiterating how awful the bag searches had been before. I accepted her apology, but told her it wasn't necessary – it wasn't her fault that Pebbles had clambered into her bag. She'd been charming ever since, the snapped response clearly being a one-off.

Saturday passed without hitch and Sunday arrived without any word from Tom. I probably should have tried him again but he'd have seen a missed call from me and I'd have hoped that would have prompted him to make the next move. I'd try him again tonight.

Macey had been true to her word and kept pestering me with messages asking if I'd resolved things yet. I told her I'd decided it would be better to have a face-to-face conversation and I couldn't do that until Monday at the earliest when the café was closed. She responded to say that was a cop-out and she was right. I was in avoidance mode big time. I didn't want to hear that Tom was with Brodie now and I didn't want to hear that our friendship was over.

Late on Sunday afternoon, we'd served our final sitting of the day and I was in the kitchen wiping down the surfaces. There might be a couple more orders for drinks but it was unlikely there'd be any more food requests.

We'd had a good day at the café with lots more lovely customers. Eliza had nipped in with a couple more of her hand-crafted felt Christmas decorations – this time of Heathcliff and Babushka. She was exceptionally talented and I didn't have the heart to tell her I didn't actually have a Christmas tree upstairs. I'd need to get one, even if it was just a small tabletop one, so I could hang the cat decorations on it. Imagining a tree dedicated to my fifteen cats made my heart sing.

When it was dark outside like it was now, the café looked so gorgeous decorated for Christmas with the fairy lights on. I'd been playing a Christmas playlist across the week – mainly instrumental versions of well-known pop songs and favourite carols – and I hummed along to 'White Christmas' as I wiped.

Shouting from upstairs stopped me. I glanced at the CCTV monitors but couldn't see anything untoward. There were further shouts and Amelia came running down the stairs, shaking a tub of cat treats.

'Free the cats!' she cried as she dashed past the kitchen towards the entrance.

I grabbed for the door handle, my heart pounding at those familiar words that had been daubed across the front door.

Amelia had opened the inner door and was still shaking the treats. My blood ran cold as several cats followed her into the porch area.

'Stop!' I cried.

A couple of quick-reacting customers beat me to it, grabbing some of the cats, but Amelia had already pushed open the outer door and several of them ran out into the street.

'Serves you right for stealing my boyfriend,' she cried, tossing the treat pot to the ground, where it spilled open, and sprinting off down the cobbles.

Freyja, Winnie and Cloud stopped to lap up the treats, but others scattered.

'Stop the cats!' I cried into the throng of shoppers, trying to keep my eye on which cats had escaped and which direction they'd run as I did a sweeping grab of the three by the treats.

'We've got them.' Lena took Winnie and Cloud from me as Arwen took Freyja.

I needed to find the others but my legs wouldn't move. Stars swam in front of my eyes and I struggled to catch my breath. To my right, a woman lunged for Viking but he leapt over her arms and disappeared into the crowd.

So many people. And dogs. And darkness. My babies would be terrified.

Somebody put an arm round me and led me back into the café. I was eased into a chair and a sea of concerned faces faded in and out in front of my eyes.

'Give her some space,' a woman commanded. 'Put your head between your legs.' Someone pushed me forward. 'Take deep breaths. That's it. Good. And again.'

'The cats,' I murmured.

'It's all right,' said the woman. 'We think we've got most of them. Your staff are checking.'

'The flat.'

'I'll get your keys and will check now.' I recognised the voice as Lena's.

'Can someone make me some tea with plenty of sugar in it?' the woman in charge asked.

'I'll do it,' a man said.

I had no idea who these people were but I couldn't be more grateful to them for taking control when I couldn't.

'Ooh! They've got one!' another woman said, followed by the sound of the door opening and closing.

I needed to know who it was and slowly raised my head, relief flowing through me at the sight of Effie cradled in a customer's arms.

'How are you feeling?' the original woman asked.

'Okay.'

'Drink this.' She pressed a mug into my hand and I took a few sips, wincing at the sweetness.

'I'm Martha,' she said. 'I'm a nurse. You were about to faint.'

'We've called the police,' another customer said.

'Who's missing?' I looked around to see whether any of my team were downstairs but I couldn't see anyone.

'They're checking,' Martha said. 'There's nothing you can do at the moment. Drink your tea, please.'

Feeling like I might get told off if I didn't do as she asked, I managed half a mug, by which time Lena was back downstairs with one of the laminated photo albums I'd created for customers and a Sharpie.

'Arwen and Hattie are checking the flat,' she said, before I had a chance to ask her who was missing. 'I just need to confirm who we have down here.'

I ran through the names of the ones I could see and Lena placed a tick against each. A customer pointed out one I'd missed.

'I'll be down again shortly,' she said, running back upstairs.

I closed my eyes for a moment, my stomach in knots. Despite the various well-meaning comments from the customers around me about them all being safe, I knew that wasn't the case. There were definitely three or four who'd run off in the commotion.

When Lena returned, she confirmed what I'd feared. Babushka, Viking and Smudge were unaccounted for.

In my mind, the worst thing an animal lover can ever experience is when a beloved pet crosses the rainbow bridge. To us, they aren't 'just a cat' or 'just a dog' – they are members of the family. I'd deeply mourned for every cat I lost and completely understood why some people chose not to have more pets, finding the loss part too hard to handle.

What was happening right now was a very close second and I prayed the outcome wouldn't be that I was mourning the loss of one, two or three members of my beloved fur family.

Several customers offered to walk the street and check alleyways so I sent them out with tubs of cat treats to shake, but I wasn't hopeful they'd find them. Babushka, Viking and Smudge would be so scared that they'd have gone into hiding somewhere. I hoped they'd headed towards the pedestrianised precinct instead of the other direction towards the road. The rest of the customers looked dazed and I stood up, realising I needed to step up as the business owner.

'Thank you to everyone who helped and I'm so sorry your lovely cat experience has ended like this. Although you're all very important to me, my priority needs to be with the cats so I need to get them all back up to the flat. I appreciate that cuts the visit short for most of you but I won't take any payment.'

There were several protests to that but I quashed them. 'I can't do it. You came for an experience which you haven't fully had. I'll do an automatic refund of the entrance fee for anyone who booked online. Thank you.'

Lena and Sienna were downstairs with me so I asked them to coax the cats down here back up to the flat. I went upstairs and asked Max, Arwen and Hattie to do the same while I repeated my customer speech.

'I'm really sorry,' I said, looking round the room. 'What happened this afternoon is completely unexpected and out of my control. I'll take the financial hit. I don't care about that. All I want is my three missing cats back so if you can keep an eye out for them as you leave, I'd be really grateful.'

My voice broke and I raced back down to the kitchen, leaning against the counter and taking deep breaths, willing myself not to cry.

The kitchen door opened and I looked up, hoping it was someone with good news.

'Lena phoned me,' Tom said. 'I came as soon as I heard.'

He held me tightly, giving me strength.

The customers who'd been out on the search returned empty-handed one by one. Soon after, Lena returned with my keys.

'They're all in the flat now and I've deactivated the cat flap,' she said.

The rest of the team joined us. Hattie looked like she'd been crying, Arwen was clearly on the brink, and Sienna and Max looked shell shocked.

'Thank you, all of you,' I said gently. 'Do you want to get your stuff and head home?'

'The tables...' Lena said.

'I'll sort them. You've had a shock. Please go home.'

They went into the kitchen to retrieve their coats and bags and I wished the customers would take a hint and leave too. They had to have all finished their food by now as we were past what would have been closing time.

'Do you want me to kick them out?' Tom murmured, standing beside me in the shop area.

'I'm not sure what to say without sounding really rude. I thought they'd have left by now.'

'Have you put a missing notice on the socials?'

'Not yet.'

'I'll do that in a minute, but that gives me a reason to ask them to leave.'

Tom stepped forward and raised his voice. 'Thank you again for all your support this afternoon. We need to lock up the café now so we can get out and search the streets. Before we go, we'll be putting a missing post on our social media channels. We'd be really grateful if you could watch for it and share that far and wide, especially if you're from the area or have contacts here. The more people who see it, the more likely we are to find Babushka, Viking and Smudge.'

He glanced at me and I gave him a grateful thumbs up so he went upstairs to deliver the message there too. It worked. Five minutes later, the café was empty.

On autopilot, I started clearing the tables while Tom pulled together and posted a missing poster with photos of each of the cats and my mobile number. Money had been left on several of the tables, which was touching.

A knock on the window made me look up. Tara waved and pointed to the door.

'Hattie just told me,' she said as I let her in. 'I'm so sorry. What can I do?'

I didn't have time to answer as Carly and her sister Bethany arrived.

'Jemma's just locking up and Sarah will be here shortly,' Tara said. 'We can round up more bodies if you need them.'

Tom suggested a coordinated search round town with pairs going off in different directions. Word had spread and a few more traders arrived so everyone was allocated an area to search and sent out with a tub of treats, the names of the missing cats and photos on their phones so they didn't snatch any that didn't belong to me.

As Tom and I were about to leave, a couple of police officers arrived so I sent Tom on ahead and ran through the details with them, giving them a copy of Amelia's CV.

'She shouted "free the cats", which is what was graffitied on the door,' I told them. 'It could be a coincidence, but it's a big one if it is. And she seems to have some sort of vendetta against me. She said it served me right for stealing her boyfriend, but I don't have a boyfriend.'

'Do you have an ex-boyfriend who she could be referring to?'

'I do, but I didn't steal him from anyone. We split up a couple of months ago but we'd been together for five years before that and he didn't leave his ex for me. Besides, her name was Mimi and...' I broke off, clapping my hand over my mouth. It couldn't be her, could it? After all this time? Leon had always said that she was jealous of our friendship and convinced there was something going on.

'Isn't Mimi short for Amelia?' one of the officers said.

The other one shrugged, but it was. I'd employed Leon's 'psycho ex' Mimi and she'd got the payback she'd been after for over five years. What was that saying about revenge being a dish best served cold? She'd bided her time and, in exchange for falsely believing I'd taken her boyfriend from her, she'd taken my cats from me.

'Yes, it is,' I said. 'I think it's my ex-boyfriend's ex-girlfriend and I'm now convinced she's the one behind the vandalism. She's probably responsible for the comments on social media, the bad reviews and the food safety officer's visit.'

I gave the officers details of the various incidents and they gave me an email address to send in links to the Tripadvisor reviews and screenshots of the negative comments I'd hidden on Facebook to help build up a picture if it was all down to Amelia, or Mimi as I was sure she was now.

After they left, I rang Tom to find out where he was so I could join him on the search.

'That's a long time to hold a grudge if it is her,' he said when I found him shortly after and gave him an update.

'From what I heard about her from Leon, it sounds like the sort of thing she'd do. She hounded him constantly after they split up. I hope they can hang the vandalism on her. It would be such a relief to know they'd caught who did it.'

* * *

The search for Babushka, Viking and Smudge was unsuccessful. Our Facebook post had been shared stacks of times and Tom made some tweaks to the original post to add in a little more detail about what had happened, confirmation that all the cats were microchipped so could be connected back to me if taken to a vet, and how to approach them if they were spotted.

We sent messages to all the veterinary practices in the area along with photos of the three missing cats, and I contacted Laura from *Bay News*. She shared the post on their Facebook page too, widening the coverage even further.

Finally, I sent a message to Leon.

TO LEON

Have you had any contact with your ex, Mimi, recently? It's urgent

He responded immediately.

FROM LEON

Random question. Why?

TO LEON

Because I employed someone called Amelia to replace you and she coaxed several of the cats outside today. Three of them are still missing. She told me it served me right for stealing her boyfriend and I realised that Mimi is short for Amelia

My phone rang minutes later.

'I wish I could say she wouldn't do something like that,' Leon said, 'but I told you she's a psycho.'

'Is her surname Sharpe?'

'Yes.'

'I thought you said she was blonde.'

'She was when we split up, but it was bleached. She's a brunette.'

She must have reverted back to her natural colour. 'So has she been in touch?' I asked.

'She sends me a message every few months. I've tried blocking her but stopped bothering 'cos she only sets up another profile.'

'Do you ever respond?'

'No.'

'So you didn't tell her we were going to set up the cat café?'

'No. I don't tell her anything, but we both know some of the same people. She could have easily found out.'

'She smashed my window and chucked paint everywhere,' I said. 'I had to put back the opening day to get cleared up. We don't have proof it was her yet, but there's no doubt in my mind that it was.'

'I don't know what you want me to say,' he snapped. 'I'm not in touch with her. I haven't been for years.'

'Okay. No need to get shirty with me. I'm just trying to gather as much information as I can for the police. I thought she might have threatened to do something to the café or the cats if you didn't take her back, or something like that.'

'Yes to wanting us to get back together, but no to the threats. Which cats are missing?'

'Babushka, Viking and Smudge.'

'I hope you find them. How's Marmalade?'

'Loving his new home in Little Sandby.'

'Your parents have him? Why?'

'Because he's been miserable since you left and it broke my heart to see it so I thought he might be happier there and he is.'

There was a pause and I waited for him to object, but what could he say? He'd washed his hands of the responsibility so he couldn't criticise me for any decisions I'd made which were in Marmalade's best interests.

'I'd better go,' he said. 'If it is Mimi, I'm sorry she's targeted you now and I'm sorry about the cats. That's low even for her.'

'One more question before you go. Does she love cats and think they should be freed or was this just about me?'

'She can't stand cats. If you recall, it was her shouting at Marmalade that made me leave for good.'

The call ended and I shook my head at Tom, who'd heard the whole conversation over speakerphone.

'Did you ever see her mistreat the cats?' he asked.

'No, but it explains a few things. She didn't gush over them like the others and she hardly ever referred to them by name. It was always *the one with the black tail* or *the really fluffy one*. And she thought Pebbles was a boy when she tried to steal her.'

'She tried to steal Pebbles?'

'Oh, yeah, I haven't told you about that yet...'

Just after I'd relayed that tale to Tom, my phone rang. I thought it might be Leon calling back because he'd remembered something about Mimi, but it was an unknown number.

'Hello?' I said.

'Is that the cat café?' asked a woman.

'Yes. I'm the owner.'

'I saw your post on Facebook earlier about the missing cats and I think we've found one of them.'

My heart leapt. 'Really? What colour is it?'

'White all over with a black tail, so we think it's Viking. He was in our back yard and was pretty easy to spot, being white.'

'That sounds like him. Where are you? Can I come and see?'

'We're on Swan Street, but I've just put the baby down for the night so I'd rather not have visitors. My partner can bring him to you now if you're at the café. We have a cat ourselves so we have a carrier.'

Fifteen minutes later, we had Viking back. Tom gave him a once-over while I hugged him, but there didn't appear to be any cuts.

'I'm so relieved,' I said, kissing Viking's head and scratching under his chin. My heart broke for him. First that horrible customer pushed him off the table and now this. I hope it didn't make him skittish.

'I'll update the socials and then I'll go home and get my stuff,' Tom said.

'You're staying?' I asked.

'If that's okay. I don't want to leave you on your own tonight after—'

'I don't want you to either,' I confirmed. 'But we do need to talk at some point.'

He nodded. 'We will. I promise.'

46

Sadly, there were no more good-news calls on Sunday night. On Monday morning, I put an updated 'missing' post on the socials with only Babushka and Smudge on it, seeking vigilance and further shares. I felt sick thinking about the two of them all alone and afraid in the cold. They were indoor cats. The outside world was alien to them.

While Tom worked, I obsessively checked Facebook. There were lots of comments from people expressing relief that Viking had been found and hoping for a similar outcome for the other two, but there weren't any sightings of either of them.

The police came round with the news that Amelia had been arrested last night after a friend of hers, disgusted after Amelia had gleefully shared what she'd done, had alerted them to her whereabouts. They picked her up in a pub and an altercation resulted in assaulting a police officer being added to her charges. Presumably fuelled by the drink, she'd spilled the beans on everything. The vandalism had been her and she was very proud of it, and she had tried to steal Pebbles to hurt me. She was behind some of the Tripadvisor comments and several of the Facebook rants, as well as being the one who'd made allegations to the food safety officer. Apparently she hadn't been able to believe her luck when I'd advertised the job, giving her the opportunity to cause further mayhem.

I couldn't get my head around what she'd done. Even if I had 'stolen' Leon from her, it still didn't justify her actions, especially all these years later. Clearly she'd been building up a tower of hate towards me, blaming me for the break-up between her and Leon instead of looking at herself and accepting that she'd pushed him away with her jealousy, mood swings and erratic behaviour.

When the police left, I returned to the socials. Early that afternoon, news circulated that a dead cat had been spotted on the approach road to The Bay Pavilion, presumably struck by a car. It was a cat, not a kitten, so that ruled out Smudge, but it was fluffy, which ruled in Babushka. If Babushka had run down the street rather than towards the main precinct, she could very easily have made her way to that area. I kept asking about the colour but nobody seemed to know. Frustrated, I was about to go down there myself when a comment appeared saying the cat had been removed. It was agonising waiting for more information but finally someone confirmed the colour – mainly brown with black streaks. Babushka was silver with black stripes. My heart broke for whoever the poor little mite belonged to, but it wasn't my cat. And so the waiting game resumed.

* * *

'I feel so hopeless,' Tom said, slumping down beside me on the sofa bed around mid-afternoon. 'We've got a good hour left of decent light. I'm thinking another lap round town.'

'Sounds good. This is driving me mad.'

'How many spoons do you have left?' he asked, looking at me with concern.

'I'm running on borrowed spoons at the moment, but they're worth it.'

He nodded. 'Get your coat on and we'll give it a try.'

We still hadn't talked about what had happened, but this wasn't the opportunity. Ducking up alleyways and calling out names wasn't conducive to chat and I couldn't have focused anyway. I was far too worried about Babushka and Smudge. I appreciated that Tom respected that and didn't try to push me. I also appreciated how worried he was about them.

* * *

I couldn't ignore the fact that I had a business to run and, despite a green-strength flare-up, I had to return to the kitchen on Tuesday to bake cakes. Everyone I knew had been on the lookout. Alison, Aidan and his parents had explored South Bay and my parents had explored the streets where I lived with Leon, where Viking had been found. Even Macey had been out with Hudson in his buggy searching for the cats but there was no sign of them. A couple of sightings on social media had turned out to be false alarms.

At half twelve, I went up to the flat to join Tom for some lunch, but I couldn't stomach anything substantial and only managed to force down a yoghurt. I hadn't been back downstairs for long when a call came through from a veterinary practice in town. My heart pounded, hopeful for good news.

'We've had a kitten admitted and a microchip check has confirmed he belongs to you – Smudge,' a woman said, her voice sounding very serious.

'Is he okay?'

'Smudge was struck by a cyclist and I'm afraid his injuries were too severe. He didn't make it. I'm so sorry.'

My legs buckled and I gripped onto the worktop to hold myself up.

'You're sure it's him?'

'Certain.' She continued talking but I could only pick up the occasional word – something to do with what I wanted them to do with the body. The body? It sounded so cold. Smudge was a gorgeous, loveable kitten – not 'the body'.

'I'll call you back,' I muttered, disconnecting the call.

I sank down the units onto the floor, my body shaking with sobs as I cried, 'No!' This shouldn't have happened. He'd only just turned six months last week. He should still be here with his whole life ahead of him. What had my beautiful Aztec kitten done to deserve this?

* * *

I crawled under my duvet early that night, my body limp with sadness. Smudge hadn't been in my life for long, but that didn't lessen the impact he'd had. I swear the fur family knew what was going on as they all seemed subdued and I'd never had so many of them join me on the bed at one time before.

'I'd ask if you wanted company,' Tom said, leaning against the door-frame, 'but it doesn't look like there's any space for me.'

'I'm all right,' I said. 'I'm not going to be great company anyway.' He'd already been exceptionally generous with his time, helping me with the baking after I alerted him to the tragic news and giving me plenty of hugs.

'Is there anything you need?' he asked.

'You know those felt Christmas tree decorations one of my customers made me? Can you get me the one of Smudge?'

Tom returned moments later and passed me it. 'It looks just like him.'

I ran my fingers lightly over the felt. 'It really does. I'm glad I've got this. I need to get a tree at some point so I can display them all.'

'Anything else you need?'

'No. You get back to your work and thanks for everything today. I don't know what I'd do without you.'

'You don't have to be without me,' he said gently, holding my gaze for a moment before turning and leaving.

I turned onto my side and held my Smudge decoration tightly in one hand while stroking Winnie with the other. She touched her head against my forehead and purred softly and I imagined her words – *Don't you be feeling guilty for wanting to be with Tom-cat, my lover. It's what Smudge would have wanted.*

I closed my eyes and tightened my hold on his decoration, so grateful that Eliza had made one in his likeness in her first batch. What a special gift to remember him by.

47

I didn't want to open the café on Wednesday. I wanted to barricade the doors and hide my remaining thirteen fur babies inside where they were safe, warm and loved, and keep bad people out.

'Nobody would judge you if you didn't open,' Tom had said before I came down to make scones.

'I'd judge me. I'd have let her win if I close. I'd be letting customers and the team down. And Smudge would have died for nothing.'

Wendy, Mark and Fay had all been in touch earlier in the week, asking if there was anything they could do, and they expressed their shock today – the first time I'd seen them in person. I hadn't shared with anyone that Smudge hadn't made it but I thought it only right to let my team know, apologising for the sombre start to the day but asking them to do their best to stay cheerful and positive in front of the customers.

Shortly before we opened, Alison arrived.

'I figured you might need an extra pair of hands,' she said, giving me a hug. 'I'm so sorry.'

'I can't believe she did it. I trusted her. I thought she was my friend.'

'She fooled us all. I'd *never* have dreamed she was capable of something like this.'

'I shouldn't have recruited her without taking references.' I'd been so surprised to find someone with the skills and experience I'd hoped for that my focus had been on getting her in rather than conducting further checks on her suitability.

'Please don't blame yourself,' Alison said, shaking her head. 'Even if you had taken references, would this have come up? Absolutely not. The only one to blame in this is her.'

I told her about Smudge and she hugged me again. 'That's all on Amelia. She might as well have been the one on the bike. There's nothing you could have done to stop this.'

Deep down, I knew she was right. I'd gone over every conversation with Amelia from her interview to her shifts, and analysed everything I'd seen her say or do to the staff, customers and cats and the only possible red flag had been Pebbles in her bag, but it seemed so ludicrous that a member of staff would steal one of the kittens that there was no reason for me to have been suspicious. It was perhaps a little comfort that none of the team had any doubts either. I'd wondered if I'd hear, *Ah, that explains why she...* but they'd all been genuinely shocked by her behaviour.

We were only five sleeps from Christmas Day but I couldn't feel less Christmassy. The team were absolute troopers, keeping everything going and ensuring the customers had a great experience. I don't know what I'd have done without Alison and her amazing gifts of warmth and enthusiasm, stepping up as manager and keeping everyone motivated when all I wanted to do was hide away from the cruel world.

I sat on a stool in the kitchen with a tray of brownies in front of me. I was meant to be cutting them up, but was staring at the fairy lights in the bay window instead. It would be the first Christmas for all the kittens but Smudge hadn't lived to see his first one. Christmas Eve on Sunday would be Babushka and Heathcliff's seventh birthdays. Would Babushka make it to hers? Would she be home to celebrate with her brother? Or was it already too late?

'We need to get you upstairs.'

'Mmm?'

'Tabby, you need to take a break.' Tom pulled off some kitchen roll and dabbed my cheeks. I hadn't even realised I was crying, but I hadn't noticed him coming into the kitchen either.

'The café,' I muttered. 'Who's going to...'

'I'll sort it,' Alison said. 'Tom's right. You need to rest.'

Tom removed my apron and picked up my phone and the pair of them bundled me up the stairs to the first floor. Alison took the till keys from me, reassuring me she had everything under control, and Tom led me up the next flight to the flat.

I had the strangest sensation as we continued up to the bedroom, as though I was outside my body, watching down.

'So tired,' I murmured, flagging against him as we reached the top.

'It's all right. You'll be in bed soon.'

He led me into the bedroom. I had no energy to undress and crept under the duvet fully clothed. Heathcliff jumped on the bed and curled up beside me. My heart ached for him. He'd been lost without his sister, roaming from room to room looking for her. I longed for nothing more than to be able to reunite them but three nights had passed so it wasn't looking good.

* * *

'Tabby?'

Tom's voice was soft, but it was definitely him.

He said my name again and I tried to open my eyes, but they were so heavy and the room was too bright. Why hadn't I thought to close the blinds? I drifted off to sleep again.

It was dark in the bedroom when I opened my eyes later, and I thought Tom must have closed the blinds for me but they were still open as I could see the glow from the streetlight outside.

I felt for Heathcliff and found him still beside me, but my hand stroked over another cat who didn't feel so soft. I frowned at the matted, gritty fur and opened my eyes wide, trying to adjust them to the gloom. It couldn't be!

Heart thumping, I flicked on my bedside light and blinked several times but my eyes weren't deceiving me. Babushka was curled up next to her brother – dirty and tangled but alive and back home where she belonged. I had no idea how she'd got here, but my heart swelled with joy as I cuddled her closer and drifted off to sleep again.

I awoke sometime later to the sound of my phone ringing – a different ringtone to Tom's. Tom must have answered it as I could hear him talking, although I couldn't make out the words. A little later he appeared in my doorway.

'Babushka's back,' I said.

'I tried to wake you, but you were out for the count, so I left her with you.'

'Did she just turn up?'

Tom perched on the bed beside me. 'No. Someone found her near Hearnshaw Park and thought they recognised her from the post on the *Bay News* page. They took her to a vet to check and the microchip came back to you. I picked her up this afternoon.'

'I can't tell you how relieved I am.'

'I can imagine. She needs a bath, but I thought you'd rather have time with her first.'

'Thank you. What time is it?'

'Quarter past six.'

I pushed myself up onto my elbows, shocked at that. 'I've slept all day?'

'You obviously needed it. How's the fibro?'

'I'm not in pain at the moment, but who knows tomorrow? Who was on the phone?'

'Your mum, checking how you're doing. She says to call her back if you're up to it but she'll speak to you tomorrow if you're not. Your cousin Fiona phoned earlier too. She wanted to check in as she hadn't heard from you in ages and wanted to make sure you were listening to your body whispering to slow down.'

'I need to call her. I've kept meaning to, but it's just been one thing after another. How were things in the café today? Did Alison manage okay?'

'She had some help. A woman whose name I've completely blanked on came in around eleven and offered to help. She said she's a regular. Late fifties, maybe? Curly hair. Great with cats.'

'That's Shelley. Aw, bless her. She doesn't usually come in until the end of the day.'

'She told Alison that she'd heard what happened so wanted to drop by sooner to see if she could do anything.'

'That's so good of her.'

'Alison's coming back tomorrow and Tara's lending us one of her staff until the end of Friday to give you a couple more days to rest. She's also making some scones and cakes for you and says she's – and I quote – *not interested in your protests, so accept it because it's happening*.'

I smiled. 'That sounds like Tara.'

The kindness from everyone was overwhelming and, even though I found it hard to accept help, I knew I needed to while I processed everything that had gone on and what I wanted to do next. I had some big decisions to make.

48

I had expected a flare-up the following day but my fibromyalgia was predictable in its unpredictability and I was spared. My number one priority was Babushka. I wanted to get her clean, groom her and shower her with attention. Heathcliff had barely left her side since she arrived home and, when I took her into the bathroom for a bath, he followed us.

I placed a baby bath inside the normal bath and filled it with warm water. Heathcliff hopped into the bath and sat beside the baby one, not taking his eyes off his sister, while I cleaned Babushka. She loved bathing and grooming so was happy to let me pamper her.

Mum rang while I was brushing Babushka's fur so I called her back when I'd finished grooming and reassured her I was taking things carefully and had plenty of cover in the café thanks to Alison and Tara.

Tom nipped out for a couple of client meetings but otherwise spent the day in the dining room, working hard. With Babushka home safe and no more cats on the loose, it had to be time to address the situation between us. While it hadn't been awkward since he'd moved back in, I was now very much aware of it being the elephant in the room, but sensed he was waiting for me to approach it when I was ready. Hopefully he wouldn't have to work too late and we could have that conversation tonight.

I rang Fiona and apologised for not being in touch since our last chat, a whopping six weeks ago.

'I wanted to make sure I hadn't overwhelmed you with too much information,' she said.

'No, you hadn't. It's been so helpful and I've needed it so much since opening the café.' Conscious that we could be on the phone for hours if I told her everything, I provided a brief version of what had happened, how I'd made some huge steps towards accepting my fibromyalgia diagnosis, and how my biggest challenge was working out what my life looked like now that I'd done that.

'The café doesn't work with my fibro,' I told her. 'I've been thinking about it a lot since we opened but the last week has really hammered it home. So, as well as accepting that I have fibro and my life needs to change to work with that, I've accepted that I can't have fibro and a cat café, which puts me in a bit of a pickle.'

'Aw, Tabby, I'm sorry, but I'm not surprised. I thought it when you told me about the café but I wasn't going to rain on your parade. I can't help you with what you do next, but I can continue to help you with the acceptance side of things if you need any more advice.'

'I appreciate that. You don't think I'm giving up, then?'

'Definitely not. You've given it your best shot but you've gone, *hang on, this isn't right for me and my body*. That level of acceptance takes guts. That level of acceptance is about trying to work with your fibro instead of fighting against it. You can't do better than that.'

I felt reassured when I came off the phone. I still didn't know what I was going to do or when I was going to do it, but I was absolutely clear that I couldn't continue to manage the cat café. And instead of feeling upset about it, I felt relief. It had to be the right decision.

* * *

'I cannot look at another column of figures today,' Tom said, emerging from the dining room rubbing his hands down his face at half six that evening. It would normally have been five-a-side football night but, being so close to Christmas, the lads all had too much on so were taking a break until the New Year.

'I've just boiled the kettle,' I said. 'Cup of tea?'

'Yeah, but it's all right. I'll make it.'

'No, you won't,' I said, planting my hands on my hips and giving him a stern look. 'You look shattered. Go into the lounge and I'll make the drinks. Also, there's no food in the house so I've ordered some takeaway pasta from Mario's. I'm picking it up at seven. Don't say you'll do it because I won't let you. It's my turn to look after you for a change.'

Tom gave me a weak smile. 'You star. I'm so hungry, but I can't face cooking. If food's ready for seven, I might jump in the shower first to wake myself up.'

The temperature had dropped and there was quite a breeze as I walked the five-minute journey to Mario's. Nonetheless, it felt so good to be outside. One of the things I hadn't considered when moving into the flat was how little exercise I'd get – other than up and down the three flights of stairs – and how infrequently I'd leave the premises. I missed walks along the seafront and through the countryside in Little Sandby. This lifestyle really didn't suit me.

I hadn't paused to look at any of the Christmas lights in the main part of town when we'd been out searching for the cats, but I stopped on my way back from Mario's and looked up and down the main precinct. The enormous Christmas tree outside the shopping centre had multi-coloured lights on it and there were colourful lighting arrangements suspended between the shops showing various Christmassy items. From where I was standing, I could see candles on one, gifts on another, holly, stars and baubles. I'd suggest to Tom that we come out one evening, spoons allowing, to properly look at them. I wanted to capture some positive Christmas memories to balance out the sadness.

* * *

'That was so good,' Tom said, licking his garlicky fingers then wiping them down his jeans, which made me smile. Rylan always did that too. It drove Macey mad.

I reached for his empty bowl but he took mine instead. 'You have to at least let me clear the dishes.'

He returned moments later and sat down beside me. 'How was it not spending the day in the café?'

'Surprisingly good. I needed some space and I can't tell you how relieved I am to have Babushka back. I've done a lot of thinking and I've made a big decision. Running the café isn't for me. I don't want to do it anymore.'

Tom nodded slowly, and I sensed he'd been expecting me to say this.

'Because of what Amelia did?' he asked.

'That was the final straw, but this has been building up for a long time. When I got upset about the Tripadvisor reviews, I told you I wasn't sure if I could do this anymore and now I know I can't. It's not about what Amelia did. It's not even about the bad reviews, a few nasty customers, or the staffing issues. It's about me and how I live with fibromyalgia. I've got to stop fighting it and listen to it instead. The only way this could have worked was if Leon had run it with me because I can't do it on my own – too many hours, too much pressure and stress, too many nights going to sleep in fear that I'll wake up with a flare-up and nobody to cover for me. It's time to let go of this dream and find a new one.'

I thought I might get emotional telling Tom, but I felt strangely calm. Was that because, the moment Leon stepped away, I'd known deep down that it wasn't just the end for our relationship?

'What if...?' Tom paused and chewed his lip. 'What if I ran the café with you? What if I did what Leon was meant to do?'

His expression held such sincerity that I did now feel emotional.

'What about your job?'

'I could cut back on my clients and work on evenings.'

'You'd do that for me?' I asked, my voice tight with emotion.

'I'd do anything for you, Tabby-cat. I don't want you to let go of your dream, especially when there's something I can do to help you hang onto it.'

'But you love your job.'

'I love you more.'

Tears pricked my eyes as I registered his words. 'But you left.'

He grimaced. 'I know. I shouldn't have done that. I wish I hadn't.'

'Why did you?'

'It was awkward between us after what Rylan said and I didn't know what to do or say.' He paused and lowered his eyes. Sensing there was more to come, I remained silent.

'I analyse accounts for a living and I love it,' he said eventually. 'For me, a world of numbers, spreadsheets and accountancy software makes sense. It's a comfortable place to be. You put the numbers where they're meant to go and it all adds up. Analysing my life is a different kettle of fish. It's a dark place that I prefer to avoid so I've tended to go through life just accepting what happens and not trying to do anything to change it. I'm the guy who moved into my apartment intending to get a cat, discovered that I couldn't have one and, instead of pulling out, accepted that no cat was how it was.'

He chewed his lip once more, looking uncertain.

'Go on,' I encouraged gently. 'I'm listening.'

'Recently, I haven't been able to stop the analysis of my life. It started when I found you in your parents' garden and you told me what Leon had done. It made me so angry and that's not like me. I couldn't stop thinking about it when I got home. I even went for a run to try and work out the frustration, and I hate running. I couldn't work out why it had affected me so much. I put it down to a fiercely protective big brother thing but this voice in my head kept saying *but you're not her brother*. I didn't know what to do with that.

'A fortnight later, you showed us how bad your fibromyalgia really was and the anger was back – with Leon for abandoning you when he knew about your pain, and how hard running the café was going to be without him. I was angry with your diagnosis and with myself for not noticing how bad it was, and I was desperate to do something to try to make it better.'

'Which is why you offered to move in,' I suggested.

'Exactly. When I went home to pack, I was so tense that I went for another run and I had all these questions in my head about why my reaction was so strong and why I'd suggested moving in with you so quickly and the answers scared me. I realised that it wasn't just me being a caring friend. It was because I cared for you in a different way. I wanted to help you but I also wanted to be with you.'

'I had no idea,' I said, placing my hand gently on his thigh. 'You never said or did anything to suggest that you were feeling like that.'

'Are you surprised? This is me we're talking about – track record of being worse than useless when it comes to this sort of thing. So many times that first week, I psyched myself up to saying something but I just couldn't do it. When we had the food fight, I came the closest. I thought there was something sparking there, but I talked myself out of it.'

'There *was* something,' I said. 'I felt it too.'

He rolled his eyes. 'The one time in my life that I don't just go with it. How typical is that? Anyway, the weekend arrived and it was crunch time. I wanted to stay but you were so insistent I went home that I convinced myself you'd had enough of me and I was stupid to think that we'd have any chance of a future together. Being away from you was hell. I was so worried about you and I was annoyed with myself for putting my feelings first so I gave myself a good talking to. I needed to stop this emotional crap that was tying me in knots and just be a friend helping out a friend going through a tough time. Easier said than done. When I FaceTimed you to ask if I could move back in, I've never been so scared in my life. I thought you might say no.'

'Aw, Tom. If it helps, I'd missed you so much too and not just as a helping hand. I missed *you* and it scared me as well. I tried to convince myself that it was a combination of gratitude for your help and relief at having someone here after the window was smashed.'

His eyes lit up at that admission and he placed his hand over mine. I so badly wanted to kiss him right now, but it was obvious it was difficult for him to open up like this and I didn't want to get distracted. Besides, this could be the most important conversation of my life and it needed to happen. I encouraged him to continue.

'Every day I spent with you, my feelings got stronger but so did the life-analysis. I had so many thoughts in here...' He tapped his forehead,

'...about how to handle it. What if I said something and you laughed? What if I kissed you and you were repulsed? What if we did get together but it didn't last and it caused a rift in your family? Or what if your family didn't like the idea of us being together? And that really freaked me out.'

I shook my head slowly. 'Which is exactly what happened.'

'Yep. If my best mate – the man I think of as a brother – couldn't accept us, what were your parents going to think? I could lose my family and I could lose my job. And that's when the analysis took an unexpected turn.'

He ran both his hands through his hair and exhaled loudly. 'This is hard.'

'It's okay,' I said gently. 'Take your time.'

He sat forward with his head in his hands for a few moments, presumably trying to work out how to word it. My heart raced, nervous about where this was heading. With another deep exhale, he sat up once more.

'When we were putting the Christmas decorations up, I mentioned Tracey and you asked me if I wanted to talk about her. I said I was good and there'd been no lasting damage. I thought that was the case but, after what Rylan said, everything I'd tried to bury about my childhood bubbled to the surface and spewed out everywhere. I've never said this before, but I have a huge fear of rejection. My own mother didn't want me. She was never physically abusive, but the emotional abuse was horrific. I spent my early childhood being told *I wish you'd never been born* and *I should have let them keep you at the hospital*. She had pearls of wisdom too, like *Don't have kids, they're such a drain* and *Don't fall in love 'cos everyone leaves eventually*. Although the sting in the tail on that one was *Although I wouldn't worry too much about that one – you're never going to find someone who loves you because you're not very loveable*.'

'Aw, Tom, I'm so sorry.'

'She was obviously a very messed-up woman. When I went into care, I was relieved to get away but I had some wounds, the biggest one being rejection. Moving from one foster placement to another didn't help that. No matter how many times the social worker told me that the moves were just until they found a longer-term placement, I was convinced it was me and these people were rejecting me too. And then Nanna Betsy took me on and I became part of the Walsh family and, for the first time ever, I knew what it was like to be loved.'

His voice cracked and tears filled his eyes.

'Sorry,' he said, swiping at the tears. 'I didn't think I was going to get so upset by it.'

'Hug?' I asked, desperate to comfort him like he'd comforted me so many times.

'Yes, but can I have it when I'm done? I need to get this out.'

'Of course. When you're ready.'

'Actually, I need some water.'

My heart broke for him as he powered across the room. I could completely understand the need to have some space. He'd never opened up about his childhood before so this was huge.

'Sorry about that,' he said, returning a few minutes later with a glass of water for each of us. He bent over to put the drinks on the coffee table and, when he straightened up, his eyes were red and puffy.

'I *will* take that hug now,' he said. 'Give me strength to keep going.'

I stood up and wrapped my arms round him, pressing my head to his chest while he rested his head against mine.

Several minutes must have passed before he loosened his hold. 'I needed that. Thank you.'

We sat down again and he continued. 'Your whole family were incredible. You accepted me from the off, had me to stay at Christmas, took me on holiday. All these things I'd never had before, I had with you and I threw myself into it. But there was always this fear at the back of my mind that I'd get home from school one day to the news that I needed to leave, that you'd all had enough of me and that Tracey had been right about me – nobody was ever going to love me.'

'But we did all love you. We still do.'

'The logical side of me knows that, but the emotional side is a bit delicate. So when Rylan said what he said, it just all came back to me. This was it. This was the moment when your family were going to reject me because they knew I wasn't loveable and therefore wasn't worthy of you. If your brother rejected the idea of us being together, it seemed likely your parents would too and that would make you realise you'd made a huge mistake and...' He shook his head. 'As the week progressed and nothing happened between us, I thought it was a matter of time before you told me to leave, so I took myself out of the game before you could reject me.'

'I wouldn't have rejected you. None of us would.'

'I can see that now, but I couldn't at the time. As I said, numbers are great but I'm not so good at the emotional analysis. Looking back, I can't believe I packed my stuff without talking to you. No wonder you had a go at me.'

'I'm so sorry about that, Tom. I shouldn't have snapped at you like that. Yes, you'd packed, but you did try to explain and I didn't let you. I should have. I've regretted that ever since and I really regret my parting shot.'

Tom shook his head. 'Don't. When you said it was no wonder I'd stayed single all these years, it was actually a light bulb moment for me. I realised that my fear of rejection had controlled my love life – or lack of it. I think that I deliberately messed up any dates I had because I couldn't face getting close to anyone, only to have them reject me down the line. The only date I've ever enjoyed and the only time I've ever truly been myself was our practice one. That was what gave me the courage to kiss you.' He smiled at me. 'Well, that and Celine Dion. When I moved out, I had that song on a constant loop. I know all the lyrics now. I kept imagining that was us, happy together years and years down the line having faced all life's tough challenges together. I picked up the phone so often, but I couldn't make that call. I couldn't face the rejection. I couldn't bear to be what Tracey said I was – unlovable.'

'She was wrong. You're not unlovable. My family love you. I love you.'

He gave me a weak smile. 'But as a friend.'

'Once upon a time, yes. But not anymore. I love you as so much more and I believe that song *is* about us.'

Tears glistened in his eyes again. 'You mean that?'

'I mean every word.'

He smiled at me so tenderly. 'In case it wasn't clear from that outpouring and from what I said before about loving you more than my job, I don't just mean as a friend. I love you too.'

I'd waited a long time for another kiss from Tom and had feared it would never happen again, but as his lips met mine, it was so worth the wait.

49

We lay on top of my bed a little later, propped up on our elbows, facing each other. Heathcliff and a clean and fluffy Babushka had joined us, and Rubix and Cloud were both draped over Tom.

'I think the cats approve,' I said, smiling at him.

'Maybe we should send them to Rylan's to plead our case.'

'I think Rylan will be fine. Macey says he's mortified by his reaction and thinks it would be cool if we were together.'

'Macey knows?'

'She brought Hudson to visit and interrogated me. You know what she's like. I didn't tell her I loved you, but I did admit there were feelings there. Didn't Rylan say anything to you at five-a-side last week?'

'There's a crowd of us so there's no way he'd have brought up something like that. I don't think he believed Macey anyway.'

Babushka stretched out, padded her paws on the duvet and changed position, nuzzling closer to me. I stroked her, relief flowing through me once more that she was back safe.

'I've got a question for you,' I said. 'I kind of don't want to ask this but it'll niggle if I don't. If you knew you wanted to be with me, why did you go to Brodie's Christmas party?'

His eyes widened. 'You know about that?'

'Yeah, and I don't want to make an issue of it because we weren't together at the time, but it's—'

'I didn't go with her,' he said.

'But she came into the café looking for you. She said you were her plus one.'

He sighed. 'I wasn't. It was all a big misunderstanding. Brodie messaged on Friday night inviting me. I'd got back to the apartment after moving out and my head was exploding. It was an easy no for me but I was thinking about rejection and how much it hurts so I stupidly sent her this non-committal *I'll think about it* reply. It sounds awful but I completely forgot about it – other things on my mind – until I got this phone call from her on Saturday afternoon to tell me she'd given me the wrong venue and I realised she'd taken my reply as a yes. She was fine about it, but I'm so sorry you thought I was going out with her again. You must have been cursing me.'

'I was a tad insulted that you'd moved on so quickly.'

'You really think you'd be that easy to get over?'

I shrugged. 'I was for Leon.'

Tom brushed his lips against mine ever so softly. 'He wasn't right for your future, but I think he was right for you at the time.'

'That's a nice way of looking at it. Feels like it wasn't a wasted five years. Speaking of the future, we got a bit distracted from talking about the café. You know I can't let you leave your job just for me?'

'I want you to be happy.'

'And I want you to be happy and this isn't the way. I know you enjoy baking and I know we'd work well together, but you'd be giving up on your dreams to help me achieve mine and I've already made that mistake with Leon. There's no way I'd make it with you. You've got a partnership in Mum and Dad's company and one day you'll take over completely. That's what I want for you. Besides, the cat café isn't my dream anymore.'

'What is?'

'I don't know, but it's out there somewhere. As for what happens next with this place, I need to do some sums and a lot more thinking.'

He gave me a cheeky smile. 'Ooh, if only we knew someone who was good at sums.'

I laughed as he kissed me once more.

'Whatever you decide to do, I'll support you,' he said. 'I have a question for you. You know when you described my ideal woman to me, did you realise you were describing yourself?'

I frowned for a moment, recalling what I'd said. 'No. I didn't realise, but I see it now.'

'You got emotional. Why?'

'Because I so wanted that person to be me and not Brodie.'

'It was you. It *is* you. When you said that thing about the balance sheet and about family, that was the moment I knew I'd fallen in love with you.'

I pressed my body against his, melting into his kiss. I might not yet know what my dream job was, but I'd found my dream partner and I actually had Leon to thank for it. That eleventh-hour telephone call from him at Mum and Dad's was what had triggered a shift in our friendship. And, weirdly, I had my fibromyalgia to thank for it too. Without that, Tom would never have moved in. Who knew fibro would actually bring me a gift?

50

'This isn't helping make the scones,' I reprimanded Tom, giggling as he wrapped his arms round my waist from behind and nuzzled my neck the following morning while I was trying to roll out the dough.

'I'll stop if you *really* want me to.'

'Maybe I deserve a quick break.' I spun round and kissed him, wishing we could spend all day doing that.

'But now I do need to bake,' I said, reluctantly pulling away. 'And I think you'd better leave me to it because I can't concentrate with you here. Up to the flat, please. I'll see you later.'

With another kiss, he left me to it. I wiped my hands and put some music on, unable to resist Celine Dion's 'Another Year Has Gone By'. Singing (very badly) along to it, I felt happier than I had in a long time and so much lighter for sharing the decision with Tom that the cat café wasn't right for me, for having his unwavering support on that, and for getting our relationship back on track.

Despite the happiness, I ached for Smudge, as I still did for my other fur babies who'd crossed the rainbow bridge over the years. They all left a gap in my life and their pawprints on my heart.

Tom and I were anxious to let the family know that we were a couple and had invited my parents, Rylan and Macey round for pre-Christmas drinks and nibbles this evening. I couldn't imagine my parents would react negatively and I desperately hoped Macey had been telling the truth about Rylan coming round to the idea, otherwise it could be an uncomfortable evening and cast a shadow over Christmas. Better to face that now than risk it happening when everyone was together on Boxing Day.

Alison was helping again today, but couldn't work over the weekend due to family commitments. Wendy, Mark and Fay were all in and I had my last day with Tara's team member so we should be okay for staff. We didn't have a huge number of bookings, although I anticipated a lot of walk-ins – fraught-looking customers seeking a spot of relaxing timeout with the cats between tackling the Christmas shopping.

Alison arrived half an hour early, saying she thought I might need a hand. 'I can't stop thinking about Smudge,' she said, hugging me. 'How are you holding up?'

'Not great,' I admitted, locking the door behind her. 'It was such a senseless loss of life and should never have happened.'

'How are Viking and Babushka doing?'

'Babushka's doing amazingly well. Viking's a bit skittish still, although that started when a horrible customer shoved him off their table. He hasn't been back down to the café since Amelia let him out, although that could be because I've been in the flat most of the time. It'll be interesting to see whether he comes down today.'

'People can be so cruel.'

We went into the kitchen and I started piping icing across a lemon drizzle cake while Alison removed her coat and pulled on her apron.

'How's the fibro today?'

'It's a good day.'

'And how are things with Tom?'

I turned round and grinned at her, icing bag still in my hand. 'I wondered how soon you'd get to that! Things are amazing with Tom. We've finally had a talk and we're together. We're telling the family tonight.'

'Oh, my God!' she squealed, flinging her arms round me once more and making me squirt some icing out of the bag. 'I'm so thrilled for you both. He's lovely, Tabby. Aw!'

'And I do have another piece of news, but this has to be strictly between us. I don't want any of the team to go into Christmas thinking they might lose their jobs, but I'm going to put the café up for sale in the New Year.' I narrowed my eyes at her. 'Tom didn't seem surprised and you don't look it either.'

'I'm not – not after our recent conversations. Do you know what you'll do instead?'

'Absolutely no idea, but I've got time to think. It could take months to sell this place, if at all. The fantasy is that there's an ailurophile with a catering background and deep pockets already coveting it. The reality is that we've only been open for five weeks so there's no track record of success. We're doing brilliantly so far but it's the run-up to the Christmas season when the town is busy and the café's still a novelty. Who knows what will happen when January hits? It's a massive risk and I doubt many would take it, especially when I didn't spare any expense when I did the place up, so I mean it when I say deep pockets.'

'Someone will want it,' she said. 'Like I said to you before, you've already done the hardest part. They just need to step in and keep doing what you're doing.'

'And bring some cats with them 'cos they're not having any of mine.'

Alison laughed. 'Ooh, by the way, the gift bag over there has your Christmas present in.' She pointed to a large bag with a cat on it wearing a Christmas hat.

'I'm so sorry, Ali, but I haven't managed to get your present yet.'

'I'm not surprised with everything you've had to deal with. No rush. I quite like after-Christmas gifts – extends the whole festive period. Right, what do you need me to do?'

* * *

As I'd anticipated, we had a lot of walk-ins across the day and they did all look frazzled, but refreshments and a little cat time meant they left with a smile on their faces, looking a lot more relaxed.

After the team had welcomed the 3.45 p.m. customers into the café, Alison joined me in the kitchen. 'I was thinking about Christmas gifts. You said you haven't bought my gift yet, but have you done any of your Christmas shopping?'

I shook my head, grimacing. 'Not a single gift. I was going to do it on Monday but I had other things on my mind. I've already apologised to everyone that they can either have a gift after Christmas this year or a voucher.'

'Why don't you go out now? We've got eight tables booked for the last sitting at four and I doubt there'll be many walk-ins. You could get an hour in – maybe two, as some of the high street shops are open till six.'

A break and some fresh air would be good, even if I didn't actually do any shopping, so I slipped off my apron and dashed upstairs for my hat, coat and scarf.

'Things have calmed downstairs so I've been sent out Christmas shopping,' I said to Tom. 'I don't suppose you fancy a break?'

'I'd love one.'

'It'll mean my gifts for you still need to wait until after Christmas,' I warned as I wound my scarf round my neck.

'I've already got the only gift I want,' he responded, drawing me into a gentle kiss.

* * *

'Crikey, it's cold out,' Tom said, whipping his phone out to check his weather app once we stepped outside. 'Two degrees. They could be right about that snow.'

The weather reports had warned that the current cold snap would continue across the weekend, and that we might have snow on Boxing Day.

I tightened my scarf and pulled my hat down a little lower to cover my ears, then linked my arm through Tom's as we set off up Castle Street.

'I haven't looked in any of the windows this month,' I said, pausing in front of Seaside Blooms next door. 'This Christmas has been such a blur.'

A stunning Christmas floral display took pride of place, surrounded by wreaths and Christmassy gifts. Next to that, Bay Babies had faceless mannequins standing or crawling in fake snow and wearing the most adorable baby and toddler clothes. On one side of the window were party outfits and, on the other side, there was an angel, snowman and Santa costume. Warm white lights twinkled round the window.

'I might get some clothes for Hudson,' I said, pushing open the door. 'Have you got anything for him yet?'

'I was planning to do the classic stereotypical man thing of shopping on Christmas Eve and panic-buying rubbish gifts.'

'You do *not* do that!' I cried. 'You always give really thoughtful gifts and I know you're organised well in advance.'

'Not this year. Cats and accounts only and, before you start feeling guilty, I wouldn't have had it any other way.'

He looked at me so tenderly that I longed to kiss him. I'd hold that thought for later. For now, we had some serious shopping to do. An hour would hopefully be enough to whizz in and out of the Castle Street shops as I wanted to shop local if possible. It helped that I didn't have many people to buy for. Outside my immediate family, I only needed gifts for Alison and Madison. I also wanted a gift for my cousin Fiona as a thank you for all her help, but would have to post it after Christmas.

As we looked through the clothes in Bay Babies, I had a warm feeling in my stomach with the realisation that I'd finally found the person with whom I might have a family one day. We could be standing in this very shop at some point in the next few years choosing outfits for our own baby. Tom glanced at me and gave me another tender smile and I wondered whether he'd had the same thought.

We found the cutest sleepsuit for Hudson with a picture of a cat on the front (of course) and the words 'Crazy Cat Baby', which made us laugh, and a few other clothes for him. I also bought the sweetest pink pinafore dress with a cat face on it for Madison.

Over in Bear With Me, I completed Madison's gift with a gorgeous lilac squishy cat toy and bought Hudson a lovely soft teddy bear wearing a Christmas jumper.

In Charlee's Chocolates, I purchased several boxes of chocolates –

one for each team and family member – but it was Yorkshire's Best where I managed to buy most of my gifts. Run by Tara's partner, Jed, it was partly a gallery of his amazing artwork and partly a showcase for locally crafted gifts. Tom and I chose one of Jed's framed pictures for Mum and Dad and another for Rylan and Macey. For Alison, I found a gorgeous scarf and a trio of sea salt candles, and bought a second set of candles for Fiona. Finally we nipped into Forget-me-not Cards for some gift bags and Christmas wrap.

'I think that has to be the quickest and most successful shopping trip I've ever been on,' Tom said as we crossed the cobbles and returned to the cat café before 5 p.m., laden with bags.

'Me too. It's my kind of shopping trip.'

Shelley the cat whisperer was settling her bill with Alison.

'Perfect timing,' Alison said, smiling at me. 'Shelley was hoping to have a quick word with you before she left.'

'I'll take these upstairs and get the gifts ready for...' Tom tailed off, giving me a knowing look, and I appreciated that he knew exactly what was needed – wrapping Alison's and Madison's gifts and a box of chocolates for each of the team members who were working today, as I wouldn't see any of them again until after Christmas.

'That would be brilliant. Thanks, Tom,' I said, as he took my bags and headed upstairs.

'Lovely to see you, Shelley,' I said, steering her towards one of the clean tables and removing my hat, scarf and coat. 'I can't thank you enough for helping out the other day. That was so good of you.'

'It was a pleasure. I loved every second of it.'

'How's your mum?'

She shook her head. 'Not good. She's had another fall and broken her arm this time.'

'I'm so sorry.'

'Thank you. She was actually still in hospital so they got her fixed up quickly. She's very confused so she now needs specialist care. She's got a host of health problems and, sadly, I don't think she'll be with us for much longer, so it's also time I started to reclaim my life. I don't expect an immediate answer as I'm sure your head is all over the place at the moment after everything that's happened recently but, if you're looking for any more staff in the New Year, I'd be ever so grateful if you could consider me.'

'You can buy the place if you want,' I joked.

Her eyes widened. 'You're selling?'

I clapped my hand across my mouth when I realised what I'd just said, the high spirits from the successful shopping trip getting to me. 'Please don't say anything to anyone. That should *not* have slipped out. The staff don't know and I have no intention of saying anything until the New Year. I don't want any customers knowing either.'

She leaned in a little closer. 'Don't worry. Nobody will hear it from me. You're not letting that awful woman drive you out, are you?'

I checked behind me to make sure nobody was within earshot but there was only Alison running a mop around. The others were obviously still cleaning upstairs. 'That didn't help, but it's my health. I have fibromyalgia and I just can't run this place with it. It wouldn't have been an issue if my ex-boyfriend had run it with me as planned, but he dumped me and I've had to rely on friends and family since then, which isn't sustainable.'

'I'm sorry to hear about the fibromyalgia. I have a couple of friends with it so I can imagine the challenges you have.'

She fished into her cat tote bag and removed a notepad and pen – both with cats on, of course.

'I'll give you my mobile number and email address,' she said. 'If you're serious about selling, I'd love to have first refusal.'

I remembered her telling me the first time she came in that she'd love to run a cat café. I also recalled that she'd run a restaurant with her former husband, so she had a catering background too. Was my fantasy purchaser sitting right in front of me?

'Shelleythecatqueen,' I said, smiling at her email address when she handed me her contact details.

'My friends used to call me it and it stuck. Cat queen, cat whisperer, cat lady – I'll answer to them all.' She rose and pulled her tote bag onto her shoulder. 'I'd best get back to the hospital.'

She wished a happy Christmas to Alison and I followed her out onto the street.

'You're serious about this?' I asked, her contact details folded up in my hand.

'Never been more serious and don't worry about the financial side. I've got the money. I'd have done this myself years ago, but I lacked the vision and the time. You've provided the vision and, with the way things are going with Mother, I'll soon have the time too. Have a think about it and work out a price that reflects what you've spent on this place, and drop me a message when you're ready. No rush. Enjoy your Christmas and New Year first – you absolutely deserve to. But please know I won't change my mind. I was hoping for a job but if I can have a café and a home too, all my Christmases will have come at once.'

With a wave, she left and I stood there for a moment, oblivious to the cold. I glanced up and down the street at the late shoppers and the beautiful lights in the windows, then looked up at the zigzag of lights between the buildings and, beyond that, at the dark sky. *Did you send her to me, Nanna? If so, thank you.*

Shelley said all her Christmases had just come at once. With Tom's admission that he loved me and now this, it felt like mine had too.

'On a scale of one to ten, how nervous are you?' I asked Tom as 7 p.m. approached – the time the family were expected for drinks and nibbles.

'Twelve,' he said. 'You?'

'Same. I swear the cats can pick up on it.' Pebbles hadn't left my shoulder for the past hour, Winnie wouldn't leave Tom's side, and several of the fur family were pacing restlessly.

A message pinged through.

> **FROM MUM**
>
> Just parked so we'll be with you in 5 mins. Got my key so will save you doing the stairs xx

I showed it to Tom and he breathed in deeply and exhaled slowly. 'I feel sick,' he said.

'It'll go well,' I reassured him, squeezing his hand. 'They love us both. They'll be happy for us.'

'God, I hope so!'

Minutes later, we heard voices on the stairs and I opened the flat door. Hugs were given as we welcomed them inside. Hudson was asleep in his carrier, so Macey took him through to the lounge and placed him beside the sofa bed.

'Everyone make yourselves comfortable,' I said, watching them all select a seat as Tom and I stood together with our backs to the lounge door.

'We'll take your drinks orders in a moment but, before we do, there's something Tom and I want to tell you.'

I caught Macey's eye and it was obvious from her expression that she knew what I was about to say and was stifling an excited squeal.

'Having Tom staying here with me has been invaluable. The help he's given me with the café and my fibro has been above and beyond so thank you, Mum and Dad, for agreeing to him taking time off work and flexing his hours for me at what I know is a really challenging time of the year for you all.' I paused to take a breath, wishing the butterflies would stop chasing each other round my stomach.

'We've always been friends but spending so much time has brought us closer together and...' I glanced up at Tom, wishing I wasn't finding this so difficult. Doing the speech thing had seemed like a good idea at the time but having four pairs of eyes on me was so daunting that my mouth had gone completely dry. I hoped Tom could see my silent plea for help.

His eyes softened and he put his arm round my shoulders. 'This might come as a shock to some of you and others might not like it, but I've fallen in love with Tabby and it's mutual. We thought you should be the first to know.'

'Well, about time too,' Dad declared. 'I win!'

I glanced at Macey but she shrugged, her expression bewildered, so she evidently hadn't said anything to my parents.

Mum stood up and hugged Tom and me. 'I'm so pleased for you both. We've been hoping for this for years.'

'You've had a bet on it?' I asked when she stepped back.

'Just a little wager with your dad. I reckoned it would happen before you hit thirty but your dad said thirty-five.'

'But how did you know? We didn't.'

'Parents know everything,' Mum said.

'Give over, Joanna,' Dad said. 'We didn't know, but we hoped. We could see you'd be perfect for each other.'

I looked over at Rylan, whose cheeks were bright red, head hung. 'What about you, Rylan?' I asked.

He looked up, expression serious, shaking his head, and my stomach plummeted to the floor. Macey was wrong. He still hated the idea.

Tom's hand found mine and gripped it tightly. 'I can't say sorry, Rylan,' he said. 'And I'm not letting her go. I hope you can—'

But he didn't get to finish as Rylan was out of his chair and heading towards us. Surely he wasn't going to hit Tom. But, to my relief, he grabbed him in a tight bear hug instead.

'I'm sorry, Tom,' he said, his voice all choked up. He reached for me and drew me into the hug too. 'Sorry, Tabs. What I said in the hospital was awful. I'm mortified.'

'It's all right,' I said, hugging him back. 'Just as long as it's not what you think now.'

'It isn't. I promise.'

'What did you say?' Mum asked.

'You don't want to know,' Rylan muttered.

'He got a little bit confused between being like a brother and actually being a brother,' Macey said, joining us for a hug. 'I'm so pleased for you both.'

'Shift, the lot of you,' Dad said, joining us too. 'My turn!'

All the hugs were a bit much for me, so I escaped into the kitchen to sort out drinks.

Tom joined me a few minutes later. 'Getting a bit overwhelming in there?' he asked.

'Just a tad. I can't believe Mum and Dad had a wager going, but how lovely is it that it's what they'd always hoped for? I hope that helps alleviate your rejection fears.'

'It does. I don't think it could have gone better, although your brother's getting a right earbashing from your mum just now so I thought I'd leave them to it. And perhaps steal a little kiss while I'm at it.'

I snaked my arms round his neck. 'I think I can manage that.'

On Christmas Eve, I said goodbye and happy Christmas to the weekend team, sending them off with their boxes of chocolates, then closed and locked the door.

'Done!' I said to Tom as I joined him in Cat Castle. 'A whole nine days off!'

I'd initially been hesitant about closing between Christmas and New Year but a lot of the Castle Street traders took the time off, saying it was a rare and welcome break, so I'd followed suit. We'd be open again on Wednesday, 3 January. Tom would need to do some work but was definitely taking the next three days off.

'Have you got many spoons left?' he asked.

'A few. I took as many rests as I could today. Why?'

'I thought we could feed the cats then go for a walk and pick up a takeaway.'

The shops had all closed when we ventured out into the cold evening. I linked my arm through Tom's and we did a circuit of Castle Street, looking in all the beautifully decorated shop windows and discussing which were our favourites. There were some other gorgeous displays around town, but the Castle Street traders definitely put on the best.

There was a giant illuminated teddy bear wearing a Santa hat in the middle of the pedestrianised high street, so we took photos and selfies with him and in front of the enormous tree outside the shopping centre.

Lots of people were still around, a few with bags of shopping, but most dressed up for a night out. The atmosphere was light with lots of laughter.

As we headed back towards home with a Chinese takeaway, something wet hit me in the face, startling me. I looked up.

'Oh, my God! It's snowing!'

There were only a few flakes slowly floating down but, by the time we made it back to the café, they were tumbling thick and fast.

'Looks like the forecast was right about snow,' I said, hastily unlocking the door and shaking the flakes from my arms as we stepped inside.

'Happy?' Tom asked, smiling at me as he dished up the food.

'Happier than I've been in a long time. The final piece of the puzzle is to figure out what to do next and then my happiness will be complete. I'm such a planner and it's weird not having a plan.'

'Something will present itself eventually.'

'You sound like Nanna.'

'It's what she always said, and she was usually right.'

I lit candles in the lounge and we ate in there on the sofa bed with the only light coming from the candles and the fairy lights round the tree Tom had nipped out to buy for me so that I had somewhere to hang my felt cat decorations. Eliza had called in today with the final ones so I now had a full set of fifteen cats on the tree, Smudge taking pride of place at the very top where the angel would normally sit.

When we'd eaten, Tom cleared the plates away and I moved over to the window to watch the snow. The cobbles were now fully covered and the street was deserted.

'It's quite thick,' Tom said, slipping his arm round my waist as he joined me. 'I love it when it's all quiet like this.'

A man hurried along the street, collar on his coat turned up, baseball cap on, carrying a cardboard box.

'He looks a bit shifty,' Tom said, as the man kept looking behind him.

He stopped by the café doorway and we both leaned forward.

'What's he doing?' I muttered.

'I can't see.'

'He'd better not be having a pee in my doorway.'

Next moment, the man ran off in the direction of Castle Park.

'He hasn't got the box with him,' I said.

Tom and I frowned at each other, then ran across the room and down the stairs. If there'd been paint in that box and he'd graffitied my door...

From the inside, there didn't look to be any damage, but I yanked open the external door to check the outside and my stomach dropped to the ground as I heard a plaintive mewing. I was right back at that day when I was seven and heard the abandoned kittens singing to me. Heart thumping, I opened the box lid and gasped at the sight of seven tiny kittens, eyes closed, clambering over each other.

Tom ran out into the street.

'Forget about him,' I said, picking up the box. 'He's long gone. We need to get these inside and warmed up.'

Tom took the box from me while I locked up, and carried it upstairs to the kitchen. The kittens weren't as cold as I'd feared so presumably they'd been born in a house locally and brought straight here. If we hadn't been watching the snow... I shook my head, not wanting to go there now. I needed to focus.

'They can't be more than a few hours old,' I said. 'Can you grab me a fresh bath towel and a hand towel?'

Tom ran upstairs and returned moments later. I instructed him to place the hand towel on the worktop and help me lift the kittens out onto it. I unfolded the bath towel and laid it in the bottom of the box and scooped the kittens back into that, adjusting the folds to keep them warm.

'I need a stack of stuff but it'll be easier for me to grab it rather than tell you where it is, so can you boil a full kettle, then watch them?'

Without the warmth and protection from their mother, newborn kittens couldn't regulate their body heat so needed help in keeping warm. I had a heat pad I used across my lap to help with my fibro which would be perfect with a fleecy blanket over it. The cardboard box they'd been left in was okay for now but it had got wet in the snow and wouldn't hold out for long, so I grabbed a long plastic crate and loaded the heat pad and several fleecy blankets into it along with a baby bottle steriliser and a smaller crate containing my kitten feeding kit – bottles, teats, syringes, a bottle brush and a small set of weighing scales. Fortunately Ruby and Marmite had come to me as abandoned newborns who I'd hand-reared, so I had all the right equipment.

Cats couldn't be fed cow's milk and, after six to seven weeks, they only needed water to drink, but young kittens needed special milk formula and I fortunately had an unopened can of it which was still in date.

'What do you need me to do?' Tom asked when I returned to the kitchen, arms laden.

'Wash this lot with warm soapy water,' I said, handing him the crate containing the bottles. 'Plug the steriliser in. I'll set up their bed.'

We worked quickly together, me issuing guidance every so often. The kittens would need 2 ml of milk every two hours, including through the night, until they were three weeks old and they'd need to be stimulated to go to the toilet, wiping their private parts with a piece of damp cotton wool after each feed to replicate their mother licking them. With seven kittens, we certainly had our work cut out, but I was determined we'd do our absolute best to save all seven lives. I hadn't been able to save Smudge, but I could save these.

53

'Happy Christmas,' Tom said, smiling at me as the alarm sounded for the 12.30 a.m. feed on Christmas morning.

'Happy Christmas,' I said, rubbing my eyes. 'Have you slept yet?'

'No, but I probably will before the next feed. I'm tired now.'

'How are they doing?'

'All good. The kettle should have cooled to the right temperature for the formula.'

Tom had brought the coffee table up to my bedroom and moved all the equipment, including the kettle, into the cat lounge. We figured it would be easier to both sleep in my bed with the kittens nearby – not exactly the most romantic of first nights as a couple, but practical for the current situation.

I went into the cat lounge to test the water temperature and prepare the formula and, shortly after, Tom and I settled into feeding in the bedroom. He'd never done it before but I'd been impressed at how quickly he'd picked up the best way to hold the kitten on its belly and get it to suck on the teat. We were starting with syringes but would move onto bottles once they'd gained their confidence with the sucking.

'They don't look like they're from the same litter,' Tom said, as he moved onto his second kitten.

'If a female is in heat, she might breed with lots of different tom cats so there could be two fathers or even a different father for every kitten in the litter. It's known as superfecundation. Isn't that a great word?'

'Looking at this lot, there might be some super superfecundation going on,' he observed.

Their markings and colours would come through more strongly over the next week but it looked like we might have three tabby designs – two grey and one ginger like Marmalade – a black kitten, a white one, another white one but with black or grey patches and a mixed-colour kitten. My early thoughts were four girls and three boys but they needed to be bigger before I could be sure so there was no point in thinking about names just yet. Besides, if Shelley really did want to take on the cat café and had the means to do so, we might have her 'starter pack' of kittens right here and the naming honour should go to her.

'Not the Christmas Day we expected,' I said to Tom as I dampened a piece of cotton wool to stimulate the bowels of the second kitten I'd just fed.

'You're in your element, though, aren't you?' he said, smiling at me.

'I am. And I think I might have just found my new dream. There isn't a cat rescue centre in Whitsborough Bay. What if I established one?'

'If anyone can do it, you can. But what about the through-the-night feeds when you have fibro? I mean, I'd help, but I'd hate you to feel that you were back to a commitment you're struggling with, just like running this place.'

'When I was hand-rearing Ruby and Marmite, I had a couple of flare-ups including a red one and I managed to keep going. I think it was knowing that they were completely dependent on me and the only thing I had to do was feed and toilet them. I could sleep in between and they were my only focus. It didn't matter if I stayed in my PJs and didn't wash my hair because it was all about them. I could do it, Tom. I really could.'

'You don't have to convince me. I know you can do it, and I'm in with all the help and support I can give.'

Tears pricked my eyes and my words came out hoarse. 'I love you.'

'I love you too.'

My kitten had been to the toilet so I placed it back on the heat pad and picked up my third one to feed, feeling all warm and content. This was what I was destined to do. It was meaningful and rewarding and I could manage it with my fibromyalgia. I'd get what I'd always wanted – to spend every day with cats rather than watching other people spending all day with them – and I'd prepare them to move into their 'furever' homes. I'd found the final piece of that puzzle – or at least the idea, anyway. There was a lot to do and I'd imagine setting up a rescue centre would have way more red tape than a cat café. I'd need charitable status too as I'd need to fundraise to keep the place running, but I couldn't wait to get started – purr-fect project for after Christmas in between the feeds while Tom was working.

* * *

After the 8.30 a.m. feed, I FaceTimed Mum.

'Merry Christmas!' she cried, echoed by Dad, who poked his head into shot.

'Merry Christmas to you too. We have an unexpected Christmas gift.' I panned my phone round to show them the kittens.

'Where did they come from?' Mum asked, looking shocked.

'A man dumped them on my doorstep last night after it started snowing. Luckily we saw him.'

'How many was that?'

'Seven. We weren't going to name them yet but we couldn't resist. We've temporarily called them Dasher, Dancer, Prancer, Vixen, Comet, Cupid and Blitzen. We left out Donner 'cos that's a kebab.'

'So tiny,' Mum said, shaking her head. 'How could somebody do that, and in the snow too?'

'I know! Don't get me started. I hope the queen's okay.' Queen was the name given to a pregnant or nursing cat. 'This scuppers our plans for today and tomorrow as they're on two-hour feeds and I don't really want to move them with all the stuff.'

'We'll come to you,' Dad said. 'I cooked the turkey last night as usual, and I can bring everything else to cook at your place. If that's okay.'

I glanced at Tom, who nodded enthusiastically. We had no food in the flat, so this was the ideal solution.

'That would be brilliant. Thank you.'

* * *

It was certainly a different Christmas Day, but lovely. Dad timed Christmas dinner between the feeds and having four of us meant feeds were quicker and we could give the rest of the cats more attention.

Mum and Dad loved the framed print we'd chosen for them. Their gifts for me were mainly cat-related – clothes and items for the flat – and I loved every single one. Mum was always really tasteful with what she chose.

When they left after the 4.30 p.m. feed, it was time for Tom and me to exchange gifts.

'I've only managed to get you one thing so far,' I said, when he placed a large gift bag in front of me full of presents.

'You haven't had any time to shop. I'm surprised you've even managed one thing.'

The first gift I unwrapped was a pair of EarPods.

'I know you love reading but you find it hard to concentrate when you have a flare-up and you get tired holding a book, so I've bought you a year's audiobook subscription. I thought you might enjoy listening to books instead. You can still fuss the cats while you're doing that.'

'That's such a thoughtful gift. Thank you.'

He'd bought me a set of relaxing bubble baths, an incredibly soft hoodie with cat ears on the hood and another cat planner.

'I know you already have one for the café,' he said, 'but I thought you'd like a new one for whatever you did next. And now we know what that's going to be.'

There was some perfume, some chocolates, and the final gift was a beautiful silver necklace with a pair of cats on it with our names engraved on the back.

'A Tom-cat and a Tabby-cat,' he said, fastening it for me and giving my neck a soft kiss, sending my heart racing.

'It's so funny you've got a Tom-cat and Tabby-cat gift,' I said. 'Great minds think alike!'

My gift to him was one of Jed Ferguson's prints – a pair of cats, one of them a tabby, sitting on a cliff top, cuddled together, with Whitsborough Bay's South Bay in the background.

'It's purr-fect,' he said, smiling at it. 'I didn't see this when we were in Yorkshire's Best.'

'You were looking through the prints at the other end of the shop when I spotted it on the wall and I asked Jed to put it away for me without you seeing. He delivered it yesterday.'

Tom propped it up against the wall and we both gazed at it. It would look great on the wall of the flat for now and could have pride of place in our new home, whenever and wherever that might be.

'I've got one more thing,' Tom said, jumping up. 'It's not wrapped because I bought it a while ago but didn't get a chance to give you it.'

He left the room, returning moments later with something behind his back. 'I saw these and I thought of you.'

I laughed as he produced a set of Top Trumps.

'Most mischievous cats,' I said, smiling at the cover. 'Thank you.'

'Do you want a game?'

'Have you already been into the pack and reordered them so you'll win?'

'How very dare you! As if I'd ever do anything so underhand.' He laughed as he showed me the broken seal. 'I might have tampered a little bit. It's a habit.'

I opened the pack and shuffled the cards. 'Time to get rid of old habits and start afresh. I'm looking after my fibro from now on and you're not listening to any of the poison Tracey's put in your head. Agreed?'

'Agreed.'

'I know it's not that easy but, if we talk to each other about it, we can get through it together.'

He kissed me once more. 'Definitely agreed. Deal those cards, Tabby-cat!'

'As you wish, Tom-cat!'

54

ONE YEAR LATER

I stood in the beautiful kitchen of the sympathetically extended eighteenth-century four-bedroom farmhouse Tom and I had shared for the past six months, a contented smile on my face as I watched Pebbles and Cloud, now fully grown, batting a catnip toy back and forth, while I stroked Rubix, who was pacing up and down on the worktop beside me.

We were four days into December and I was almost ready for Christmas. Tom and I had put up the Christmas decorations at the weekend, including a large tree in the grand entrance hall and another by the inglenook fireplace in the lounge, my set of felt cats from Eliza distributed round the branches. Cards had been written and sent and I only had a couple more gifts to buy – very different to last year and so much more relaxing.

Relaxing had been the word for our move. As soon as we'd landed in the countryside, I felt like a different person. I'd always love Whitsborough Bay and have an affinity forever with Castle Street, but living in a town wasn't for me. Being surrounded by lush fields and gently rolling hills absolutely was.

Our new home was so much more than a farmhouse. It had land and outbuildings and the most important of those was our cat rescue centre. We'd been alerted to it by one of Tom's clients. A friend of theirs had bought the farmhouse and former cattery in a converted barn, intending to keep the business going with her husband. In a scenario reminiscent of my own situation with Leon, the husband had decided it wasn't for him after they'd refurbished the farmhouse and the barn – and neither was the marriage anymore. Things had got so bad between the couple that they just wanted rid of it, even at a significant loss, so they could move on with their lives separately.

The end of their dreams had been the start of ours. I'd already been in the process of transferring ownership of Castle Street Cat Café to Shelley and the sale of Tom's apartment was also progressing.

Shelley had been amazing and had said we could stay in the flat with our fur family until the sale of the cattery completed, which was just as well because I have no idea where we'd have gone otherwise. She'd become a great friend and I still often visited the café, but as a customer. Our Christmas Eve rescue kittens had indeed become her 'starter pack'. All seven had survived and I'd been right about there being four girls and three boys. Shelley had planned to re-name them but had decided that the reindeer names were so appropriate for seven kittens delivered to the café on Christmas Eve that she'd kept them. It was wonderful being able to visit them there, knowing Tom and I had saved their lives.

Running the rescue centre had been everything I'd hoped for – a role which worked with my fibromyalgia instead of pushing against it, meaning I could spend my days with cats, just as I'd always wanted. I hadn't ditched my second love of baking either. We regularly held open days and sold cakes, scones and bread to raise valuable funds.

* * *

Tom arrived back from a client meeting a little later with a stunning bouquet of festive flowers for me.

'What are these for?' I said.

'Just because,' he responded, taking me in his arms for a tender kiss.

'They're beautiful. I'll pop them in some water.'

He followed me into the kitchen and I added water to the vase that Alison had bought me last year before opening up the packaging.

'I can't believe we'll have been open six months on Tuesday,' I said, cutting the stems. 'That time's flown. In fact, the whole year's flown.'

'Celine Dion called it.'

My heart leapt as the opening notes of 'Another Year Has Gone By' filled the kitchen.

'You remembered it's the...' I turned round with a smile on my face and gasped. 'Oh, my God!'

Tears rushed to my eyes at the sight of Tom kneeling on one knee on the kitchen tiles, Winnie nudging up against him, with a ring box held out in front of him.

'The anniversary of our first kiss to this song,' he said, finishing what I'd been about to say. 'Another year *has* gone by and it's been the best year of my life and I want to spend next year with you, and the one after, and every year after that until we're old and still laughing and cheating at Top Trumps.'

I laughed through my tears.

'I love you, Tabby-cat, and I always will. Will you marry me?'

'Yes!' I cried, rushing over to him and sinking onto my knees beside him as I kissed him. 'Yes, please!'

He removed the ring from the box and placed it on my finger. It was stunning – a twisted vine white gold band with a diamond either side of a blue-violet coloured stone.

'It's beautiful.'

'It's tanzanite. It's one of the December birthstones and December was the birth of our relationship, our new dream to run this place and now our engagement. The trio of stones indicates our past as friends, our present as a couple, and our future as husband and wife.'

'That's so thoughtful,' I said, wiping my cheeks and kissing him once more.

'My knees are hurting now,' he said, laughing. 'Can we get up now?'

'Gladly!'

He helped me to my feet and, as he took me in his arms and kissed me again with several cats now weaving round us, I didn't think it was possible to be happier than this moment. I thought my dreams had come true when I found the empty premises on Castle Street, but they'd just been a stepping-stone to my real dream and my dream man. Who knew he'd turn out to be the boy my wonderful nanna fostered when I was only seven? She'd made everything we had today possible, so it was only appropriate that we'd named our business Betsy and Smudge's Cat Rescue Centre. She'd rescued Tom and given him a home, Tom had moved into my home and rescued me when the fibro became too much, and now we rescued cats and kittens together. Purr-fect.

ACKNOWLEDGMENTS

It's believed that as many as one in twenty people might be affected by fibromyalgia. That's huge! But until seven years ago, I hadn't heard of it. I met and became friends with Nicola, who told me that she had fibro. Not long after that, a colleague of mine, Carol, shared that she'd been diagnosed and, through my research for a different book, I met Angela, who also has fibromyalgia. I wondered who else might be unaware of it and whether I'd have an opportunity to shine a light on the condition in one of my stories. I had no sense of a character or plot, so the idea floated for a while.

For several years, I've wanted to write a book set in a cat café. Visiting the fabulous Steampuss Cat Lounge in Scarborough and Kitty Café in Leeds strengthened this desire. My fictional cat café would obviously be on Castle Street, but I had no sense of who would run it.

Sometimes two seemingly separate ideas combine beautifully and this was one of those moments. What if my cat café owner had fibromyalgia – a condition which would make managing the café difficult but not impossible if she had a supportive boyfriend running it with her? And what if he decided he didn't want to do that anymore and left her in the lurch? Tabby and the Castle Street Cat Café were born.

As with all of my books, I undertook a substantial amount of research. I interviewed Nicola and Carol about every aspect of their experience from the triggers to seeking a diagnosis through to daily living with fibromyalgia. I'd also picked up a lot from conversations with Angela, so my first thank you goes to Nicola, Carol Margerrison and Angela Jennison for their honest insights into their experiences of fibromyalgia. A special thanks to Nicola for reading an advance copy to make sure I hadn't misrepresented anything. I'm so very grateful to you all for your time.

I also undertook research online – reading research papers, exploring charity websites and watching real-life videos. There are many fibromyalgia symptoms, they can present differently, and not everyone experiences them all. If you have fibro or know someone who does, Tabby's experiences might be different. If you would like more information on fibromyalgia, you can check out Fibromyalgia Action UK at www.fmauk.org.

My second thank you goes to Chloe and Matthew at the fabulous Steampuss Cat Lounge in Scarborough for some really helpful insights into the highs and lows of running a cat café, and for sharing their passion for their adorable fur family. Sadly, Steampuss will have ceased trading by the time this book is published, the pandemic and the cost-of-living crisis making the business unsustainable. Chloe and Matthew hope to open a cat rescue and animal sanctuary in the future and I wish them well with this new venture. I'd already decided on the plot for *Christmas at the Cat Café* – Tabby no longer running the café and opening a cat rescue centre instead – when Chloe shared this information with me. Talk about a spooky coincidence!

Readers who are familiar with Castle Street will notice a few new businesses have appeared in *Christmas at the Cat Café*. Several businesses came from my imagination but I turned to the amazing members of my Facebook group, Redland's Readers, for further inspiration. Thank you so much to Pamela Viti Byrne for Forget-me-not Cards, Claire Woolf for Nibbles & News and to everyone else who came up with such fabulous suggestions. You are all awesome! If you'd like to join my reader group, please search for 'Redland's Readers' on Facebook.

An enormous thank you and huge hug goes to Sharon Booth. I had a shocker of a start with the story and couldn't seem to make any decisions. Sharon was an incredible help with dissecting it, working out the crux of the story and getting it back on track. She also came up with the name Tom for me, which was just perfect for my Tom-cat. Sharon, you are incredible and you saved this book! I owe you a lot of cake! xxx

My other book saviour is my editor, Nia Beynon, who always sees exactly what's missing or needs work when I can't. I'd sent the first draft of this book to the naughty step but she gave the insights to turn it into a story I love so much now.

As always, my thanks to everyone in Team Boldwood – such an incredible publishing family. I don't have cats myself at the moment. I had siblings Felix and Pixie who crossed the rainbow bridge, but I've already immortalised them in The Starfish Café series, so I needed some new names and really appreciated the team letting me use their cats in *Christmas at the Cat Café*. A huge thank you to our head of marketing, Claire Fenby, for the support with this and all the amazing feline marketing materials.

My final thanks goes to you for choosing *Christmas at the Cat Café*. Whether this has been your introduction to my work or you've read/listened to everything I've written, I'm incredibly grateful. If you're new to my writing and have enjoyed this story, there's a huge backlist available for you to explore, including several more visits to Castle Street. Reviews are invaluable, as are recommendations to friends, family and colleagues.

Big ailurophile hugs, Jessica xx

ABOUT THE AUTHOR

Jessica Redland writes uplifting stories of love, friendship, family and community set mostly in Yorkshire where she lives. Her Whitsborough Bay books transport readers to the stunning North Yorkshire Coast and her Hedgehog Hollow series takes them into beautiful countryside of the Yorkshire Wolds.

Sign up to Jessica Redland's mailing list here for news, competitions and updates on future books.

Visit Jessica's website: www.jessicaredland.com
Follow Jessica on social media:

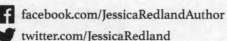 facebook.com/JessicaRedlandAuthor
twitter.com/JessicaRedland
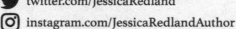 instagram.com/JessicaRedlandAuthor
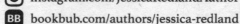 bookbub.com/authors/jessica-redland

ALSO BY JESSICA REDLAND

Welcome to Whitsborough Bay

Making Wishes at Bay View

New Beginnings at Seaside Blooms

Finding Hope at Lighthouse Cove

Coming Home to Seashell Cottage

Hedgehog Hollow

Finding Love at Hedgehog Hollow

New Arrivals at Hedgehog Hollow

Family Secrets at Hedgehog Hollow

A Wedding at Hedgehog Hollow

Chasing Dreams at Hedgehog Hollow

Christmas Miracles at Hedgehog Hollow

Christmas on Castle Street

Christmas at Carly's Cupcakes

Starry Skies Over the Chocolate Pot Café

Christmas Wishes at the Chocolate Shop

The Starfish Café

Snowflakes Over the Starfish Café

Spring Tides at the Starfish Café

Summer Nights at the Starfish Café

Escape to the Lakes

The Start of Something Wonderful

Standalones

The Secret to Happiness

All You Need is Love

Healing Hearts at Bumblebee Barn

Christmas at the Cat Café

Boldwood

Boldwood Books is an award-winning fiction publishing company seeking out the best stories from around the world.

Find out more at www.boldwoodbooks.com

Join our reader community for brilliant books, competitions and offers!

Follow us
@BoldwoodBooks
@TheBoldBookClub

Sign up to our weekly deals newsletter

https://bit.ly/BoldwoodBNewsletter